UNAUTHORISED DEPARTURES

Also Available From The Terminal Press:

The J.G. Ballard Book
Deep Ends: The J.G. Ballard Anthology 2014
Deep Ends: The J.G. Ballard Anthology 2015
Deep Ends: The J.G. Ballard Anthology 2016
Deep Ends: A Ballardian Anthology 2018
Deep Ends: A Ballardian Anthology 2019
Deep Ends: A Ballardian Anthology 2020
Deep Ends: A Ballardian Anthology 2021
Deep Ends: A Ballardian Anthology 2022
Deep Ends: A Ballardian Anthology 2023
Dominika Oramus - Grave New World:
The Decline of the West in the Fiction of JG Ballard

Lawrence Russell - Radio Brazil
Lawrence Russell - Outlaw Academic
Lawrence Russell - Temple of The Two Moons

Rick McGrath - Straight Man: Rock Star Interviews,
Reviews & Photos From The 1970s Underground Press
Rick McGrath - The Disenchanted Forest

UNAUTHORISED DEPARTURES

Trippy Tales for the Adventurous Mind

Edited By Rick McGrath

Published By
THE TERMINAL PRESS
3399 Cariboo Avenue, Powell River, BC, Canada V8A 5K1

First Edition: March 2024

Print Edition ISBN: 978-1-990682-07-0

Visit us: www.facebook.com/theterminalpress

The Road to Woop Woop by Eugen Bacon was first published in
The Road to Woop Woop & Other Stories, Meerkat Press, 2019
Scars of Grief by Eugen Bacon was first published in *Bukker Tillibul*,
Creative Research, Swinburne University, 2014
Autonomous by Lyle Hopwood was first published in *Aurealis* #157, 2023
Pace Car by Lyle Hopwood was first published in *Interzone* 290/291, 2021

Cover Photographs: Rick McGrath

The Second Door

By Elana Gomel

As a child, Rose would sneak out onto the balcony despite her mother's stern warnings. She would clasp the shaky railing and look up into Day, squinting into its perpetual radiance. She saw, or thought that she saw, indistinct blue shapes swimming in the circle of blinding light. She asked her mother if these were Day-fish, like the fish bred in the City's aquariums. Her mother shrugged; her face folded into a permanent shape of vague discontent.

Rose tried to talk about the Day-fish to her elder brother Reggie, even though she knew it was useless. Eventually, she relegated them to the special place in her mind, which she inhabited alone. There was no room there for her mother's tired, lined face and for Reggie's jerky motions, as he sat in his corner, stacking up his old wooden blocks. The blocks had lost their original color long ago and were now of soft uniform gray, the same shade as the landings' walls. Reggie would stack them up, contemplate the resulting tower, and then destroy it with a single blow of his pudgy hand.

Reggie became a Night Flier when Rose was thirteen. She did not think he had it in him. Reggie never spoke. Though he had learned the basic survival skills, such as turning on the light in the bathroom and closing the kitchen faucet to prevent the leakage of water, he was like his blocks: monotonous, predictable, and passive. But one day when Rose came back home from school, she found Reggie gone.

School was Miss Peabody's cramped Twilight Apartment, below Rose's floor, where the youngsters of the building met every third watch for their lessons in reading, writing, and arithmetic. Rose rode the elevator up to her floor as she always did, punctuating the formlessness of her waking with the predictability of clanging doors and groaning movement. But this predictability was broken when she entered their apartment and found Reggie gone.

His corner was empty, a gray smudge on the wall marking the place where his head always rested. In the kitchen, two open lunchboxes with sliced cucumbers and tomatoes sat on the cracked counter. Outside on the balcony, the drooping vegetable garden sweltered in the glare of Day. Rose could see the broken stems and scuff marks on the railing. She touched the rusty metal where her brother had gone over the edge of the world.

The infinite buildings of the City curved around her in a hollow cylinder five hundred meters across. The balcony-studded walls soared into the pitiless fire of Day that shone above her head, unchanged and indifferent, as it had done for generations. And below her, the walls dropped into the dusk, congealing into the empty pupil of Night. The Twilight apartments marked the lower limit of human habitation on the boundary between the soft glow and the blunt darkness. Unable to sustain agriculture, their balconies were piled with the mysterious junk found throughout the City.

On the periphery of her vision a dark-robed pilgrim crawled slowly down the fire escape, his—or maybe her—gloved fingers glued to the creaky beams. In many places the ladders had come away from the corroded walls, supported only by a thin strut.

A watchman, walking on one of the catwalks that encircled the City, stared disdainfully at the pilgrim and made a sign as if pushing away something unclean. The pilgrims, just one step above the Night Fliers, were feared and despised for their courtship of falling.

Rose felt an overpowering tug of loneliness. The balcony below hers contained only a tangle of desiccated stems. The apartment was empty; its furniture plundered by the neighbors after the owners had disappeared into Night. Their grasshopper cage, painstakingly woven from salvaged wires, hung open.

Rose rushed out into the landing and kept her finger on the button of the elevator until she heard the rumble of its ascent and then the clanking when the door of its cage slid open. Inside were the familiar gray walls and the bank of buttons numbered 1 to 45, the magic number of the human life-zone.

Her mother was working on the Twenty-Third, at the fish farm. The walls of that apartment had been ripped out and the entire floor space stacked with glass boxes, in which swam fat-bellied guppies with slack mocking lips; black-and-white striped panaques; and mustachioed catfish.

Mother was in the bathroom, carefully filling a bowl. The Second Door, the mystical portal into Day according to some or the demonic temptation into Night according to others, was lit up by the pale electric bulb behind her back. Every child tried to open the Second Door until they learned that it could not be done or more likely, were spanked by their irate parents and desisted. Some grew afraid of it, scurrying in and out of the bathroom as quickly as possible. Others became fascinated by the electricity and would spend hours on the toilet seat in meditation, staring at the bulb. Sime even pointed out that all the rooms in every identical apartment had electric fixtures but only the ones in the bathrooms produced light. There were lively debates as to why it should be so but no consensus.

The bowl shattered on the tiled floor when Rose's mother saw her face. Rose tried to tell her that it would be easier for the two of them to survive, now that they had no useless mouth to feed, but she could not find the words.

Several watches later, Mother sneaked out of her bedroom and having left a lunchbox and "I love you" scribbled on the kitchen counter, vaulted over the balcony's railing.

There were not many orphans in the City. When a parent turned Night Flier, he or she often took the children as well. But here was Rose, the last of her family, stubbornly clinging to life, even though she had to endure the superstitious dread of her neighbours, the greed of the aldermen, and the privation of a Twilight orphanage.

In the orphanage, crushed by the unwashed bodies of her mates and grimly tended by tight-lipped women, she often thought of Reggie. Not of her father who had succumbed to the pull of Night before she was born; not of her mother who had chosen to follow her firstborn; but of her silent brother whose eyes had often followed her as he sat in his corner. What wonders was he witnessing on his infinite journey?

And would he ever forgive her for wishing him out of the way?

By the age of eighteen Rose grew up into a pudgy, red-haired, morose girl who rebuffed infrequent friendly overtures and even less frequent attempts at wooing. At least, she did until she met Sander.

It was at a get-together for young people. Theoretically, all unmarried persons had to attend; practically, the aldermen's children had their own decadent parties somewhere in the Day apartments. The rumours flying Dayward and Nightward insinuated that the aldermen had some mysterious means of moving from one building to another without risking the catwalks, perhaps with the help of the mythical Red Elevator that was supposed to be able to go beyond the forty-five human floors. But Rose believed in the Red Elevator as little as she believed in love.

She was sitting in the corner alone, eating a dish of fried grasshoppers, when a boy plunked down on the shaky settee by her side. Rose glanced at him askance and was surprised to see an unfamiliar face. She did not often meet people from other buildings.

The boy did not look very impressive: reedy, with an apologetic smile and large clumsy hands. However, he had a nice voice. His name was Sander, and he was from the Third Building. Rose's birthplace was the Fifth, though nobody knew how and why the identical buildings, locked in the perfect cosmic circle, had acquired their numbers. Certainly, the First building was no better and no worse from the Twenty-Fourth.

He lived with his father on the Fifteenth Floor and was now visiting his cousins. Even though he did not say so directly, she guessed that he was sent out to scout for a bride. She was not even in the running; a family like his would look for a girl with a dowry: a chair, a table, perhaps even a bundle of precious and irreplaceable clothes. She had none of it. Her family's entire stock of possessions had been given into the "temporary keeping" of the aldermen and she had no hope of ever seeing it again. Nevertheless, despite her blunt admission of her penury, Sander did not leave her side.

At some point he suggested they go out onto the balcony. Standing there, he lifted his face into the brassy light of Day.

"You know," he said, "when I look out into Day for a long time, I think I see moving shadows. Do you think there are creatures living there?"

This was the moment Rose fell in love.

When Sander proposed, Rose could hardly believe her ears. She had schooled herself not to seek happiness but only survival. After a kiss that was simultaneously intoxicating and vaguely disappointing, she tried to steer the conversation back to practical matters.

"Tell me about your family," she said. "Are we going to live with your father?"

He shook his head.

"No, no! Our aldermen already promised me a new apartment when I get married. They wanted me to," he added with a wink, "they knew I'd bring somebody special."

Rose blushed, which, she knew, did not suit her complexion.

"What is your building like?"

Sander shrugged.

"All buildings are the same."

"Why?" Rose blurted out.

"What do you mean?"

"I mean … didn't you ever wonder what lies beyond the kitchen wall?"

"Beyond …" Sander frowned, trying to visualize an abstraction.

"Or what if we could open the Second Door?" Rose continued, emboldened by a flush of desire.

"What an imagination you have!" Sander was shaking his head—she hoped, in admiration.

There was something faintly offensive in his voice, but she had no time to think what it was because he kissed her again, and this time she suddenly felt what the other girls in the orphanage had been raving about.

Weddings in the City used to be grand celebrations, with several aldermen presiding over a crowd of guests squeezed into the new couple's assigned apartment. But recently, with the increase in Night Flying, the mood in the City had turned brittle and sour. The aldermen clung to their precious vegetable gardens and avoided going Nightward. Rose did not mind; she wanted an inconspicuous ceremony.

Her orphanage mates unexpectedly organized a bridal shower for her. She boarded the elevator laden with gifts: an all-purpose box made of recycled chair-wood; a child's shirt let out at the seams; and a rusty key, of a wrong shape and size to fit an apartment door, one of the inexplicable odds and ends salvaged from Twilight.

All this sudden goodwill made her feel self-conscious and she was glad when the elevator reached the Forty-Fifth Floor where the alderman who had robbed her of her family's inheritance performed a brief ceremony, fidgeting under her unflinching stare.

Sander, now her husband, called the elevator that was to take them down to the middle floor with access to the catwalk. From there, they would embark on their journey to Sander's building. He seemed jittery. It surprised Rose, just as her own calm did.

Sander jiggled the button; the growl of the elevator came up the shaft from way down below, somewhere on a Twilight floor. The moment seemed to stretch forever.

Finally, the cage-door slid open. Sander pushed her in. The pile of gifts she was holding fell apart and scattered on the floor. Rose bent to retrieve them, as the elevator rumbled into motion and she lost her balance and crouched stupidly on all fours, dizzy with the sense of monumental wrongness.

The elevator was rising!

It could not rise; no elevator went beyond the Forty-Fifth Floor. But Rose's body, trained from her earliest childhood to know instinctively how far Dayward or Nightward it was moving, was telling her loud and clear that it was.

She was so stunned that she remained in her undignified position while her eyes slowly took in the impossible color that filled her field of vision. Expecting the muddy brown of the elevator floor, they were blinded by bright scarlet.

Slowly, she got up, still clutching the gift key, the only solid and reassuring object in this liquid nightmare. She touched the plushy scarlet wall.

In front of her was a bank of buttons. The buttons were arranged in two columns as in all City elevators and numbered in the same way. But underneath them and slightly to the right was a fat red button. The symbol on it looked like an 8 lying on its side.

She remembered she was not alone. She turned and faced Sander who stood in the corner like a scraggly plant.

"Yes," he said. "It is the Red Elevator."

Rose kept her eyes on him.

"I couldn't very well tell you, could I?" he said whiningly. "Would you believe me? But anyway, here we are. We're married, you know!"

Rose felt the improbable miracle of love shrivel into nothing and was relieved to let it go.

"Where is it taking us?" she asked. The elevator kept climbing.

"You'll see. Soon."

But it was not soon; at least, she did not think so. In the City time was measured by sleep cycles announced by the watchmen; by the slow ripening of plants; by the birth of babies and death of old and sick. But here, in the elevator rising into infinity, with no familiar markers of duration, she suddenly felt that time stopped. It terrified her more than Sander's betrayal.

The elevator clanked to a stop and pushing Sander aside, she rushed out into the landing.

Except it was not a landing. It was a room and this distortion of the familiar laws of space made Rose's head spin, so she swayed like a drunkard.

The room was big, as if several walls had been knocked down. There was no furniture and no windows or doors apart from the elevator. It was also creepily dark, as if they were in Night. The only light came from the crack in the curtains on the far wall.

Rose rushed and drew the curtain aside. Sander gave an outraged squeal.

"You stupid idiot!" he cried. "We could have had some time together!"

The pitiless brightness made her squeeze her eyes shut. But then she opened them stubbornly and wiping away tears, stared into the gulf beyond the window, slowly accepting the impossible.

The light was not uniform.

The light was the one fixed and unalterable aspect of the City. Everything else occasionally changed: catwalks sagged and fell; balconies burgeoned with new shoots or gaped bare in famine; the cladding peeled off, revealing the rough concrete underneath. But these trifling changes were always bracketed by the glare of Day above, the darkness of Night below. Each altitude had its unique illumination, from the golden flood of Noon, through the brassy tinge of Afternoon, into the crepuscular lilac of Twilight, and the dull darkness of Night.

But here the luminosity outside was streaked and marred with moving shadows. In the pool of Day giant silhouettes were circling, dipping, and diving. Their V-shaped bodies cut Day into slivers of varying brightness.

"Day-fish!" Rose whispered, awed.

"Move away!" Sander cried. "Draw the curtain! They may not have seen us yet!"

But they had.

One of the winged creatures above canted and sheared, falling through the air, and hovered in front of the glass. A blunt, blind head curving into a meaty hook nudged the window.

Sander grabbed her shoulder and pushed her down onto the floor.

"Pretend you're dead! They don't eat carrion!"

Rose found herself with her face in the musty carpet. Sander scrambled to the window and pulled down the curtain.

They lay side by side in the stuffy murk.

"Are they really Day-fish?" Rose asked after a while.

"Yeah … Well, we call them Day-masters."

"And you are their pet?"

"I was a Night Flier," he said. "Just seven. My mum decided she couldn't go without me, you see? But they saved me. Plucked me out of the air, brought me here."

"Where's 'here'?"

"Upper floors. Above the Forty-Fifth. Humans can't go here, and they don't go down below."

"Why not?"

"I don't know. Afraid of Night, I think. Anyway, there are several of us here. Mostly younger Night Fliers like me. They treat us well; we have plenty of food."

"An in exchange?"

She could see his eyes now, as flat as buttons.

"You know, don't you?" he said. "We have to bring them people. We go down on the Red Elevator and … well, bring people up here with us."

"What do they do with us?"

"What do we do with our fish?"

For a heartbeat, Rose was still. And then she rushed to the elevator's door and jabbed the big concave button.

"You can't do it!" Sander said calmly. "They do something to us, so we can ride the Red Elevator. Nobody else. But listen, I can make a deal with them. Really! I was thinking about it. I … I mean, you are my wife! I can talk to them … sort of. You can stay with us here. Be one of us."

Her fingernail broke, as she stubbed the button.

"It's a good life!" Sander insisted.

"And in exchange?" she whispered.

"I do it. So can you. We survive."

She felt his tentative touch. Turning around, she closed her fist around the gift key and drove it into Sander's stomach. He doubled over, clasping his hands over a spreading stain on his shirt. And Rose ran back to the window and tore at the curtain.

The Day-fish were still swimming in the hot glare outside and Rose's action attracted one of them. The furrowed dome of a giant head butted the glass, the pale, corrugated skin squashed into a neat circle. There were no eyes, but she felt the Day-fish was looking straight at her.

The toothless beak-like jaws clacked open, revealing the blood-flushed lining. The window exploded inwards, and she was showered with glass fragments.

Rose flattened herself against the wall. The room went dark again as the creature pressed its bulk against the empty window-frame. It was too big to get in, she saw with a thrill of hope; perhaps it would frighten Sander into calling up the Red Elevator …

The creature unfolded a slender segmented limb and reached into the room. A bony clawed hand groped among the glass on the floor, grazed Rose's sweatshirt, and grabbed.

The old over-washed fabric ripped, and she was free. She threw herself on the floor, rolled, saw the clawed digits dig into Sander's forearm as he was dragged, kicking and screaming, toward the window, leaving a bright streak of blood on the dingy carpet. The beak-jaws stretched wide, and Sander slid into the stinking maw.

The skeletal arm snaked back into the room.

Rose leaped to her feet, ran to the window, squeezed past the hovering body, and jumped.

So, I became a Night Flier, after all.

This was her first coherent thought. It sneaked in past a jumble of wordless impressions: the hot blinding glare, the intoxicating feeling of lightness, the constant susurrus of the wind against her falling body. She flexed her arms and legs and tried to grasp the air. Fear came and went.

She thought of her family and imagined herself chasing them forever. The idea repelled her. She wanted an end. She realized this with a sudden astonishing clarity. No matter what the end would be; she wanted it; a conclusion, a closure. This is why she had followed Sander whose flat dead eyes had been there all along to act as a warning. But even a bad end was better than none.

This is why she had jumped.

Had Reggie wanted an end too, an end to his pointless, monotonous survival? Had he jumped in search of time?

The Day-fish had not tried to pluck her from the air. Why not?

She discovered she was still clutching the gift key and carefully tucked it into her pocket.

She was falling through the tube of the City like a drop of water through a pipe. Endless identical sash-windows stared emptily at her; endless bare balconies grinned toothlessly as she floated by; endless fire-escapes clung to the gray walls like barren vines. But there were no faces in the windows, the balconies were bare of vegetation, and the ladders' rust undisturbed by any pilgrim's progress. She was far above the human zone. The light had softened a little, but it was still too bright.

Rose closed her aching eyes. And then she fell asleep, sweetly and soundly, splayed in mid-air.

Rose woke up because she was cold.

She was shivering in her torn sweatshirt. The air rushing past her cut her like a knife. She was in deep Twilight, so deep that it was almost Night. Some light still bled from the distant circle of Day above but all it showed were the same empty balconies and blind windows.

Rose cursed. She must have slept throughout the plunge through the human zone! How stupid of her! Somebody might have seen her as she flew by; might have waved farewell …. But then she remembered there was nobody whose farewell she wanted. Her family was gone, and her husband had never existed.

She curled up into a tight ball, trying to keep warm. Below her, spread the unrelieved darkness of Night.

Except that it was not unrelieved. The black eye of the City tube was speckled with golden sparks. A giant net beaded with quick moving lights expanded to meet her, tough strands giving and then bouncing back. She had her wind knocked out of her and was entangled in cold and dripping cables that twitched, as if made of raw muscles. Rose glimpsed something unutterably strange, like an enormous light bulb with a human face. And then she passed out.

She opened her eyes and saw Reggie.

"Hello, sis!" he said.

His voice was a little rusty and a little squeaky, just like the voice Reggie would have had, had he had any. But it seemed to her quite natural to be greeted by him.

"Are we dead?" she asked.

"No. Dying."

The cables were digging into her bruised back. She sat up.

And saw what Reggie's face was attached to.

In the City some people bred grasshoppers to supplement the scant diet of vegetables and aquarium fish. There were also cockroaches skittering in the corners. The hard wings and segmented thorax of the creature reminded her of these insects. But it stood upright, on the long stilt-like pair of hind legs, while its upper appendages were small, and jagged, and twitching. The thorax flowed into a lumpy head with a shock of red hair and Reggie's face. The entire thing was the color of pasty human flesh dusted with freckles on the lower segments. It shed a pale silvery radiance.

Rose reached out and touched the thorax. It was warm and yielding. Reggie—somehow she did not doubt it was him—smiled bashfully. She had seldom touched him when they were kids, even though their mother had sometimes asked her to give her brother a hug.

"How long have you been like this?" she asked.

"I don't know," he sounded surprised. "Why does it matter?"

She did not know why, but felt that it did.

"Come on!" one of his twitching appendages touched her cheek lightly. "You can't stay on the Net; she doesn't like it. I told her to leave you alone."

"She?"

The tough grayish-pink strands beneath her, each as thick as her forearm, were contracting and relaxing in a complex symphony of movements. The strands' intersections were marked by round knobs that looked familiar. She squinted: they were human heads encased in transparent tegument. The nearest head that belonged to a middle-aged man blinked sluggishly and returned her stare.

"The Net takes the old and the feeble," Reggie said, nodding at the heads. "And it changes us, the young, I mean. Gives us wings, so we can hunt in Twilight. You'd be surprised at what lives down here."

"Mum?" Rose asked. "Dad?"

Reggie turned away and hopped dexterously across the strands toward a balcony. Rose followed. The Net beating was under her feet like a heart.

She vaulted across the balcony's railing and followed Reggie into the apartment. It was the same as any other apartment, except that the furniture was not scuffed and worn by generations of use. She thought that it was a waste. Her brother in his present condition did not need a bed to sleep in or a dining table to sit at. Indeed, he dropped onto his belly, craning his lumpy neck up to look up at her.

In the corner there was a small pile of objects. She picked up a gray wooden block.

"Yeah," Reggie said shamefacedly. "I still like them. And there are enough of them. See, in the Forty-Five they have moved things around, from one apartment to another. But here it all remains as it was originally. If I drop my blocks Nightward, I can just go to the next building and get them."

Rose shook her head; it made no sense to her.

"How come you can speak?" she asked.

"The Net fixed me."

"So," Rose said dully, "some Night-Fliers are hunted by the Day-Fish, and some end up in the Net … and when she gets hungry, do you help her like those Day-fishers do?"

Reggie did not answer.

"Are you hungry?" he asked after a while.

Rose realized she was ravenous. She had not eaten anything since her wedding breakfast, and it had happened to another person in another lifetime. But she shook her head.

"No," Reggie said sadly, "it's not what you think. I told you, we hunt. Only … can you cook?"

"There is gas here?"

"And electricity. Of course. I told you, we are still in the City. Only there is no City. Not really. Just this one building."

The creature he put on the kitchen table looked like a miniature version of the Day-fish that had killed Sander, with a sinuous naked body and eyeless head coming to a point. Perhaps they breed here, she thought, in the depth of Night and only then climb up into Day. But she had no compunctions skinning the creature like a mudfish and putting it into a familiar aluminum pot to boil on the familiar gas stove. There were no vegetables to go with it but the saltcellar was full.

"Do you cook?" she asked and then realized Reggie's feeble upper appendages could not handle such tasks.

"What do you mean, there is just one building?" she asked quickly, trying to fill in the awkward pause.

"This is what the Net told me. There was just one building. Forty-five floors. The rest … the City … they are just like mirror reflections."

"But people live in all the buildings!"

"Yes … but … See, Day and Night were once moveable. They changed places, so half the time the world was light, and half—dark."

Rose tried to imagine Day and Night sliding like giant elevators along the shaft of the City.

"And then there was something … like a great fight or maybe like a giant explosion. You know, like a gas leakage that blows up sometimes. Only this was much worse. The building—our building —was destroyed."

"What are you talking about?" Rose cried irritably. "It's still standing! We are in it, aren't we?"

"No," said Reggie, "we are in the last moment of its existence. Just before the final annihilation. This moment is the City."

They ate the cooked Day-fish in silence. Rose cut the chewy meat into bite-sized portions and fed her brother with a fork. He looked profoundly touched. In the past, their mother had done such menial tasks for her disabled son alone.

"So what are the Day-fish and the Net?" she asked. "Did they also live in that … that original building?"

"No, I don't think so. I think they have evolved here. Just as humans have evolved and adapted. The fish we eat … the original tenants had kept fish in aquariums just for fun. They had so much food they threw it away on useless pets."

"But how can it be?" Rose cried impatiently. "How could one building wrap around itself and become an infinite City? How could time just drag on and on and never come to an end?"

"Maybe," Reggie said, "because they did not want it to end."

Rose thought about her childhood in the orphanage, the succession of grim monotonous days, keeping her head down, doing the aldermen's bidding for fear of losing the precious moment of survival. She thought of Sander, fishing for men to feed his masters. She thought of Reggie adapting to the Net that had killed their parents.

"What is outside the City?" she asked.

"Death, I think," he said. But he did not sound sure.

"What will happen to me?" But she already knew the answer.

Reggie's tough cockroach wings clicked in excitement.

"The Net will fix you!" He cried. "I can talk to her … sort of. But she'll do it, I know! And you'll be one of us!"

A Day monster or a Night monster, she wanted to say; that's my choice.

But blood is thicker than water. Reggie is my brother.

But I loved Sander. He loved me. Maybe.

"Listen," she said, "I'd like to take a shower. Is it working?"

She knew there was no need to ask: every apartment had the same amenities, the same furniture, the same clothes and knick-knacks it had had in the moment before its destruction. The moment of infinite duration that would never end.

Until somebody put an end to it.

The water was hot and the towels exactly the same as they had been in their family apartment. Some alderman was now using them—or their infinitely multiplied reflection.

Drying herself off, Rose stood with her back to the mirror, not wanting to see the human body that might not be hers for long. Her eyes fell on the Second Door.

Every bathroom had one, but it was locked, inaccessible, believed to lead nowhere. After a while, one stopped seeing it. It was as familiar and worn-out as everything else in the City, dissolved into invisibility by the endless routine of survival.

Rose stood still.

Her clothes were thrown in a heap on the floor. She rummaged in the pocket of her jeans, found the key she had used to wound Sander. It was spotted with his blood.

She pushed it into the keyhole and turned.

The Second Door opened.

The Follower
By Ana Teresa Pereira

I'm afraid I have fallen in love with a country church and a graveyard; I don't think I could rest anywhere else. I go there nearly every day, and the long morning walk is like a godless pilgrimage. I take a bottle of water, my sketchbook, and some pencils: I can always use leaves and spit. In the middle of the afternoon, I'm back at the studio in the backyard—it used to be a shed, listening to Charles Mingus, reading a detective novel, and smoking. There are a lot of unfinished paintings here, and I am supposed to have an exhibition in London next month. I don't paint many things: the moor, heather, heather flowers, a spring, the lake with its deep blue water. No one else recognizes them on the canvas; apparently, things that pass through me are always transfigured.

When dusk comes, and it comes very early this time of the year, I return to the house. It gives us a sense of security, having breakfast in the kitchen, coffee and a bun, and then he going upstairs to the back room with the two steps that are like the threshold to another world, and I crossing the garden with its layers of wildness, and entering the shed. Two normal people, that go to work every morning and come back in the evening. Sometimes he is waiting for me at the kitchen door, and we enter the house solemnly; it has always been a sacred place, even when it was rather empty: the paintings and pieces of furniture with any value had been sold. After he married Stella, things didn't change much, and that surprised me. Stella, with her incredible beauty and all that money, was expected to surround herself with nice expensive things. But then Stella could always surprise me.

When I think of us, it is often as three children playing blind man's buff in the fog: a little boy with dreamy blue eyes, a blond girl that seemed to get dirtier than the others and always have her knees wounded, and a skinny girl with short brown hair, who was the best climber and the best swimmer. Three children pursuing each other in the fog, and our voices, and all our sinister songs.

Today, our cat hadn't come with me. He shares his life between Alan's studio and mine, our miniature tiger. I put on my black jacket and locked the door, but I don't think anybody would trespass; the noble house they had once revered is now a place where something happened that no one dares to mention. For us, it's still sacred, with little shrines here and there, a corner table with a vase of flowers and some stones, an old icon he has brought from one of his travels, a moonstone.

I walk slowly among the shadows; it's autumn now, and the world celebrates it, as we do. He is waiting for me at the kitchen door, and our cat is sitting on the windowsill among the pots of violets. Oh, my darling, to be here with you …

I had never seen the ocean before my mother and I came to the village, and I hated it: it was grey and quietly menacing, not blue waters turning into green. It was on the other side of the street, and the grey wall and the grey beach were not enough to keep us apart. I could hear it humming during the night; sometimes it kept me from sleeping. I longed for the village where I had lived before, the cozy house, the children next door, the bells of the nearby church, the small gardens, and laundry drying in the sun.

I was never as lonely as in that first autumn. I had no friends at school, and anyway I hated it; but nothing was worse than returning to that nightmarish street, to the grey flat with no light on. I delayed the moment as much as possible. I stayed in the local library for hours and stole a few books, when the pretty red-haired girl was flirting with some boy. Then I discovered the back door of the cinema was never locked and spent the evenings watching movies, English and French old movies, mostly black and white.

Near Christmas, I began to notice Alan in the cinema; I didn't know, but he was home from school. He was about my age and looked like a boy in a book illustrated by Lilian Buchanan. When we met years later in London, he said I looked like Audrey Hepburn in *Green Mansions*: my hair was long and well-treated, my dresses simple but deliberately simple, a kind of nakedness, because people only notice your body. I always sat in the back of the cinema, by a column, to hide in the intervals, though I suspected the old employee was aware of my presence. Alan and I became friends the night we saw for the first time a film with Robert Ryan and Ida Lupino, that would become one of the films of our lives. And, as in the movie, he brought me the world outside, a handful of flowers, the branch of a tree.

A few days later, I took the bus that went up the hill, crossed the moors and got to the next big village. I went down just before the moor; he was waiting for me at the bus stop. You couldn't see the house from the road, only the iron gate among the trees. The old house, with its red roof and the almost bare rooms; his father working in the library; and the long studio at the end of the corridor: the bookshelves, the table with notebooks and sketches, an easel near the window. The piano was downstairs, in an empty room. Something his teachers told him at college was that he dispersed himself, writing, painting, playing music. They understood nothing.

We went for a walk on the moor. It was winter, but he seemed to know his way even with the fog; he knew the plants, and often the names of the plants were the plants themselves; there weren't many birds, mostly curlews. And the lake surrounded by heather. I fell in love with the lake, with the tone of blue of the apparently frozen water.

I fall in love easily. I could fall in love with a man because of his hands, or the way he sat on a bed, or the way he held a cigarette. When we met in London, I had slept with many men, and I knew he had slept with many girls.

Stella entered our lives when he came home from school on spring break. We only had two days alone, to see his studio and his work, to walk on the moor, and return to the hidden lake: the dark waters that didn't move, not with wind, not with gale, but seemed to tremble with the rain.

Stella was the most beautiful creature we had ever seen. She was the daughter of Alan's father's best friend, who had built a holiday house nearby. It was natural that she spent most of the time with us; so, she arrived in the morning, a few minutes after the bus had left me in front of the gate, with her ash blond hair shining and a nice dress, and I felt like the tomboy I had always been. But she seemed to resent that perfection; she pushed her hair back and held it with a string; it took me some days to realize that she deliberately dirtied her dresses and wounded her knees. That was Stella.

She seemed content to hear Alan play the piano, to watch him drawing, to play hide and seek in the garden when there was fog, to follow us in the narrow paths of the moor. She was as afraid of the dark lake as I was of the grey sea, but she swam a little near the margin. It was one day, when Alan was showing her a sketch, and her blond hair, blue eyes, and white skin looked almost unnatural, that I decided to grow up beautiful. And I did.

He had travelled during the holidays, earning some money with his music and his drawings. I was happy enough sitting near the Thames and painting the fog again and again, lonely people in the fog, small dark shops, where one could enter a darker world. I loved the river; I love all fresh water; it's the sea that disturbs me; it's not the same element.

Now I go to the village once or twice a week, to buy fresh bread and vegetables, coffee, buns, some fish. A bunch of flowers, lavender polish, even though we don't receive anyone. The cinema has closed long ago. The library is often deserted; the girl with red hair is a spinster with glasses, who follows us with inquisitive eyes: she must read too many mystery novels. The books are the same, and it's easier to order a few or buy them when we go to London.

Alan and I didn't look for each other when we were studying in London, as if we had been too close, and needed to breathe for a while. Then one Saturday morning, not long after the opening hour, we found ourselves alone in the Rothko Room. I had arrived first and was sitting on a bench, when he sat by my side. His hand caught mine, and I remembered we once had been to the village chapel together. A few minutes later, a bunch of children and their teacher entered the room. We went out to the sun and walked by the river, and it was then he said You look like Audrey Hepburn in *Green Mansions*. My long straight hair was loose, and I was wearing a dress I could have made myself, just a bit of green tissue, the breasts barely covered, the arms and legs naked. He hadn't changed much; the boy from the illustrations would have been a man like that; he was that strange mixture of writer, painter, musician, but he looked like a wanderer, an adventurer.

"Do you have daffodils under your window?"

He stopped.

"No. Do you?"

"No. But then I am not at Oxford."

He laughed silently.

"But you have violets in the kitchen window," he said.

"How do you know?"

"You always loved stories with violets."

My room was small, but perfect for us: the narrow bed full of blankets like in a fairy tale, the working table, the easel near the window. I had painted the walls thinking of him, as I had made the cheap curtains and bought the two pots of violets: one had violet flowers, the other crimson.

When Krzysztof Kieslowski was writing *La Double Vie de Véronique*, he looked for the best puppeteer in the world. He found him, but the puppeteer was doing something else; couldn't earn a living with his art. And I was afraid the same would happen to Alan. He didn't separate things, and that is right, things are not separated; nobody wrote like him, always on the point of revelation, and then he interrupted it to draw; he spent a few days listening to the singing of a bird, he took a train to some remote place because of a picture he had seen: a lighthouse, a water course, a street covered with ice. He was following something and that was his task. He would go away for months and then come back to college and start studying for his exams; after all, he wanted to be a teacher and earn his living; maybe he could even keep his house.

I did sell some of my paintings, but no magazine accepted his stories or his drawings. I saw him the rest of his life in Oxford, with the ghost of Charles Ryder, but without daffodils under his windows.

One day, I pretended to meet Stella by chance. She was as gorgeous as anyone would have expected, with long blond hair and perfect transparent skin. But when she came back to us, she cut her hair and started combing it back, wearing jeans and cheap T-shirts; she would hurt her elbows and her knees if she could. She was studying languages and literature, but didn't seem to give a damn about it. She would bend over Alan's shoulder as in the old days, to follow his writing, his drawing; and I knew I only had to step aside. I started going out with other men again. I loved Alan's hands, but I've always liked tough hands in other men; and I fell in love easily, with the way they held a cigarette or sat on a bed. It was not really falling in love, but I liked sex, and it was almost relaxing, those other hands on my body, without the anxiety and the pain Alan's proximity brought to me. He was waiting for me once or twice near the building, even though he had a key, and I pretended not to see him. I pretended I was not in a Cornell Woolrich story, with a man on the other side of the street under the lamp, while some stranger with tough hands was sitting on my bed.

I had worked hard during those two years. I rented a small attic room in the building where I lived and turned it into a studio. I painted the walls and the ceiling that on one side came down to the floor and washed the big window. I could jump it easily and sit among the roofs with my tiger cat; I often put my canvas to dry against a chimney. I stayed in the studio even if I was not working but simply reading a novel, and at the end of the day I came down two flights of stairs with my cat on my shoulder. I warmed a soup or ate some bread and cheese, and, like Philip Marlowe, I fed my cat. Sometimes I spent the morning in a gallery copying a painting, once or twice a week I went to the movies, or, if I had money, I saw a play. There were no men, now that he was married to Stella.

They lived in his house. I imagined he had made all the repairs necessary, bought new furniture. I even imagined they received visitors and gave parties. The idea that he was with Stella did hurt, but he could spend his days studying the singing of a bird, reading detective novels, drawing quietly near the lake, going on those expeditions from which he came back with some leaves or stones, or a plastic bottle with the water of a distant spring or river; he could go on following the thing, the hidden thing he had sensed all his life.

I was not surprised the morning I found him waiting for me at the door of the building. It was raining, and I was wearing my old grey raincoat and no umbrella, and he said You look like Audrey Hepburn at the end of *Breakfast*. He took the bags with bread and fruit from my arms, and we went upstairs to my room. He sat on the bed; his hair was wet, too, and he looked like a little boy. I stood near him, and for a moment there was no physical desire; we were the two children that loved each other innocently. Then we took our raincoats off and looked at each other's bodies; we slowly recognized ourselves.

"I won't be apart from you again," he said.

"Have you been working?"

"Yes."

"That should be enough."

"It isn't."

"I like the way you sit on a bed."

He drew my body to his knees.

"I like the way you're always half naked even with your clothes on."

"There aren't many."

"I know."

He came to London from time to time, and, as when we were students, we slept in my narrow bed; one of us went out early to buy fresh buns, while the other made coffee. We had breakfast and spent the rest of the day working, I upstairs in the studio, he at our working table.

One evening, Alan looked rather upset when he arrived. But only when we were sitting at the kitchen table, with a bottle of wine in front of us, he said:

"Stella wants you to come and spend some days with us."

For a moment, I didn't understand.

"But did she know you were coming to see me?"

"Apparently. She drove me to the station and, just before the train left, she said Ask Jennie to come here for a week or two. The daffodils are starting to bloom. She loves daffodils."

We looked at each other, very solemnly.

"Do you want me to come?"

"Yes."

Suddenly, I realized how much I had longed for the house, the garden, the moor. Our lake. To bring a bottle of water from the lake to use in my paintings.

"It will be good for my work."

He nodded.

"For mine, too."

"I wonder."

"It was through you I felt the presence of things. The connection between things."

"No. You were like that when we met."

"It was blind man's buff before we met. But it was through you I began to get closer."

I tried to laugh.

"So, it was all my fault."

"In a way."

One Sunday afternoon, I went down the bus on the other side of the road, this time coming from the moor. Stella was waiting for me near the gate. Her hair was shorter and straightly pushed back, she wore a dark blue skirt, knee-length, and a white shirt, a jacket on her shoulders. She wasn't wearing any make-up, and her lips were thinner. We said hello rather coldly.

The house looked the same, and it moved me. The red roof, the walls covered with leaves, the yellow daffodils appearing miraculously on the front lawn. The garden looked as always, beautiful and cool but in need of a gardener. I guessed it was only Alan who worked in it. And I noticed the bareness of the rooms. The lady of the house didn't feel the need to show her riches, after all. There were no signs of parties in the big saloon, but the piano was tuned, and everything seemed cleaner, shinier. A faint smell of lavender polish and some dispersed vases of flowers. I learnt later that a girl from the village came every day, to clean the house and cook lunch.

We managed a simple dinner between ourselves. Then I washed the dishes, and Stella dried them. We didn't exchange more than two or three words. Only when she was hanging the towel, she looked me in the eyes and said:

"You are finally here."

"You invited me."

"You would come anyway."

I sat down, my hands clenched on my knees.

"I was in London, doing my work. You were the ones who came for me."

"You were calling us."

"Are you mad?"

"You never stopped following us."

I found nothing to say.

Her blue eyes softened.

"It was always the three of us, wasn't it?

"We were two. You were the intruder."

She closed her eyes for a moment.

"I tried not to be."

"We are not three children anymore. Why don't you take off the disguise?"

She looked at her skirt, her flat shoes.

"It doesn't work."

"Only from a distance. When we get closer …"

"What?"

"You are still the fairy tale princess."

A faint, sad smile.

"The fairy at the top of the Christmas tree. That's what Alan used to call me."

"I remember."

How could I forget?

The next day, after breakfast, I went to the moor with my sketchbook. Everything looked closer, our path, the heather, and finally the lake with its dark still water. I didn't come back for lunch. I took the bus and went to the next village, had a coffee and a scone and, in memory of some children's books I had loved, a strawberry ice cream. Then I went for a walk and was suddenly inside a new place: an old grey church, a quiet graveyard, abandoned flowers and a silence of birds. I took my sketchbook from the bag and sat on a stone.

Those were strange days: Stella playing the housewife, Alan closed in his studio, and I exploring the countryside. At night we sat together; we listened to music or read children's books—we were still partial to children's books. Sometimes we watched old TV Series, with actors we had been in love with, who had disappeared into the wings of obscure theatres or second-rate films.

Did any of us really believe it could be the same? Days of splendour in the fog? Or would we quietly go mad and end up singing *Here we go round the Mulberry Bush, the Mulberry Bush, the Mulberry Bush*, in the garden submerged by the fog?

And then, one evening, Stella didn't appear for dinner. She had been around in the morning, wearing a blue flowery dress, her hair loose, her eyes dark blue, her skin transparent, the most beautiful creature … I had thought for the first time that she was the more mysterious of us. The fairy at the top of the Christmas tree, the dancer in the music box.

They found her in the lake at dawn, no longer beautiful, no longer one of us. When the policeman told us the news, we looked at each other for a moment and his eyes were absent, darker; I shuddered. We both knew who had killed her.

The verdict was of suicide—as if our fairy tale princess would ever destroy her beauty, beyond some scratches or a bad haircut. We kept away from each other for a few months. I tried to work, but something was missing; I mostly read and walked in the streets. Then one day, in the beginning of autumn, autumn had always been our season, he was waiting for me on the sidewalk. He didn't say I looked like Audrey Hepburn; I thought for a moment I did, like Audrey Hepburn in *The Unforgiven*, with a long skirt and a brown jacket. He just said Let's go home.

I'm afraid I have fallen in love with a country church and a graveyard; I don't think I could rest anywhere else. I go there nearly every day, and the long morning walk is like a pilgrimage, but I don't know who or what I am trying to save. I sit on a stone and sketch: writing ink, a leaf, spit, water from the sacred fount. I have an exhibition in London next month, but it doesn't mean anything.

Dusk makes everything nearer, sadder. I close my jacket, as if I was cold, and walk towards the house. We have worked all day, and now I go back to him. The light of the kitchen is on. I can see him on the threshold; our cat is sitting among the violets. My heart warms up, this is my house, this is my place, and my man, and my cat. I fall in his arms, and he kisses my hair.

Oh, my darling, to be here with you, what a long, strange way I had to take.

Thin Suit

By David Quantick

Travis went to the audition but he didn't feel good about it. He didn't feel good about many things these days—his apartment, his drinking, his landlord, his bowels—but this was a worse not-good feeling than usual. Travis used to think he was a good actor but he'd fucked up so many auditions and calls in the last six months that he was beginning to think that maybe it wasn't the booze and the drugs and he was no good as an actor.

The notion that he could act had kept him going for a long time. As another girlfriend left the apartment sobbing that he was a piece of shit, Travis always consoled himself with the thought that, yes, she might have a point, but at least he could act. He wasn't sure how the two things—him being a piece of shit, and him being able to act—cancelled each other out, sometimes they felt more like a Moebius strip, meaning perhaps two sides of the same noose, but in his mind they did.

And when his father left messages on the machine, all *She's dying, you heartless fuck* and *She knows you took the money, that's what broke her*, he could just erase them, secure in the knowledge that, gold-standard shit-heel he might be, but he had a talent, and everything is forgiven when you have a talent. But lately, when he looked over at the snapshot that curled like a sail on his shelf, and peered at the letters on the stone in the picture, he began to suspect that the talent might be departing, might in fact have already departed and closed the door on its way out.

Each audition served to confirm this suspicion. The time he forgot what monologue he was supposed to be doing at the Everyman. The time he lapsed, for no reason whatsoever, into comic Uncle Tom dialect during his Othello piece at the Margrave. The time he pissed himself for real halfway through his Willy Loman at the Fulmar. Travis wasn't so much losing it as leaving it on the bus and getting off at the next stop without it. Time after time he found new ways to screw up the one thing he was good at. It was like whatever had found a reason to nest inside Travis and make him different and better had one day turned round, looked at the fleshy shithole it was inhabiting, and decided to just fuck off out of there.

But Travis needed rent, and food, and booze, and so he kept going to the auditions, and the auditions kept getting worse, and so did he, and it was all becoming more and more futile, until he heard about the thin suit.

It was like this.

Travis turned up at the Mortimer, which was holding an open call, and he was feeling particularly not ok. He'd been up until three trying to juggle learning his lines with drinking something that claimed to be Scotch whisky but was possibly lawnmower fuel. When he woke up the next day, he had been so violently sick that he'd actually checked his vomit for lung matter: but he hadn't puked up his lungs, just the burrito he'd eaten for dinner and an incredible amount of green bile.

He showered, shaved, ate some cereal without milk, and put on his cleanest clothes. Then he looked in the mirror. This was a mistake: either the mirror was in the pay of his worst enemies or he looked entirely like shit. Travis's face was the colour of week-old steak. His eyes looked like a bowl of yoghurt in which several thin-legged spiders had drowned. And his hair had been drawn on by an epileptic with a broken hand. His entire head resembled a kind of carnival waxwork that had been pulled out of the furnace at the last minute. *At least I look how I feel*, Travis thought as he pulled a comb through his hair like a human sacrifice being dragged to the altar. He shrugged, pulled on a jacket with many of its buttons still present, and left his apartment.

Ten minutes later he was outside the Mortimer, looking at a cigarette and wondering if his need to smoke it would be offset by the strong chance it might make him throw up again. He tossed a coin in his head, lit the cigarette, and managed to keep his breakfast down until someone with a clipboard came out of the building and said, "Hi everyone, um, we're seeing the first three people in line."

Before Travis could turn around and establish that he was, by some fluke of destiny, first in line, everyone else outside began to move towards him.

"I was here first!" he shouted, and maybe it was the despair in his voice or the reek of bile in his breath, but everyone moved back and let Travis pass through the door.

Maybe I do still have it, he thought as he made his way into the auditorium.

Even though he was still feeling not OK, Travis was experiencing a mild adrenalin rush. Twenty years of failure had not completely eroded the excitement of going up for a part. Here he was, again, still, in a real theatre, auditioning for a real part in front of a real director and a real producer. It was happening, still, again, and it was real, and he was here.

Travis scoped the room. There was a table and a chair onstage. The seats in the middle of the front row were occupied by the people whose show it was. And that was it. There was him and the other two hopefuls, who were standing next to him now.

Travis scoped the competition. Like him, they were male, white, in their thirties, and giving off a faint aura of panic and hope. Unlike him, they were clean-cut, better-shaved, and were clearly the first people to own the clothes they were wearing. Travis hated their guts.

"Hi!" he said, sticking out his hand, "Travis."

The others responded in kind, although Travis immediately forgot their stupid names. As it was clear that the director and producer or whoever weren't ready yet, the three of them fell into desultory chat.

"This would be a great role for me," one said.

"I have no chance," said the other.

"Best man win," said Travis.

"Look at me," said one. "I got no chance."

"You?" said the other, laughing like actors do, "You're fine. You'll get it, I know. Me? I'm screwed."

Travis, who actually was screwed, narrowed his eyes. The other guy seemed normal to him. He was even fairly good-looking, bar a very slight potbelly.

"How do you mean?" he asked, "Screwed?"

"I'm too old, too messed-up, and too fat," said the other, pointing at his almost invisible gut. "I need a—"

And he paused, as if he'd embarked on a sentence whose ending he didn't know and was waiting for the end of it to arrive. It must have come, because then he said, oddly:

"I need a thin suit."

There was a short silence.

"A what?" said the first guy.

"A thin suit," the other one said, sounding a bit embarrassed. "Like a fat suit, you know, only in reverse."

"Oh," said the first guy. "Oh!" he added, and laughed.

Travis joined in, although he didn't see what was especially funny. But people like it when you laugh, so it's all good.

Travis' audition did not go well. His stomach began to churn halfway through the speech—Loman again—and this made him conscious of his physicality in an unwelcome manner. It was like the noise in his gut woke up every unhappy fibre in his chaotic body. His head hurt, his joints ached, his ears itched, his eyes felt gritty, he wanted to piss, he wanted to sit down, he wanted to fart, he wanted to sleep… He felt ugly, and ill, and dumb, but most of all, he felt fat.

Travis had never felt fat before. He was just a man of slightly overweight build with a beer belly and, as he'd always gone up for parts where the person he was playing could conceivably be slightly overweight with a beer belly, his size had never been a problem. But now? As he stood onstage reciting lines with no more or less feeling than the scene required, Travis was suddenly aware of every single ounce of flesh that he was carrying. In his mind he could see every chunky limb, every neck roll and ring of belly fat, and he could feel the weight of it all.

He made it to the end of the piece, muttered his thanks, and headed out into the morning sunshine without even leaving his details. He walked straight down the road into the nearest coffee shop, bought a bottle of water, and sat down.

Travis' mind was racing. He was a blimp! How had he not noticed before? He was a barrel of pork on legs, a disgusting balloon of farts and blubber. No wonder he couldn't get work! No wonder his talent had abandoned him! He was just too gross to look at, too fat to fuck and too enormous to even contemplate. It all made sense now.

What I need, he thought, and it was if the idea had been waiting all his life for him to think it, *is a thin suit.*

Travis had no idea where to get a thin suit. It didn't seem like the kind of thing you could buy in a store. He put the words into his computer but nothing came up; nothing useful anyway. Travis considered putting an ad in the paper, but that would probably just mean a lot of cranks would call him up. So he tried to forget about it and got on with what even the most optimistic of men would have had difficulty in calling his life.

The idea would not go away, though. Sometimes he imagined himself starring in a play or even a movie, with starlets cooing over him and awards coming at him like bricks, and he'd be saying to some chat show host or other, *All it took to get here was a lot of hard work, some talent—oh, and a thin suit.* And everybody would laugh, and only Travis would know the truth.

On other occasions he'd be cleaning the bathroom in a fast food restaurant—by now, Travis had passed the point where he could attend auditions—and a gob of bile would rise in his throat as he watched himself poke turds back into a toilet bowl, and think *this wouldn't happen to a guy with a thin suit.*

But mostly he just lay on his bed and dreamed of the unattainable, the indescribable, thin suit.

Some time later—a long while after that morning at the Mortimer—Travis was entering his second day in the temporary employ of his third boss of the month, a company who kept the public areas of bus stations free of piss, shit and syringes, when he heard a phone ring.

He looked around. Travis no longer had a cellphone, and the station was deserted. Then he realised the sound was coming from a payphone in a cubicle behind him. Travis had never seen this phone before, but that didn't mean anything: at this point in his decline, a mammoth in a silver bikini could have lain down in front of him and he wouldn't have thought it odd.

The phone continued to ring. Travis tried to get on with his work, but the ringing was getting to him, so he picked the receiver up from its cradle and put it back down again. The phone immediately started ringing again. Travis picked it up and set it back down. The third time this happened, Travis spoke into the receiver.

"Hello?" he said.

A voice replied:

"I have it."

"Have what?" asked Travis.

"You know what," said the voice.

"No, I don't," Travis said.

"The suit," said the voice, "The thin suit."

Travis felt a tingle run down his spine.

"How—" he began, but the voice just said: "See you later."

Travis put down his broom and walked out into the street. He continued to walk for six or seven blocks, not thinking about where he was going, until he came to a small side street, the kind where every building is the back of somewhere else and the walls are crisscrossed with fire escapes.

One of the buildings had a door in it, propped open with a cinderblock. Travis went in and climbed the stairs to a room on the second floor.

"Come in," said a voice. It was the same voice as the phone call.

Travis went in.

The room was sparsely furnished, to say the least. There was a plastic garden chair, faded and white, which Travis sat on. There was a large trestle table, covered in pins and random fabric shapes. And there was a dressmaker's dummy, made of some unpleasant pink foam-like substance. Standing next to it was a man. He was, in Travis' opinion, a weird-looking kind of a man but in what way weird it was hard to say.

"It's nearly ready," said the man. And he lifted the thin suit, which Travis hadn't even seen, from the dummy and held it up for Travis to look at. Travis didn't know what to say, because he'd never seen a thin suit before and had nothing to compare it with, so he just nodded and grunted.

"Here, put it on," said the man, and the next thing Travis knew, he was wearing the thin suit.

"How is it?" the man asked, the tone of his voice suggesting that he knew full well how it was.

"It's great," said Travis: and it was.

"I thought so," said the man and he sounded pleased.

"Can I—" Travis said, then stopped. The thought was too much for a man who'd been through what he'd been through.

"Can you keep it?" said the man.

Travis felt foolish. Of course he couldn't keep it. When had Travis ever been allowed to keep anything good? And the thin suit was good, make no mistake. It was more than good. It made him feel like he could do anything. Be anything. Be anyone. Fuck anything and anyone. Say and do what he liked, and shit on the consequences. It was like being high, except it was real. And no way was Travis going to be allowed to keep something this amazing.

"Of course you can keep it," said the man, "It was made for you."

Travis almost cried with gratitude.

"Thank you," he said. Then fear overcame him.

"I can't afford this," he said. "It must be worth a fortune."

The man shrugged.

"Pay me later," he said. "You'll know when."

For the last time in his life, Travis felt like a lunk. Not knowing what else to do, he stuck his hand out.

The man shook his head and made a face, as though Travis had taken his dick out instead. Then he smiled. It was the best smile Travis had ever seen.

"Enjoy it!" he said, and dismissed Travis with a wave.

And that's it, if you're asking—or even if you're not. You think things need your permission to happen? Travis walked out of there, and never looked back. What do you mean, what happened to him? You know what happened to him.

You saw him. You saw him everywhere.
You followed his career.
You watched his show.
You laughed at his stand-up special.
You rooted for him.
You played his song on your phone.
You downloaded his movie.
You jacked off to his picture.
You voted for him.
You're going to die for him.

Maybe you should have got a thin suit, too.

Autonomous
By Lyle Hopwood

It wasn't immediately apparent why the autonomous vehicle notified Surya that it wanted to hand over control to a human. Surya, sitting in his cubicle in the Faraday data centre, struggled with the camera views before he realized the person in the driver's seat must be incapacitated. Surya could tell they had slumped over from the way there was no head between the rear-view mirror and the car's internal camera. Drunk, asleep, giving head … It wasn't his place to figure out why. His task was to get the vehicle to safety and hand control back to the autonomous system.

He checked the external views again. The car had been reversing into a parking spot. He took over the wheel, accelerator and brake and continued backing into the space. The parking lot markings were US standard and the buildings to his and the driver's left were the stucco-clad, beige mini-mall buildings of Middle America. There were grackles on the asphalt, but they'd get out of the way by themselves. There were abandoned carts in view but not in the way, no people, only a sickly sapling planted in a concrete-kerbed rhombus of dirt. Surya backed the car into the space, watching the reversing camera, and stopped with the rear bumper about eight inches away from the struggling little tree.

With the car now out of traffic, Surya touched his controls to get the Highway Patrol online, simultaneously activating a line to the AAA. Triple A answered first, and Surya gave them the car's details. It was a Midnight Magenta Faraday SUV, license plate 2GAT123. He read off the parking spot location and gave a description of the occupant's apparent incapacity. He used his American name—Stuart.

The dispatcher chuckled. "Thanks for the heads-up, Stuart … is that your real name? What time is it in Delhi?"

Surya switched off the Faraday's engine. The system had noted that the first vehicle was stationary, and the emergency services had been called. His activity screen was already flashing to indicate another vehicle needing his help. He had twenty seconds to pick it up or be reported to his supervisor.

In his excellent Queen's English, Surya said, "It's pretty late here in Gurgaon, dispatcher. I'm looking forward to a bloody good night's sleep in a couple of hours. I'll be sleeping better knowing I've got a good man on the job!" He cut the connection before the dispatcher could make any more small talk.

His system patched him through to another vehicle. Surya massaged his temples as he got a read on the new vehicle. He tried to ignore his heart, which was pounding from defeat, loss and rage. Not because he'd parked a vehicle, he reminded himself. That was the easiest auto-to-remote-driver hand off imaginable. No, the depression was coming from inside the house, to use a phrase he'd learned from American films. He was bringing his internal anger into his job, and his job was stressful enough without personal issues intruding.

The newly connected vehicle was speeding down a US freeway. The Faraday self-driving system was out of specification and signalling it needed to hand control over to a human. The cause of the parameter excursion was illegible signage above the lanes. Surya's heart continued to race, now exacerbated by adrenalin. The latency period, the time between the car's video reaching him and his reactions getting back to the car, was almost a second. The Faraday AI always handled the issues requiring a quick reaction time, such as brake lights appearing ahead of the vehicle. This had been drummed into him during training, along with the conceit of calling the vehicle occupant "the driver," characterizing the onboard person as the final decision maker. This, Surya felt, took no account of reality. Surya knew, deep in his pounding heart, that the 'drivers' never read their manuals, and his body reacted as though he was the last line of defence. It insisted on preparing itself for a series of fast decisions and irreversible actions.

He reviewed the signage rapidly. The signs were in place, the lanes weren't coned off, nor had the lane markings been altered since the last time the freeway had been surveyed. There were no vehicular accidents or slowdowns. The AI had failed to read the overhead sign because someone had sprayed reflective graffiti over it. A few ounces of glitter had defeated the billion-dollar artificial intelligence. The Faraday network normally handled overhead sign problems by displaying jpegs of the signs to people doing online shopping. "Prove you are not a robot," a little box would say before they could check out. "Type in the words you see in this picture." After eleven to seventeen answers (the trainers told him) the new interpretation of the sign was propagated throughout the network. There must not have been time for that process to complete, and so the system was requesting the help of the data centre human personnel. He prompted the AI to stay in lane. Machine-readable signage appeared ahead, and he and the AI agreed the vehicle was on the road the driver had selected. He signed it off as returned to safety.

He looked at the clock on the wall. He had one, maybe two, more incidents to handle before his ten-hour shift was over. Before a vehicle could be assigned to him, he picked one—another West Coast US issue. He was good at them. He'd had the practice.

Surya walked back to his lodgings in the morning to save money. He was originally from a small town near Chennai, and the main breadwinner for a poor family there. He lived and worked in Gurgaon, in Delhi, because that was where the money was. It was the Indian centre of BPO, Business Process Outsourcing. Working the phone lines, providing support to customers thousands of miles away, was a huge and growing business. Americans did not want to pay a real Stuart from, say, Kentucky, to bill customers or fix their laptop trackpad problems. That could cost $8 an hour or more. Surya earned $2 an hour for the first forty hours and $3 an hour for overtime. He calculated he could earn $5000 in a year, five times what his cousins earned in the village back home. The trick was to earn the money, keep his nose clean and live in the cheapest hostel he could find so he could send cash to his parents. He'd been sending money to Anjali's family as well.

The walk from work to his hostel wended from the Faraday data centre, behind the mesh fence of the luxury car dealership with the armed guards at the gate, past four tower blocks that sprang unexpectedly from level, unimproved ground, and around the cricket pitch into the town itself. It was hot, even this early in the morning. If he wasn't at the hostel by sunrise he would bake. He quickened his stride, walking past several cows who turned to watch, and he reached his room just after dawn.

Surya had been sending half his money back to Anjali's father for their wedding next year. They'd been sweethearts since he was a boy and up to last week nothing suggested that would change. Then Anjali had sent him a letter 'regretting' that she had found a local boy who would be her beau. He'd spoken to her on his cell only a few days before that, and she hadn't mentioned any dissatisfaction. Ugly thoughts and images surfaced in his mind. She was a liar! She had taken his money and spent it on a man! He tried to fall asleep on his pallet in his hostel. There were hundreds of young men there, all working BPO jobs for foreign firms, all coming back to sleep in the man-warehouse at night, all like him sending their money to their families back home.

A year ago, when Surya had left his little village for the Big City, he was following in the footsteps of his uncle. Uncle Hari took a course to become a worker at a BPO centre. Companies all over the world paid Indians to handle billing disputes, technical help and call routing, he said. There was one drawback, he explained—Indians spoke dozens of languages. Uncle Hari had grown up speaking Tamil, so he promised a company his first three month's salary upfront to sit in a tiny, airless room in the high-tech district, learning English. He graduated, went on to Billing Process, made it through the first few months of no pay and started earning real money.

Following the same plan, Surya signed on at the English school. He read a grammar book on the train and expected no trouble picking up colloquialisms, but the school proved harder than he expected. The teacher was a tiny woman called Monica, who had a short temper and wore a different bright-coloured pantsuit every day. The lessons included repetitive drills designed to force him to lose his accent. Early on, Surya had raised his hand and hesitantly asked if he could learn to speak American.

"No! The goal of this teaching is to make your accent neutral. You must be understandable to the Aussie and to Brits. They must not think of you as an American."

Between each cobra-strike "No!" whenever a student got a sound wrong, there were vocabulary exercises and pop quizzes on life and culture in Australia and the US.

"Dayanand, give me three minutes about life in New York City. Keep vowels neutral. Keep your head up."

"In New York City," Dayanand began, "We eat hot dogs, and we have to line up at the DMV to register our automobile. It is snowing on the ground …"

He went on for his allotted time, and the teacher turned her basilisk glare on Surya. "Three minutes on a baseball game," she said. "Now."

Surya had read up on baseball and managed to get through a description of his "favourite" team, the Red Sox. He had never seen a baseball game. If the teacher were so jolly keen about being multi-national, he thought, she could have asked about cricket.

Getting ready to dismiss them for the day, the teacher said, "I want you all to eat an American hamburger. Remember, when you are in the call centre, you will not be Indian. You will hate Indian things. You will love American things. You will love the Queen and Australian Rules Football. Your village is nothing. The customer is everything."

Surya passed a food stand on the walk home. He wondered if anyone in the class would eat a beefburger just because the teacher told them to. He bought a *paneer dosa* wrap instead. It was delicious. His walk took him past a tiny pool of shade where the local cows gathered. "Don't worry about me," he told them, showing them the wrapper, green for vegetarian. "I won't eat you." He crumpled the wrapper up and put it in his pocket, mindful not to litter.

After twenty days in class, Surya graduated. He looked forward to his placement in Billing Process, which was in one of the nearby multi-story buildings. He called his uncle, who congratulated him. Uncle dropped his voice and told him the real money was in Fake Process.

"What's that?" Surya asked, sweating under the limping fan of his hostel room.

"We scam the Americans," his uncle said. "We are taught a list of things that will get an American to give you her credit card number, or her log in details. Then you pass them to the group that uses them, and you get ten percent of their proceeds."

"Is that … is that ethical?"

"Americans are rich, Indians are poor. It is bringing balance, which is always ethical."

"Why would they give you their financial details?"

"There are fifteen ways, but my favourite way is number eight, which is I tell them that there are millions of dollars waiting in dormant accounts. I tell them the government seizes the account after a year and a day without transactions. I tell them that our bank has permission to share it out to people with current accounts in other banks instead of giving it to the government. I tell them I need their bank account number to initiate the transfer."

Surya thought it over. Back then, almost a year ago, he decided that Billing Process would be the better path to follow, morally.

Unfortunately, there had not been enough turnover in Billing, and the young Sikh man who did the induction duties told Surya he would be assigned to Collections Process.

"What is the difference?"

"In Billing Process, you help people with questions about their medical bills and auto loans and so on. In Collections Process, the people have not paid their bill and you explain they must pay. When you really think about it, it is the same thing."

The training period for Collections Process was only three days. "Americans are rich," the trainer said on the first day. "They are not paying their bills because they want to hold on to their money. We are telling them they have received the services and now they are paying." He had not had Surya's training in how to lose his Hinglish language rhythm.

He began to call Americans and ask them to pay their bills.

Collections Process was a nightmare. Surya called the rich Americans and ran through his script, intended to guilt them into paying whatever medical bill or auto loan was past due. He could hear those around him going through their scripts and inputting credit card numbers. It was clear that they enjoyed the work, as much as anyone enjoyed being in a call centre in the middle of the night in New Delhi's frequent heatwaves. The first few he called promised to think about it. The next one swore at him and hung up. The next one said he did not have the money.

"It's three hundred dollars," Surya said, as if that would settle the matter. That was nothing, surely. Americans are rich.

"They repossessed the car last week. I haven't eaten in two days. I can't get any work because I don't have a car. I'm going to starve, Stuart."

"You can put it on your credit card."

"I don't have a credit card, man. They made me cut it up. I just have the debit card and there's nothing in the bank to back it up. I mean nothing."

The next call was to a woman in the south of the US. Surya found her accent difficult, even after all his training, but she couldn't pay either. "They cut out things in my belly they said I wouldn't need no more, but it's a year later and it hurts like hell. I ain't been able to work since the operation and they been chasing me for twenty thousand dollars ever since. Where am I going to get twenty thousand dollars? I don't got fifty."

"We can put you on a gentle weekly repayment plan, miss."

"Like the bail bondsman offered me? You owe a hundred, you pay twenty a month and after six months you owe two fucking hundred. I been there."

Surya typed in his own figures. She was exaggerating only a little.

At the end of his first harrowing day in Collections, Surya was invited out to a club by the Billing and Collections guys. His group piled into a Maruki Suzuki Alto hatchback that wended its way through the dust, traffic and street traders to Hotel Marchpane. The driver, Ashok, threw his keys to the valet and the five of them—four experienced city dwellers earning five times the national wage, and one newbie—walked through the frangipani-scented marble lobby to the neon-lit door of the bar.

Surya had never seen girls like the ones in the bar, nor heard sounds like the electronic dance music that pulsed across the floor. It was the sound of Detroit, of London, of Coachella, with touches of non-western scales that marked it as Indian. The drinks were strong. And on occasion, a discreet man in a suit came around to check if you needed anything. That man was the dopeman.

Drinking with his new friends, Surya tried to raise the subject of his Collections calls, the misery and poverty of the Americans he'd called, when he demanded their money. The others did not take his bait. Eventually Ashok bellowed in his ear: he would have to learn to ignore the excuses if he were to become successful. And if he were successful, he could apply to work in Fake Process—the phishing department. But Surya remembered his Uncle Hari telling him about his work in Fake Process. It was not ethical. "I would very much like that," he lied, red-faced from the heat. Or was it the drink?

After working three months to pay off his English lessons, money began to flow. He was able to hire cabs, bribe bartenders and call over the dopeman with a sly wink. He'd become a success in Collections. He did not call over the slinky girls who sat in the corner nursing lemonades and making eyes at him, because he had Anjali back home. Her picture was beside his mattress at the hostel, in an ornate aluminum frame. He sent money to her father and to his own. He lied, very slightly, about his total income and used the surplus to buy drink as well as a little cocaine. And on occasion, when the shrieks of anguish from the American debtors got too loud, he even had a little dab of heroin.

Surya had watched Americans, and the British and the Aussies, on film and TV. But he had particularly watched the Americans. They were loud, they were outspoken. Their women wore few clothes. Above all they were rich, with new cars and giant SUVs. Those cars were fast, and their roads were wide and endless and an American could drive his V8 forever down the two-lane blacktop to the Promised Land, which was beyond the red-striped mesas of Utah and Arizona and deep into the marble canyons of New York. Yet when he phoned them, they reacted with fear and horror. They had not intended to get sick and they had no money to pay the hospital. They'd leased the car, yes, but after a month they'd fallen ill and missed a week at work, and no work meant no car payment.

Surya got out of Collections into Billing within three months. He still had to deal with the quiet sobbing of the poor, but the incoming calls were more positive.

"Hello? Billing? At last. I've been on hold for nine minutes. How the fuck do I input my date of birth into that third box down on your stupid website?"

"Hello, miss. This is Stuart. I'm available to talk you through the date of birth entry process on our website. Do you see a logo in the left-hand corner?"

Once he knew which billing system was confusing the customer, he could talk them through it, line by line in his unaccented English.

Afterwards, in Delhi's early morning, he'd have some coke to perk himself up, and still sometimes a little dab of heroin, to keep the nightmares away.

Later, he'd got his job with the autonomous vehicle company Faraday. He heard no more from the crying people. This job was his dream. He would be alerted by his console to look at his screens, and then he helped drive a luxury car through the American highway system. He saw the granite towers of New York first-hand. He learned to recognize Chicago from the city silhouette. He discovered that 8 Mile, in Detroit, was not just a rap lyric. Los Angeles was truly a sunny paradise. He drove over the Golden Gate Bridge, from which he could see Alcatraz. California's Coastal

Highway 1 appeared regularly on his screens, not just to watch, but to drive. He saw the breakers on the west coast that epitomized the American Dream of catching the perfect wave. On more than one occasion he was privileged to see Route 66 signs as he chaperoned out-of-specification vehicles into the correct lane for their turnoff. The beauty of the US was his to drive.

But now, six months in, the American Dream was sloughing away in fragments, as dreams do when you wake. What had been bright and meaningful and all-consuming was just a disco ball of lights and nonsense, shrinking back in the rear-view mirror of reality. That evening he walked back towards the Faraday building, past the cricket pitch. He thought over his life choices. He was earning a lot of money, and if he did not have to send any to his ex-fiancée Anjali, he could move out of the hostel. His journey took him past a crowded food court, with its wall-sized colourful placard displaying the dishes available. He sniffed the air, and the smell of fried spices whisked his mind back to his days in the BPO call centre. They even sold *paneer dosa* wraps. And with that recollection, there came uncalled memories of nights out with his Billing and Collections buddies and the cocaine highs they had shared. He made a call and ordered a cab, detouring by his old dealer's spot, where he bought enough coke to keep dark thoughts away for a few days.

He had a hangover and to clear his head, he used a little of his coke. It would be instant dismissal to be found with it at work, of course, and he wavered for minutes before wrapping some in a piece of notepaper and putting it in an inner pocket. The armed guards weren't in front of his facility, after all. They guarded the places with tangible things to steal.

He sat down. The screens spread out before him were displaying tracking information for vehicles that were at the edge of the parameters for the self-driving AI but had not yet requested the data centre humans take over. He felt the familiar cold rush as his body prepared itself. His nerves were convinced that if he were truly geared up, he could beat the latency period, like a superhero switching into super-speed.

All the vehicles stayed in self-driving mode as he attempted to calm himself down. The cocaine was not conducive to relaxation and the hangover was getting worse. A stray thought of Anjali arose, and he slapped it down viciously. As he struggled to remain focused on the screens, he saw Tasnim, a girl who worked a few spots down from him, enter the room. She stood in front of her cubicle, pulled off her scarf and took off her outer top, leaving her arms bare to the shoulders. Surya had noticed this before—some Muslim girls like Tasnim would come to work fully covered, but when they were through the door, they took off their headscarves. Some even changed into western skirts.

He looked at his screens, tried to concentrate. "You have to learn to hate India," his teacher had said. "You have to learn to love America." He shook his head to clear it. The sight of Tasnim's bare shoulders summoned a vision of Anjali. At this time, almost midnight, what would she be doing? She was not waiting chastely for her beau to come back and propose marriage. She could be anywhere. With a man.

He wondered about the driver of the vehicle he had parked outside the Walmart yesterday. Why did he not have his hands on the wheel? Was something wrong with him? You never found out what happened to the people who entered your life for a minute or less and then were gone forever. He could be dead.

Telemetry came up on his right-hand screen. A Faraday SUV was signalling for live assistance. Its map did not match the road and it could not read the lane markings. He took over, forcing to the back of his mind Anjali and his hangover and the cows he'd begun to eat and his rich uncle who cheated old people out of their savings. The car was on a freeway. A huge construction project was underway, and Caltrans had taken to moving the concrete triangular prisms of the Jersey barriers every few days, creating new lanes of varying widths atop a rutted, uneven pavement. Surya pointed the car in the right direction and made it recognize the barrier as a type of lane marker. He slowed the car to prevent its wheels catching in the ruts, which could have run it straight into the concrete blocks. The AI signalled it was clear to restart autonomous driving; he signed it off.

He sent the new road information off to be checked and downloaded to the other vehicles in the area. For all he knew, he was the fifth or tenth to get a car through that re-routed off-ramp today. Eventually information reached the threshold, and everything would change for the cars in the area. They would run efficiently in new lanes, ones that had not been there before. The old ways would be wiped clean, and they would drive as if there had never been an old road.

He rubbed his eyes. He felt used, weak, like a brake pad worn beyond its tolerance limits. He opted to take a rare restroom break. He was allowed two fifteen-minute breaks a day, along with a half hour lunch. If he took his breaks, then he was expected reduce his downtime between tasks to less than a few seconds for the rest of the shift. It was better not to take the breaks and to use the precious extra few seconds between duties to calm himself down and get centred.

In the restroom he sniffed a bump of coke. A thought hit him. Prove you are not a robot. But he couldn't prove he was not a robot. He could read a Captcha like a man, but in the school, in that hot little room, the woman in the cerise and saffron pantsuits had reprogrammed him like an automaton.

"You must learn to hate India," Monica, the teacher had said. "You must learn to love America. Have you had a hot dog from the food court yet? Surya, have you ever eaten a hamburger?"

His mind had driven along the old roads and ramps of India, and she had shifted the lane markings, made him run in the new lanes. She had made him forget the old street map and instead be constrained between shifting concrete barriers. She had twisted and distorted his inner atlas until even Anjali had not recognized his new road plan. The same woman must have poisoned Tasmin's mind, destroyed her Indian dedication to modesty. And his Uncle Hari, a great man of his town, an elder, an upstanding member of the community, had been taken apart by call centre algorithms and repurposed as a venal man who preyed on the innocent.

He looked out of the restroom window at the crowds of ordinary people outside. Over there were the half-empty skyscrapers. The ground between was undeveloped, flattened, tamped and infertile. Over here, the packed food court, in an atrium filled with small businesses, issued strange foods: sushi, Kentucky Fried Chicken, Thai curry.

Further out, he knew, the roads were covered in dried mud and the swarms of motorcyclists drove carefully over the hardened ruts. The patient cows stood there in twos and fours under shade trees. The sidewalks were stained crimson from betel-spit and the spicy smell of lunch would rise at mid-day from the tiffin boxes being delivered to businesses and stately ancient households run by spinsters.

He earned more in a year than those spinsters had accumulated in their lives. If really wanted it, he could buy one out and live in her stone house with its herb-filled garden. He was richer than the Americans he'd phoned by the dozen, daily, in Collections Process. He had been told to love America, land of rock and movies and great cars, but he had listened to Americans speak of their deprivation and lack of opportunity. Men with no legs and no jobs, women abused and in hiding, divorced men with wives to pay for and nothing for themselves. In the meantime, his uncle was getting rich on ten percent of every bank account whose details he could scam out of the uneducated couch potatoes he called.

His uncle had recently bought himself a Faraday with the profits. The biggest, baddest, reddest coupe, top of the line. It was festooned with cameras and a sound system that rivalled an in-home cinema. Surya had ridden in it once. He had almost drowned as he sunk into the soft leather, half dozy from the smell of high-end tanning and lambswool floor mats. His uncle had joined him on the backseat while the autonomous car had taken them from Surya's meagre hostel to his uncle's top-end hotel.

The coke had cleared his head. He combed his hair with his fingers and checked his nose. He walked to his cubicle, replaced his headset and, taking a shaky breath, let the system know he was back. I am operating within my specification, he thought. I have returned to my reprogrammed lane layout. He touched the keyboard. There were a dozen cars in his system, the rows of text representing each vehicle rising up the list and dropping down the screen as problems developed or were solved. He felt detached from the process, watching his own actions as if they belonged to someone else. He was mesmerized by the shifting levels of dilemmas the AI faced. The vehicle coming to the top of the list most frequently was a Faraday SUV, in Southern California, driving south on the I-5. Its tires were correctly pressured, and its brakes and power pack were nominal. The roads were readable, dry and good quality. The issue was the driver, who was gripping the wheel and occasionally trying to override the AI. The next one down was a small, overpowered coupe. It was in Michigan in icy conditions and the AI's assessment of its anti-lock brakes' readiness was flickering between 97% and 93%, the difference between roadworthy and service required. It had notified the driver by lighting up the instrument panel, but the driver had not relinquished control.

He understood all this in a glance. He knew the standard responses. What he didn't know was what was happening to the bloody driver. Was the man (or woman) with the failing brake system trying to get home in a hurry and couldn't brook a delay? Was the man in the SUV fighting the AI's steering because he was drunk, or didn't know how to disable self-drive, or did he really know the road better? And what was the problem with the driver of the car he'd parked at Walmart yesterday? Maybe he was dead!

One of the problem cars on his screen jumped to the top, lighting up with a contrasting red background, signalling an emergency. He touched the keyboard and the camera feed came up on his monitors. The vehicle was travelling fast, southbound on a highway, the US-101. The driver's trip plan showed that he wanted to take the SR-85 southbound. Most California off-ramps are to the right of the road. This one was unusual. It was on the left.

The vehicle was a red luxury coupe, like his uncle's. In the land of people who could not afford a dentist or a doctor, someone had bought the same overpriced vehicle his scammy relative had acquired with his ill-gotten gains. Surya glared at his screens. The autonomous AI had determined that a particular marked lane constituted the turnoff, but part of its system had flagged the appearance of unknown white and red stripes ahead. Coupled with the unusual leftward lane change, it found itself outside its operating parameters, required to ask for human assistance.

Surya could tell that the AI was misreading the marking. The "lane" led up to a crash cushion, a row of water-filled plastic barrels with white and red warning stripes. Beyond the barrels would be the blunt end of the chest-high concrete wall that separated the freeways after the turnoff. What the vehicle thought was a "lane" was what Caltrans called a "gore", a no-man's land that Caltrans often marked up between drivable lanes. To the left, a turn off; to the right, the continuation of the freeway, and straight ahead, the impact attenuator. It was a Clever-Cushion 125MG, a very efficient device for slowing down cars that failed to make a choice between two traffic lanes.

If someone hits a crash cushion, then Caltrans, alerted by the Highway Patrol, comes along the next day to replace it. A line of smashed plastic shards without water-filled bins no longer constitutes an effective crash barrier. Surya saw, as the car approached it, that the crash barrier had been hit, but Caltrans had not yet replaced it. It was simply a line of colourful plastic wreckage in front of the concrete wall.

The vehicle was heading for the crash cushion. With one touch, Surya could move the vehicle to the left and into the offramp lane, off the US Highway and on to the 85, as thousands of vehicles did every day.

Surya sat back and folded his arms. "This is what you get, rich man," he said to the screen. You clone of my uncle, the man who robs the poor of their rightful earnings, you doctor who bills the poor, you man who eats beefburgers from the drive-thru every day. The car raced towards the crash cushion.

The vehicle smashed into the plastic shards, throwing them to either side like a boat ploughing through rough sea, and hit the concrete barrier. The vehicle somersaulted into the air, gracefully, landing on its back on the 85.

Surya looked at the car from all his cameras. The driver was visible in the twisted wing mirror, slumped over the top of the driver's window. A complex tracery of blood stretched from his ear to his chin.

He even looked a bit like Uncle Hari. Surya measured out another bump of coke. There'd be an investigation. He would have to get rid of the cocaine. But the crash itself was a work of beauty, and unlikely to be attributable to himself. Perhaps Faraday would be sued. Maybe not. He thought about hamburgers and India and Anjali, sighed, and selected the next vehicle that needed his human touch.

A Bend in the Road

By Thomas Frick

It's been said by many claiming to possess the secrets of the ages that, from the perspective of higher dimensions, our lives can be seen whole, laid out from before our births until after our deaths, each moment able to reveal its particular truth without contamination by causality. Even if such a belief is true (and I'm inclined to accept it), it gives me no guidance whatever regarding where to begin this tale of something that happened long ago. Indeed, the enigmatic events I'm going to relate might have been lying in wait throughout my life, or even from before it began, until the appropriate time and place for them to manifest.

Puzzling over all this, I remembered what Ivor Madsen, my favourite English professor, once said, trying to console a distressed freshman, in tears, in the hall outside his office at term paper time: "Start anywhere, and just keep going," he told her, with all the kindness he could convey through his carapace of brilliance. I doubt if this advice helped her; but in any case I will start with Madsen's Modern British Novel class on a certain blustery October afternoon in 197–.

The large wood-framed windows in the old classroom rattled in the wind. The light dimmed, brightened, and dimmed again as fast-moving clouds repeatedly crossed the sun. The tempestuous weather that day contrasted sharply with the studious atmosphere in the room as we made our way through five novels in a single semester: *Sons and Lovers, Nostromo, A Passage to India, To the Lighthouse,* and *The Good Soldier.* The demands of the class, I felt, were unfair—to us; but even worse, they were unfair to the authors (if one can be unfair to the dead). But maybe that's what youth always looks like from the standpoint of age: too full, too fast, unfair—at odds with time itself.

On this particular Friday we were wrapping up our discussion of *A Passage to India.* Specifically, we were debating the central puzzle of the novel: what actually happened to Adela Quested in the Marabar Caves? E.M. Forster introduces this peculiar landscape feature in the book's early pages: "They are dark caves. Even when they open towards the sun, very little light penetrates down the entrance tunnel into the circular chamber.

There is little to see, and no eye to see it. An entrance was necessary, so mankind made one. But elsewhere, deeper in the granite, are there certain chambers that have no entrances? Chambers never unsealed since the arrival of the gods?"

Adela Quested, a visiting British schoolteacher, wants an encounter with "the real India" before deciding if she will marry the Magistrate of Chandrapore. This is Ronny, the son of Mrs. Moore, an older friend with whom Adela is traveling. A tragicomedy of British colonial life unfolds, through awkward introductions, interminable bridge parties, and various seemingly preordained misunderstandings. Dr. Aziz, a sympathetic young Muslim physician, befriends Mrs. Moore, and arranges to lead a small group visit to the famous caves. Forster, in a sly bit of thematic satire, couches the primordial landscape itself as the "real India," a geological fundament prior to all culture: "The Ganges, though flowing from the foot of Vishnu and through Siva's hair, is not an ancient stream. Geology, looking further than religion, knows of a time when neither the river nor the Himalayas that nourished it existed."

During this visit to the network of caverns, Aziz loses track of Adela Quested. Apparently she has wandered off alone and gotten lost. Calling out her name produces only echoes. The assistant guide assures everyone that shouting is useless: "A Marabar cave hears no sound but its own." Eventually Aziz glimpses Quested in the distance, driving away with another woman. Stepping off the train back at Chandrapore, he is arrested at the station for "indecorous advances." This charge provokes great confusion and anger throughout the Anglo-Indian community.

Adela Quested, disoriented, perhaps ill, is sequestered during Aziz's trial. Attempts to visit and question her are deemed improper. Finally she admits that she can't be certain what really happened in the caves. Aziz is freed, yet questions remain unanswered. This is where Madsen came alive, prodding us to examine possibilities unresolved in the novel itself. Had Adela truly gotten lost? Had she been tricked by someone and abandoned? Did she misinterpret an innocent remark or gesture? Was she fundamentally an unstable fantasist? Or worse, trying to entrap Aziz? Was he to blame for not more carefully handling a delicate situation involving a "proper Englishwoman"? How much was what occurred, or didn't, a colonialist projection? The trial is settled legally, but Forster notoriously avoids commitment to a definite narrative conclusion.

I think some of us, certainly I, thought Madsen's metafictional probings were more interesting than the novel itself. That there might be crucial problems in a literary work left unsolved by design was a new and provocative concept at the time to many of us. *Inherent* undecidability, a *permanent* not knowing—Madsen proposed that these weren't failures or bad faith on Forster's part, but were exactly the point he was making: "Might a *purposeful* obscurity, in effect, most clearly represent Forster's view of Anglo-Indian relations during this late-colonial period?" Madsen's favoured pedagogic technique was tossing one idea on top of another like logs on a bonfire. "Before *A Passage to India*, Forster hadn't published a novel in fourteen years. And it would be his last, though he lived another forty-five years. So I think it would be a mistake to view it as any kind of 'summing up.' But consider his deeply metaphorical descriptions of the caves—doesn't this perfectly symbolize the unheard echoes inherent in any colonial relationship? Or perhaps any relationship—Yes, Stefany? What have you got for us today?"

Stefany Scheim was by far the brightest person in the class, a fact I couldn't help but see as connected with her wildly tousled red hair. That afternoon she'd prepared a report on geological symbolism in George Eliot's *The Mill on the Floss*, not a modern British novel to be sure, but Stefany was a star, Madsen's favourite. Generally she was forthright, sometimes even strident, but that afternoon an occasional quaver of diffidence crept into her voice as she read, which elicited my sympathy, though many in the class resented her.

"Maggie's favourite place to walk (though it had frightened her as a child), was hidden by a ridge, quote, 'which was hardly more than a bank; but there may come moments when Nature makes a mere bank a means toward a fateful result,' end quote. Below, the land is, quote, 'broken into very capricious hollows and mounds by the working of an exhausted stone-quarry, so long exhausted that both mounds and hollows were now clothed with brambles and trees,' end quote. Maggie's name for this special place is the Red Deeps. *Obviously*" (and here Stefany looked over at one of her rivals in class, daring disagreement) "this signifies menstrual blood, and therefore the unknown female interior. The Red Deeps is where Maggie meets up with a hunchback named Philip. Having to confront his traumatized body forces her to acknowledge her own body's traumas, which include her unexamined sexual feelings." At first I was tempted to object: Stefany was wrenching Eliot's nineteenth-century symbolism to fit contemporary mores. But in fact, I thought her gloss was illuminating. In discussion she underlined various parallels to the Forster's book, and I admired her critical boldness.

As the class drew to a close there was some aimless discussion of "Quested" as a preterite verb, and different senses of the word "passage," before Madsen adeptly reined us back in. Holding the novel in one hand, gesturing cryptically with the other, he quoted the mystic Professor Godbole, a Hindu character for whom he had obvious affection: "'I am informed that an evil action was performed in the Marabar Hills, and that a highly esteemed English lady is seriously ill in consequence. My answer is this: that the action was performed by Dr. Aziz.' Godbole stopped and sucked in his thin cheeks. 'It was performed by the guide.' He stopped again. 'It was performed by you.' Now he had an air of daring and of coyness. 'It was performed by me.' Godbole looked shyly down the sleeve of his own coat. 'And by my students.'" At this point Madsen looked theatrically around the classroom for a long moment before resuming. "It was even performed by the lady herself. When evil occurs, it expresses the whole of the universe. Similarly when good occurs.'" He clapped the book shut, smiled somberly, and said no more. It was a memorable class.

As we dispersed, I knew I'd have to hurry: apparently sometime during the hour I'd decided to go home for the weekend. My girlfriend Abby and I hadn't quite broken up, but she was avoiding me, and the prospect of two aimless days on campus wondering about our relationship was a good reason to skip town. Actually, though, such spontaneous trips weren't rare. My parents still lived in the same house, in the same small town, where I'd grown up. It was eighty minutes away by bus—a straight shot on the freeway that crossed the lower part of the state. A Greyhound left from the student union every day at 5:15, and after one brief stop halfway, dropped me at the Citgo station on the edge of town. Almost always I was the only one getting off. A half-hour hike through typically empty streets got me home around 7:00. I didn't always tell my parents I was coming. In those days they left the back door unlocked, and if by chance it wasn't, and they weren't home, I'd climb the mulberry tree behind the garage and cross the roof to my bedroom window, always propped open with a book.

On this visit, as soon as I walked in the door my mother said, "Oh, I wish I'd known you were coming. We have tickets to see Itzhak Perlman tomorrow night at Foster Auditorium. Do you want me to try and get you one?" I said "Sure," though I wasn't hugely interested. We were a musically attentive family, but each of us had our own interests, and a solo violin recital wouldn't have been at the top of anyone's list. My father favoured symphonies; my mother never tired of Verdi opera highlights, and I was devoted to psychedelic rock.

My mother got through to the box office the next morning and secured another ticket. "They've opened up the top balcony, so there are still plenty of seats. You won't mind sitting by yourself, will you? Do you know anyone else who wants to go?" As I was in a general social retreat, I didn't. Foster auditorium was at the other state university, not very far from my own. These two bustling college municipalities, along with my hometown, formed a squat triangle encompassing a region of small farms carved out among low rolling meadows, largely undeveloped, that were dotted with random copses and sometimes strangely precise lines of trees. On summer afternoons the cornfields were golden-green and bucolic. Now, in late October, they were pale tracts of stubble, already announcing the approach of winter. The wan patches of color remaining in the trees would soon be gone.

I'd never known any other landscape, so this one, whatever the season, had the comfort of familiarity. Nonetheless, I'd always been aware of a witchy aspect. We lived on a long, dead-end street that meandered through small wooded thickets. The houses were not close together, and whenever I walked home alone at night, random clumps of trees and bush, pleasant enough in daylight, became concentrated knots of blackness that emitted malign vibrations. Even now, visiting from college, I felt an embarrassingly childish urge to run past them, not feeling truly safe until I'd locked my parents' door securely behind me.

The only route to the concert was via Old 32, a two-lane highway that ran directly north until it took a long, graceful turn to the east near the halfway point. As we drove, the day began to slowly fade, and a landscape gloom came over me, familiar since childhood. Despite the occasional tidy farm and rural homestead, along with a few half-hidden trailers and tumbledown shacks, the land felt like a realm that humans had barely mastered, had hardly even charted. Most of the county roads had names like D Drive North, J Drive South, 26 Mile Road, abstractions with no trace of history, legend, or human presence. Notoriously America don't honour her poets, but surely, I grumbled to myself, we could muster an explorer, a college president, at the very least a mailman or dogcatcher? On the evidence, I thought, the vegetable world deserved to reclaim everything.

Traversing the bend in the road at moderate speed took no more than thirty seconds. During a dozen previous trips, an abstract sense of it had become part of my nervous system, but I'd never really observed its unfolding details. This time I noticed, on the outer edge of the arc, right at the central point, a house so unusual I couldn't believe I hadn't seen it before. It was a single-story structure, covered in brown shingles with an almost furry appearance. The peaked roof, a rich storybook green, was comically steep. But the most noticeable thing was the house's extreme depth. It could only be a concatenation of single rooms, one after another, running from a small gravel parking area near the road all the way back to the dark edge of the woods behind. Though the house was clearly well constructed, the eccentric proportions gave it a handcrafted look. To either side, wide, rough-edged margins of mown grass were bordered by tidy shrubbery and small boxed beds of flowers. Beyond this verge was the usual untamed scrub and bush, which paradoxically gave the house and yard the air of a protected island. As we exited the curve, I looked back and counted nine identical small square windows, equally spaced along the length of the house, charmingly lit behind light blue curtains in the thickening dusk. As it receded into the wooded distance I had the fleeting impression of a passenger train passing through the lonely night. What sort of people would live in such a dwelling, I wondered, which had the air of a picture in a forgotten book of fairy tales.

The busy auditorium, the prospect of a crowd and musical entertainment, chased away the gloom and buoyed my spirits. We'd arrived early, but I was eager to see what the view was like from on high, so I took my ticket and began the long ascent. At each level the stairs grew narrower and less populated until, at the top, there was no one around, and I felt I had climbed out of the auditorium altogether. Finally a student usher appeared and pointed me to a door at the far right, where another handed me a program and led me down the steeply raked aisle to a small box containing four seats, attached to the front of the balcony proper. An identical box hung suspended at the far left. Strange! I couldn't imagine what purpose they were meant to serve.

I took my seat in this front row beyond the front row, feeling oddly honoured yet also uncomfortably exposed. The front wall of the box was four inches from my knees and only about eight inches higher. Resting my elbows on the ledge, I leaned out, trying to spot my parents, but the distance was too great for my myopic eyes. I'd never been as high up in a place where it would be so easy to jump. It needn't even be a jump; just a daring forward tilt might do the trick. I felt a sick thrill in trying to find the exact point where vertigo took hold. Just beyond that point, I imagined, the world would shift ninety degrees: I wouldn't be falling anymore, I decided; I would be flying.

For reasons that elude me, I'd recently read Edgar Allan Poe's "The Imp of the Perverse" several times, and it had coached me for this sensation: "We stand upon the brink of a precipice. We peer into the abyss—we grow sick and dizzy. Our first impulse is to shrink from the danger. Unaccountably we remain. By slow degrees our sickness and dizziness and horror become merged in a cloud of unnameable feeling. Upon the precipice's edge, there grows into palpability, a shape, far more terrible than any genius or any demon of a tale, and yet it is but a thought, although a fearful one, and one which chills the very marrow of our bones with the fierceness of the delight of its horror. It is merely the idea of what would be our sensations during the sweeping precipitancy of a fall from such a height." *The fierceness of the delight of its horror*: I couldn't decide if this phrase was a protective charm or a dangerous goad.

I was startled out of these baroque musings by an attractive young woman, about my age, approaching the box and settling in the seat to my right. As she wriggled out of her coat, I looked around stealthily: there was no one anywhere near us, and I felt the instinctual discomfort Auden describes in a bit of doggerel:

Some thirty inches from my nose
the frontier of my Person goes . . .
Beware of rudely crossing it:
I have no gun, but I can spit.

She seemed perfectly at ease, but I decided that if we were still surrounded by empty seats at showtime, it would be proper for me to shift to a more gentlemanly distance. Just then our elbows bumped while negotiating the single armrest between us; bumped and stayed put, firmly touching even as they nudged around, finding space to rest. I was wondering how to break the ice, when she turned toward me and said, "I didn't really plan to be here. My friend got a ticket at the last minute, then suddenly he couldn't go, and he offered it to me."

"Same here," I replied. "I went home on the spur of the moment, and my parents had tickets. My mother felt bad and managed to get me one."

"My name's Lorna." She put out her hand and we shook, awkwardly; at such close quarters it was mostly rubbing fingers. She was attending the university in this town, living with her parents to save money. Since she was at State and I was at U, we exchanged obligatory comments about the notorious football rivalry, but soon moved on to more fruitful topics: classes, teachers, campus politics, vacation plans.

"This isn't really my kind of music," I confessed, "but it was nice of my mother to invite me, I guess."

"Yeah, when Sam gave me his ticket I thought, well, what have I got better to do?" Those last few words made me realize that I absolutely had nothing better to do at this moment than sit next to her. I thought of telling her so but decided not to. It risked sounding like smarmy flirtation from a forties film. Besides, I didn't know the significance of Sam.

Lorna was funny and sharp-witted, spoke with confidence, and knew what a conversation was. I gradually sensed that both of us were invigorated as well as comforted by a matrix of instant mental and physical comprehension. How confused and deadened I'd become during my dubious time with Abby! How luxurious the sensation of starting something new, however transient.

I looked at the program: Bach Partitas and Sonatas for solo violin. I knew nothing about the music, knew nothing about Bach except for a crazy factoid I'd read or heard: that there were more than seventy musical Bachs in a family extending across two centuries. I told myself I should read the program notes, but what I really wanted was to get Lorna's take on an idea I'd recently been mulling over.

In general, solo performances, with their displays of virtuosity, had never appealed to me, though they seemed to thrill most people. Rock guitar geniuses, even in groups I liked, left me cold when they broke into fretboard histrionics. The undeniable beauty and prodigious mastery exhibited by some outstanding solo artists was nonetheless missing something; so I felt. Granted, this was an era of various kinds of communal experiments, but it was also a time of exalted subjectivities. I'd taken a seminar on Jung and had to confront the idea that it was me who was missing something. My aversion to single-handed virtuosity could well be, I had to admit, the projected shadow of an inflated self-regard. As I laid these ideas out to Lorna in a somewhat tangled manner, she looked at me more and more intently. Her eyes widened, then narrowed; it was like she was deciding whether to accept a perfect stranger's invitation to tea.

"I just read a book I think you might like," she said carefully. *Jung and the Story of Our Time*. I'd heard of it, and recalled the author's name: "Van der Post? I saw a BBC thing he narrated—might have been based on it?" "I saw that too." Lorna had suddenly grown cooler, more serious, proceeding cautiously, it seemed. "You know, people are going to have to wake up. The shadow is such an important idea. Important in the world, not just in personal psychology. Just think, if the concept of projection was brought into politics ..." She stopped abruptly, perhaps abashed by this effusion of earnestness.

While talking, I'd been looking her over. Lorna was modestly dressed up for the evening in what looked to be resurrected high school clothing. There was a small, faded tan stain on the collar of her white blouse. Her black slip-on flats had old-fashioned buckles. Several bits of lint clung to the side of her navy skirt, and I had a strong desire to pluck them off. Her knees, protruding several inches below the hem, were knobby, like mine. Such homely details produced a reality-effect I found intoxicating: cupping my right hand firmly over her left kneecap would be a regal gesture of recognition and amity. Daring, and yet so eminently possible, such an act had an abstract inevitability—perhaps akin to the bend in the road? Surely Lorna would understand and welcome the bold approach.

But once again the memory of Poe's Imp gave me a warning: *We peer into the abyss, we grow sick and dizzy; because our reason violently deters us from the brink*. To distract myself from the delicious abyss of Lorna's knee, I steered the conversation in a different direction, mentioning the town I was from. But this didn't go as expected. She drew back a few inches. Her eyes narrowed suspiciously, though there remained a glint of curiosity.

"You must have driven up Old 32," she said hesitantly. I nodded. "Then you went right by my house." Of course I knew exactly where she lived, but she told me anyway, still almost reluctantly. "You know where the road curves? Right in the middle there's a long brown house with a steep green roof ..." Though this should have been a zestful fortuity, Lorna seemed to harbour an odd mix of alarm and awe. She sank back in her seat and withdrew, as if she'd brushed against something slithery under the lake's surface and didn't know if it was an eel or merely seaweed.

Dulcet warning chimes sounded before we could reestablish a friendly equilibrium, and a few seconds later the lights began to dim. I was almost panicked. I wanted to say something more—the mood would be very different after the music. But it was too late. Though maybe not. After so many years it's impossible to be certain, but I'm pretty sure that, just after the house lights went dark, in the midst of the pregnant hush, Lorna leaned toward my shoulder and whispered very softly, "Come visit me."

The stage lights came up, and Perlman entered quickly to tremendous applause. He bowed slightly, forearms braced on his metal crutches, which he dropped to the side as he sat back in a plain wooden chair. I threw a quick glance toward Lorna, but she was intently focused on the stage. Perlman smiled at the assistant who brought out his violin, placed a folded white cloth between his chin and the instrument, raised the bow, paused to adjust his right leg slightly, then began. I wasn't prepared for what happened next.

With the very first notes I was pulled into a calculated, devilish, inescapable game. The sawing arc of Perlman's bow magically (it seemed at a distance) set loose repetitive sequences of notes—up and down the scale, rapidly, then slowly, then rapidly again—which became an invisible staircase-labyrinth. There was beauty in the timbre of individual tones, but their structure as a whole turned the vast auditorium space inside out and trapped me in what I had never imagined, even in the wildest frenzies of rock guitar: a cage of music, though a cage in which I was still vulnerable to vertigo. I closed my eyes, gripped the armrests (Lorna's elbow was now gone), and braced my feet against the balcony wall in front of me.

It sounds ridiculous now, but I was terrified that the relentlessly cascading, almost cruel notes had the power to pull me out of my seat and pitch me over the edge: down—down—down. *What would be my sensation during the sweeping precipitancy of a fall from such a height?* Would it seem fast or slow? Almost at the panicked point of grabbing for Lorna's hand, I felt something bump my right knee; then, very lightly, what had to be her calf rubbing slowly, up and down, against mine. It was so soft a touch, and muffled by my clothing, I had to wonder if it was really happening. And if real, was it intentional? And if intentional, was it an attempt to comfort me or a calculated seduction? Against all instinct (*the frontier of my Person*) I kept my leg rigid. The sensations came and went in an exasperatingly indeterminate fashion. The more I concentrated on this barely liminal signal, the more it was like staring at a word until it becomes alien, impossible to drag into meaning. But then all at once things became distinctly palpable: the slow stroke, up and down, of Lorna's shoeless toes, a reality that couldn't be denied.

Behind my closed eyes this electrical contact must have engaged some visual circuit. I saw myself floating out above the auditorium, then following the course of Old 32, retracing the earlier drive. It was marvellous to soar, bodiless, high above the road, free from landscape gloom, and then descend, gently guided, to the fateful bend in the road. I drifted peacefully, without hesitance or hurry, three or four feet above the walkway, then up four wooden steps to the small porch, which was roofed but not enclosed. With no sense of physical contact, I penetrated first an outer screen door, then a wooden front door, painted blue. All these details were as clear as in waking life. Once inside the house I realized that this floating world was entirely silent, and I had no way of knowing if anyone was home. The lights in the front room, past the vestibule, were dim, and there were faint traces of illumination all the way down the long hallway. I passed room after room opening off to the left: living room, dining room, kitchen, bathroom, what obviously was Lorna's parents' bedroom, then past two rooms that were cloudy to my sight. Then a laundry, and another bathroom. Finally I approached the back of the house and a door, slightly ajar, facing me at the far end of the hall. The end of the journey: Lorna's room. A patch of brightly lit blue carpet was the only thing visible through the crack. But whatever force was guiding me refused to carry me any farther.

Instead, I was painfully jerked back into my body, aware of Perlman again. My calf still vibrated from the memory of Lorna's foot. Reluctantly accepting bodily reality, I wondered if there would be an excruciatingly awkward moment when Lorna and I reengaged. But no—remembering the auspicious inception, I was confident that we'd overcome it.

The first half of the program came to an end. Wild applause broke out. While my eyes were still shut, a hand briefly cupped my genitals, squeezed firmly, then withdrew. "Well, that raises the stakes," I thought, aroused and now very cheery about the next few moments. It was wonderful to feel the difference between vertigo and giddiness! I opened my eyes, blinking at the lights. I turned to the right—and Lorna was gone!

How could she have vanished so quickly? I hadn't sensed a thing. Oh, but of course!, I reassured myself: she's dashed off to beat the bathroom rush. But there was no trace of her, no purse, no jacket; surely we'd reached the stage where she'd have asked me to watch her things? Or at least told me where she was going? Then I remembered that my mother had the habit of always taking her jacket and purse with her to the restroom.

Maybe, given the musical ambivalence we'd both expressed, she'd had enough, left early, and didn't want to disturb me? As far as she knew my eyes could have been closed in ecstasy. I might myself have left if I'd had a car; though I'd certainly have suggested that we adjourn somewhere to continue the conversation. Throughout the intermission I craned my neck around in every direction, but as the audience slowly reassembled, I had to accept the truth: she'd departed without a word, which stung. I hoped she hadn't suddenly been overcome by shame, afraid to look me in the eye after her (admittedly somewhat louche) behaviour. Oh, well (those curious words, bland charm against despondence). I reminded myself that though I couldn't know what her disappearance meant, she had invited me to visit, and she'd made sure I knew where she lived. Would she now regret that invitation? If I showed up on her doorstep would she refuse to see me, pretend ignorance, never be home, use her parents as a bulwark? I rode back home in a funk, barely able to converse with my parents about the recital.

The following week was hard to get through. Again and again I floated down that long, dimly lit hallway, but I could never get further than the door to Lorna's room. Something diverted me, shut me out, then dissolved. Of course I began to doubt myself as the events receded. Had I made it all up? Memory is such a frail thing. But I had a burning need to know and gave my parents some plausible reason for borrowing the car the following Saturday.

Sometimes it's hard to remember the days before cell phones. Now it seems implausible that I drove to Lorna's house without further corroboration or confirmation of plans, without our phone numbers being lodged in each other's devices. It was a couple of days after her sudden departure that it dawned on me I didn't even know her last name.

Ten o'clock on the Saturday morning felt right: not too early to knock unannounced, but early enough that Lorna might not have left for the day. The partly cloudy morning had an entirely unforeboding aspect, and the trivial normality seemed auspicious. The drive went by swiftly. I realized that Lorna had lived not very far from me for years. Entering the long curve, I scanned ahead, saw in the small paved parking area a newish yellow station wagon, and a scoured red pickup. Neither seemed what Lorna would be likely to drive. She hadn't mentioned siblings. There seemed no way to calculate the possibilities, so I stopped trying.

I'd rehearsed a little intro, in case one of her parents came to the door. *"Hi. I sat next to Lorna at the Perlman concert last Saturday at Foster Auditorium. We had a nice talk, and she invited me to visit. Somehow, I forgot to get her phone number."* I tried to be ready for anything: Lorna might not have mentioned me at all, she might have warned her parents against me, they might have their own ideas. Impossible to know.

Oddly, the mailbox near the road had no name on it, just a bold five-digit number. I parked next to the station wagon. As I walked to the front door, I felt a rush of frivolous optimism: if things went well, I might be in her bedroom fondling her knee within twenty minutes! I pressed the doorbell but heard nothing. Remembering the length of the house, I counted to twenty, then knocked firmly. Silence. I pounded the door with the side of my fist and thought I heard a stirring in the distance, but it stopped, or else I was imagining it. Just as I was screwing up the courage to knock again, even more assertively, I was startled almost out of my skin by the door opening, suddenly and silently. A couple stood there, older than I expected, with no expectant or curious or even wary expressions. Instead they looked somber, caved in, maybe ill. The woman stood halfway behind the man, peering over his shoulder, as if seeking protection.

I must have breezed through my introduction, though I don't remember it. What I didn't expect, and can never forget, was the man's gruff, choked, overloud response: "I don't know who you are, or what you're doing here." "Oh, John," came the muffled, plaintive voice of the woman, whose face was now burrowed into his shoulder. His next words were harsh, yet almost formal. "In fact I don't know what you're trying to pull. Our daughter *died* last Saturday in a car accident on her way to a concert and I think you'd better leave. *Right now.*" He slammed the door with seeming finality. Stunned as I was, I have no memory of walking back to the car. All I remember is the door opening again, and the man shouting a hoarse afterthought: "Her name isn't Lorna!"

What else is there to say? You, reader, undoubtedly have the same questions I do, face the same dearth of answers, confront the same inherent undecidability, the permanent not-knowing. Though it was broad daylight, I was terrified on the drive home, nearly running off the road when, in a sudden panic, I tried to make sure nothing lurked in the back seat. I pulled onto the shoulder to lock the doors, catch my breath, and calm down. The day outside was still unremarkable, the landscape harboured no dark messages. But I remembered a haunting detail. When I'd told Lorna about Madsen and my decision to major in English, she said that she wanted to concentrate in parapsychology, though she'd have to go elsewhere to do so.

In December, approaching exam time and the end of the term, Abby tried to reengage with me, but of course there was no going back. As time moved on, there was no reason to keep in touch, and I have no idea what became of her. If I mention her here, it's because in a way she might be said to have initiated everything that followed. A long while ago, I came across a prominent review of a book by Stefany Scheim: *The Geography of Sexual Indulgence*. It was on its way to becoming one of those unlikely academic best sellers that captures the attention of the general public. Of course I'm curious, but I haven't let myself read it. I'm sure it would only provoke me to write her an unbalanced and pointless letter.

Once in awhile, even now, I let myself wander through the Marabar Caves, hoping to hear a word—even just an echo—from Lorna. One day, perhaps, she'll whisper in my ear, telling me what happened in that primeval place, even though it hears no sound but its own.

Scars of Grief

By Eugen Bacon

The story starts here. This is a work of fiction. The author is struggling, he finds his story rigid. He wants to write about a thing he once read in the paper, an article about a bad tabloid that gained from victims of murder, hacked into their phone lines. Anything for a juicy caption, right? Wrong. The tabloid marched into trouble. Frankly it was shut down.

The author wants to build a set of events. Not around the tabloid and its shutdown, but around the families that were harmed. He makes the choice to write about the families because he understands his talent. He has a knack for people stories, no aptitude for institutions. He wants to be true to his learnings on the art of suspense. He wants to make sure that all is not revealed at the start. He worries. If he manages the use of suspense well, what if the reveal comes too late? He is nervous. What if he runs out of story? He is restless. What if the reader gets unhooked?

He looks at his cast.

Ralph:

Ralph Patton avoids their eyes. His wife Trinity sits haggard, listless. Withdrawn into herself. Marble Norman handles it best. Her husband Dane cradles a tempest. Time leaks perilously, frightening and consoling.

It is a common grief, reborn. It unites two couples who lost two little girls nine years ago to a murderer. Trinity finds her question. "Why?" There is a dead twig in her voice.

"Because journalists are knobheads," snaps Dane.

"Cookie ... " Marble reaches across the table to calm his fists. Despite her composure, Ralph knows, her anguish is undiminished. Her grief is the kind that spills inward.

It seems minutes since Detective Vera Downs came to see them, first the Normans, then the Pattons. To alert them to the phone-hacking, to stress again her regret at finding the girls too late. Yesterday. The detective came yesterday; brought them a day that opened up grief, that awakened the one thing that stirred the Normans, the Pattons, to seek each other out. Now they sit together at the Norman house in Halls Gap, Victoria. Same way they sat those many years ago when tragedy snatched their children.

Trinity lets out a sob, rises from her chair, flees the room. Marble chases behind.

"Bleeding freaks," Dane Norman says.

The author pauses at this stage, feels like he is scratching an itch. Should he dump the Normans? He notices that, with this story, he asks himself a lot of questions. Regarding the Normans it's … it's not that he is insensitive to Dane's rage, his despair. But he … he wonders if the story is better served focusing on a single family. A typical short story has a small cast at a single point in time. The author feels he can achieve more fleshing out the characters of Ralph and Trinity Patton.

Undecided, he continues typing.

Ralph understands the freaks. They are monsters bold as gold but septic inside. That same tabloid, a glimpse of hell, already once prospered on a story, the Patton and Norman story: two six-year-old girls curled ten-foot deep in a ditch at the mouth of Mount William ranges. How the press bled it.

The curtain flaps. Slowly, Ralph understands it is raining outside. A determined drizzle grows into slanting rain. He has never set foot near that bushwalk in the Grampians again. Neither has Trinity; they both want to forget. But Marble visits it annually like a shrine. Ralph never thought he could feel a knife so deep, so twisted in his breast.

He doesn't know why the news scandal has thrown him into the pit again, why so bottomless. But it has. Each word the detective said curved the blade deeper. "I am sorry they targeted you," she said. "There may be more families."

The press stopped at nothing, disregarded whose privacy they breached. Just the ready money a hot yarn cashed. The tabloid's ugliness is personal. Stolen conversations of trauma, of gloom, distorted on front pages. Intimate words shouted to the world, vilifying everything, sparing nothing. Ralph wants to climb to an edge and leap from the world.

At this stage the author pauses. He has hinted about the tabloid, about the children's murder, more than hinted. He has unveiled that a grief almost healed is now again torn open. But he is not sure … Is he indicating well what exactly is doing the tearing? So the press hacked the parents' phones, nosed into their grief. All for back story. But the coppers just found out now titbits of press data. Leaks, like how Trinity wanted to down a palmful of pills. Like how Dane was going to quit the marriage. It was all too thorny for them, barbed enough without the press. The author wants to show, not tell. He wonders how much detail to contain, how much to tell. Should he spell out what the tabloid did with the conversations it stole?

Less is more, he decides.

Ralph:

With the phone-hacking scandal, *Hot off the Press!* has slashed open scars that began to heal after that trial in August 2005 at the Magistrate's Court. Ralph thought the torment was abridged when Chief Magistrate Gray handed the monster two life terms. But what he feels now is wolfing him alive.

Even so, those same shock-and-awe tactics that saw the tabloid thrive since 1901 have proved the tabloid's own undoing. 113 years of scandal flushed down their rotten drain. That infected ink will never hurt anyone again. Not after one week today, the publication date of their last edition ever.

The end.

But—wait. The author sees how this ending moves away from the parents to the tabloid, how it is rather rigid. How can the story be over?

The phone tapping is part of Trinity's sorrow. The author wants to build on this, make it her recovery. So he deletes "The end".

But the tabloid's disgrace, and then closure, cannot patch what has happened.

It cannot fix open scars. The Normans and Pattons part yet again as they did years before, no longer allies, no longer able to feed as one the grief that joined them in the first place. It is as if they can no more bear looking at each other, being together.

Weeks after that parting, fog remains in Trinity's eyes.

Ralph takes to writing. He sits at his desk by the window. Trinity pours herself into works of charity: baking, resourcing, fundraising, publicizing ... Now with the Salvos, the Vinnies, the Givewells. Philanthropy. Bugger that. Ralph types, types, types into his computer. Ideas jotted down on a shoddy notepad in the dead of the night, in that stretch between midnight and dawn when sleep eludes him the most.

He writes about Apple and the swell in his heart the first time his eyes set upon her. As he writes, the child invades his dreams. She is so tiny, so rosy, her face scrunched like an old woman's. Now it's a strong little mouth, she smiles. She is so vivid, her baby smell, still now, apricot and honey soap. She doesn't say a word, but chuckles when he ruffles her furious curls ... a tangle right there on the crown of her head, an island of red.

Sometimes, gazing at windswept grass in the fields beyond the gate—it needs new paint—he thinks about what to write. Other times, he presses his nose against the window and an eye toward the horizon and can't think because his mind has slipped off. Just as well. He gets stuck in his head too much. But often, words swirl like waves and he cannot type fast enough.

His writing this morning is charged, stimulated. A whiff of melting butter, lime rind and fresh blueberries fills his nostrils. Trinity is baking. The waft of cookery is like a therapeutic balm. The smell stirs fond memories. Apple loved cookies, macaroons, turnovers, brownies ... gobbled chunks whole without chewing.

Now and then, on difficult days, a sting of tears escorts his writing. Other times like now, memory massages his heart, lifts something inside him. Elation swells his being. He feels merry, surreal even.

Apple, always a scrawny thing, no matter what. Always wandering, investigating her world full of butterfly, ladybird and garden snail surprises. He watches her dazed expression at each find ...

"Look Papa! I gots a new friend." The trapdoor spider escapes but Apple finds a Goliath stick insect to replace it. "She hungry, Papa. I ask Mama for a cookie."

"Why not, kiddo."

The moment her eyes, and then hands, lock on Jojo Norman, their love is instant. Without question, as if destined, Jojo reciprocates. She follows Apple everywhere. They toddle with hitched up skirts in grasslands near home, run—their delight giddy as summer rain.

"Me and Jojo see a wolfie near the park, Papa." Ralph experiences again the fork of fear in his gut, but it's a neighbor's European Wolfdog—completely tame—on a run.

The girls' lust for adventure steers them into trouble.

The author pauses. Is there a better story out of building the characters of Jojo and Apple? Then bringing in murder? Or maybe … How about looking individually at Ralph, Trinity, Marble and Dane now? How each responds in a different way to news that their privacy has been breached. Maybe exploring if that breach is as important to them as the way their daughters were treated in the original news reports. Yes, emotions directed at themselves, at their feelings of exposure, instead of at their daughters loss.

Still … he questions the angle, understands that this kind of feeling may not be true of Dane. Or Marble. Or Trinity. Or Ralph. After all Ralph has been writing, a cathartic way to deal with loss.

The author asks himself why he cannot put away "The scars of grief" for three months, give it another look then. It is too raw right now, he knows. But, then again … He is in a hurry to bed it down. He likes where he is going with Ralph.

Look behind you, Ralph, he says. Forget the blinking cursor on my screen.

Thanks.

"Do you remember when Apple made toast in your brand-new stereo?" his wife speaks quietly to his hair. She is right behind him. "How you lost it and scolded her to tears but stopped short because Jojo bawled so loud?"

Ralph looks up from the computer, startled and then awed. Fog has lifted from Trinity's eyes. What brings about her change? Is it reading his writings?

"Clearly it works," she says softly. "It works very well." He stares at her. "You bring her back each day … Apple, she is right here." She presses his hand to her chest.

"I missed you." He nestles his head against her breast.

"And I you. Dreadfully."

Their coupling is … animal.

Later, Trinity showers his face and throat with kisses that cool and burn. Wrapped in her arms, Ralph speaks against her wet skin, bedraggled hair. "I thought … maybe.. Marble and Dane … I thought maybe we could go and see the Normans tomorrow."

"Okay."

The author settles to this unauthorized departure from his story, and quite likes it.

Springtime In New Orleans

By Maxim Jakubowski

He was a man haunted by death.

Ever since he had lost his wife to dementia, he had been travelling through life without an anchor. In outward appearance, he looked much the same as before, but his mind oscillated wildly between grief and loneliness, carrying along an inescapable mental suitcase full of regrets. Friends, as a way of complimenting him, remarked he appeared to never age, but he knew they were sorely mistaken.

He could feel the years he had left racing by inside. His eyesight was beginning to fail; his teeth were in a bad condition, and he had lost two in the past eighteen months; he occasionally experienced strong muscular spasms in his left leg at odd times that made him want to scream and woke up to five times a night to go pee. Worrying irregular pains in his knees and hips. A feeling that the writing was finally appearing on the wall.

When reading his daily newspaper he would always head straight to the obituary page, hoping against hope it wouldn't again feature people he had known or other minor personalities who happened to have been younger than him. His way of counting the days down to his own inevitable mortality. He just hoped it would, when the day came, happen quickly and he wouldn't suffer or have to navigate infinite physical pain and anguish.

In the meantime, he travelled.

A lot.

To places he and D had been to, which always caused his heart to stutter; to new cities or landscapes he was curious about and that they had not managed to visit in the time they had been together and, he felt in retrospect, not made the most of.

He sailed off the coast of Newfoundland, walked Water and Duckworth Streets in St John's Harbour, navigating the beggars, the cannabis stores, the Dildo Brewery and the Fat Bastard Tacos; he cautiously navigated the ice-strewn byways of Reykjavik, visiting the Penis Museum; ambled through the cobbled alleyways of Montreal and Québec City; he watched hardy surfers fight the mighty waves off Bondi Beach and roamed the streets of Paris, New York and Amsterdam unendingly in search of both memories and he knew not what. Sometimes a place he had almost forgotten would fortuitously be one they had strolled through together and it would bring tears to his eyes and his heart tumbled into some awful pit of despondency.

In his callow youth, he had written a novel in which the obviously autobiographical protagonist travelled the world in search of the truth, love and all that jazz. It was never published. Not only had he not yet lived properly or stored enough in the way of experiences, but his evocations of places foreign stemmed in their entirety from books and films and were utterly superficial. He had always been something of a romantic, but in unfocused ways. Had romance smacked him in the face, he wouldn't have known what to do about it.

So why was he now travelling so much? Solo cruises, beach holidays, city breaks. Indulging in memories, a sliver of hope against hope at the back of his mind about a final fling, a redemptive love affair? All of that and more. And filling the days until he would inevitably die, trying to make some sense of his life and the little he had achieved, all the things he should have done and said better. He was in his detached manner trying to keep ahead of the inevitable, or was it even the Devil?

Eventually he ran out of places, destinations, harbours in the storm.

It wasn't even a city, let alone one set in Mississippi or bathing in the splendored shadows of swampy bayous. And luxuriating in the scent of spices.

Someone had long ago suggested they call the place Samarkand, but it was nowhere near a desert, let alone sited in the footsteps of Marco Polo. So the name had not curried favour. But one of the first to settle here had once visited the real New Orleans and his taste buds still carried a lingering and affectionate nostalgia for gumbo and oysters on the half shell and he had suggested the name. No one had forcibly objected and the moniker had somehow stuck.

It was actually set in a plain on a sizeable island set in the very centre of the sea of Exopotomia. An island that appeared on few published maps. And which didn't even have a name.

This is where they had all converged. Some had arrived on their own while others had been part of random groups which had then splintered, but they had remained on. They trickled in and never left, as if caught in a spider's cobweb. One dotted with empty skies, personal dreams and memories the exiles kept carefully hidden.

A town that did not officially exist, with a borrowed name. But, for now, it was home. Their other New Orleans.

It didn't even have a church. Not that it was a place God had forgotten; more like he had never become aware of its existence.

Nor did it have a jail. Neither God nor law in these heathen parts!

A bunch of them were enjoying coffee at the Café des Philosophes one evening. Sharing silences, aimless conversation and killing time.

It was Vernon who brought the subject up.

"Does anyone know who was the first to arrive here and stick around?" he asked.

"An old timer once told me it was Melody..." Sullivan responded.

They all sighed.

Everyone knew of Melody, but none had actually met her. It was long before their time. A whole generation or so of travellers ago. It was rumoured she was the first owner of the Hotel Marseilles, where most of them now stayed. Some preferred the river boats, or the caravans, most of which no longer even had wheels, but the Hotel Marseilles had hot water which the sturdy embarkations moored by the nearby lake with no name hadn't.

By all accounts, Melody Nelson had been an incomparable beauty. She hailed from Nova Scotia, had fled an abusive relationship and settled here to hide from either bad men or foreign authorities. She had acquired a plot of land and had the two-storey hotel built by local labourers.

"Was it her decision to call this place New Orleans?" Marie, the pianist who never smiled, asked.

No one knew the answer.

A portrait of Melody still hung behind the hotel bar. She wore a green silk jacket with ornamental buttons which looked somewhat Chinese in the way its collar surrounded her neck. Her blonde hair flowed down to her shoulders and her eyes were violet. There was a hint of a smile on her lips, almost mischievous, knowing, drawing you into some form of complicity. Like a modern Mona Lisa.

We all knew the story: Melody's first customer at the hotel had been a French jazz trumpet player and they had fallen passionately in love. But the trumpet player had a hole in his heart and the couple were forlornly aware from the very beginning they had no long-term future. He barely lasted past their first summer together before he collapsed while improvising on Gershwin's 'Rhapsody in Blue' on the hotel's forecourt, just a stone's throw from the nearby river Mersey. Melody had been heartbroken. Two years later, she had picked a bunch of black flowers that bloomed by the shore and that all knew to avoid. She ate them and succumbed to their poison within a week, in terrible agony. She left a child, Fleur, from their liaison, who was the present owner of the Hotel Marseilles.

Another of the itinerant musicians who had travelled to New Orleans alongside the man with the hole in his heart had written a song, which he'd performed at her funeral: 'The Ballad of Melody Nelson'. But it was now considered in bad taste to ever play it on the bar's juke box.

"I heard say that while they were still together, Melody and the trumpet player with a hole in his heart managed to fuck in every single room of the hotel…", Prince Rupert said. He was allegedly from minor European royalty and had fled his family home in disgrace and landed here many years later. He considered himself something of a lady's man, although none of us were aware of any women in our group of misfits and refugees from reality having actually been bedded by him. Let alone felt an iota of attraction to his unctuous manners and persona.

"Next you'll be telling us their rutting ghosts still haunt the hotel rooms…" someone remarked, debunking him.

Night was falling as most of us departed the Café in single file. For our respective hotel rooms, our rental apartments or the houseboats. The sun was fading across the faraway mountains of the sea, that shimmering, liminal zone where the sea faded into the line of the horizon and merged with infinity. It was autumn, but in our hearts we still wanted it to be spring.

I watched as Lora walked hand in hand with Tristan to whichever sofa they were squatting on tonight. I sighed. I had briefly thought I had a chance; that she might become my final passion. But she was too young and I was too old, and who can win when the other guy in the triangle happens to be a poet. At any rate, I had plans to write a story about her soon. It would be my last story. It would be perfect. That would be the way to go. Prose survived and poetry died, transient as it was. The literary odds were weighted in my favour even if the real-life ones had me pegged as a non-starter! I already had the first paragraph drafted and was determined to begin writing the imaginary tale in earnest the following day.

The only problem was that I had no idea what I should be writing about. Yes, Lora or a young woman resembling her in every detail, would feature. That it would be a love story with bizarre characters. But beyond that, I was completely at sea. In truth, I had nothing left to say, I had run out of stories to tell. Running on fumes, vague shards of my past tales full of sound, fury and sad endings. Maybe I should accept the evidence that my writing career had come to an end. All my stories told and the world remained the same: I had made no noticeable difference.

Little did I know that the movie makers would be arriving in town. And that our surreal ballet of stuttering relationships would be shattered once and for all.

We were some thousand miles East of nowhere and never more than three hours from the sea.

Our ramshackle city had begun with a gas station.

Which soon went out of business as there were no roads nearby. Just dirt tracks leading in and out of a small forest. No cars.

The pumps remained. Rusting. Like minute Stonehenge or Easter Island figures. Marking our Equator, the centre of our circle of abandonment. Later someone raised some shacks made of wooden blanks and with coruscated metal roofs to keep the elements at bay. It never rained around here but the winds followed seasonal patterns and sometimes raged. Albeit always at night, as if cannily aware they were keeping the settlers awake throughout.

There was talk on the island of a possible railway line that would be built bisecting it and the rumour attracted further folk and the town grew in small increments. Dreamers, rapscallions, cloud poets, would be captains of enterprise, fugitives, singers hoping to craft the perfect song, tattoo artists and scoundrels. You could always count on artists to make up the numbers. Some pretended to be composers of unwritten symphonies, others were dancers about architecture; a tribe of fools and their entourage, men and women who held on with ferocity to their original sense of innocence like babies refusing to relinquish their rubber dummies as they grew older and heavier, sycophants and soldiers of fortune seeking out a new, improbable war.

I came much later and inadvertently became a repository for the tales, the lies and the stories about the growth of the other New Orleans. Of how, building by building, it began to spread, branching out in a circular motion away from its heart, the Hotel Marseilles and backing up to it, the obligatory bank, the Baxter and Sons Bank, which also doubled up as a post office.

An unreliable old timer had related the story of how Melody Nelson's father had arrived a couple of generations back, with his child bride in tow and, allegedly, sacks of gold, after eloping with not just her but her valuable dowry, only to see his wife succumb in childbirth.

And then there was the Butterfly Kid, who hailed from San Francisco, whose real name was Chester so who could blame him for adopting a different sobriquet? He opened the Stone Museum, and later helped build the theatre where all our artists performed once they had been vetted by the Council of Contrarian Philosophers, a group of freaks who steadfastly refused to step foot in the Café des Philosophes because of a long-standing rift between their respective creeds, Sartre vs. Nietzsche or Lacan vs. Husserl, or something like that. When they drank too much, which was often the case, they would come to blows, settling their differences in the wounding fields by the creek, in the south-eastern fields on the edge of the ever-growing town.

It must have felt like being on the set of a spaghetti western, contradictory buildings rising almost overnight, seemingly in geometrical opposition to each other, crazy patterns outlined against the night sky, battling shapes and materials, a gentle form of anarchy, of madness that was more quaint than dangerous. The only thing we lacked was a town sheriff, a hangman or domestic animals roaming the dusty streets to conform with Sergio Leone western standards!

And, somehow, I became its involuntary chronicler. What else can a writer do when his job is done and has run out of narratives?

It could be that word of our haphazard enclave leaked and reached the outside world, and soon arrivals doubled, more dreamers, more lost souls. And someone had the bright idea of setting a movie here. The railway never came, but the mirages of the silver screen did.

Their metal silver trailers, their money, the giant generators, the cranes, the carpenters, the gofers, the hangers-on and the grips. The suits amongst them marvelled at the environment, the creatives gazed in amazement, but following the initial wave of enthusiasm their moods darkened when they realised the script they had brought with them could not be filmed here. Some major mistake at the production head office!

The actual producers who flew in weekly by helicopter had bought the movie rights to an obscure French novel with a surrealist bent, titled 'The Red Grass', but the director soon came to realise that a - the script some Hollywood hack had come up with was unfilmable her, b - that it made no sense either, and c - that they would not be allowed to dye the limited patches of grass that circled the town red, or any other colour for that matter.

Eventually, the executives and the big name stars left, but much of the minor 'talent' remained, charmed by the lazy rhythms of our laid-back existence here. Or all too aware that life on the outside presented no improvement.

Lily was a waitress from Québec City. She always wore black and had a tattoo of a tree branch running down from her shoulders to her sublimely-rounded bum cheeks. Or maybe it was a weeping willow? I had never had the opportunity of viewing its roots in her holy of holies. She had come to New Orleans to work make-up on the movie that was never made, but had also been promised a small walk-on part by one of the executive producers who wanted to get inside her pants. He didn't. But that did not deter us single men around who persisted in that wonderful ambition.

Lily stayed on when the movie bunch retreated to more propitious terrain. This was as good a place as any to live, she reckoned.

She now worked behind the counter at the Café.

She had come off shift. It was night, the fragrances of the island drifted by, bougainvillea here, exotic smells of cooking from the campsites crisscrossing the town, a delicate cocktail that caressed the senses, and one of the reasons I had some years back decided to remain here, so unlike the scent of big cities full of decay, stale beer and silent despair.

Lily was sad tonight. I did not dare ask her why, afraid she might tell me she missed her old life and might be contemplating a return to the mainland.

I raised my glass to her.

"Long day?"

"I guess so. Sometimes I get tired having to be so polite to customers and forcing myself to be cheerful throughout," she said.

"I wouldn't want to work as a waitress, let alone a waiter…"

Her skin was porcelain white, her cheeks flushed, the black of her work outfit clinging to her skin, highlighting its pallor. She had green eyes. The patterns of her visible tattoos flowed like small rivers across the length of her body.

"Sad?" I asked her.

"More like dreamy, you know. Feeling a bit lost. Not sure I can explain it properly."

"The blues?"

"Maybe. Why do they call it that? That particular colour? Should be more like the greys, no?"

"I'd never thought of it that way.."

"What about you, Mister Storyteller, what makes you remain here. Unless I'm mistaken, you're not particularly happy either?"

"Ah, the million-dollar question!"

"I can't quite afford that much," she remarked. She dug into her pocket and pulled out a coin and offered it to me. "I'm a cheapskate sort of girl. Will that pay for a story?"

"Now we're talking. A man can't live on royalties alone…"

"Deal!"

"So what sort of story appeals to you today, Miss Lily from Québec City?"

"A sad one."

"Those are the only ones I know."

"How did I guess?"

"Any plans for the night?" I enquired. "Can I be your Scheherazade and serenade you with stories until dawn breaks." I pocketed the coin she had proffered.

“And if your tales displease me, might I have your head chopped off when morning comes, if I remember the legend correctly?”

“A risk well worth taking…”

At worst, if I ran out of stories to serenade Lily’s angst, I could always rely on ChatGPT to galvanise my imagination, I knew.

But would I last a thousand and one nights?

We settled on seven nights only. If I could make her cry she would come to my bed. Should I fail, it was off with my head; I was uncertain how serious she was, but nothing ventured, nothing gained—or lost—I guessed.

There was the story of Colin and Chloé. He had fallen for her in a big way. But Chloé had a venomous flower blooming inside her lungs and no medicine known to man could nip it in the bud before it grew even more deadly and killed her. Colin hoped against hope but Chloé knew all too well what had given birth to the flower that was eating her up from inside: it was the ghosts of all the other men she had foolishly gifted herself to before, each of which had stolen a further inch of her soul and left a barren patch in their wake. Men, users who had not even loved her truly, but had taken advantage of her, plundered her body, enjoyed the pleasure of penetrating her without even imparting an ounce of joy. Their presence lingered, malevolent, spreading, like a shadow against the sun of her heart and no medicine man the couple consulted in their desperation could find a solution, an antidote. Tears had no effect. So, they partied extravagantly with their friends, a collection of endearing eccentrics until time ran out. There was only one way the story could end. With grief.

“I read the book,’ Lily declared, “but your version is too nihilistic”. She took a kitchen knife and gently pressed it against his throat. “Try again.”

In a city called New Orleans, which bore little resemblance to ours and luxuriated by the shores of the mighty Mississippi river, a young Italian woman called Giulia was fleeing her demons and was followed there by her older lover, while the rest of the country was overtaken by a bitter civil war, and the state of Louisiana (as well as California, Maine and a few others) declared independence and seceded from the rest of the United States. However, by the time he reached the city following picaresque adventures on the river, she had now become the captive of a local magician and had her memory erased and no longer recognised him. In a bid to save her, the older man volunteered to relinquish his own memories in the hope they could meet again as new people altogether and somehow rekindle the flame that had once burned so strong. But, by then, the new Giulia had married a local journalist, closer in age to her, and blanked him when he engineered a meeting, as if he were a total stranger.

“Do I note some autobiographical elements and, in your apocalyptic tale, does Louisiana become a Republic?” Lily the waitress from Québec asked, the sharp end of her knife caressing the wafer-thin skin of his neck. “Try again.”

He briefly wondered what it would feel like to be decapitated. How long his consciousness would survive, thoughts, pain, white lights and all?

On the third night Lily was not wearing waitress black, but a short white linen dress that didn’t reach further than her mid-thigh, offering a tantalising glimpse of the multi-coloured ink and foliage running down her right leg, raising terrible lust in his heart as to where it took root above, between her legs.

He told her the story of the trumpet player.

He was a man with too many talents. As a result, people wouldn't take him seriously. Just an entertainer, a dilettante, they said. He was a gifted musician, whose love of traditional jazz ran deep through his veins. He dreamed endlessly of travelling to New Orleans, the city on the Mississippi, the birthplace of jazz in Basin Street, that mythical street where Louis Armstrong, Sidney Bechet and so many others had practiced their early craft and he sat in awe at the feet of the American musicians who had serenaded him and a whole generation of post-war French intellectuals in the smoky cellars and crowded clubs of St Germain des Prés. But he also wrote. Novels that didn't fit anywhere and didn't conform to the parameters of his acquaintances Albert Camus and Jean-Paul Sartre in the heyday of existentialism; his books were just not serious enough, bizarre, unrealistic; he translated pulp American novels, hardboiled stuff and science fiction; wrote avant-garde plays and song lyrics. He even adopted a pseudonym to pen a schlocky thriller in the American-style which everyone assumed was the real thing and managed to attract the attention of the censors and outsold all his other books, those that came from the heart. How ironical for a man whose heart suffered from an irregular beat. And still he had ideas for more. When his pulp novel sold to the movies, he knew they would fail to understand its innate sense of irony and would just come up with a literal, vulgar adaptation. Which they did. And he died of a heart attack one morning in a screening room on the Champs Elysées in Paris, just as the producers were about to screen a preview copy of the movie for him. He was still much too young.

Lily the waitress remarked "Isn't it always the case that genius is seldom recognized in its lifetime?"

He nodded.

She was a hard nut to crack. With not an inch of sentimentality to spare.

But the pressure of the kitchen knife she had been moving from hand to hand while he recited his story abated against his carotid artery. She wouldn't cut him tonight, he realised.

On the fourth night, he elected to tell her a story full of magic and colour. It was the tale of a mysterious costumed ball that had been going on for a few centuries, migrating yearly, and that had become the stuff of legend. Ball? Orgy? Ritual? Tales would fly from ear to ear, speculation brewed, but only past participants knew the truth about it, and they were sworn to secrecy. All that was known was the fact the Ball had a Queen, the Mistress of Night and Dawn, and every generation a new Queen was crowned in a public ceremony that was as shocking and beautiful to behold and that even millionaires and true royalty would not dare to repeat in its savage splendor. She was selected when still a child by the courtiers of the ball, who carried the flame and dictated the rules which remained unchanged through the passing of the centuries. Usually an orphan. Her life was closely monitored until she became of age. Until the night of the ball, she would remain a virgin, although her education had carefully emphasised that the pleasure of the senses was the most wonderful of life's attainments and it was seen that the future Queen would, until the day came, be kept on terrible edge, her body aflame with lust and desire, craving for the little death of consummation. Then, as the night of the Ball finally arrived, she would be led naked to the altar around which the festivities were about to be triggered, laid out, washed, placed on satin sheets and tied into position. Then, at the stroke of midnight, when the music began, every man present, each a suitor carefully selected both for his amorous skills and his girth, would approach her crucified body and gently mount her. But through the miracle of the Ball, on every occasion the future Queen would orgasm, a tattoo would appear, risen from unknown depths, and flower across the unbelievable pallor of her skin, in a furious frenzy of wild colours, patterns, images and the most exquisite of calligraphies. First, a teardrop, below her left eye. Then, as she came for the second time, a scarlet rose above her heart. Men would breed her in quick succession, with a soft soliloquy of love reaching her ears while they thrust inside her. Wonderfully obscene words in a parade of languages dotting her body, a wide-open eye between her navel and her bruised cunt; a painted heart surrounding her spread labia; a spider's web circling her nipples; a dagger along her side; on and on the images appeared as she sighed, writhed, cried tears of joy, wet herself, invoked God as a concentric wave of abominable pleasure raced outwards from her genitalia and rushed like electricity through her body, every limb and extremity on fire and her mind ablaze as she gradually assumed her royalty. Until, at dawn, every man spent, her bindings were severed and she rose to her feet to stand in her terrible nudity, her people below her, with not an inch of her body unillustrated, unpainted, with the exception of her face, still flushed with every emotion she had travelled through between night and dawn, where the legacy of her very first orgasm, the delicate, miniscule tear-drop, was the only tattoo to be seen. And then the Queen smiled…

"You have a talent for dirty stories,' Lily said. He blushed. "That was wild… But a bit unrealistic, hey? No woman could… hmm…entertain… that many men without a serious risk to her health, not to mention delicate parts of anatomy, no?

"God only knows what it says about me… That I'm a dirty old man?"

"Let me be a judge of that."

She had left the knife on the table throughout.

Night five. A delicate night breeze blew through the Café's terrace. Lily was wearing black again and in the penumbra he could see goose pimples spreading across her bare forearms.

"So what has the dirty old man have in store for me tonight?"

It was the story of a man who felt he no longer had valid reasons to live any more. He was tortured by grief, loneliness and guilt for all the times he had done the wrong thing. His home was a repository of memories, things, object, clothes, thousands of books, photos, much amber jewellery, all the detritus that the years accumulate. So, he travelled. For a short while, the lure of exotic places partly filled the void inside him but he quickly ran out places to visit, to roam. Once you've seen the walls of one old city or two or more or observed the sun set in the tropics like an orb of fire crowning the line of the horizon, night after sultry night, you feel you've seen them all. Quickly, cities, beaches, islands all merged in his mind and brought him no joy. He had read too many novels full of crass romanticism in which the main characters travelled in search of truth, or experience or salvation. He had actually attempted to write one himself. He was on the balcony of a cheap hotel in a city in the southern hemisphere watching the waves and surfers cascading between them as the early morning distant, cold sun attempted to break the barricades of the clouds, when at the opposite end of the beach he spotted a curious shape. It looked like a mermaid. He cleaned his glasses and looked again. It was most definitely a real-life mermaid. She sat there, forlorn, her head bowed, water lapping her outstretched body. No one else appeared to have seen her. He walked down to the beach and approached her. She looked up at him, her hair was tangled with thin strands of seaweed and her tail shimmered like a wake of diamonds. He couldn't help but stare at her breasts; they were just perfect; firm, small, dark-nippled, like ripe fruit begging to be harvested. She was called Megan. She had cheekbones to die for. Over the following fortnight, he fell in love with her. He knew it made no sense, but as the cliché goes, the heart has its reasons. They found an isolated cove where they could not be disturbed. She allowed him to touch her, they kissed and as he expected she tasted of salt water. He brushed her hair with all the delicacy he could summon; she took his manhood in her mouth and remarked his emissions reminded her of oysters. But there were limits to their lust, the obstacle of contrasting anatomies. She sulked. He hurt inside. Then, one day, as they lay in the sand, listening to their respective heartbeats, she told him there was a way. But he would have to sacrifice his penis in the process. He knew better than to ask further questions or query the details. Arrangements were made; Megan knew of a willing surgeon in the nearest coastal town who could operate on him. Then, she revealed, he would be able to follow her beneath the sea. He agreed. The doctor castrated him. It was agreed that it would take a fortnight or so for him to heal properly and then he and Megan could meet again and be together. The endless hours went by all so slowly. But the day came. Early dawn, he descended to the beach in their isolated cove, shed his clothes and stood there naked, emasculated, uneasy. In the distance, he could see Megan the mermaid waiting. She was more beautiful than ever. She was smiling. Or was it more of a satisfied leer? He stepped closer to her. And saw she was now wearing a heavy necklace. He neared. And his heart missed a beat when he had full sight of the necklace. Around a rough piece of rope hung a dozen or so men's cocks in all shapes and length. His eyes were drawn to his own, fixed to the string holding them by a hook through his ball sack. He was frozen to the spot as Megan retreated and disappeared through the rising waves without as much as a farewell. The mermaid from the southern seas had completed her necklace.

"Wow," Lily the waitress from Québec. "That's truly wicked."

"You liked the tale?"

"Absolutely… I just hope it's not autobiographical…"

He lowered his eyes.

On their final night of storytelling, Lily invited her purveyor of sad stories to the caravan which she rented and which was parked in the Café's car park. She normally shared it with another waitress from the Café, but her friend was absent tonight. She allowed him to chastely sleep beside her until dawn broke across the simmering sealine. I had an affair with a married woman called Kate. I was also married at the time. I'd come across her at a conference and had immediately fallen in lust with her and brazenly written her a letter declaring the fact. We worked in the same industry. In nine cases out of ten, this sort of approach never works but there must have been a confluence of moons and moods and she did not answer negatively. We met up for a drink, in a pub by Cambridge Circus, skirted the subject endlessly but it was immediately apparent that she was not immune to me, and was unsettled in her marriage and my indecent proposal out of the blue had her similarly not so much lusting after me, but craving for something different in her life. As I drove her to her railway station following our first meeting, she took hold of my hand and, in a low voice, just said "Yes, I will." I was overjoyed. We booked a hotel room by Heathrow airport and I brought along a bottle of white wine and a punnet of strawberries. The affair began. My office after hours, rutting over the carpet in the staff room; holding hands at bad movies in darkened cinemas where no one knew us; at another conference in Brighton where we only left the room to eat and spent all our time fucking with the energy of despair. The sex was good, as to be expected from sensualists who had respectively been in long marital relationship that had inevitably become a tad stale. One evening as I was inside her, she asked me to hold her hands down harder, to be rougher with her. It went against my natural instinct but I did, enjoying the rapture it brought to her face, her lips trembling, her whole body responding, her wild Medusa-like hair a maelstrom of curls in disarray. Another time, she asked me to choke her gently. It escalated quickly. Until the day we were faced with choices about the way ahead. I was willing to jettison my marriage, my children. Kate hesitated. We were apart the time of a long business trip to Omaha in Nebraska, a place I found out to be the dark hole of nowhere. By the time I returned, Kate had opted to remain with her husband. And called a halt to our relationship. I screamed her name silently in my sleep; I raged against my fate; I wrote terrible pornographic stories in which her avatar suffered the worst of indignities. But life went on. I began reflecting on our time together, how she submitted to me in such intimate ways beyond the vanilla sex we had both previously been accustomed to. I began to speculate about the nature of sexual submission, how one person could offer themselves so completely to another, with no limits, no shame, no sense of decency. I had always been a particularly sexual person and the memory of Kate and her hidden nature was like an itch I couldn't scratch. I sought other women, other affairs, but none could match the beauty of Kate and the gift she could orchestrate of her body and mind. One twisted thought led to another. I had often speculated what it felt like for a woman to take a man's cock into her mouth and suck it. An itch, I knew. One day, I succumbed to a Craigslist ad and met another man and got down on my knees and opened my mouth. I had never been attracted to other men in the slightest, but I found out, to my surprise and shame, that I was attracted to their penises, had an out of body experience watching myself sucking anonymous cocks, belonging to men whose faces I would never even care to remember. It was a kind of submission. In my folly, I identified with Kate and all the other women who had once fellated me. One thing would lead to another and soon I submitted fully to strangers. Was taken anally by them, mounted in the same sexual position Kate had always preferred. I hadn't become gay, but somehow feeling myself being filled to the hilt, past the initial pain due to my tightness, I began to understand the women I had known, those with whom I had sex. My own sexual history had begun, years ago, in France, where I lived and feasted on the books of Boris Vian, Mandiargues, Drieu la Rochelle and Aragon; all men who loved women intensely. I justified my increasing number of anonymous sexual encounters with strange men – very seldom was I used by the same one more than twice – by the fact that I could now understand how women felt and therefore the unknowable minds of women, and now felt so much closer to them by virtue of being used as they were so frequently. The Internet is a great enabler and I had great success in advertising myself as a mature submissive and making myself available for free to all-comers. Both pimp and whore. On the FetLife website, a social network for active BDSM practitioners, I perved on others with the same cravings, on both sides of the sexual divide and also that ravine that stood between, full of every kink under the sun. Of late, I had been following a sub in Antarctica who called herself Cloudpoet and developed a strong attraction to her. Touched myself to photos of her in lingerie, naked, genitalia and openings, on occasion in the process of being used by men only the members of which could be seen penetrating her. She posted regular poems, naïve but touching, almost like haikus of lust and cravings, sometimes misspelled, but my heart opened up to her and her quiet radiance; I read her wish list of advertised kinks which she was slowly ticking off: being fucked inside a car, in the rain, at a party, as part of a threesome, roughly, and all the things she still aspired too: a delightful catalogue of sex, excess and deviance I could easily count as my own in my submissive role. Bizarre thoughts of contacting her and making an indecent offer to join her as part of a couple and enjoy our submissive status together and enjoy the same users, cocks, and rude attentions. But she lived half a world away, was more than half my age. My sister soul in submission. Beauteous curves, red hair, a slightly boy-ish face with a definite touch of humour in the curl of her lips, almost demure in appearance, her repository of cravings concealed from the outside world. So, one day, I wrote a story for her in hope of reaching out n some unconventional sort of way, on the assumption that poets and writers went well together. I sent it as a lengthy message through the website. She blocked me and I lost all possible contact with her!

"Oh, that is SO sad," Lily the waitress said. "I can't think of anything sadder," she added.

"Neither can I," I admitted.

And then Lily finally took me to her bed.

Discretion is the better part of valour. But she was the first woman from Québec I had mated with, and no doubt the last. I know my performance that short night was poor; I had difficulty even achieving an erection, but I can now die happy knowing that Lily, the waitress from Québec was momentarily mine. And I fell in love with her enigmatic smile and the twinkle in her eye when she muttered "I want you inside me' and opened her legs to me. Although I half reckon it was also an act of charity.

Maybe I should now learn to play the trumpet and let my sounds float like clouds over New Orleans, surrounded by the sea of Exopotamia. Or, alternately, I could go travelling again and visit Peking in the autumn? No, not Beijing as it is now known, but the Peking that never was.

Tribunal

By D. Harlan Wilson

Dramatis

P. Torque, F. Torque, D. Celina, S. Hackwith, R. Dankly, A. Fibb, A. Fibb's Secretary, L. Inez, E. Leviticus, B. d'Oria, N. von Klempt, J. Constantine, V. Jung, B. Coleco, W. Grimoire, and I. Ishmael.

Extremities

"Fingers."

"How many?"

"Two."

"Which ones?"

"Doesn't matter."

"It matters."

"Not if I say it doesn't."

P. Torque flailed as I clutched his left wrist and clipped off the thumb with straight-blade scissors. He didn't scream—he never screamed. Blood hemorrhaged from the wound and he instinctively shoved the nub in his mouth, biting down to stop the flow. He clenched his teeth too hard, sprung backwards like a cat. There was nowhere to go. He ran in circles until D. Celina punched him as hard as he could.

"A thumb isn't a finger," D. Celina observed.

"Shit," I said.

It took awhile to get the fingers off. There was a lot of blood and I couldn't see what I was doing very well.

"Gimme those things." D. Celina grabbed the fingers from me and put them in a paper bag alongside his flask. He constricted the bag at the neck and took a swig. As P. Torque nursed his wounds in a fetal position, D. Celina said to him, "You're done, get me? I'll keep these digits on ice until the end of the week. Do as you're told and maybe you'll get them back in time to stick them up somebody's ass again. Not the thumb; you lose that. This is what happens when you act like a shithead. Understand, shithead?"

P. Torque passed out and had a dream about D. Celina and I. In the dream, everything that just happened happened again, only there was a cow in the room, and D. Celina fed P. Torque's thumb to it.

Conjugation

He awoke next to his wife.

She slept so soundly, he couldn't hear her breath. Her eyes, in contrast, were loud, clicking against the skull like marbles as they pulsed behind the lids. His hand throbbed in pain, but he was afraid to look at it.

"Spouse?" he whispered in a nasal drawl. "Are you there, Spouse?"

The eyes pulsed harder and her mandible fell open. Gently P. Torque tried to close the mandible. It fell open again.

In the bathroom, he inspected his hand. The thumb was growing back, although it looked like a talon, black and sharp. Assuming history remained true to itself, he wouldn't have the same luck with the fingers.

It was difficult putting on argyles. P. Torque found it most efficient to use his smallest fingers to lift the fabric over his anklebones. Getting on pants, shirt, and cravat wasn't that hard. Luckily, he didn't need to shave: a feral moustache consumed most of his central faceplate and he only attended to his cheeks and neck once every week or two.

He didn't bother trying to tie his shoes. He simply removed the laces.

"What are you doing?" said F. Torque, dazed. She sat up in bed. Across the room, hunched in a chair, her husband fidgeted with the laces in a stylish pair of dress shoes. He was a small man and looked like a frustrated child in the chair with his feet dangling above the floor. "I said what's going on?" implored F. Torque.

"Nothing," P. Torque replied.

"Nothing? What's wrong with your hand?"

"Go back to sleep."

"I deserve to know what's happening."

"It's fine. It's early."

"Isn't it too early?" She squinted at the flickering walls. "It's definitely too early."

"It's never too early."

"That's ridiculous."

"Are you sure you're awake?"

"I'm sure." She closed her eyes.

"You'll feel better when you wake up."

"I feel fine."

"Damn these things." One of the laces had a knot in it and he couldn't disentangle it. "You pay this much for shoes, you figure they'd be more user-friendly."

"A perfect shoe has never been made," noted F. Torque. "Nor will it be made. Ever."

P. Torque said, "I have to go."

"Okay."

Still sitting upright, F. Torque snored obscenely as P. Torque abandoned his dress shoes for a pair of moccasins. Bougie vs. boho chic—either style would do.

Waterfowl

I was staring out my office window at a badling of ducks when I saw P. Torque march down the path that curled out of the woods. His little legs seemed to have a mind of their own, drawing the torso atop it forward, and yet he proceeded with machinic purpose, arms moving like pistons.

The ducks were fighting again. I often watched them skirmish in the pond. One duck out-sized the rest and almost looked human, with a head in the shape of a fedora. This veritable Spartan stood tall, as if posing for a camera, its chest pushed up and out, and it manhandled the other ducks with ease, tossing them in the air, biting and cracking their necks with its great bill, and performing awkward wrestling moves.

As P. Torque passed the pond, the ducks grew uncannily still, and every duck that wasn't floating dead in the water observed him intensely, vigilantly, aligning with the Spartan like soldiers on a battlefield.

Distressed, P. Torque's pace quickened as the cattails and reeds in the pond quivered in the breeze.

The Spartan emitted a loud, drawn-out quack. The proles that flanked it mimicked the warcry.

P. Torque broke into a sprint …

The ducks were faster and pounced on him all at once, just as he was about to enter the building. He fell down and rolled around the grass as if on fire. The Spartan stomped on his groin and delivered a series of one-two punches with its wingtips. P. Torque never broke character, not even to call for help, even when his pants came halfway down. I had seen the ducks accost people before, but never like this.

I recalled my favourite line from Walt Whitman's epic poem "Song of Myself": "Nature without check with original energy."

Pathos

"What the fuck?"

Loud footfalls in the hallway …

D. Celina appeared in my office door. He was a huge man. Everything was too big on him—too-big head, too-big hands, and a stomach that seemed to have been inflated with a tire pump. Like most of my colleagues, he was more of a grotesque caricature than a believable character, let alone a human being. Even his voice, affected and over inflected, didn't seem real.

"Did that little shit come into work today?" he intoned.

"He did," I said.

Shaking from some kind of neurological condition—nobody knew what it was—D. Celina gesticulated in consternation. "He's a sociopath!"

"Autistic and schizo-affective, too."

"Sonofabitch. I already threw his fingers in the trash. Fuck those fingers."

S. Hackwith sidled next to D. Celina, startling him. A new employee, we hired her because she was the best of the worst in a pool of candidates that was All Bad. "What fingers?" she asked. "Who are you talking about?" Whenever S. Hackwith sensed negative energy, she assumed that she generated it.

D. Celina sort of brushed her aside and fixed his round eyes on me. "We gotta get that asshole."

S. Hackwith jockeyed for position in the doorway, her bramble of wild, gray-streaked hair seeming more and more like a wig that might pop off.

I said, "He'll just keep coming back. He doesn't learn. He doesn't listen. He doesn't care."

"Who?" panted S. Hackwith. "Me?"

"You're a woman," I said. "*He* means *man*."

"He means P. Torque?" said R. Dankly, somehow manoeuvring himself into the doorway. "P. Torque is always himself." R. Dankly was also a new hire. There were very few of us oldsters left, in fact, so almost everybody knew next to nothing, possessing no institutional memory, perspective, or wisdom.

D. Celina subtly tried to muscle S. Hackwith and R. Dankly out of his orbit, but subtlety was impossible for him: every move he made was a grand gesture whether he wanted it to be or not, and he accidentally knocked both of them over. Unfazed, they clamoured to their feet and back into the doorway.

"Look," D. Celina consternated. "There are only two things you need to know regarding the issue of P. Torque. First, the most horrible kind of administrator is the administrator who wants to be an administrator. Second, this variety of administrator only wants one thing: to please the administrator above him. Always bear in mind these seminal guidelines, if only to protect your own psyche." Then, to me: "Be in my office at 2 p.m. I have sixteen meetings this morning, and I'm taking a two-hour lunch for mental health purposes. I'll be drunk off my ass at 2 but we can still figure something out."

After D. Celina, S. Hackwith, and R. Dankly extricated themselves from each other, S. Hackwith lingered and stepped into my office, keen on having a conversation about an impending feminist movement that would ostensibly integrate certain Krav Maga techniques. Not one for idle exchanges, I pretended to have a meeting and politely asked her to die.

Conjugation

He awoke next to his wife.

Feathers on the duvet. He hesitated to look under the comforter.

F. Torque lay on her side with her face turned away from him. P. Torque couldn't hear her eyes. He poked her shoulder.

"Spouse," he drawled.

When was the last time they had done sex? He couldn't remember. He knew they participated in sexual relations on a regular basis, multiple times per week, but he couldn't envision a re-cent interaction on his mindscreen.

The walls illuminated her contours ...

As he mounted her, P. Torque put too much pressure on his wounded hand. His elbow buckled and he collapsed on his wife, who cried out and rolled onto the floor. Disoriented, F. Torque scurried around the bedroom, standing and tripping and falling down again repeatedly. P. Torque barked at her to stop, but she was in a fugue. Even when he pushed her against the wall and entered her from behind, she continued to make weird noises and pace forward, like a toy robot that can't turn around.

P. Torque lost track of time.

At some point, he staggered back to bed … and awoke sitting at the kitchen table trying to eat a boiled egg. He struggled to manipulate utensils. Numb and prickled, his good hand wouldn't wake up, and the fingers on his bad hand were still gone, although the thumb had grown back, dark and smooth and cold as obsidian.

Defibrillation

One of A. Fibb's teeth fell out as we entered her office and sat down. She didn't stop smiling. She picked up the tooth, placed it in a drawer, sat across from us, pushed a glass jar of chocolates across her desk, and tapped on the lid.

"No thank you," I said.

D. Celina stared at A. Fibb with crisp blue eyes that seemed out of place above the swollen cheeks marked by splashes of broken blood vessels.

"Are you sure?" urged A. Fibb, fixating on me. "Who doesn't like chocolate?" Still smiling, she rolled her tongue around her mouth and stroked the wilted skin of her neck.

I shrugged. "I only eat sweets once a week. I prefer salty things. But I don't eat those either. Look at me." I pointed at myself. "I'm healthy."

"You're too skinny. You look sick. You have body dysmorphia. You need to fatten up." She turned to D. Celina, who had wedged himself into the chair. "Right?"

D. Celina looked me up and down, perplexed.

A. Fibb unwrapped and ate a chocolate. "Ak!" She spit the chocolate into a trash can. "Christ that hurt." Speaking into an intercom, she asked her secretary: "When's the last time I've been to the dentist?" The inaudible response seemed to emanate from some tomb. "That long? Heck. Go ahead and make me an appointment. Bring me a bottle of water, too." A string of drool fell from her smile onto the lapel of her cheap gray suit. A. Fibb hissed, "Heck, shit, and fuck!" She wiped it off with tissue and the tissue came apart on the fabric.

A doleful secretary entered the office. She looked Amish, with a solid-color dress, long sleeves, and a ragtag cape. "Look at what's happening!" A. Fibb barked. "I need a washcloth now! I'll take that water first. Don't get any on me."

The secretary solemnly paced around us to the other side of the desk and fed A. Fibb several sips of water, like a bird feeding her young. After each sip, she swished the water around her mouth, then spit it into the trash.

As the secretary left, A. Fibb reminded her about the washcloth and told us, "I don't like to touch store-bought drinking receptacles, if possible. Factory workers ejaculate on them and so forth." She smiled, groaned. "Christ that hurt. It hurts to smile now. I'm not going to smile for the rest of the meeting. Don't take it personally. Don't read into it. My lack of a smile means nothing in terms of what I think about you, what my mood is, and all that. I like to think of myself as a source of reliable positivity, but sometimes life gets in the way."

"Smiling is a symptom of the devil's fuckery," said D. Celina. "One should never smile. It's a waste of time and face, as is positivity in general. Positivity and productivity have dick to do with one another."

"I respectfully disagree." Pointedly, A. Fibb said, "Now then. It's come to my attention that P. Torque—"

"Let me stop you right there," I interrupted. I didn't have anything else to say. I figured D. Celina would chime in. He didn't.

"If you please," said A. Fibb. "It's come to my attention—"

"There's nothing worse than being trapped somewhere you don't belong," said D. Celina.

"I respectfully agree," I said.

A Fibb continued, "I have not spoken to P. Torque. Nor did he come to see me. But I know what's happening. I know—"

"P. Torque is a broken and fucked-up sociopath who lords over everybody and is fully empowered by you and your bosses because you don't know how to do your job," explained D. Celina. He wasn't lying, but the truth never solved anything. He added: "P. Torque fucks people over on a regular basis at the behest of your bosses. Your core desire is to please your bosses at all costs. Hence you fully empower P. Torque to act as he pleases. As a result, people suffer. The world suffers. Reality suffers. Everything suffers and everybody knows this. Even you, sitting there playing dumb like a big fuckin' dummy. That said, I have no idea what you're talking about." By now, D. Celina had forgotten I was there. It only took a few sentences for him to lose himself in himself. Under different circumstances, he might have gone on for hours.

"P. Torque is a good boy," she claimed. "He does a lot of work for me. Give him some grace."

"That sonofabitch does *all* your work for you, the little freak. Operating at his very best, he's an obstacle. At his worst? Well, he's much worse than an obstacle. He can grace my ass with grease."

I said, "Do you know what P. Torque did to me?"

A. Fibb growled, "I don't care what he did. Be fucking nice!" She clutched her jaw. "Ouch … Listen. P. Torque has got a job to do. We all got jobs to do. Things are weird enough without you two barbarians making them weirder. Why can't you be happy?"

D. Celina and I blinked at one another.

A. Fibb hugged us before we left. She hugged me so hard, her shoulder dislocated, and she lurched back to her desk, slanted and slot-mouthed.

Extremities

"Toes."

"How many?"

"Four."

"Which ones?"

"All of them."

"There's ten toes."

"Actually there's nine."

He was right. Kind of. The second toe on P. Torque's foot extended from the base, but it didn't have a nail, and I couldn't see a knuckle. "There's a protrusion," I said. "Looks like brachydactyly. He was probably born like that."

"Born bad," said D. Celina, eyeballing P. Torque.

P. Torque mumbled something. D. Celina punched him squarely, soundly, knocking him over. We had tied him to a chair. In one undulant lunge, D. Celina scooped up P. Torque like a doll and replanted him upright. Occasionally D. Celina's largeness escaped me until he abused somebody with such a show of strength, and he was deceptively spry despite being clinically obese.

P. Torque flailed as I clutched the foot with five toes and cut one, two, three, four … I used garden shears instead of scissors this time and they came right off.

Thoroughly intoxicated yet ever-functional, D. Celina leered down at us. "Your body is not your friend," he slurred.

As always, P. Torque passed out. It was a lame exeunt, but he didn't know how to behave, and ultimately, he was a coward. I could empathize with him. As a child, I used to play dead in dreams when things went sour and monsters closed in. Oneiric disavowal. In the game of existence, you can't get killed if you pretend you're not there.

Conjugation

"Nobody likes me," P. Torque informed his wife. "I wonder why."

"I like you." F. Torque talked in her sleep more than when she was awake.

"I'm not convinced that you matter vis-à-vis me being liked by people."

"I think I matter."

"You know what I mean, Spouse."

"Do I?"

P. Torque lost time again. It had always been this way. Idle pathology kept his nerves at bay—technically, he never really "worried" about anything, no matter what happened, and this above all distinguished him from his peers. If he worried about anything, it was his worry-free disability.

"I should probably kill myself," he announced, returning to himself. "If nobody likes you, there's a chance you're probably worthless. Can you think of a notable historical figure who nobody liked? Even tyrants had friends. Hitler and Stalin and Pol Pot all had a lot of good buddies. My only good buddy is you."

"Do you want to be a notable historical figure?"

His foot bled onto the sheets as he thrust into his wife. On his mindscreen, the blood went back into the foot …

Cravat

S. Hackwith and R. Dankly were complaining about Administration in the hallway. This produced a sociochemical reaction wherein multiple personnel gravitated towards them, magnetized by the exfoliation of Angst. L. Inez and E. Leviticus attached themselves to S. Hackwith and R. Dankly, drawing B. d'Oria, N. von Klempt, J. Constantine, and V. Jung into their orbit.

“They don’t know what they’re doing,” S. Hackwith was saying, “and nobody will listen to me. I know what they’re doing wrong, too. It’s hard to stand by and watch people screw things up when you know what they’re doing wrong.”

“They don’t respond to logic or reason,” R. Dankly remarked.

“Who?” asked L. Inez.

“Who?” echoed E. Leviticus. “*Them*.”

N. von Klempt said, “They’re all the same. They don’t know how to communicate. They don’t know how to behave. They don’t know how to exist.”

“You only have to sit there like a cunt on a log to exist,” said J. Constantine. “Anybody can do that.”

“Some people exist better than others,” added V. Jung.

J. Constantine snorted. “How do you exist better than somebody else? That’s a stupid thing, what you said.”

“I’m existing better than you right this second.” V. Jung poked J. Constantine, who poked him back. “That’s assault,” said J. Constantine. “You all saw it.”

N d’Oria said, “You poked him back. You’re both guilty.”

D. Celina turned a corner and trudged down the hallway like a rolled boulder. “Get the fuck outta my way!” he barked. Everybody tried to give him room, but the hallway was narrow and he took up too much space; predictably, he flattened them against the walls in passing. “Fuckin’ slugs,” he carped, and disappeared into his office.

“Geez.” R. Dankly’s essential tremors flared for a moment, rendering him spastic, then receded to normal.

E. Leviticus worried that her ribs might be broken. J. Constantine assured her, “You’d know if you broke a rib or two. It hurts like a cunt.”

They fell back into discussion, adding B. Coleco and W. Grimoire to their corpus. Nobody noticed that P. Torque had colonized the ceiling. On his knees, with his unravelled cravat hanging down like a do-rag, he deftly crawled past his colleagues like a garden-variety poltergeist.

Spartan

I stared out my window at the pond.

There was only one duck. The Spartan. More than ever, the multicolored gradient of its feathers made it appear like a beaked gladiator in uniform, with a discernible chestplate and subligaculum.

Self-righteous and statuesque, the Spartan stared back at me.

Had it killed the other ducks? Where were all of the proles? Did it eat them? Are ducks cannibals?

I tapped on the glass. The pond was a good distance away, but the Spartan saw me all right, and it pointed at me with a mindful wing as if threatening to hit the ball out of the park.

Similitude

A. Fibb sent a message to everybody. The message read:

All:

Good morning! It has come to my attention that many of you would like to have more meetings in order to better keep up to date with policies and procedures. I think this is a wonderful idea! Let's schedule three additional meetings per week. Dates and times will be sent out directly. The first of these new meetings will take place tomorrow morning at 8 a.m. in room 102. Attendance will be taken. Thank you!

A. Fibb, Chief Administrative Officer

It was a child's lie, and clearly her secretary wrote the message; A. Fibb couldn't string together a coherent sentence in writing given word enough and time. But child's lies were the status quo. And A. Fibb only called ad hoc meetings for two reasons: 1) to control an interoffice narrative that she feared would reflect poorly on her image, and 2) to punish everybody for not being happy enough in accordance with her definition of the concept of happiness.

For the most part, every meeting unfolded in precisely the same way. First, A. Fibb castigated us for being miserable and not smiling or speaking in jovial tones on a regular basis. This manner of invective started as pleasant encouragement and evolved into an hysterical rant wherein various body parts fell off as she bullied us. Next, she ordered us to respect and obey "My Dear Number Two," assuring us that P. Torque had everybody's best interests in mind. She often paused during this phase to ask if anybody required snacks. Finally, A. Fibb adjourned the meeting with a promise that nobody's job was in jeopardy, even in the absence of good moods, although such an absence invariably resulted in penalties that ranged from demotions and paycuts to various forms of public humiliation.

Typically, D. Celina became frustrated, picked a fight for the sake of it, and the meeting devolved into another episode of Korean parliament. For some reason, at the first "new" meeting, he kept his cool. B. Coleco, on the other hand, who was six-months pregnant and generally mild-mannered, broke down and charged P. Torque, who stood with A. Fibb at the front of the room, hiding behind the vast shoulderpads of her business suit. Reality skidded into slow motion as B. Coleco leapt in the air and pounced on the "Little Darkness," as some employees referred to him, knocking aside A. Fibb.

I try to remain detached, if not more or less invisible, at all times. I have found that drawing attention to oneself in any way tends to result in pain and suffering, but sometimes one has to get involved, and I have a soft spot for children, even when they're still in the womb.

As B. Coleco pummeled P. Torque with an impressive execution of blows—like S. Hackwith, she clearly had martial-arts training—I pulled her off of him and accompanied her to the office nurse to ensure that both she and the baby were okay. I would likely be penalized for leaving the meeting early in spite of the surety that no issue would be (re)solved and everything would stay the same.

If nothing else, we can always count on similitude.

Conjugation

He awoke next to his wife. Shadows flowed across the iridescent walls like a timelapse of consternated nimbus clouds …

"Where are we?"

"Home."

"Where's home."

"Here."

"Where's here."

"Somewhere."

He paused, reflected. "That's illogical. All of it."

"But nonetheless true. All of it."

He lost himself in reverie as he enfolded her in his embryonic lobes like an insect whose internal drives dictate terms. He absorbed her into his skin as if through osmosis, and he tasted her cells with the tongues of his wounds. Base synesthesia—he was no stranger to this uncanny affect, and the pragmatist in him suspended his disbelief, per usual. But he was sheer pragmatist; there was nothing else inside of him; cold, machinic, Soviet, rational … Not everybody believed him to be rational. Nobody did. His purview seemed rational to him, though, and while he did not consider himself to be a sage, or even a person of import, he did think he possessed special wisdom, knowledge about the job and the world that nobody else had logged in their epistemological register. All he had to do was keep doing what he was doing. Eventually people would come around and see things his way. The Universe would prove him right. He never expected anybody to be "happy"—he and A. Fibb fundamentally disagreed on this point—but he did anticipate a less hostile work environment, or at least less hatred for his bedside manner.

"Fuck me."

"I am."

In the meantime, he would continue to make the hard decisions and do his due diligence. He would not give in to the whimsy of D. Celina, I. Ishmael, or anybody, no matter what they did to him. Nearly everybody was his moral inferior in any case. He cheated on his wife habitually. He broke the law habitually. He had even committed murder, but that only happened once, and it was mostly an accident. All told, everybody else's shortcomings far outweighed his own.

"Fuck me."

"I said I was fucking you, Spouse. I'm not convinced I'm doing a good job at it."

"You're doing fine."

"Then why do you insist on telling me to fuck you?"

"I'll try to be quiet."

"I don't understand."

"I'm fine. You're fine."

He didn't believe her. He manoeuvred and finessed his appendages so that they more effectively hit their marks. A thick, oily mucous began to build beneath their snarled bodies. It got into their mouths—a bitter, acerbic substance that tasted like absinthe gone sour. The clouds on the walls didn't like it; they shrivelled into themselves even as they vomited themselves anew …

Later, P. Torque viewed the corpse of F. Torque with mild curiosity. She lay naked on the bed, arms and legs broken in places, bones jutting out of the flesh. There was no blood. Her mandible looked more like a proboscis than a human thing.

I need new argyles, he reminded himself.

Conjugation

He awoke next to his wife.

"Are you real?"

"No."

"And yet there you are."

"There I was."

Conjugation

He awoke next to his wife.

"What day is it?"

"Today."

He stretched out his legs and repositioned himself so that he straddled the city. Maintaining balance was a problem. One false move and he would fall backwards, impaling himself on spires and turrets and bell towers.

At this height, the air smelled clean, free of all impurities. But clearly there were ample impurities up here. The clean-smelling air was an illusion, like life. He just couldn't see and experience the molecules.

"Where's my cravat?"

Caesarean

D. Celina and I sat across the desk from A. Fibb and P. Torque. They were in bad shape. Both administrators, however, donned their signature frontages: respectively, a delirious grin and a pursed smirk.

"You two look like fuckin' retards," said D. Celina.

A. Fibb exaggerated a laugh, and her ear fell off. "Goodness fucking gracious." She picked it up and scrutinized it, then put it in a drawer and cocked her head. "Let's not start on a bad, ugly note now. Good, cheery notes are the finest notes."

D. Celina groused, "You have weaponized Good Cheer. Everybody is miserable because of you. Shame on you both."

P. Torque cleared his throat nervously. He resembled a dilapidated mummy with all the bandages, yet vogue had not escaped him: he had been careful to give his cravat primacy. D. Celina and I had only worked on his hand and foot as of late. I wondered where the other injuries came from. It could have been that he was merely posing for sympathy.

"Listen to me," said A. Fibb. "This is no good. We need to come to some sort of agreement. Like it or not, we have to work together." She smiled too hard and several teeth fell out, clattering against the desktop.

D. Celina made a fart noise. "My ass. This is a world of your making and it's a world of turds." He rearranged his girth in the chair and pointed a thick finger at A.

Fibb. "Let me be clear. You're a turd. That turd behind you is a bigger turd, and all of your bosses are turds that try to turn everybody beneath them into turds. Nothing matters in your turd-infested dystopia. Nothing changes, either. It keeps going on and on and nobody learns or listens or grows."

What A. Fibb said next was garbled in light of her mouth falling apart. My translation would go like this: "There's something to be said for stability. But I think you're being too hard on P. Torque. He just [*sic*] does what I tell him to do."

D. Celina heard the last part. He replied, "P. Torque makes his own rules. And you don't have a fuckin' clue what he does. You don't even know what you do. Nobody does."

"I do plenty. All day I do things." Again, garbled. And now P. Torque was starting to come apart as well. He tried to say something but only a death-rattle came out.

That afternoon, we performed the Ides of March again, cornering P. Torque outside near the pond. D. Celina went first. Then S. Hackwith. Then R. Dankly. Then L. Inez. Then E. Leviticus. Then B. d'Oria. Then N. von Klempt. Then J. Constantine. Then V. Jung. Then B. Coleco. Then W. Grimoire. Then me. Then a few others. We all had our own knives. Even a few ducks chipped in, pecking at his legs, and the Spartan kicked him in the groin. P. Torque oscillated between hysterical consternation and something like aloofness, if not complacency. The latter reaction incensed D. Celina, who finally cut his head off, then collapsed from overexertion. We ushered D. Celina to the bar quickly, though, and he was himself again in no time.

Tai-otoshi

As a boy, I practiced judo for years. My parents made me. I was uncoordinated and awkward-looking, but not without grit. Still, bullies antagonized me endlessly at school. Mother and father thought judo would give me an edge. It just gave more boys more leeway for hostility. And these boys were bully candy, too, with parents of the same mind. Most of them, in fact, were meeker, weaker, and clumsier than me. Despite myself, however, I allowed them to beat me, every time. I could have countered every hip throw, every body drop, every foot sweep, every knee wheel, every choke hold ... but I let myself lose. Every time. Because even as a boy, I knew that every narrative must culminate in loss. That's what an ending is, after all: the loss of everything that precedes the ending, brought to a close like a guillotine of naught.

Absentia

"Snap out of it."

"I'm all right."

"You're fucked up."

"I'm okay."

"No you're not."

"I don't want to be here, is the thing. I don't belong here, is the thing."

"None of us do. Hence we're right where we belong."

D. Celina seemed to have shrunk or deflated in recent days. Slouched over like a mammoth buzzard with his neck pushed out, he swayed back and forth on disproportionately small feet, trying to bring me into focus. He was no more drunk than usual, but he seemed particularly distant, disconnected. The nystagmutic movement of his eyes didn't correspond with his stance.

"This has always been happening," he said.

"Yes," I replied.

"Nothing strange is happening here," he added.

"No," I replied.

He braced himself against the wall. "There will be no denouement. Everything is denouement. Or it's not. You know."

"I know."

He sunk to the floor, wheezing. I helped him take sips from his flask. He dropped onto his belly, nose and chin pressed into the carpet. "I'm not here," he whispered.

"I know," I said. "Nobody is."

"Absence is more valuable than presence."

"Absence, is the thing."

"I mean, this isn't a fairy tale. Humpty Dumpty can always be put back together again. It's the nature of reality."

"You mean the culture of reality. You mean the cult of reality."

D. Celina said something else, something about "negative triangulation," then slipped away and back again.

Conjugation

P. Torque awoke next to his wife as his body liquidated all of the ducks in the pond, including the Spartan, which he killed with a hatchet, chopping the torso into cubes. Then he drained the pond like a bathtub and machine gunned every living thing that glanced at him from the basin, including fish, frogs, and one presumably herbivorous alligator. On his mindscreen, the head watched the body enact the scene in stop-motion animation. The stump of the head mimicked his grown-back thumb as the neckbone formed into a kind of silicon tusk. This unnerved F. Torque, who insisted that the stump was "profoundly absurd yet perfectly normal." P. Torque thought this thesis was weak and asked her to revise it as she gravitated off the bed, crawled up a wall, and stepped across the ceiling on long, thin feelers.

"I'm not convinced that your view of my person is accurate," said P. Torque, who was in no position to pass judgment on his person, which he could neither see nor properly assess. In response, F. Torque spread her legs and descended on him like a spider. The maw of her vulva opened and swallowed the head, incubating it. P. Torque continued to express his discontent with her angle of incidence even as uterine acid dissolved his flesh and skull and brain tissue.

Tableau

Tableau of a headless body splayed out beneath a mythical tree with flowered branches that extend into eternity. Beat. A tributary of black blood flowed from the neckhole across the grass. Once the body emptied, it decayed and disintegrated in a furious timelapse. Flowers and fungi erupted in its wake.

Tribunal

Fully empowered and unchanged, entirely deranged and sound of mind, P. Torque arrived to work early, canvassed A. Fibb's office, and made certain that everything was in place, ranging from the geometric alignment of the landscape portraits on the walls to the tactical positioning of writing utensils on her desktop, and he was sure to dust the room from top to bottom, including ceiling tiles, one by one. There were never any daily tasks for her to complete—A. Fibb's job was a concerted façade, like all of our jobs—but he knew she counted on him to curate her false image, ensuring a continued supremacy of the status quo. P. Torque had no hope for a brighter future. The future was bright enough. And he didn't need hope: every day was the same, a begotten tribunal. If anything ever changed, it would be a matter of perspective wherein everybody would awaken to a world that authorized his due diligence to reign supreme.

The prospect of such futurity was almost enough to dilute his evolving happiness.

Pace Car
By Lyle Hopwood

The road ended abruptly just beyond the turnout, and I set the Mustang's parking brake with care. I eased myself out of the stifling car and walked a few steps to the edge where the road started again, fifteen feet lower down the parched hillside where the earthquake had dumped it more than ten years ago. There's a palm tree down there that had landed on its side as the falling road twisted and flexed. About thirty feet of it was horizontal. After it landed it started to grow straight up again, and the heavy mass of green fronds was now almost level with the old road. No wonder the asphalt was split and dry here at the dead end, after lying more than a decade unrepaired in the Southern California sunshine.

In the little turnout at the side of the road, there was the usual fifty-five-gallon drum of gasoline, half empty. I began the familiar task of filling the tank and the gas cans that occupied the back seat. The mechanic said he'd be here by noon. I kept looking up at the sage-covered hillside as the sun got higher, but no one appeared over the brow of the hill.

I was deep in thought and not expecting it when I heard the sound of stones dislodging on the shallow path. I looked up again, shielding my eyes from the glare. I couldn't tell if it was the mechanic at that distance, although it wasn't likely anyone else was trekking here from the Gate behind the roadless hill. The figure was sandy-haired, a little shorter than I expected, and he was picking his way with excessive caution between the dry, spiny plants and loose stones. He was wearing a short leather kilt and a jerkin, and, of course, had brought no tools. As he got closer, I realized why he was walking so slowly and carefully. He had hooves.

I straightened up, dismayed. He was clearly part goat, his thighs covered in short, curly blond hair. His ankles were like a goat's, which would be fine if he were four-legged, but as he walked on his back legs like a man, he was not as nimble as either of his natural bloodlines. In lieu of heels, he used a long staff to balance his weight. I tried to keep the dislike out of my expression as he came close enough to hail.

"You must be Ben."

"And you must be Alisa," he said. Then, indicating the Mustang, he added, "Nice car."

I nodded. "It's my daily driver. The collectibles are in the garage, waiting for your gentle ministrations."

"Driver," he said, coming up to it and running his thumb along the bodywork. The black paint had sun-crackled, giving it the texture of keeled scales, as though it was in transition from a boulevard car to a Beaded Lizard. "It's in good condition. It's a '66, right?"

I nodded again and began to coil the tube I'd been using as a siphon. He seemed to notice what I was doing for the first time.

"There's a polythene drum of gasoline just waiting here in the chaparral?"

I smiled. "Don't ask me how it gets here. Someone brings a new one from the Gate for me every few months. When I've used all the gas, someone takes the drum away for their own purposes. It's one of those arrangements."

I wondered if he was as surprised by the sight of me as I was by the sight of him. When he heard I collected California muscle cars, he probably didn't expect a woman. Even more unlikely, I was young, too young to remember when the Southland was packed with cars, a skein of connected tar plains. Then again, after twenty years in this climate, I must have looked forty. My skin was bronze and beginning to show signs of sun damage. My long hair, formerly black, wasn't grey, but it was colourless, sun-bleached. At least I'm human, I thought, and then tried to push that to the back of my mind.

"Do you want to drive?" I said, as I opened the door. It was baking hot inside and a rush of heated air rose past me. The black coupe just invited the California sun in to stay.

"I couldn't possibly impose," he said, and walked around to the passenger side. Opening the door, he placed his long staff between the front seats and climbed in. I closed my door and turned the ignition key. Unused to having someone beside me in such an enclosed space, I reached for the handle to wind down my window and open up some room, letting in gritty air and reducing the scent of our bodies. There wasn't a lot of water around here for me to wash too frequently, and he, of course, smelled of goat. He was taking some getting used to.

The little engine—little compared to my other cars, anyway—ran quietly. There was about six miles of cracked but passable blacktop from the bottom of Gate Hill to my home and I drove slowly. He was a famous automobile mechanic from Boston, after all. It was unlikely I could impress him with the performance of the self-maintained driver vehicle. I'd impress him with the Corvette instead.

My house sat in a valley beside a dry arroyo. It was well camouflaged; there were palm fronds on the sloping flat roof and the outside walls had weathered to the same colour as the brush around it. There was always a danger that the winter rains would raise a flash flood, but so far so good. Not that there was much in the house to ruin. I used it as shelter and a home for my books and tools. The garage was a few dozen paces away, on a flat gravel apron. I drove carefully off the paved road and on to the gravel, parking with a satisfying crunch just outside the doors.

The mechanic got out stiffly and bent over to reach for his staff between the black vinyl seats. He straightened and stretched while I unchained the wooden double doors of the garage and threw them open. He did a double take. The sudden jaw drop was mighty gratifying. He trotted forward a few paces to touch the bodywork, unable to stop himself from reeling off a description.

"It's a Corvette Pace Car Replica. You said you had a collectible '78 and I thought the Silver Anniversary Edition would be crazy enough. Not like this." He paused a moment. "But this can't be the original paint job. It's not weathered at all."

"Oh, it is."

He ran his short-nailed fingers over the detailed perfection of the body. The flowing, carnivorous Corvette lines, originally designed to capture the beauty and fleetness of a Mako shark, curved from the imposing hood over the T-Tops to the fastback rear window. He touched the red pinstripe that separated the black upper section of the body from the silver lower. "You don't have the decals that came with it?"

"They're in the house, with the driver's manual and the sticker."

"Cool." He touched it again, almost reverently. "It's a beauty. I'd say there are only about half a dozen Pace Cars left."

"How many did they make?"

"Around six thousand."

I chewed my lip, thinking of what to say. "Well," I said, "in many ways the world is a lot smaller now than it was in 1978, so maybe that's about the right number."

I left him with it and went to prepare some food. Yesterday I'd baked, so I had bread, some cheese and onions and plenty of herbs and greens from the bed down by the stream. When I came back with a tray of bread and orange juice, I found him on his back, slid under the Corvette, looking at the underside.

"I have jacks," I said. You could find them all over the place. This was the mecca of car culture, of course, Southern California. Or had been, once upon a time, when the Beach Boys sang about their 409s and their Corvettes and their Deuce Coupes to tanned, eager surfers and their curvaceous girls.

He slid out from underneath. "You wouldn't jack this up, would you? You need a lift for it. To protect the fibreglass body. Is that food? I'm so hungry."

He reached out for the tray and as he did so, I saw that two short horns were nestled in his hair. He began to eat without another word.

When the light started to fade, I built a fire in the grate outside the house and let it blaze up. He came out to sit on the ground beside the grate, legs crossed, arms wrapped around his knees and his staff at his feet.

"How are you going to get your tools?" I was suddenly worried that he expected me to be some sort of post-apocalyptic hotrodder driving a JATO-equipped De Soto festooned with desert roll bars and an array of lethal projectile weapons. I wasn't outfitted to scavenge for gear myself. I was a female homesteader with steady work in civil engineering.

"They're on the train already. I'll pick them up in San Juan Capistrano on Tuesday."

I looked at him. "We route them around the Gates so easily. It makes me wonder what They thought They were accomplishing by building them in the first place."

He looked back at me, his yellow but apparently human eyes glinting in the firelight. "What do you think They were doing when they built the Gates?"

I sat back a little. Why, punishing the decadent civilization that could engineer bridey monstrosities like this goat-man beside me, of course. The hybrids. I didn't say that. "To send us back to the stone age. I think we were getting too tricksy for them." This cosmic conspiracy theory sounded lame out there under the clear sky which was, as I spoke, burgeoning into colour, black-brown corrugated clouds like a celestial ploughed field filtering the red-gold of the classic sunset. There was, after all, nothing to indicate that They knew their gift would lead to the destruction of society. There's no obvious causal connection between a world-spanning chain of matter transmitters and the death of almost every human born. "Why, what do you think They were doing?"

"Stopping us from killing ourselves," he said.

"What, by murdering five and a half billion people themselves? Cure was surely worse than the disease."

"You have to thin out seedlings if the mature plants are to grow. The world was choking on its own waste. There was no will to change anything. We'd have been back to feudal times on our own by now. And we'd be without the Gates to help us grow toward the light."

I recognized the phraseology. It was a religious mantra I'd heard before. I didn't agree, to put it mildly. "Five billion dead is not a 'thinning', it's genocide."

"So, how many did they actually kill?"

I laughed, without humour. "You mean like, name three?" I rattled off the names of about twenty family members, dead and mostly unburied in the Great Unrest that had followed the sudden appearance of the teleportation Gates.

"I bet all of those people died from something another human brought with him through the Gates—diseases, revolutions, wars—"

I sighed heavily, signalling the end of the conversation.

Reading that correctly, he changed the subject. "Where do you get your tires?"

"Huh? Oh. Sears. They're getting more brittle every year, but I don't drive them fast. The Camaro and the 'Vette, I get new manufactured tires from China. It can take weeks of labour, but …" I trailed off.

"You do business for China?"

"Just Barn Raising, I guess," I said shortly. I liked to keep myself to myself. Answering questions made me feel exposed. Out here in the sagebrush, two was a crowd.

"OK." He was silent a moment, changing mental gears. "What do your vehicles need?"

"The V8s need tuning, is all—checking the distributors, plugs and wires. Balancing the carburettors."

He looked at me. "I know you can do all that yourself."

I shrugged. He didn't look away, and I gave in. "All right. I think I've lost confidence. I've been doing it myself for years and I worry that what I'm doing is drifting, if you know what I mean. I want someone to check, someone with an outside standard to measure my work against."

He looked into the fire, thinking.

"And …"

"Yes?"

"Can you look at the 'Vette? There's something wrong. I can't put my finger on it. It runs perfectly. There's just something there that doesn't add up."

He nodded and sniffed the air. "I can smell fish."

"I'm not cooking any fish. I don't have any."

"No, live fish. Muddy smell, like Louisiana fisheries."

I shook my head. "You're mistaken. This is virtually a desert. The streambed's been dry for months."

He sniffed the air. "What's that, then?"

I took in a deep breath through my nose. "It's the local vegetation. Sagebrush, mostly. Sometimes you can smell orange blossom, but the wind's blowing the wrong way today." I got up. "You can sleep in the house. I'll sleep in the garage."

He got up too, leaning on his staff, and smiled. "You can keep your bed. I've slept in garages all my life. Good night."

And with that he crunched off across the gravel.

I woke up to the squeal and cough of a starter motor. I'd never heard it from outside the garage before; it took a while to interpret it as the L72 starting. It was light outside. I'd overslept. I threw on the previous day's clothes and headed out to the garage. Ben was leaning over the engine of the '69 Camaro, checking the hoses and belts. The air cleaner was on the floor by his hooves. I didn't flinch at the sight of his misshapen legs and wondered whether I should hate myself for my previous reaction or hate myself for getting used to this hybrid horror. The engine was running at about 1200 rpm, and I walked a little faster.

"It'll overheat."

"What?"

The noise was shaking dust from the rafters and I had to move closer and raise my voice. "It will stay on cold idle until it gets some gas."

He felt alongside the carburettor and tugged on the accelerator cable. The big block paused like a surprised animal, and then suddenly roared, bouncing the whole car as gas poured in. It settled down smoothly to its 700 rpm idle.

"Sensitive little miss, aren't you?" he said, speaking to the car. He touched the cable again, more lightly. The engine snarled, rocking the car with torque, and settled back again to its happy purr, modulated with the cam's distinctive lope. "That's better."

He finished checking under the hood and shut it off. "How does it run under load?"

"It misses occasionally."

"There's a bad plug lead?"

I nodded. "There comes a time when stripping leads out of 70s cars that have been sitting in the open for twenty years gives you diminishing returns."

"When do you think that time will come?"

"I think it was about ten years ago."

He laughed, took off the distributor cap and began cleaning it. "I can get new leads when I go into town. How far is it to Capistrano?"

"SJC." He looked up at me, so I clarified. "No one calls it Capistrano. It's SJC. It's about eight miles over the hills or about fourteen if you follow the streambed. Can you really walk that far on those—" and here my voice shrank and cracked "—feet?" I felt my face suddenly burning.

He sat down abruptly, leaning against the front left tire of the big muscle car. He tugged on my hand to get me to sit down too. I did.

"Am I scaring you? I don't mean to."

"You're fine, I guess. I'm just having a hard time learning to get on with someone who isn't … fully human."

"I'm plenty human."

I nodded.

"You blame me for the destruction of your culture. But I didn't do it, you know. I was four years old."

"That was … you're talking about my parents' beliefs, not mine. I was only three myself. Even they didn't think you people did it. They taught me that the scientists who made you went too far, and that's what brought the Gates. But that was their generation." I was speaking very slowly, not only because I wanted to choose my words with care, but also because I wasn't sure what I wanted to say. I certainly didn't blame the brideys for the Gates; that made no sense. "For me it's something else. It's not hate, it's some sort of … emotion. When I see people like you I feel sad. I don't know why." As I spoke, a wave of melancholia washed over me, and for the first time I looked at my cars and wondered if nostalgia was a vaccination against the other horrors, a tame infatuation with the lost past to keep the wilder nightmares away.

"We can go for a ride in the Corvette today," I said.

He shook his head. "I'm not sure it's a good idea to start the Corvette. Did you loot it from a dealership?"

I nodded. "Up in Anaheim."

"Near the Gate?"

"Yes, near the Gate. That was before the big earthquake so there were paved roads all the way. I found the key and drove it out. I was maybe fourteen and it seemed worth it at the time."

"That was before you pulled in your horns?"

The mention of horns knocked the breath out of me. I couldn't answer.

"I'm sorry." He looked genuinely contrite, too. "I meant, before you mellowed and started this homesteading life?"

"Youthful exuberance. But don't try to change the subject. Why won't you start the car?"

He shrugged. “I think the engine block needs attention. With the compression ratio that thing’s pulling down, you could crack the block. Wait,” he said, seeing my jaw drop. “You can sinter blocks of metal to make them solid again.”

“Sinter?”

“It spent years near a Gate. The field the Gates produce is an unsinter field, right? And it’s had time to go to work on the engine. Good choice to pick a car with a fibreglass body rather than sheet metal.”

I leaned back against the Camaro’s fender. My beloved cars. The Gate was eating my cars.

When the matter transmitters had appeared, dropping from the sky all over the Earth, they’d been welcomed as manna from heaven. Walk up to one, squeeze through it in a slightly sideways, uncomfortable sort of push, and you were somewhere else, thousands of miles away, exiting an identical Gate. And you could learn to navigate quickly, as though the twisting through hidden dimensions was a part of us, an instinctive knowledge, just as a man whose ancestors hadn’t flown in a hundred million years can learn to hang-glide in a few minutes. The Gates had been a godsend to the human race—apparently quite literally.

Suddenly, there were no barriers to travel. People moved away from governments and economies they didn’t like and migrated to those they preferred. They moved away from famine and disease and civil war and settled new colonies inside old ones. There was one restriction—you could not take anything through the Gate. They accepted only organic matter or a few grams of inorganic matter if it were completely covered, such as a water bottle wrapped in a leather cloth or a silk scarf. If something inorganic came near a Gate, it began to disintegrate. They produced a field that rotted the item to dust in minutes. The effect dropped off rapidly with distance, so that a house or a mountain top a few dozen miles away seemed unaffected.

The unsinter field seemed to be a protective measure. You could bomb a Gate (and many governments had) or bury it under rubble or shell it from a thousand tanks, and it would remain, untouched, eating the stone and the steel around it and producing fine dust that blew away in days, sometimes choking the army that had brought the storm of steel and brass.

The age of anarchy and freedom lasted a few short years before it became increasingly clear that the gift was a kind of genie’s trick. The Gates had punched holes through boundaries, and society was leaking like a spaceship holed by micrometeorites. The leaks led not to equality for all, but to a homogeneous mess in which there were no distinctions between cultures or nations. Eventually, increasing entropy led, like water flowing downhill, to a state of low energy and low information—the lowest common denominator. Societies crashed. And as they crashed, refugees streamed away carrying disease but not medicine, famine but not food, hatred and ignorance but not books, and the result was the deaths of almost all of Earth’s inhabitants. Eventually the population density was too low to support epidemics or armies and the world stabilized once more.

The Gates remained; pinpricks ready to let the air out of any society which puffed itself up again. And the unsinter field remained, also. In some places they gradually wore down the hills beside the Gates, leaving them sitting on a field of dust. In California, they sometimes cracked the bedrock, producing waves of earthquakes. The ones I'd visited all sat on a flat plain already. I envisaged the eventual end of the world, when the Gates had flattened everything, and there was no weather, just an eternal stasis of homogeneity.

And now They were after my cars.

My mother said that the way to reach your goal is to focus on the next task at hand and push away the thoughts about how many steps there were before a project was complete. I'd always found that to be woefully inadequate advice, but now it proved useful. Psychologically, it was exactly what was needed. If I thought about the ultimate fate of cars, mankind, the earth … nothing would ever get done. But the next task was something I could come to grips with.

"How are you going to pull the engine?" I asked him. "I don't have a cherry picker."

He scratched between his horns with a thumbnail. "I'll think of something. I need to pick up my tools from Cap—I mean, from SJC, on Tuesday, and strip the engine. The train doesn't return for two weeks, so we have time to think about that. A block and tackle is hardly rocket science."

I drove him in the Mustang to my next-door neighbour's, a few miles down the valley, where he borrowed a horse. Riding presented no problem for him, although he cut a strange figure to my eyes. Moreno, my neighbour, didn't remark on my visitor's appearance at all. He took the dried herbs I bartered for the rent of the horse, exchanged about five words of lukewarm pleasantries, then bid goodbye. That's the way people were around here. They weren't very open to new people. I drove back to the broken road by the Gate hill to fill up on gas, and there was a new drum waiting there. I siphoned the remnants of the old one into my tank. The empty drum would be gone in a few days, and for the first time I wanted to know who brought them. Someone coming from the Gate, of course—the Gates moved hydrocarbons and soft plastics without breaking them down—but how did they bring the huge drum over the hill without a cart?

On the top of the full barrel was a piece of paper, weighted down with one of the smooth brown rocks that eased themselves out of the earth around here. I picked it up and pitched the rock away, getting the red-brown dirt on my fingers. The note was an invitation to a Barn Raising way up in cold northern California.

I looked at the hot sky, thinking about the note and what plans I would have to make. I watched a turkey vulture circling above, signalling to others that there was a meal down below. Insects made the strange, inorganic high-pitched whine that filled the summers here. The sound seemed to come from every direction, punctuated by the rattlesnake buzz of grasshoppers in the brush. It was time for a change. I got a yellowed piece of paper from the glove compartment and pencilled a note back in block letters that I hoped let them know I'd be out there within a week. I pinned it down on the top of the drum with a nice lump of sandstone and drove back home.

I'm a bridge-builder by trade, a journeyman civil engineer. The big community projects, colloquially called Barn Raisings, were fun; a chance to share stories, educate the children, eat a great deal and work from dawn to dusk for a few weeks. Ultimately, it satisfied. It paid off psychic debts to the larger society. I didn't pay for the gasoline someone brought me, and I didn't get cash for being a quantity surveyor. The locals could find me tires, or fenders, maybe I'd teach the kids math for a few lessons. With so few people stretched so thin over the Earth, a community wasn't a geographical entity, but a totem tribe. I was a bridge-builder. Ben was a motor mechanic. People all over the world knew our names and asked for us when they were in need.

Ben got back late the next day. He found me at the well, pumping water up into the shallow pool at the top of my property. He took over while I rested in the shade. He had brought his leather sack of tools, which unnerved me; I wasn't ready to see the Corvette's L82 taken apart. As I watched him work the pump, I realized I'd never be ready. It could never be the same somehow, afterwards. Different seals may weigh only a few grams, but they constituted a change. In a fundamental way, it would no longer be the original rare collectors' item.

When the pool had a few inches of water in it, I ran up and opened the sluices. He put his arm around my shoulders, I put mine around his waist and we watched the water trickle down into the plant beds below. I supposed mechanics don't nurture growing things much and he may have had a romantic notion about it. Certainly, with the setting sun behind us casting long shadows on the parched ground, we only lacked a pitchfork in his hands and a stem between my teeth to look like quintessential farmers. Though I don't suppose much of America was settled by pairs of goat-men and gear-head women.

Over a meal of grits and soaked dried meat, I found the courage to ask him about himself. "Do you remember how you were made?"

"Made?" He raised an eyebrow. "I was born, like everybody else."

"From a woman?"

"Yes, even I have a mother, Alisa."

The questions didn't seem to be making him mad. "So how come the—?" I indicated his legs with a vague handwave.

"I'm told I'm a chimera."

"Aren't they lions and eagles?"

"A man-made chimera—it means a mixture of two different cells in the embryo."

I hoped he didn't see me shudder. "Do they still do that now?"

"No, it's a technology thing."

"Thank God," I said.

"Wasn't I worth it?"

I looked at him. His legs were under the table and in the feeble light of the kerosene lamp he looked like any other male visitor. "It's not you. It's the process that created you. I don't like to mix things. It's a compulsion with me. I like clear lines between things. I don't even mix the types of plants in the beds."

"You're an Old Testament Christian?"

"My dad was."

"Maybe that explains it. Purity laws. A childhood horror of mixing sheep and goats." He was smiling, big, flat, masculine teeth showing.

"No," I said, suddenly realizing something about myself. "It's not that. I think I'm afraid of being obsoleted. The last of my marque, like the last C3 Corvette. There are new ones, but you can't directly compare them."

"I'm not doing that to you," he said.

I snapped. "I didn't say you were. You know, my world did fall apart. It's not some teenage cliché. The world really did end. I think dread is an appropriate response, not something I need to be argued out of like a child who refuses to eat cabbage."

He put his hands up, palms out, for calm, and I took a deep breath. I had a lump in my throat and couldn't continue eating, so I got up to check in the mirror and comb my hair. He was finishing the bowl of grits, tipping it away from him to scoop up the last grains as I got back.

He watched me sit down, his yellow eyes glinting. In a different, deeper voice, he said, "You are so very lonely."

"Oh, dear God," I said, "don't try to seduce me."

He huffed a laugh. "I am a goat, after all."

"Keep it under your kilt."

He smiled in reply, and when I'd finished, he cleared the table and went to clean the dishes.

He tuned the two cars the next day, new caps and rotors and leads, and they sounded so sweet. There was a rocking couch on the porch and in the afternoon we sat there to discuss stripping the Corvette's engine. He'd brought some wine from the town, so we were working our way through a bottle. I was lying on the rocker, my head resting on his thigh, rather woozily describing my haphazard childhood spent keeping ahead of waves of unrest and disease, when I remembered I'd promised to go to the Barn Raising. I had to break it to Ben that I was going to abandon him here, leave him working on my cars with no one to help and no one to take care of him. Suddenly I felt very selfish; and then, just as suddenly, I blamed him for the social obligation I had to him. That was why I *preferred* to be lonely. It was impossible to disappoint a friend if you had no friends.

He felt me tense. "What?" he said. He passed the bottle of wine, but I couldn't figure out how to drink it lying down and I didn't want to sit up.

Keeping emotion out of my voice, I said, "I have to leave tomorrow. There's a Barn Raising in Northern California and I'm requested to attend."

He sagged against the faded stripes of the back cushion. "You're going away?"

"Two weeks, maximum. How long were you planning to spend here?"

He sighed. "I thought you were asking me to leave. I can stay here and finish?"

"If you want to."

"Of course. Once I have a project, I'm committed."

"Me too."

"We're going to have to move sooner or later. Either you sit up and drink your share or I have to get up to bring an oil funnel so you can pour it down your throat while you're lying down."

I sat up and drank my share and passed it back.

The Barn Raising went well. I was only there for project initiation, so I put on a hard hat maybe twice in two weeks. Most of my work was on paper. The digging and grading and mixing and pouring part of the bridge would come later. It was a big span, too; the foremen were expecting more than two hundred people to work on it in total, and while I was there more than forty people came through. The crush of people bothered me at first. Those more used to it than I had a 'social face' that they kept on in public, and I didn't. Crowds like this reminded me of famine and camps, and I relaxed only with difficulty. Once I got used to it, I began to take a sort of pride in it. It was unexpectedly uplifting to be around other people. I'd spent a long time alone and had begun to imagine that there was nothing left for humanity. I'd started thinking there was no one left; we were finished as a culture, a few hunter-gatherers sifting through the garbage dumps and looting stores for scraps they no longer knew how to make. Here, people worked together and created something. Forty people who could read, and figure and measure working in concert for the greater good.

The labourers started arriving in the second week, a selection of people from all over the world mingling with locals. There was at least one goat-man, I saw, with a reflective jacket on his bare back, and a couple of other types of … people. My subconscious proposed the word 'brideys' but my mind suppressed it as a slur.

By that time, I was comfortable amongst a crowd and didn't want to leave. I tried to focus on my cars. They'd be finished by now. Then I thought of Ben and my feelings seesawed between desire to see him again and the existential anguish of what his kind represented to me.

"I need a word?" someone said. They touched my elbow.

I whirled, ready to snap at them for presumption. But I immediately realized it was Dr. Chan, the architect of the bridge.

"Yes, doctor?"

"Just call me Chun-Man. I don't know if doctorates count for shit anymore," he said.

He had some questions regarding his design. The bridge was less than thirty kilometers from the nearest Gate and he had some formula he wanted me to check to see if ferro concrete would hold up in the unsinter field.

I didn't know offhand, but the chance to talk to someone about engineering was inviting. We sat down in the bamboo hut that the builders had designated as the executive office. We went over some of his suppositions about the two nearby Gates and the field that emanated from them, slowly eating away the fabric of the earth around them. When he was happy, if that's the word, with his calculations, he closed the notebook on his desk and mopped his forehead with a cloth. He folded the cloth and, putting it into his pocket, he said, half to me and half to the universe, "I don't think people know how fucked we are."

"Excuse me, but I think five and a half billion ghosts could tell us how fucked we are."

"They're dead," he said. "It's that people don't know what those Gates are doing to the planet."

"The planet?"

"The geology. They'll keep on wearing the local rock to dust and returning metal to ores forever unless we find out how to switch them off."

He was worried about the geology? "Do you know how nerves work?"

"No?"

"They have a membrane, and they pump ions from the inside to the outside until the nerve builds up an electrical potential. When the potential is great enough, the nerve fires, and passes the need to fire to its neighbours."

"I had heard that."

"All living cells do the same. Potential is everything. A tire works because there's pressure inside it. You have a valve to get air in, but if you have a hole, the air pressure equalizes, and the tire is useless. If you have a battery full of energy and someone puts a jumper lead across and shorts it, you have no more energy. The Gates punch holes in the borders, so that people on either side are no longer have enough differences to produce change, never mind push for innovation and revolution. Just like nerves, or any cells, if there's no difference between outside and inside, there's no life. Things can't get concentrated. It all becomes a grey goo, a sameness."

"Entropy," he said.

"That's it. Everything runs down, reaches the same state. You used to be able to store energy and knowledge and cash and goods in one place and utilize it as a force for change. Now we have a much-of-a-muchness and how did that ever lead to change? The Gates destroyed our potential and whoever put them there knew it would."

He looked at me for a long moment. "You're a bridge-builder. How come you see more connection between people as a force for evil?"

"We planned the bridge. Communities on both sides voted for it. Nobody voted for the world to become porous."

I walked back to the Gate the next morning. I'd tried to get a ride in a car first. This area had roads in good repair, and there were some later model vehicles traveling on them. A local told me they'd discarded the useless chip-based electronic fuel injection and retrofitted carburettors. They kept them away from the gates nevertheless, so I took shank's mare instead.

There was nothing recognizably metal in a radius of several kilometers from the Gate itself. Dust was being sucked into it in the weak, wheezy way it always was, and the smooth black circular wall of the Gate, built of whatever star stuff the builders alone knew, was planted askew on a hill that was half ground down, flattened and muddy. I didn't need to carry tools, but a number of my colleagues were visiting the train station first to send their theodolites and sledgehammers as freight back to their own homes. I checked my clothes and pockets for inorganic matter and stepped through, aiming for SJC.

The warmth and familiar smell of sage brush almost bowled me over. The Gate here was blowing moist air weakly into the mudstone hills and a few drips of condensation had blackened the ground around the wall. I walked down the hill towards my road, shuffling down the sagebrush slope, grabbing at stalks of sumac and monkey flower for support as Bill had.

The recently delivered drum of gasoline was half empty now, and for the first time I saw something working behind it. Much bigger than a man. When I got closer enough to make the shape make sense, I realized it was an elephant—who was, presumably, also a human.

I hailed him. "You're the person who takes the empties?"

He nodded. "I don't need the fuel myself. Help me with this, would you?"

He directed me to help him lift the empty barrel into a basket on his back.

"Kids' swimming pools?"

"Hardly. I farm catfish. Every time you empty one of these barrels, I get a catfish pond." He dipped his trunk into a canteen and curved it back to drop water in his mouth. "I'm surprised you haven't smelled the farm."

I sniffed, but the smells of sage, buckwheat and gasoline was all I could detect.

He trod heavily off down the valley, and I followed the road back to my place.

I walked down to the garage first, to see if Bill was still at work. There was no one there, and the doors were chained. I opened the lock to check on the cars and they were all there, looking great. Sunlight was sloping in through the door, the perfect time of day to check for dust and oil, and everything passed muster. The cars shone. The Pace Car was sitting half a meter or so away from where it had been, suggesting he'd moved it at least once. It was spotless, and when I peered in the window, I saw he'd detailed the interior. A faint smell of wax emanated from inside and I knew he would not have cleaned it until he'd replaced the engine. Presumably, the world beating L82 had been disassembled, sintered and reassembled. He would have started it up here in the valley, while I was a thousand kilometers away, and I'd missed out on its stentorian roar.

I backed out and headed for the house. There had been a little rain since I'd left and there were goat hoofprints in the dried mud, along with the round imprint of his walking stick. He'd been foraging in the green bushes of the valley, and I wondered whether he could eat like a goat, or whether he'd been keeping to the plants the Indians of the district had seeded all over the valleys hundreds of years ago.

I opened the house door and the smoky scent of the kerosene lamp hit me, along with the smell of cooking and the faint musk of a goat. Bill was sitting in the chair reading a book, and he jumped up seizing his stick as the door came wide open.

"I'm sorry!" I said.

"You could have knocked!"

"It's my house. But, point taken, I should have knocked. I kind of forgot you were here. Well, not that you were here, but that you probably felt you were responsible for the defence of the place."

"It's cool. There's coffee on the stove."

I was hungry, and the coffee—it was made from dandelion roots—was a delight after the walk in the dusty heat.

"How was the Barn Raising?"

I told him about it as I prepared some food. Flatbread and fish. He'd gotten fish from somewhere. It took me a moment before I remembered that I had a fish-farming neighbour. Tomatoes, peppers, beans. Apparently, he'd been tending to the garden and harvesting produce as it ripened.

I sat down with the coffee and a full plate.

"How did the thing with the L82 engine go? The sintering doesn't remove the engine block number, does it?" I was suddenly afraid I'd done something irreparable. It was a numbers-matching car, obviously. The whole list of serial numbers was on the dealer's sticker. The number stamped into the engine block matched the VIN number visible in the vehicle's window.

"It was fine," he said. "Good as new. Your neighbour helped me pull the engine."

"The … elephant?"

"He's a man, like me, but strong enough to lift an engine block."

"I first met him today. I've never seen him before."

"Top man. Gave me some catfish."

"And the block is okay now?" The rarity of the car was important to me. But after a moment's thought I realized the purity of the car was more important. It was unique. It was celebrated. It was an item that would no longer exist if it were changed in the slightest. I'd agonized over permitting new gaskets, fifty grams of rubber or, nowadays, silicone. If the engine had changed in some fundamental way, it wouldn't be a 1978 Corvette Pace Car Replica, one of 6,200 ever made.

"Why were six thousand two hundred made?" I asked.

"I guess there were that many Corvette dealerships and there was some sort of internal politics, so they decided there should be one car for each."

That made me stop breathing for a long moment. There were over six thousand dealerships? And now you'd have to be a mastermind to get six thousand living humans in one group, let alone six thousand luxury car dealers.

He got up to refill our cups and sat down next to me to stroke my hair as we sipped the bitter root drink. I lay my head on his chest and my body was considering that late night move, unapproved by consciousness, whereby you twist and lie down, resulting in the man lying down upon you. I caught it in time, sat up and glared at him.

"Do you really hate me?" he said. "I could go soak in the pond if it's the pheromones that are putting you off."

"I don't hate you," I said. The pheromones—by which I assumed he meant the smell of animal—wasn't what was making me hesitate. "I've said before I don't blame you for anything. How could I?" I paused to think. "But now we'll never know what we could do. What the human race could do. I wanted to see what we could do unaltered—by ourselves. On our own. Test our limits. Now the edges are all blurred, it's all running together." I twisted my fingers in my hands. "I wanted us to remain pure."

"You lost that when you first contemplated a tool. Never mind a Corvette. You haven't known what you could do alone since the first caveman picked up a rock and threw it."

He was right, I knew, but the unfairness and not being given a chance to see the human world play out still consumed me. He went outside for a bottle of wine and opened one, waving the neck at my empty coffee cup.

"No thanks," I said.

He got up to get a cleaner cup. "I need to talk to you about the Corvette, and you should drink some wine first."

My heart beat against my ribs. I took the proffered cup. "What is it?"

"It's fine, and you should think of what I'm going to tell you as a plus. Do you remember—obviously you do—that there were more than six thousand Corvette Replica Pace Cars made?"

I nodded and drank half the cup. He refilled it.

"They were beautiful, with the black upper half, the T-Tops, the grey lower half, the red pinstripe between the colours. The 25th Anniversary Car that year had the silver top and the grey lower half. The other Corvettes sold that year had the same body type, the same packages, the same fastback window."

He was stalling. "What are you trying to tell me?"

"It was possible to buy a regular 1978 Corvette, in black or silver, get a spray gun, attach a couple of spoilers, upgrade the trim in the cabin, fake up some decals and you'd almost have a Pace Car."

I choked on a mouthful of wine. "But … are you saying … but I have the sticker with the listing of numbers and everything. It's a Pace Car."

He put his arms around my shoulders. "It's not a Pace Car, Alisa. It's a 1978 Corvette with a spray job."

"How did you find out?"

"The Pace Car, to put it simply, had 1979 seats rush-ordered and installed. The regular Corvettes had 1978 seats. If you see both seat types together, you'll see how different they are."

I took the bottle from him and drank straight out of it. Easy come, easy go, said one part of my mind. What's it to you if it isn't a collectible? The other part was saying, over and over, *it's a fake, a mixture, something that looks real but it's man-made. Counterfeit. Imperfect. Not the real thing. A dupe, a substitution, a copy. Not as originally built.*

He brought over a joint he must have rolled earlier and lit it. He puffed smoke into the cabin and took a deep breath. "Here," he said in the squeaky voice of someone trying not to lose air. I took the joint and inhaled. "I want you to look at this differently. There were a bazillion Pace Cars made."

"Six thousand two hundred," I said in a blue cloud of smoke.

"All of them preserved in museums until the world ended." He inhaled and passed me the joint again. "How many counterfeit Pace Cars, carefully crafted by men and secreted into the world do you think there are?"

"No idea."

"Men—man—the human race—produced the so-called counterfeits with their own hands, in order to make a thing that people loved. You have what is probably the only one left. You have the real deal. The carefully crafted work of art in your garage is the unique expression of a human ideal. For that alone, it's worth so much more than if it were one of a dozen remaining items from the output of a giant corporation."

Easy come, easy go, I thought again. I'd made my stand. I'd drawn a line between the showroom-quality Pace Car and the regular cars I drove. Now that clear, bright line was disappearing, blowing away like the dust from the Gates. The wine and smoke filtered out the thoughts that would otherwise have filled my head. It was getting cold in the cabin. I went to light the kindling in the fireplace. Bill was in the kitchen, finding more wine. We could sit in front of the fire and we would cuddle, and as long as I didn't touch his horns by accident, I could be happy with this man.

It's Cob Day!

By Hunter Liguore

> *"If all humanity minus one, were of one opinion, and only one person were of the contrary opinion, humanity would be no more justified in silencing that one person, than she, if she had the power, would be justified in silencing humanity."*
> John Stuart Mill

September 4—The meeting house smelled of sweet roasted corn, as pots of cooked cobs were placed on all the picnic tables. Everyone in town was present, not a space empty on the benches. From left to right, a mass of ages and races and abilities, decked out in lemony shirts, scarves, and hats, incited a buoyant roar of chatter.

Cobs were passed out in no special order. Ma Catsby, the oldest resident, encouraged everyone to take two.

Soon, every plate that had one cob, had two—the mayor noted the Mohars and Sargossas had taken three to a plate!

Keep the butter and sugar moving! The ushers patrolled the tables looking for empty butter dishes quick to slap down another hunk of the yellow stuff.

Salt and pepper shakers were passed hand-to-hand, a sacred sharing between neighbours.

The sugar bowls stalled beside most children. The girl with the marigold shirt, especially, took her time sprinkling her cob; some might've thought she lingered a little too long, putting a damper on the spirited momentum.

It wasn't until the bell rang, and Ma Catsby said the annual Cob Day prayer, that the feeding commenced. By then, even the cooks had taken seats with their families.

The streets would be empty; stores vacant; cars stilled; dogs and cats napping; front doors left open to let the summer sun and air volley through the deserted halls and rooms.

With everyone eating, the chatter came to a lull, leaving just the churning of chews and gobbles, and the occasioned clink of a shaker against a dish, a beautiful harmony of munching, like a steady fan in the background, time stilled.

It was natural for people to look at their neighbours eating.

Each scanned the rows in anticipation on whether a victor would come quick like in 1946, the shortest day on record, happening in under ten minutes, or if they'd be at it for hours, like in 1982, the longest Cob Day, according to Ma Catsby, who kept impeccable records, since she'd inherited the task from her great-great-grandma.

"It can fall to anyone!" She loved to encourage, especially to the young ones, attending their first year, and eager to play a part.

Right before the bell ring, Ma Catsby secretly whispered to her husband that she felt lucky. "It could be *my* year, right?"

Her husband kissed her cheek. "Have faith, Ma."

More munching. More sweet corn cobs passed.

The empty husks piled up on the table and floors like bones, and yet the silver axe still rested ceremoniously on a yellow pillow beside the bell. People checked it, in between gobbles, and rallied that it might still fall to them.

"Aren't you hungry, child?" The mother asked, adding two more cobs to her daughter's plate. The girl in marigold had hardly eaten one, feigning a smile when her aunties and uncles, and the town baker and her family pressed her to gobble faster.

She had no choice, chewing haphazardly—*chewchewchew!* She had three cobs mauled and on to her fourth, spurring the rest of the table to also eat faster.

"We're getting low!" announced the baker's wife, hand inside the tall pot, her fingers swirling the salty water at the bottom.

On it! An usher pirouetted into the communal kitchen and was out like lightning, placing a toppling pot of cooked corn in front of the girl in marigold.

One ear sputtered out.

An omen!

It's meant for you!

Everyone grew eager to take it from the girl ... a few even poked at it, as if to prod her to hurry up, or they'd claim it.

All eyes were on it—sure it meant the silver axe was only a bite away.

They'd missed the moment when the girl in marigold gave a timid sputter, her mouth filling up with blood, raining from the corners, spawning two red rivers onto the plate; she dropped the cob.

Her mother grabbed it, inspecting it—*HERE, EVERYONE!*

An usher joined and studied the half-eaten cob, now looking like it had been dashed with ketchup, a shiny razor catching the light.

Forty-four minutes! The usher showed it off, affirming the time for the official record—

Despite the applause, the girl in marigold just sat, semi-slouching, as she dabbed the blood.

Her mother scolded her for doing so. "Hon, everyone wants to see."

What is she waiting for?

The girl animated, making her way to the front, surprised and embarrassed, just like when her middle school soccer coach put her in the last five minutes of the match, clear they'd already won, and her presence didn't matter.

But she mattered now. She felt slightly famous and part of things, especially when the mayor rang the bell in her honour.

Ma placed the silver axe into the girl's hands, reminding her of the rules and the amount of time—*forty-four minutes*—she had to get back.

The girl in marigold nodded, feeling slightly strong, but also strangely weak, as she walked past everyone cheering… all emotion faded as she left the meeting house and crossed the gravel road to the nursery.

Once inside, the first thing to do was turn on the conveyor belt to signal the meetinghouse that she'd gotten there and could expect an arrival shortly …

In the meantime, ushers would begin the clean-up, resetting the tables for the next course. Families would collect the eaten cobs for compost. Other senior members, like toothless Sooth Lanka, would strum an old-time Cob Day song on his banjo, while the church chorus sang. Married couples would dance. Young lovers would find their way to each other on the outskirts of the dance floor.

The girl in marigold bypassed the conveyor belt switch, and checked each corner of the rectangular room to ensure she was alone.

She drew the shades.

She ran back to the door to see if anyone had followed, catching her reflection in the window-glass, the blood drying and smeared, a symbol of honour, she was told.

With heart racing, the girl tiptoed to the nearest crib and looked inside, slightly shocked by the size of the naked baby. She'd only ever imagined them to be—AT MOST—15 pounds. But this one was giant! Plump as a pumpkin or pillow or her backpack stuffed with her entire wardrobe of clothes.

She reached in and squeezed an arm and leg, noting it felt squishy like rolled socks, then hurried to the other cribs, finding every baby just as giant. She tried to lift one, straining her back.

The clock was ticking—fifteen minutes of fusing, blown on finding the lightest one, but none of them fit the bill, causing her to pace, window to door, to crib, circling, the axe handle sweaty-hot in her grip.

She never really thought it'd fall to her; she pinged her forehead a couple times to feel the prick, to register she was living this moment, like it or not.

The conveyor belt!

The girl hurried to flip the switch, watching the belts *swirtle-and-peep* with movement, so sparkling clean. Hardly four-year's-old, she could remember with vivid detail the first time she'd heard the belts and asked what they were for.

It's our lifeblood.

She didn't understand, until the history of the town came alive with an afternoon play, and she was given a little crown, to show she'd come of age, and had a proper seat at the table. Later, before dessert, she'd joined the line with her father, to touch the bloody axe for good luck, a tradition, solidifying in her mind a sense of safety and love, as everyone looked on.

It was half-past, fourteen minutes remaining.

They'd soon check on her if the belt remained empty; a sickness washed over her.

She gaped into the nearest crib, noting the worn floor beneath it: centuries of footprints had scuffed the floor, standing where she did, eye-to-eye with the infant.

It gurgled and smiled, fingers bouncing like it wanted to be picked up.

Scooping the baby out, the girl cradled it on her shoulder, knees bending to accommodate the weight. Never holding a giant baby before, she noticed the way each part moved and animated, so full of energy; it both confused and marvelled her how it would magically get turned into subarbe.

Subarbe pot pie. Subarbe stew. Subarbe cutlets. Barbecue subarbe. Subarbe-kebobs. Deli subarbe. Subarbe salad sandwiches. Deep-fried subarbe. Subarbe sausages. Shredded subarbe. Breaded subarbe. Toasted-coconut marshmallow subarbe strips, once a favourite.

On Cob Day, Mom liked the leg. Papa the wings. Her uncle, the bony neck. Her sister, the liver. Grandma and grandpa split the heart. Ma Catsby said the taste was down to slow-cooking and marinating the skin with butter to make it crispy.

No one ever called it what it was, a plate of giant baby.

The girl in the marigold shirt salivated, yet repulsed, thinking back to Cob Day, three years ago, when her fork had snagged an artery, a big one, and tried to pluck it free, but it goofed with blood. No longer a child, she had the know-how to see past the commodity of subarbe to something alive, once. Her mother had plucked it out, wiping it in a napkin, then squirted mustard where it'd left its mark.

The girl had never forgotten it, though slowly wondered what she'd do if she'd ever won the cob.

No one ever made it past by Tiller's Creek.

—1.5 miles west of the meeting house, past the middle school and soccer field, the bank, and two corn fields (though the whole town was patch-worked with corn)—

By no one, she'd meant Tim Taine, a local baseball legend, who three years ago, mysteriously passed away during the Cob Day celebration. He'd won the cob the same day the rifles burst like a symphony by Tiller's Creek. No one made a fuss, and only the girl with the marigold shirt had noticed the noise—or the big, manly vein in her food.

The girl had planned to take two babes with her, but didn't think she could even manage one in her backpack; she searched again for the smallest.

If she could make it to Tiller Creek and cross the river with the giant baby, she might actually get away. First thing she'd do was set up an altar of rocks and white flowers, her own tradition, made of her own ideas; she would never speak of Cob Day.

She felt a trickle down her leg, the odour of urine mixing with the sweet-smelling corn, permeating the whole town.

Five minutes. Either she had to start chopping necks or get-a-move-on!

By now, bottles of special sauce would be placed on tables, and Ma Catsby would be halfway through her yearly retelling of the first time she tasted subarbe.

Running—she doubted her choice of babies, believing she'd taken the heaviest, and neither of them would get very far. She wanted to go back. Two—she was sure she could've carried out two! Focusing on her weakness made her all the more determined, sprinting, even when struggling for breath.

"We'll make it, baby!" Even as she said it, she had no clue how they'd live—out there, it was only other communities, a string of them across the continent, celebrating Cob Day.

The first gunshot forged a harsh splinter of sound into the summer day. A blur of yellow-dressed folk zigzagged the corn field from diverse directions.

"Just a single day on my own—we can do it, baby!"

The creek was cold; the weighted movement of water slowed her down.

Gunfire ignited, her shoulder splattering with pain, the baby suddenly heavier—but she could hear its wispy breath.

The mob called to the girl in marigold—not her name, as if forgotten, commodified already.

As her legs kicked the mud up the new embankment, she realized she was already separate, no longer one of them; a smile emerged.

Left, right...

Gunfire—

The Pond

By Ana Teresa Pereira

I watched the girl open the gate and stare at the house. There was something wrong with her; the red hair seemed even longer, the red dress shapeless, she was barefoot, but she had always liked to be barefoot. Then I realised what it was. The hair was dripping; the dress clung to her slim body; her feet and her ankles were dirty, dust or mud.

I stepped back from the French window. The drawing-room I had known all my life, the mantelpiece, the Turner watercolour on the wall, the curtains and the sofas of a faded peach colour, the old books on the shelves. The smell of the lavender polish and the yellow daffodils in the vases. She had gone away with the bluebells; she was coming back with the daffodils.

The sense of unreality grew sharper as I sat on Tom's chair, near the fire. April had gone away seven years before, she had taken the six o'clock train to London, everybody believed that, even though her clothes were in the wardrobe, and she was supposed to be getting married the next day.

I felt something like claws in my arms and realised it was my own nails, my well-cared-for nails painted in a soft pink that matched my lipstick. April's hands were dry, with short nails, sometimes a little dirty; she worked in the garden; she climbed trees and walls, swam in every stream or pond.

I thought vaguely that what a person is shows in her hands and her eyes. We were nearly alike, and the difference people noticed first was the hair. Mine blond and straight, April's in a strange shade of red, like a girl in a painting, and curly. But that was for the others. The real difference was in the eyes: mine are a pure blue, April's darker, almost grey. And in the hands, mine are nice and soft, April's thinner and scratched, like claws. But I had resented those hands; they could create things, every seed they planted would grow, when she put flowers in a vase the bony fingers touched them absently, and the thing turned into a work of art. I was the one who got good marks at school; I was a good dancer. April didn't care for studying or dancing; she went for long walks in the wood; she smelt of heather.

Everybody was surprised when Tom fell in love with April, as if the prince had chosen one of the bad sisters. He had lived in London for years—he worked in a publishing house, then came back to the cottage the aunt he grew up with had left him; he took the London train on Monday morning and came back on Friday evening. The first time we met him in the street, he only had eyes for April. It was a new experience, as if someone was enchanted with my shadow and ignoring me. Soon I realised I was in love with a man who waited at the gate on Saturday mornings to go for a walk, who rang the bell on Saturday evenings to go to the movies, but not with me.

April and I had always slept in the same room. I was born first and often wished she had stayed inside, forgotten in that other world. She was like the last kitten in a litter, the runt, almost unformed, the one we have to take care of, with blankets and milk. I felt that she watched me, like a bird on the branch of a tree watches another bird eating sweet and bitter fruits. But now I was the one watching, quiet and hungry.

The day before the marriage she went for one of her walks and didn't come back. I went looking for her. The lonely path in the wood, the rumor of a spring. The pond in the center of a clearing, heather and bluebells: an eerie place. It was by chance I noticed the coat among the flowers. Inside the pocket were her keys and a few coins. I didn't mention that, even when there were searches and people said a girl with red hair had been seen at the station with a man.

The knock on the glass startled me, as if I had believed that by keeping quiet the ghost would simply disappear.

"Go away," I whispered.

But the thing knocked again, more firmly. I went to the glass door, and for a moment it felt like I was meeting myself in a deformed mirror. I opened the door. The red hair was dirty, moss and slime, the dress was full of stains and faded, as if it had been under water, the ankles and feet covered with mud. The girl looked very young, very skinny, a girl of nineteen with small breasts and colourless lips.

"What do you want?"

The question surprised us both. The girl tried to say something, but as if the effort was too big, she seemed to lose her strength. I only had time to open my arms and receive the wet, bad smelling body against my chest.

She had started wearing her old clothes, the jeans and white T-shirts, the loose dresses. Her hair seemed redder, and her eyes, that had wandered between the blue and the grey, in a certain light were almost green. It was not that she was more beautiful; she was more fey, like a girl in a Pre-Raphaelite painting who slept with the painters.

We lived in a strange harmony. After the first evening, when Tom found us kneeling on the floor, holding each other, a twisted Pietà, we hadn't talked much. Tom had moved his things to the guest room, and April slept in her old bed, near the window.

I felt guilty, as if I had stolen my sister's fiancé. It had taken years, a shy friendship, our work together; he used to bring manuscripts at the weekend, and I read them. I made a simple dinner – April had always been the cook, her useful hands, once in a while we went to the movies. And then one night he looked up from a manuscript and whispered, You are so beautiful. It was as if he was seeing me above her shoulder, among those red hairs he seemed to have counted, to know by heart. He went on, You are made the same way, your face and your body, but you have different colours; and then we put the manuscripts aside and solemnly kissed. He moved in the next weekend. I had cleaned the floor and the stairs with lavender polish, I had washed the curtains and, as in a Jaan Kaplinski poem, had felt strangely sad, I had changed the sheets of the beds in my room, and caught daffodils from the garden, even though there were only fourteen, we never cut them before there were sixteen. I felt the old unease when I put them in the vases; I craved April's hands, the bony fingers and dirty nails among the flowers. At the end of the spring holidays I didn't go back to college. I started working at the town library. On Friday evening I went to the station to wait for him.

Now, I felt the house smelt of heather, heather flowers on a rainy day, as it used to seven years before. April had taken her place; she slept in her bed; she cooked the meals. She seemed to have a deep knowledge of plants and used strange herbs; I had the fantasy she would poison us with the soup, the fish and potatoes, the dark bread. Sometimes I caught her singing, and those songs made me feel afraid, not only the monotonous melodies I had never heard, but the language; it didn't sound like any language I knew.

April declared she didn't remember anything. The doctor said she was all right, she needed rest and food, and her memory would come back. He had seen her only after a hot bath, with a nightgown and the hair humid and clean, drinking coffee and eating toast. So, people still believed April had left in the six o'clock train with a man, she had lived in London with a man, and the fact that she looked much younger than me meant nothing. We didn't receive visitors, and when she started going out, she was her old self, reserved and quiet, and nobody really expected any explanations.

On Friday, Tom came home on an earlier train, as if he couldn't stand being away from her. He followed her with his eyes, with the old look of amazement. I once caught them listening to their song: maybe I'm amazed at the way I really need you.

A strange harmony. He went to London, I went to the library, April stayed at home. She had fetched her painting box from the attic. Sometimes when I arrived she was drying the paint from her hands in a dirty cloth.

One day, when she had left for a walk, I opened the drawer of her desk. There were a few watercolours, mist, water, and plants, and some indistinct figures; only for a moment the figures looked the same, a slim girl walking in dark streets, on mountain paths. Things had passed through her, or through water, and were beautiful and vague, remnants of a time when all was mixed together, before separation. I wondered if she had been there, in the place where things didn't have form.

She entered the room without making any noise, a little grey cat in her arms.

"They recognize me," she said.

"Some of them are not the same."

"They are. They are born again and again."

Two birds, perhaps the skeletons of two birds, on the branch of a tree, one of them watching the other eat a fruit.

I remembered the three of us playing in the garden, hiding in the fog. We sang all the sinister children's songs from the movies: here we go round the mulberry bush, we lay my love and I, beneath the weeping willow. But we had never played together; Tom was a village boy; April and I were the children of the old house. Even though our family was ruined, people still treated us with deference. My father spent the days among his books and sold a painting or a piece of furniture from time to time to keep us going. He was the only one who preferred the pale redhead, the ugly duckling as he called her; when I saw him showing her some illustration in an old book, reading her a long passage as if it were a story, I hated the fey creature that smelt of heather and had her knees wounded most of the time.

Tom no longer shared his manuscripts with me. He read some parts to her, though she only cared for children's books, the stories by Will Scott where things didn't really happen, and *The Way to Sattin Shore* and *The Other Side of the Tunnel.* Like Alice she fell down a hole, I used to sing to her in the old days, even though Lewis Carroll and mirrors had more to do with me. I spent some time getting dressed for parties, combing my hair; like cats, she seemed to feel uneasy when in front of a mirror. What had she felt when she approached the pond? The pond. *They*, too, had chosen her. All my life I had walked and lain among the bluebells—we were forbidden to cut them; they died before we arrived home. I was aware of the presence of the trees, the bushes, the birds, the water, familiar water; water recognizes us. But nothing else.

"Where have you been?" I cried one evening. We were in the drawing-room, I leaning against the window, she sitting near the fire, pretending to read a magazine.

For the first time she didn't give me that startled look I was getting used to. A slight, ironic smile passed her lips and was gone in a moment.

"Who are you?"

April stared at me, and there was no smile this time, only a cautious expression. She looked terrible lately, she didn't wash or comb her hair, and it was a dirty red mess; her hands were rough, her nails filthy. I could feel in her that smell she had never really lost, the smell of mud and slime. She looked into the distance and started humming one of her songs, and as if it was a calling, the little cat that was sleeping on the hearthrug woke up and jumped to her knees. She caressed him under the chin, and he began to purr.

That night, Tom arrived just after supper. When I entered the drawing-room, they were kneeling by the fire, his face hidden in her shoulder, a religious image. She stared at me, and there was a warning in her eyes. I turned back and ran upstairs.

I woke up at dawn and saw that her bed hadn't been touched. I took a shower and combed my hair that smelt of flowers. I wore a long summer dress, even though it wasn't warm enough for summer dresses.

His car was still outside; he was in bed holding the girl with dirty red hair and greenish eyes, the girl that looked like me, except for the hair, the eyes and the hands. I know nothing about hair, but eyes and hands are what make us unique, what doesn't really change with time. I wondered if she would stay nineteen while I grew mature and then old and died.

It was early for bluebells; there were only a few among the grass and the heather. I walked slowly to the pond. I didn't remember taking off my shoes, but I was barefoot; maybe I had left the house that way; my feet hurt. The morning mist seemed to come from the water; I licked my lips to feel the moisture. Like an animal, I was afraid to look at my image. I only whispered, "I'm here."

I sat on the grass, my arms around my knees, and waited. I had no notion of the time, only of the colours that were changing. There were more and more bluebells, as if they answered to some calling.

The day was like a circle, and it was beginning to close. When the dusk came I lay on the earth, my nails in my arms like claws, some bird roughly formed, and before I closed my eyes I had a glimpse of the other bird among the branches of heather, watching me.

Spatial Psychology

By Rick McGrath

Later, as he sat on the sun-bathed balcony, poking some dying embers in the rough fire pit, Robert Maitland reflected on the unusual events that must have taken place within this huge apartment building over the past two years. Impressed by the building's size, with its 40 floors, swimming pools, liquor outlet, and supermarkets—all now but abandoned—he was also surprised of not being aware of its existence until two days ago.

Formerly an experimental architect in a London design group—before he was injured in a serious car crash—Maitland used his lengthy time in recuperation to study social psychology and made his name a year later with a seminal study of urban unrest in London's Chelsea district, where residents suddenly transformed their upscale neighbourhood into a scene of self-indulgent property mutilation, disguised as dereliction. The media was fascinated.

Once a Chelsea resident himself, Maitland famously described the event in his breakthrough *Guardian* series as "spontaneous spatial neurosis"—a violent, yet innately positive reaction to high levels of cultural homogenization within a confined geographic area.

Maitland followed this success with a regular output of well-publicized pop psych pieces, and after a year researching and writing about social class inversion in Japanese internment camps in Tsing Tao and Shanghai, he was now back and relaxing in a fashionable London lounge, comfortably chatting about a recent project he was researching in a little town near Heathrow.

He was with his old friend Richard Pearson, once an advertising executive his firm had hired to promote a suburban shopping mall his design group developed, and who was now the sales manager for a major pharmaceutical company.

"No, no no, Richard, really, those Shepperton residents went crazy—sorry, behaved unusually—for no apparent reason. That's the interesting part—well, the part I have to figure out."

Maitland wove his wine glass in a small figure eight on the table in front of him. "I was there for a week. Sadly, I couldn't stay longer. But ..." he took a pregnant pause ..."I do have tapes from the TV coverage. Hopefully they have some video of the instigator, a bloke named Blake, who apparently emerged from the depths of the Thames and started the mass neuroses. Amazing stuff. Ponder this: the population thought they were living in a tropical paradise, some thought they could fly, and a few found it impossible to leave. Damndest thing. My first thought was an ergot infection."

Richard laughed in disbelief. "They thought Shepperton was transformed? Into a jungle? Brilliant! Christ, I could have used that marketing idea at the Brooklands mall ... my *Mad is Bad. Bad is Good* slogan worked for awhile until the whole thing became political. All I was saying is that perversion can be positive in the right circumstances."

Maitland gave Pearson a look of disbelief. "That campaign was a disaster, and you know it. You were recently divorced, your father was murdered in the mall, you fell in with a local charlatan, and you tried to equate the concept of shopping with violence and madness."

Pearson attempted to look sheepish. "Nonsense. I just woke the population up. It was all going to plan until they decided to burn the place down. You can't predict unintended consequences. And remember, as I bowed to the gods of irony, both my TV and billboard campaigns won Arrow awards."

Maitland rolled his eyes.

"But back to your project. I've been to Shepville many times, Robby—movie studios are big clients for our products. Sure, some places are crazy. That big loop in the river—bet you that's it. Perfect subject for a whatever-it-is spacey shrink like you."

Maitland smiled.

"Spatial, Richard, spatial psychologist. Ever wonder why open plan offices are managed by psychopaths?"

"Really? Hey. You're making that up. I run an open office—you bastard."

Maitland smiled again.

"Still, Richard, Shepperton doesn't fit the model. It's the homogeneous ones that, well—the town had too much social diversity. This type of mixed class mass delusion could be a whole new area of study for me. We'll see. I'm now wondering how many of these neurotic communities exist."

It was Pearson's turn to smile. "Well, wonder no more. I've got a tip for you, Roberto. What would you think about a large group of well-off people living in a self-wrecked building? Living there, fighting each other, and liking it? This high-rise I know went from new and sold out to broken and apparently abandoned in just over a year. Nobody bitched. Money just blown. Sorta creepy and cool in that psycho way you like."

Maitland was indeed interested. A vertical Chelsea? "Where?"

"Eastside, down by the Thames. Where it makes that big jog after the airport."

"And people still live there?"

"Apparently. Dunno. Maybe. There are stories. I don't cover that area anymore. Perks of a manager. Hey, you like a coincidence. Here's one. Didn't you write a paper a few years ago on that famous architect, Anthony Royal?"

Maitland took a sip of wine. Yes, he had. *Royal Revealed: Lipstick on the Bauhaus Pig*. The postmodernists had loved it.

"Well, get this. My friend Anthony Royal designed these high-rises."

Maitland's eyes flickered sharply under his dark brows, McGoohan-style. "You know Anthony Royal?"

"Yeah, I know him. Don't look so amazed, Robert. We played at the same tennis club before Tony hit the …" Richard lowered his voice, "… ahh, terminal beach. But that's not the story."

"Royal is dead?"

"Where you been, Robby? His obit ran many months ago. Oh, yeah. You're in China. All right, there's more." Richard looked around as if people might be eavesdropping. "It was just around two years ago Anthony talked me into buying a flat in his new high-rise—as an investment, mind you—and I rented it to some TV producer and his family. He was a big, boisterous bastard but his wife seemed competent. Children. No matter. His rent cheque cashed the first month, but not the next."

Richard took a slow drink to emphasize the gravity of this omission.

"I phone. No answer. Leave messages. No answer. So, Christ, I drive over to see what's the problem and am stunned by the condition of the building. My place is still fine, stunk a bit of cigarettes, but hell, the building has only been open a few months and it's already breaking down. One lift out of commission. I see a water stain seeping down a wall. My tenant is nowhere to be found. I'm pissed off. So are most of the people yammering at the superintendent.

The fast lifts are still working so I head up to Anthony's penthouse to confront the great man. We're in his glass studio on the roof. I'm ranting. He's looking ragged—there's all these white birds screaming overhead—and he appears to have no answers for what's happening on the floors below him. I finally mention my lawyer, and—I befuddle you none—right away he goes over to his desk and writes me a cheque for more than what I paid. Take it, he says, this place is a zoo. I look at his big, white Alsatian. Being a practical man, I took the money, signed some papers, and got the hell out. I wanted a long-term investment. Fast payoff! Sadly, a couple months later he was shot by one of the inhabitants. Like I say, that was two years ago—probably deserted now—no doubt any inhabitants are squatters."

"Fascinating. But I don't believe in coincidences." Maitland finished his wine, caught the barman's eye. He knew Pearson, like all salesmen, tended to exaggerate. "Are you sure the whole building reacted? The lower floors usually feel the brunt of change first. I'm not interested in slums."

"There's more." Richard adopted a face of adman sincerity. "When I was repping the new medical facility at Canary Wharf I dealt with one of the doctors who lived in the high-rise. Neurologist, if I remember. Maybe not. What was his name? Langley? No. Laing—that was it. He taught classes and ran the medical dispensary. Ordered all the drugs. Got to know him a bit—lived around the middle of the high-rise—floor 24 or 25. He was a tad odd."

"Howso?"

"Couldn't figure him out—hah … why would you become a brain surgeon to teach and dish drugs? But I started to become suspicious after dealing with him—they used a helluva lot of drugs. Heavy stuff. It wasn't that large a facility. And when I called for an appointment he was rarely there—when we did meet he looked increasingly shabby, distracted, and, somewhat sadly, a tad ripe. I had to wonder."

"Did he complain?"

Richard snorted in his martini. "Just the opposite. He looked like hell—beardy and thin—but seemed quite content. That sorta dreamy thing, the long stare. His personality changed, too—from a sort of mousey voyeur type to something more self-confident—like a lonely adult becoming a popular teen. Again, I wondered."

"Did he talk about the building?"

"Rarely. He once called his flat 'the cave on the cliff', but really, he basically talked business and seemed quite anxious to return to the high-rise after our meetings."

The following day Maitland drove down to the Thames and made his way east through an interzone of abandoned warehouses, faded billboards, empty parking lots, and auto wrecking yards. He could see two high-rises in the distance but couldn't find the way there. He finally stopped beside a photographer, asked for directions, and soon found the approach road.

Ahead towered a gigantic building, rising from a sea of rusting, smashed cars and a shoreline of indeterminate garbage, a dune of forgotten yesterdays in sun-faded plastic bags.

Opposite was a second sister high-rise, dark but not apparently deserted. It seemed to be covered in camouflage, until Maitland realized the discoloured streaks were the result of smoke from a series of balcony fires. Some clothing fluttered in open windows. Between these two were three half-completed towers, forming a rough semi-circle. He turned back to the primary target.

The entrance to the high-rise consisted of a path through a maze of wrecked furniture, faded and warped in the sun and rain. The big front doors were chained at the handles, but an adjacent window had been smashed and Maitland stepped into the main hall.

There's war in hell, Maitland thought as he carefully picked a route through the flotsam that almost completely covered the floor. He surveyed the carnage. The lifts were defaced with graffiti, bones cadavered the floor, and blood flecked in arcs over walls already defaced with crudely painted instructions and unintelligible threats.

Moving towards the emergency stairs, Maitland checked the lifts—none of the doors would open, and a vaguely sweet putrid smell increased with proximity. Sludge was seeping under one of the deeply scratched and dented stainless steel doors. He tested the fire escape doors—they opened, and he made it up one floor before being stopped by a massive structure of intertwined furniture, smashed TVs, twisted bathroom fixtures and what looked like a car's rear bumper. He tried a few pulls and was about to try and dismantle the beaverish dam when he heard what might have been a low growl from above. He retreated to the lobby.

What to do next, he wondered. The blocked stairwell. The distinct possibility of wildlife. The obvious signs of violence. *This was better than he expected.* Figuring this could be more complicated than simply exploring another abandoned building,

Maitland decided to return home to his Spitalsfield flat and prepare for a proper assault on the high-rise … after he had done some research. As he pulled away from the building his eye caught a sudden motion in the rear-view mirror. Something on a balcony around the 10th floor. A figure in blue, wrapped in a red blanket?

Back on the road, Maitland drove north and was soon back in familiar territory. An idea occurred. He knew the manager of the local HM Land Registry and decided to stop in for a quick meeting.

Once home he cleared a table, opened the just-obtained tube of blueprints, and began to study Anthony Royal's original plans for the high-rise project. He had analyzed Royal's other buildings in the past and—if the architect was true to form—somewhere in the overall design there would be an unidentified passageway Royal could use for covert access and egress. Tony liked his privacy. And there it was. A small rectangle built in the angle between two walls of the public and service lift shafts. He smiled. Happy ending.

When Maitland arrived on site early the next morning the warm June sun was butter yellow above the horizon and the three unfinished high-rises were backlit like the black stumps of a dog's broken teeth. This time he was prepared—along with ample food and water he packed a heavy flashlight, wire cutters, narcotic-laced dog biscuits, some rope, and his favourite toy, a set of lock picks. Again, he carefully made his way through the lobby debris and then stopped short.

Today a strange apparition dressed in a black cassock sat slouched in a broken chair in front of the fire stairs. When he got closer Maitland realized a dog's head had been crudely attached to a mannequin's shoulders. So, Anubis guards the stairs—fine. Not going in that direction, anyway. He turned left and made his way through the administrator's office to the back of the lift shafts.

He explored a conundrum of service corridors and demolished workrooms before he found a battered steel door, inset in the concrete behind a stack of smashed TVs. He knew the lock, and the door was soon opened to reveal a narrow set of circular steps twisting skyward beside a small, two-person lift. He looked up. There was a hint of light at the top of the shaft. He gingerly stepped inside the lift and was somewhat shocked to note the floor indicator light was illuminating "G". Was the power still on after all this time? He tentatively pressed 10 and was rewarded when the door closed and the lift slid quietly upwards. He felt a twinge of youthful excitement.

At the 10th floor Maitland exited the lift, carefully opened the service door and stepped into one of the high-rise's machine rooms, now a kind of demented pasta palace, with various pipes bent and ripped from walls and ceiling in great arcs, some of them decorated with lengths of different coloured electrical cord. A dentist's chair sat regally in one corner.

This room led to more hallways and then into the Concourse area, spread out end to end in the high-rise like a high street shopping mall. After a brief inspection of the ruined supermarket and liquor outlet, Maitland noticed with amusement that the beauty salon was still intact. The bank, with its barred-off area behind the teller's wickets, had at one time been converted into a kennel, with dog and cat travel cases stacked upon each other in the spacious safety deposit vault.

He poked his head into the vast recreation area. The stale air was faintly perfumed with chlorine, and a confusion of bones, shopping carts and wine bottles traced a strange pattern at the bottom of the drained swimming pool. The lift doors on this floor opened, but his torchlight revealed their use as a garbage disposal. A lightweight chain sealed the fire steps, and he quickly cut through it to reveal a clear passage up. By the time he got to the 20th floor he heard a faint, far-off, high-pitched howling beneath him—dogs on the hunt. Pausing briefly, Maitland threw a couple handfuls of his doctored biscuits on the steps a few floors below him. At the entrance to the 25th floor he met a major roadblock of stacked furniture.

He carefully began dismantling the wooden wall before him, and just by luck he pulled on a chair leg, which proved to be the master lever that opened a hole just big enough for him to squeeze through. The dogs went quiet behind him. Past the barrier, he surveyed the lobby—now an art gallery of greasy polaroids taped and pinned to the walls. He got out his torch and took a closer look. Most were jarred, motion blurred photos of people fighting, bloody faces, and drunken cheering, but many were of macabre scenes of dead people dressed in often surreal costumes with ornate face make-up, posed in various sexual positions.

He turned away and splayed his light around. Desiccated bags of garbage lined the walls. He noticed a slight draught playing on his face from the aisle to the right of the lift. Rounding the corner he heard a faint flapping sound, like a small bird struggling in the jaws of a bored cat. He crept along to an open door and looked inside.

The apartment stretched around 50 feet from the dull carpet under his shoes to the shining air outside. Straight ahead on the sitting room floor a notebook's pages chittered in the breeze from the open balcony. He picked it up, took a quick glance, pocketed the book and instinctively closed the large sliding glass door. He quickly assessed the apartment. Bathroom, good-sized kitchen, big bedroom, dining area and living room facing the long, large balcony. It looked expensive. And relatively untouched. He spent a few minutes looking through the bedroom, noticing there was a hole in the floor where a plank had been removed, and was somehow not that surprised to discover a bag of old letters in the kitchen, all addressed to the rather enigmatic Dr Laing.

Richard was correct about the location. He returned to the living room to ponder his next move and while staring out the window he was startled by a loud sniffing sound from the hallway. He turned to see a smallish man dressed in a torn and stained Superman costume, with the furry remains of an Alsatian's head for a hat.

Letting out a low growl, Superman revealed a dentist's drill in his right hand and simultaneously lunged towards Maitland, who stood frozen on the spot and then casually kicked a small, three-legged side table into Superman's charge. The rim caught the caped crusader on the shin, throwing him forward, arms flailing for balance as he fell face first into the bottom of the balcony's glass door. He lay, dazed, on the hardwood floor. Blood began to run from his nose. Maitland gave him a tentative kick to the shoulder then stepped over the body, out of the apartment and down the hallway, into the service area, and found Royal's personal lift door, concealed behind a bloody mattress. He had his lock picks out but the door swung open. Did Superman know? He waited for the lift to rise from the 10th floor, got in and hit a button.

At the 35th floor he stopped and made his way to the main lift lobby to find another empty swimming pool and the remains of a restaurant. He checked the stairwell going down—the landing was stacked with tables and chairs from the restaurant, and broken household furniture choked the steps down a whole floor. Apparently, no one from the lower levels was going to be invited higher for dinner and a dip. Inversely, the steps up to the roof seemed clear.

Maitland checked his watch. It was nigh on noon, and he sat down in the restaurant to review his immediate situation. It appeared the high-rise was still occupied, if only by an inept superman and a few dogs, perhaps kept. The high-rise was already revealing itself to be generally divided into territorial areas. Classic tribalism, he realized. Tree forts. That thought took him back to his youth, when rather than play and run with other kids, he preferred creeping through abandoned houses and derelict buildings. His explorations would keep him amused for hours, searching for the often surreal remains and bits of prior occupants, prior lives.

This building was forty floors of much more intriguing possibilities.

A faint creak in the hallway outside snapped Maitland from his reverie. Time to reach the top. He went back to the lift and ten minutes later he had reached the top and took the precaution of locking the lift in place. He carefully opened the rooftop door, blinking in the squinting sunlight. An unexpected flurry of large white birds briefly startled him as he rounded the lift head and walked onto the terrace. Did he also see a figure in white out of the corner of his eye?

He paused. Stretching out in front of him the roof was completed covered with white tiles, a snowy rectangle against the blue sky. Randomly placed on this grid a collection of large, geometrically shaped objects were mounted on pedestals. Off to the right were dozens of large plant pots, many with greenery, and to the left was a glass-walled room that overlooked the roof area.

Maitland stepped forward, belatedly recognizing the geometric forms as sculptures, and wondered about the flowing discolourations that stained the spheres, pyramids, cubes and the white tiles underfoot—like a demented Jackson Pollock had run amok with gallons of dark red paint. In the centre of the sculpture garden he noticed a large black, burnt area, and on either side of it sat a strange apparition which seemed to resemble parts of a callisthetics machine, but was obviously reconfigured to be used as support for a roasting spit.

Maitland looked into the glassy room—obviously Royal's office. Desk, table, sofa, chairs, filing cabinets—all undamaged. A second, frosted glass door inside the office revealed steps descending to the main apartment. He crept down. All was silent. Then he noticed—the walls were clean, the carpets unstained, curtains hung peacefully around the high windows in the slightly musty living room. On the shining dining room table stood two silver candlesticks. He found the apartment's foyer and entered the 40th floor lift lobby. It had no barricades, no garbage bags, and the lobby furniture was present and still intact. The walls had also been cleaned, although some faded graffiti still stubbornly remained. He opened the door to the fire stairs and they appeared to stretch cleanly down a number of floors.

Returning to Royal's penthouse, Maitland began a systematic search of the rambling apartment, which stretched half the length of the high-rise. In the library he found an unopened bottle of Italian wine—something red and strong from the Del Baldo estate—and off the master bedroom he discovered someone had converted the walk-in closet into a tiny bedroom, complete with single bed, side table, and a small light attached to a car battery. It still worked.

By the time he had checked out all of Royal's home and explored the top three floors the late afternoon sun was beginning to smear the towers of London into an orange haze, and giving in to some unknown impulse he decided to spend the night in the high-rise.

The tiny closet bedroom was too claustrophobic for Maitland, so he lugged the lamp and battery up to Royal's rooftop aerie. A few large white gulls circled above, finally landing on the roof's outer wall and rubbing their beaks in red-stained concrete crevices. Not trusting the lamp's battery he went downstairs, retrieved the two dining room candlesticks and pulled down two curtains to use as blankets should the night chill. Back on the roof, he laid out the contents of his backpack on a draughting table and surveyed Royal's late estate.

The lazy twilight beckoned, and Maitland grabbed a chair and the wine and wandered out into the sculpture garden. The golden air lightened the dull red patina on the various works, one of which caught his eye: three cement ovoids, stacked vertically, each slightly smaller than the one beneath it. Damn mid-century modern art, he thought, munching the sandwiches he should have had for lunch, but even now he wasn't feeling that hungry. He took a swig from the wine bottle and for some reason again felt like a teenager out on an adventure. Could someone actually live here? He eyed the big birds appraisingly.

It was becoming cooler in the twilight and he tugged his jacket closer. There was something in the right pocket. The notebook he had found in Laing's apartment on the 25th floor. It was about the size of a thin paperback novel, quite beat up, and had wine spilled on most of the back cover. Or was that blood? He opened it. The first page was inscribed at the top with a neat LAING, with 2525 underneath. A quick flip of the few pages revealed it was some sort of diary, to do reminders, recipes, and lists of names, many with a line drawn through them. He thumbed back to the beginning:

> Night. Girls asleep. Building still quiet. Sitting on the balcony pecking at the dog when all the lights went off on the 7th floor of our sister high-rise. Could hear some of the shouts from here. May have to visit soon and welcome them to the new neighbourhood. Tomorrow need to set more traps.

Not sure of the date. Does it matter? Steele becoming more dangerous at night, although being right beside him may be safest as he seems to be ranging wider, and he has a dog. Bait or food? Alice and Eleanor are becoming weaker. Time to increase the doses of morph?

Garlic. Growable?

Maitland paused for a drink. Darkness was deepening so he decided to move indoors. One curtain became a pillow, the other a sheet, and with the light on and candles lit he snuggled down on the sofa with the wine and Laing's notes. For a few pages there were just lists of names, as if Laing was keeping track of what must have been a dwindling population. Then …

Rossi's Roast Rover: a spit set over a fire pit with wood fuel is the ideal way to roast a whole dog. Can also be used for cat, raccoons, large whole poultry, or any other large pieces of meat. Trussing a whole or partial dog is very important. Then make one long slit down the back and several diagonal slits on each side. None of the slits should touch any other. Then rub the dog with any oil or fat you may have on all its surfaces. Begin cooking. Rotate the spit quickly enough to keep the juices from dropping. After about 30 minutes or so begin basting liberally with fat and any garlic you may have. Baste every 10 to 20 minutes and, when done, set the roast dog aside to rest for about 30 minutes. First remove the shoulder and hind-legs at the joints. These pieces then can be sliced to serve. Next make a cut down the middle of the back, down the spine. Then cut from the shoulder, hugging the bone of the ribs and spine, down to where the rump and hind-leg were removed. This large piece will include the rack and loin cuts as well as the dog's belly.

The next few pages were covered with what looked like a scratchy floor plan of the 25th floor, with various distances marked along rooms and hallways. Maitland scowled slightly as he read on …

Found it today! Was looking around the ground floor service lift area and finally discovered where my anomaly was hidden—behind a stack of mattresses, a small steel door. It wasn't locked. Inside a stairway and a vertical shaft. It was easy to walk down a flight to the basement, and there it was: a mini-lift. Room for two. Best: the lift's electric system was separate from the building and throwing a switch started it up. Royal was clever—big rubber wheels and the engine in the basement means the cage runs silently. Now we can escape from Steele, who has run out of bodies to dress up and has replaced his dead models with mannequins from the 10th floor's fashion shops. He's also found a storage of costumes from somewhere, which he either wears on his night raids or drapes over mannequins. Lately he's been Superman, or as he claims, "The Man of Steele". He may also be training dogs on the lower floors. The protection he claims to be giving us is costing me too much Ritalin.

Christ, they're all strung out, Maitland thought, then self-consciously smiled as he finished off the Del Baldo. So Steele was the inept assailant, and Laing had found Royal's lift and gained if not the territorial advantage, then certainly freedom of movement. His sense of control must have increased—but where was Laing now? Outside, the gulls had vanished with the night and on the horizon the lights of London glowed like an ersatz sunset through the dusty windows. He returned to Laing's notes.

Weather warmer and much has changed over the past months. The lift has allowed me to improve our supply of food and water, and this has revived Alice and Eleanor ... they're now walking around a few hours each day and becoming more insistent in their demands ... and details of my excursions from the building.

Steele abandoned his flat and moved to Wilder's on the second floor. He's claimed all the floors to the 10th and has chained the stairway higher. Aside from Steele's barricade on the first and 10th, the inferior block on the 25th and the huge wall at the 35th, many of the defensive structures have been taken apart.

Maitland didn't recognize the names, but realized the barricades were still as described. The list of Laing's various observations went on and Maitland sleepily paused from the notebook. It was dark out. His silhouette threw dune-like shadows on the walls of glass, and he was just about to turn off the lights and fade to sleep when he felt a slim hand at his throat and the oblique flash of a long carving knife.

"Shhhhsh ..."

Maitland raised his hands slightly. The notebook dropped. He whispered, "It's OK ... I'm a kind of explorer. Just here for the night. If that's OK."

A woman in white cut into his vision. A face that had recently seen a mirror. Blonde hair twisting over her shoulders. She appeared to be wearing something fashionable—silky pants and finely finished blouse. Her breasts moved heavily under the thin cloth as she warily circled the sofa.

"Who are you? Why are you here?"

"My name is Maitland. Robert Maitland. Technically, I'm a spatial psychologist and I'm interested in this building ... OK, I'm a kind of shrink about spaces. You can call me Bob. And you?"

"Anne. Anne Royal."

Maitland was surprised. "Tony's wife?"

"Ex. I'm the young trophy wife he dragged out when applicable."

"Sorry about Tony."

"Unmissed. But he was the Royal Lord of this manor, and now I'm the Lady."

Maitland lowered his hands and bowed his head. "Enchanted, m'lady."

Anne smiled slightly, relaxed and sat behind Royal's desk. The knife disappeared. Maitland flashed Anne his warmest smile.

"I'm sure we'll be the best of friends. Do you have any here? Are you alone in the castle tower?"

Anne looked wistfully out on the roof, now washed white in the moonlight. "We had a sort of women's organization that lasted about nine months. Mums and kids, living and working together. Protecting each other. The eventual shortage of food finally became a problem—yes, I know about Tony's lift—but I kept that a secret. Ultimately there were too many of us and our original ideals began to fade—or evolve. Within two months I was the only sister left on the roof. The high-rise still contains quite a few people—there are secret and not-so-secret passages cut through floors and walls everywhere. But nobody above the 35th floor—this is mine."

"How do you survive?"

"You've already met my protection—Steele. He pretty well scares the crap out of anyone who tries to get past the big blockade at the first floor. How did you find Anthony's lift? No matter. I keep Steele as the old school crazy, a reminder of our tribal time when the building went instinctual. Bears grudges. Is jealous of me. One of these days he ... won't be necessary." Maitland caught a glint of old fury in her eyes.

"Food? Protein is fairly easy to find. And cook. I'm growing veg in those pots, but water is bloody hard work to get up here, even with the lift. If I could only hook up a water pump—and I'm sure Tony had set up an alternate power source for the penthouse, but I can't find it—I'd have a little farm up here. This urban hunter-gatherer shit is OK for a while, but I'm willing to compromise."

Maitland wasn't so sure. He decided to change topics. "I'm also curious about one of the tenants here. A Dr Laing. Do you know him?"

Anne laughed. "We all know the Doctor, Robert—Bob. Hah—you both have the same first name. He was basically invisible and acquiescent during the, ahh ... transformation, but then he emerged as a kind of cranky, bossy shopkeeper. Laing ran the drugstore. Traded drugs—usually speed—for everything, but inevitably he ran out. Things got unfortunate then."

"Upset addicts?"

"Maybe, but it hit closer to home. Laing was quite pleased with his harem—two fucked up women he controlled with drugs—who earned their keep by complaining what an asshole he was. Don't ask. One of them, Eleanor, went missing, and soon after Laing's sister Alice died, possibly from withdrawal. Or an overdose. Laing hid her body."

"He did what?"

"Stashed it away somewhere—away from our psycho, Steele. He likes to take bodies and dress them up."

"I think I've already seen one. Anubis in the lobby."

"That's Steele, all right. Anyway, Laing didn't go long without a companion. A few weeks later sister Helen—who left us to hide on the lower floors—showed up at Laing's door with two kids and a bank account. She wanted out and finally convinced him to clean up, put on a suit and go back to teaching at the hospital. They moved out soon after. Last I heard Laing was back at his old job—they thought he's been on sabbatical in Africa, working on a water project in the desert. Hah. Maybe he was."

"You mentioned a transformation. What was actually transformed?"

"Everything." Anne managed a small smile. "It started with a happy, general slide … obsessive nights of drunken parties, a dead dog in the swimming pool, the odd fight … and escalated to serious wars between sections of the high-rise and then individual floors."

"Nobody called the police?"

"No … you have to understand … we all liked it! Normal, boring job during the day … live action adventure at night. We all felt, well, *alive*."

Anne suddenly froze. "Shhhh …"

Then Maitland heard it—the faint howl of a beagle echoing up the building. Distant, but still too close. Could Superman really fly? He hoped the lift was still locked—it was a long walk down. He looked at Anne.

"Is that Steele? Does he know about the lift?"

"No … but his dogs have figured out how to get either through or past the major barricades. They can get up here to the roof, and they'll howl at the door all night."

She didn't look happy and motioned to Maitland to collect his stuff. He got his torch, doused the light and candles, recovered his knapsack and both of them retreated to the wall behind the sculpture garden—he a dark shadow, she a shimmering flow of moonlight. They paused to wait. He liked the way she pressed up beside him. Four dogs appeared and pawed at the studio door. Maitland and Anne backed away and entered the waiting lift. For some reason she stopped it at the 25th floor.

Laing's flat was unchanged from this morning, save the fresh blood stains. Maitland propped a chair under the door handle and flopped on Laing's large and fashionable sofa. Anne stretched out beside him. Fatigue suddenly overcame him and he was soon in a deep sleep.

Maitland awoke in the early morning light, unsure at first where he was. His back was stiff. Anne was in the kitchen. He still had food and bottles of water left in his pack, and Anne had done a quick exploration of Laing's kitchen, finding various pots, broken dishes, a few mugs, and, surprisingly, a small jar still containing ground coffee.

She poured some water into a pot and took it to the balcony, where a handful of hypermarket flyers and some splintered chair legs soon made a small blaze in Laing's homemade fire pit, which looked suspiciously like a long metal meat tray from a butcher's shop. Coffee made, Maitland and Anne sat out on the balcony and basked in the early morning sun.

Maitland found himself straying from the vague view of London to focus on Anne Royal. She was like someone from an imaginary island. He looked to the penthouse high above. Power and water could be routed to the roof—he had the building plans, and he didn't think it would be too difficult to finally deal with Steele. Anne smiled at him.

Maybe, he thought, I could stay here a week or two …

The Alphabet Doctor

By David Paddy

"Everything you know is dying. From the cells that make up your body—tissue, nerves, organs—to the plants and animals that surround you. The planet, the universe, all is breaking down, fading into inevitable decay. Even the ideas you now possess—they will age, fall out of favour. Your youthful rebellions will soon become the stuff of stodgy conservatism. You as you are now will become just a memory, and memories change, get lost, become wholly unreliable. There is nothing about you—your body, your mind, your possessions, your ideas, your self, your world—that will last."

It is the first day of class. Students are still finding their seats, syllabi yet to be distributed. On the board behind the speaker are words in chalk: YOUR TIME TO TALK WILL COME LATER.

The Alphabet Doctor assembles the histories that have yet to be told, the histories that were told too soon, and the silences in between. With his instruments—displayed neatly across the ink blotter on his desk—he holds the unspoken words and assigns a letter. Once affixed, the letter story can be filed and placed in its appropriate box.

The Doctor's rooms are lined floor to ceiling with a grid of card catalogues—anachronistic fetishes—to house his library of silences. Unspoken or pre-spoken, the tales are given a letter, which assigns them a value, but not always a meaning. They find their place, but increasingly for him nothing can be drawn from them. He fears he has produced an immaculate order of nothing.

He has been in practice for many years. People have traveled many miles to see him with the hope he will save them. His fame has grown, as has his infamy. His printed lectures on the methods to recover language and story from the inside of silent heads have been pored over by scholars and banned by religious and political leaders in equal measure.

He has practiced his art, or rather his science, for many years. And he has become deathly tired of it. He has become cynical, doubting the very point of everything to which he has devoted his life.

And then the boy arrives.

A young boy travels on a train on his own. His mother has sent him to see the Alphabet Doctor in the city of Pér, with its winding walled streets and thousand bridges. It is known by all in the country that the Doctor is the man who fixes broken pasts and heals the histories that have been hidden. When the boy reaches him, he thinks he will be asked to tell stories so that the Doctor can put them in a new language that will help the patient understand.

But the boy, when he speaks, will utter loud silences. Acking and hoomphing. He wants to tell of the family's broken past. This past is clear to him even though he is wrong. He worries, rightly, that when he comes to sit before the Alphabet Doctor the words will not come. What the boy does not know is that this will not faze the doctor whatsoever. For in his office, there are cabinets filled with bottles of aphasia.

On the train, the boy wants to tell the passenger across from him, an elderly woman with a Pomeranian in her lap, the story of his sister, how she had also stopped speaking, and then disappeared. How his father went in search but never found her. How he leaves their home for longer and longer stretches. How he has not returned for a month, and how during this month the words started to shrivel and die in the boy's mouth.

His mother insists that he must seek help for the letters that won't come. The boy knows she did not seek such help for her daughter—and she seeks it for her son not because she does not want the same fate to repeat for him, but because she believes girls cannot be helped but boys can be, ruled, as she is, by Old World traditions. And who better than the famous Doctor? Refusing to speak of his disappeared sister or his diminishing father, she blames her son. "You chattery boy! You talk talk and lose your head. Must go see Doctor."

Still the boy worries that when he goes to meet the Doctor, he will not be able to tell this story. Just more acks and acks. Will the Doctor know how to understand him? The boy has other stories inside him, ones he has made up, that he would rather tell—of the rat children of the New Hebrides, or of the foul-toothed Angels tending the dying plants of the sloping hill gardens—but everything inside him is noise.

The Doctor thinks poetry is shit, thinks poets abase the Alphabet through their abysmal ignorance. Yes, yes, in his published speeches he has made the joke about the letter and the litter. Built against the misty gardens of poets, his office is a laboratory and testament to the developing science of the alphabet. Science, not the aimless magic of poetry.

The office, housed in Pér, is a model of busy stillness. Bookcases line several walls, and each and every case is filled with not only books—some in old leather bindings, others in cheap and yellowed paperback; some stacked horizontally like brickwork, others vertically like chimneys; some with spines showing, and others with spines invisible—but also framed photos, toy mice with toy tea sets, origami albatrosses, Guatemalan woven bookmarks and feather clumps. All an accumulation of his history, the gifts of those many from whom he has forceped words.

Here, in the office, he keeps his historical collection of tongues, though many are in constant circulation as he mails them in envelopes to admirers and enemies.

Here he keeps his skeleton grammars. Here he has the tweezers to capture the smell of the alphabet.

His greatest obsession, though, is his collection of fragmented studies of psychotic typographies. These stem from the patients suffering not from silences but those wracked by errant writings, those who intend their pens to write grocery lists and well wishings to grandparents but find instead arcane zodiacs spilling manically across notepads. Their sensibilities twist into occult symbols for dark magical rites they themselves cannot understand. The Alphabet Doctor has spent many years pondering these parallel alphabets, dream typographies that resist their writer's control. His interest lies not in translation but getting to the root of the process by which such anti-alphabets emerge against will. For all the years devoted to these endeavours, only fragments have come to him with no certain conclusions. Notebook upon notebook of daemonic signs that fascinate and elude.

Yes, yes, he has otherwise felt many successes. The trophies on the shelves claim victories. But more and more, they seem markers of vacancy, just signs of emptiness recalling his subjects' earlier aphasias.

Outside the office, in Pér, and to the lands beyond Százia, problems grow. Weak-tongued choirs no longer sing but shout clusters of sounds. Onomatopoeic yelps echo in the streets. More and more syllabic victims seek the return of the sensible sounds they once knew and pound on his door aching to stop the regurgitating linguistic backwash.

But as the cases grow, the Alphabet Doctor, jaded, finds he no longer believes in his profession. Recently failure has crept its way into his world. Healer or huckster? The letters he has amassed in the drawers and jars of his office no longer seem to do anything—placebos all?—with no relevance to the world he is supposed to serve. He placates a community of mutes who need to believe in the doctor's trade, even as they secretly distrust his practice as some dark alchemy that summons spirits we are not meant to know. Why is the Alphabet Doctor the only one who gets to rearrange people's words? Why is he their master, with his two-story apartment in the middle of the Old Town?

The boy enters the Doctor's waiting room.

The room.

More disconcerting to him is the Doctor's demeanour. If the boy could summon words to his mouth he might say the Doctor is a curmudgeonly, cantankerous ass.

But only a hiss of air comes out.

"Say what you will," says the Doctor, "but a professional of my sort need not be lovable nor even likable. And I have earned the right to be as sick of this career and of all who come through those doors as I damn well please."

The boy is caught off guard by this seeming act of telepathy, this reading of the inside of him that even he himself cannot decipher.

The Doctor approaches the boy and taps his skull with his pencil, "This head isn't good enough? You have to invent another one?"

The tests begin.

The boy lies back in the long, narrow wooden chair, his arms strapped down.

The Doctor brings out his tools and the boy shakes as he sees surgical knives and more mysterious instruments laid out on a metal tray.

Tremors take his body.

But the Doctor does not bring the cutters toward him. Instead he takes a scalpel and begins to cut into a ream of paper, marking shapes. Less writing than calligraphic drawing. In the lines carved into the paper, pools of blood emerge.

The boy feels a tremor inside his head stretching down into his throat.

A sickly bile rises.

The Doctor brings forth a small bowl as brown liquid pours from the boy's mouth, littered with amber letters.

"Ah, you have the language of trees and inferno," says the Doctor cryptically. "Not so common."

The boy tries to reply but only more fluid comes.

"Not yet," the Doctor says. "This language you have in you tells me you have many lies, lies you do not know you have."

More tests.

With the bloodied paper pile now coagulated into text, ready to be filed and assigned its letter, the boy feels shapes come up his throat.

The Doctor pats the boy's arm and with coloured pencils begins to write a series of glyphs along his neck.

Slowly words come, but not the words he wants.

"Fragrance! Baskets! Monkeypaw!"

"Good," says the Doctor. "You nearly return."

More text in more shades cover the boy's neck as the clusters in his mouth take clearer and clearer shape in his mind.

He feels the story mixed with bile come up.

"No," says the Doctor. "Yes, you have the story, I know. I know you want to tell it. But you have it wrong."

"You don't know do you?" asks the Doctor.

The boy blinks vacantly.

"What story has been told you about your sister?"

Words piling into order, slowly, the boy tells him of the great disappearance.

Says the Doctor, "Wrong, wrong. All this cursing and carving into human flesh. All this creation of new golems for new worlds. Cut your name into my head! You don't know. You don't know."

The boy gawps and words form, "Why curse and carve? What I don't know?"

"You see, what you don't know about the letters is that to read them is to know, to bring precise order to internal chaos. The letters, when you hold them, hold all of what you are. People let go of the letters because they don't want to know who they are, what they have done."

"Why curse and carve?"

"Like you, your sister lost all her words and your father considered her a dead thing. That day you think she disappeared was the day he took her out to the work shed, laid her on the workbench, grabbed a knife and carved letters into her forehead, thinking he would bring her to life again, to have her letters again."

"But she disappeared."

"She did not disappear. Your father killed her and took her body deep into the woods."

The boy recoils.

"You see, what your father tried to do was emulate my own craft. He wanted to bring the words out of the girl. But he was no scientist. He probably thought himself a poet, but what he was was a butcher. All this business with carving knives. Cutting into the flesh, cutting some accursed alphabet into the girl's forehead. Of course he could not bring her tongue out through so many wounds. Instead he carved directly into her heart. No reviving, no lingual rebirth, only clumsy slaughter.

"This your mother knows also to be the truth. Your parents are not stuck in tradition or lost in tragedy. They are just perfectly insane."

Here a strange thing happens.

Of course the boy breaks into tears, melting the colored markings on his neck. The Doctor has seen this all too many times before. He begins to tidy and stow his tools.

But then the boy says haltingly, "No, Doctor I don't think you understand."

The Doctor pauses. "Yes? I know such things can be hard to grasp. This will take time."

The boy says, "No, I do understand. I know what you tell me is true."

The Doctor is caught off guard and returns his gaze to the boy and unstraps his arms from the tall chair.

Reaching for the desk, the boy grabs a pen and the bloodied paper of his own cure.

He scrawls tiny strange spirals inside triangles across the sheets in an alphabet that Doctor has not seen before. Here lies a new psychotic typography! And yet, for once, something sensible emerges that shocks the Doctor.

The boy keeps writing and writing, occasionally looking at the Doctor.

And the Doctor can read this anti-alphabet in which the boy tells stories. Fantastical tales of horned beasts dancing in iced geographies; mermaids crossing lava bridges; Laplandic gods singing in chromium. The stories are not true yet they are not the lies the boy had been told or the truths he had refused to recognize. These strange lines and what they say resemble nothing in the Doctor's world. But he begins to believe something profound, even though he is profoundly wrong.

Is this poetry in the boy's hand? The Doctor realizes and fears that the boy's imaginary stories could be a kind of key to the psychotic typographies he has so desperately tried to understand. Damned if it is to be art and poetry that is to be the key he needed all along.

Eyeing the boy's face, a kind of light turns on inside the Alphabet Doctor. He feels a rejuvenation. The more the boy writes and fills his own head with marvelous tales the more he finally feels his cynicism and disappointment start to wane.

But at the dawn of this epiphany, the Doctor feels a shaking. The tremors he induces in his patients as part of their cure, the tremors he has just induced in this odd young boy, now come from outside the boy's body. Earthquake tremors rattle the office as bottles of aphasia fall from the shelves. The doors to his office spring open and he can see all of Pér shaking. Files and catalogue cards fly from their shelves as letters of the alphabet flow in streams out through the open doors in a river of meaningless syllables, a flood of fluid silences.

People in the winding streets come and scoop up clumps of alphabet, shoving Bs and Rs in their mouths, saving Qs and Zhs in pockets to savor later on. But these are all dead letters, tainted by silence and the dark magic of the boy's hand. This is no cure in the Doctor's mode, for the boy and his mad family's lineage turns everything into the psychotic typographies that have obsessed the Doctor for so long.

With anti-alphabets filling the streets of Pér, the Százian people—plagued in recent months by a different kind of silence only the Doctor had a cure for—drunkenly absorb this new void, this liberating silence that ends all sensibility and meaning. The abyss of the Real overwhelms them and they feel a freedom they have never known and cannot express or understand. Are they suffering or in joy? Aching or ecstatic? Unsaid revolutionary slogans: No more guilt over repressed pasts they do not want to tell. Instead the glory of inarticulate panic. No longer the prison of submissive speechlessness. Instead the sovereignty of the incomprehensible.

Psychosis fills the streets as people gather pebbles, wire, bolts, string, straw, broken clocks, dead birds, wilted flowers and egg shells to replace the old alphabets. A glorious dream of violence fills the hearts of all. They run through the streets with their mouths open, no longer needed for expression, spilling out vomit. A dreamy mayhem ensues. People grab one another, desperate to rip open the skin of strangers. Pushing and punching, thrashing and throttling. Pebbles, wire and bird beaks become tools to carve zodiac flesh tattoos. Limbs are torn from torsos. One small group seeks infants to alter young bodies that will no longer need eyes or mouths.

And the boy keeps writing.

The Alphabet Doctor stands in the doorframe of his ruined office, looks out onto the streets of blood and illness, breathes in the air of incoherence, and smiles.

Crash With Shopping Trolleys

By Rhys Hughes

Mrs Hamilton died yesterday in her last trolley-crash. During my time as assistant-manager of the supermarket she had rehearsed her death on many occasions, but this was her only true accident. I was talking to one of the checkout girls when I heard a loud screech coming from Frozen Foods. Mrs Hamilton had skidded on a wet patch left by a negligent cleaner and gyrated out of control toward one of the freezers. The lid had been left open by another customer and the impact hurled her body into the gaping compartment. By the time I reached the scene, ice-crystals were already forming in the wrinkles of her face.

Laura, the checkout girl, accompanied me and nervously fingered her blonde highlights as she peered over the side. The internal lamps of the refrigerator cast a sterile glow over her features, as if their photons had turned brittle and were splintering against the inflamed sebaceous follicles of her cheeks. Her voice betrayed numb concern. "Shouldn't we help her? I think she's still alive!"

This compassion was inappropriate. The chilly security of the freon sarcophagus was too perfect to violate. I shook my handsome head. "No, it's unhygienic. Leave her in peace with the *petits-poit* and oven-chips. She would have wanted it this way."

Gently, I closed the lid and escorted Laura back to the till where an agitated crowd had gathered, armed with credit cards and money-off coupons. Later, when I returned to Frozen Foods, the body had stopped twitching. The compartment would have to be defrosted and chlorinated after closing-time. Until then, it was necessary to block the aisle to discourage voyeurs. I ordered plastic cones to be placed at either end and positioned a security guard near the thermostat. It was a far cry from Mrs Hamilton's planned demise, in Condiments, on the jagged corners of a hundred ketchup bottles. She had mapped the tiles of the floor, calculating the number of rivulets her life-blood would form as it fled her veins. Had she seen in the haemorrhagic hues of the tomato sauce the symbolic spectrum of her martyrdom?

Until accepting my post at Safebury's, my experience of supermarket death was confined to isolated acts of aisle-rage in a cut-price chain in the centre of town. These hyperstores on the periphery of the city, rising from a landscape of concrete car-parks and weed verges, were far more lethal. Many of the staff considered the building to be a theatre of spilled organs, as if the whole process of shopping was a throwback to the ancient circuses. The trolleys themselves, mesh frames recalling the nets of a retiarius gladiator, had been designed by a committee as anonymous as the one which originated tridents and short-swords. This vaudeville of violence and sex was epitomised by the rush for reduced items in the Bakery department, where customers would compete for stale Bakewell tarts, arranged to resemble the breasts of anaemic girls, like libertines fighting over harlots.

I was introduced to Mrs Hamilton by Becker, my immediate superior. He pointed her out while we were touring Biscuits. A diminutive figure, she seemed to steer her trolley like a charioteer cracking her tongue at illusory steeds. As I watched, she struck a small child playing near the custard-creams and I was treated to a momentary shower of splayed limbs and artificially sweetened crumbs. Oblivious of our presence, she parked next to the fig-rolls and furiously began to stock up. Even then I noted that her motions corresponded to a personal algebra whose variables and constants were polyunsaturated.

"It's the inertia," Becker informed me. "The more weight in her trolley, the more damage it will do in a crash. She's one of our best customers; always goes for bulk."

Shortly after this event, I commenced an affair with Laura, timing our relationship by the speed at which her highlights grew out. When the roots had reclaimed her head she promised we would consummate our desire among the soft cheeses of the Delicatessen. With care this might even be accomplished during opening-hours. Laura drove me to distraction with her pale thighs, visible as her gingham uniform rode over her knees when she sat on the swivel-chair at the checkout. I suspect that sliding the Visa cards through the groove in the till was an erotic act for her, but one devoid of warmth and sensitivity. I wondered what her feelings were as she dealt with each customer's produce, fondling the goods to line up the bar-codes with the sensors and then discarding them with a casual flick toward a mound of plastic-bags layered as carefully as bedsheets in a hospice for the terminally ill. An urge to present myself to her in a trolley, to be similarly handled, came over me, but I managed to repress it for the sake of my job.

Laura was the physical opposite of Mrs Hamilton, yet they seemed to complement each other. Whenever the two met at the checkout, I envisaged a sperm struggling through a cervical fissure toward a reluctant ovary. Mrs Hamilton's jars of instant coffee and tins of sweetcorn, her veggie burgers and packets of tortillas, her boxes of cornflakes and bottles of balsamic vinegar, appeared to impregnate Laura's till, swelling its womb with a loss-leader foetus. Like a neon triangle born from a warping of rectilinear geometries, I expected this entity, the ultimate product of consumer-oriented evolution, to emerge from the receipt outlet in a roll of new improved flesh and non-biological bone.

At the terminus of my inaugural month at Safebury's, I witnessed my first spectacular trolley-crash. A customer who had entered the building from the adjacent

Housebase store with a mop protruding from his vehicle collided with a hydrophobe who had arranged an umbrella in an analogous position. Like jousting accountants they straightened their ties in the last seconds before impact. The handle of the mop caught the thyroid of the hydrophobe, while the tip of his umbrella penetrated the eye of his adversary. Cartilage and iris burst simultaneously, sounding like a kiss between an armadillo and a toad, and then both customers collapsed onto the mosaic floor. I was cognizant of Mrs Hamilton leering across from another aisle, tunnelling through a pyramid of baked-beans for a better view. Other shoppers arrived to gawp and I realised Laura had deserted her till and was rubbing herself against a tower of ideal-milk. There was liquid on her thighs, though whether from orgasm, ruptured tin or spraying eye was impossible to determine.

I cleared the area rapidly, wary of looters and necrophiles. Mrs Hamilton had reached the site of the accident and was lightly touching the wheels and chassis of each twisted trolley before moving her fingers to her sagging breasts, as if directly absorbing a wonky sensuality. I gripped her by the elbow and she responded by clutching my genitals. I was startled by way her fingers guided my penis within my trousers, as if she intended to steer my scrotum toward the checkout while leaving the rest of my body behind. I slapped her wrist and called for Security. Laura came to my rescue, placing her pricing-gun against the hag's face and pressing the trigger until her skull became a bargain. Mrs Hamilton, blinded by the sticky labels, disengaged with a crisp, overpackaged wail and scuttled away toward Toiletries.

Becker and I raided the damaged trolleys for the pound-coins. This was a distasteful but profitable business. I saved my share over several weeks to take Laura to the cinema. Bathed in the flickering shadows of a horror film, dipping into a bucket of popcorn like a spider fishing for sperm, I was able to consider the parameters of consumerism at leisure. The extreme metaphors of mashed-potato, tetrahedral tea-bags and castor sugar were far more disturbing than the images of blood and violation which faced me on the screen. Laura appeared to share my thoughts; she panted with disappointment at the panoply of celluloid violence which pulsed high above. The natural environment of real horror, we realised, was among the shredded wheat and pâté of Safebury's most unlucky aisles, where the greedy desires and tender fantasies of shoppers were fused in a sudden alchemy of trolley and driver. Broken arms, thighs cubed by the wire-mesh, tongues caught in axles: these were the dehydrated archetypes of contemporary fear and loathing.

The imprint of Mrs Hamilton's fingers remained on my penis like tabasco stains on a gherkin. I tried unsuccessfully to wash them away in the shower, exciting myself in the process and extrapolating a fantasy which involved Laura and a whole basement of baby-food. At the moment of climax, her face was replaced by Mrs Hamilton's and I recoiled in shock, slipping on a bar of soap and striking my head on a faucet. Blood flowed down the plug-hole like herbaceous pasta sauce. I bandaged the wound and staggered to bed, where my dreams were full of runaway trolleys speeding through an Escher-like mall, collecting bodies instead of groceries from the infinite rows of palladium shelves.

My obsession with our best customer intensified after an especially gory incident in Fresh Vegetables. A single mother had committed suicide by slashing her wrists on the edge of a ripe starfruit and her abandoned baby, perched on the collapsible trolley seat like an economy-sized sack of mischief, was howling and struggling to free its legs from the holes in the side of the contraption. I was reminded of a prisoner trapped in the stocks as Becker came up and ordered me to wheel the orphan out of the store to await suitable foster parents at the bottle-bank. While I was swerving around an edifice of bananas, a myopic hippy with a basket full of organic mushrooms suddenly lurched in my path. I braked sharply and the deceleration caused the collapsible seat to slam shut. Milk teeth and bile erupted over the hippy, smudging his little round glasses and matting his technophobic beard.

With the aid of half a cucumber, I levered the seat open to inspect the damage. The child resembled a barbecued tin of Chicken Korma. As his cloven legs dropped to the floor, followed by the contents of his nappy, I saw that his undeveloped penis was also marked with crimson sores. Was Mrs Hamilton somehow responsible for the arbitrary chaos which defined the character of Safebury's? Had she condemned me to a similar fate with her touch, like an irradiated Midas?

From that moment I checked the inside of every victim's underwear before allowing the bodies to be removed. Both male and female corpses betrayed signs of prior meetings with Mrs Hamilton. I confided in Becker but he was dismissive, claiming she had once grabbed his lingam without ill effects. As far as he was concerned, such conspiracy theories were examples of boil-in-the-bag paranoia.

"I've been driving trolleys for a decade," he said, "and I've had a couple of near misses, but nothing serious. It comes down to experience, knowing how to anticipate the actions of other consumers. I don't accept your ridiculous destiny hypothesis."

Three days later, Becker was killed when his trolley suffered a blow-out in Wines & Spirits. The shattered wheel span through the air, lodging in the head of a teetotaller, while my immediate superior tried to jump from his stricken vehicle. His tie caught in the mesh and he was dragged into an island display of imported beer. He was marooned there for nearly a whole afternoon, unable to cross the busy aisles to safety. The official cause of death was alcohol poisoning, but I believe it was a shandy of despair and embarrassment.

I decided to do some research on Mrs Hamilton. Something in the way she knotted her faded scarf convinced me she had once attended the local university. I spent an hour in the college library, checking the titles and authors of graduate dissertations. At last I found what I wanted: a doctoral thesis which Mrs Hamilton had submitted fifty years earlier. It had been rejected by the examiners as far-fetched, but as I read through it, I realised it provided formulae for a new sexuality. I photocopied relevant passages and took them to Laura.

"That old harpy trained to be a psychologist," I mused, handing her the pages. "The thrust of her argument concerned traditional similes for regenerative organs. If a car really is an extension of the penis, then a car-crash must be a symbol of male orgasm. Mrs Hamilton tried to show by analogy that the shopping trolley is an extension of the vagina and that the trolley-crash is a symbol of female orgasm, which is much more intense than the male version."

My promotion delighted Laura and her highlights started to grow out more rapidly. But I was too intent on watching the movements of Mrs Hamilton to anticipate the textures of soft cheese. She seemed to be observing me in turn: more than once I caught her seizing the genitals of other customers. Invariably these were killed in trolley-crashes and I began to perceive a pattern in her shopping habits. Often she lingered in Condiments, running her callused thumbs over the bottles of ketchup, obviously planning some monumental act of carnage, but waiting for a missing factor to prompt her into action.

Last week, Laura came sobbing to me, throwing herself into my arms and staining my shirts with tears harder than olive-stones. She had been attacked at the checkout by Mrs Hamilton. Hunkering down in the shadows of Soft Drinks, she showed me the marks on her vulva, like a desiccated steak spotted with cheap wine. It was plain we both formed part of some ready-washed matrix, an amalgam of ecstasy and additives. Laura, whose brain is bijou but piquant, like a sample tub of wholegrain mustard, was incoherent for the remainder of her shift and I decided to confront her assailant, throwing her out of the supermarket if necessary, despite the reduction in profits this would entail. I borrowed a knife from Kitchen Accessories and eventually tracked Mrs Hamilton down at the junction between Pet Foods and Detergents.

She greeted my approach with a jumbo smile of triumph. At once I was alerted to an unspecified danger. Even my revenge attack was part of her scheme. I turned to regard a pair of trolleys bearing down on me at converging angles. There was no time to avoid them. Steered by hunched geriatrics with hearing-aids, they rolled onward with the implacability of a twin-pack glacier. Suddenly inspired, I dropped my trousers and severed my penis with a single stroke of the knife, hurling it onto a ziggurat of cheese-and-onion quiches, where it came to rest upright like a radio-mast with a glans beacon.

My desperate ploy worked. The trolleys collided before reaching me, breaking the backs of their drivers and leaving them to flop among the spilled cat-biscuits, until their death throes powered them into a duck and beef sand-sea which reflected the glare of the fluorescent lighting like a vermilion beach. I glanced up, but Mrs Hamilton had disappeared. I hobbled back to Laura, handed her the serrated knife and urged her to eviscerate her own privates. She responded to my shrill tone with arched eyebrows but took the blade and poked under her gingham uniform until a waterfall of gore bearing two swollen lips flooded the floor, indicating a successful act of auto-mutilation.

When we recovered, I explained my demand. “It’s Mrs Hamilton. She’s been arranging all these accidents. I was nearly run over just now, but managed to save myself by lopping my member. It removed a vital variable from the loins of her equation.”

Laura gaped at me wordlessly, so I led her gently down the aisles of my theory. Mrs Hamilton had found a way to control Safebury’s entire clientele, probably by setting a paradigm with her own shopping habits. Each packet of sesame-seeds, carton of milk or bag of crisps she removed from the shelves determined the actions of her peers. By controlling the availability of certain items in different locations and making constant adjustments to these myriad variables she was able to circulate victims down predetermined paths to an overpriced apocalypse. Our genitals were a modulus in this web, turning our negative feelings about shopping into a positive drive of passion. Castration disrupted the sequence, like an asparagus spear thrust into a calculus textbook. Without sexual organs, the melodies of mayhem were silent.

Our sexuality was already dominated by a consumer environment. When Laura and I came to choose prosthetic replacements for our genitals, we had little hesitation. We never directly encountered Mrs Hamilton after this, though we glimpsed her often, flitting from aisle to aisle with a troubled expression. Her operation had been thrown out of phase. Instead of the multiple pile-up in Condiments which she hoped would encompass the entire population of Safebury's, like an aneurism of the sun, she came to a more modest end in Frozen Foods. In the college library, with thumbs as anaesthetised as fish-fingers, I searched through the other dissertations, discovering that after failing psychology, Mrs Hamilton had enrolled on a mathematics course. This combination of emotional and analytic symbolism proved a fatal mix, allowing her to plot a graph of human nature against sex and edibles.

Now we are free, Laura and I feel we have inherited her vision. The highlights are almost gone. Soon we will cavort among the camembert and brie. Laura will tear off my trousers to reveal a Visa card stitched in place of my lingam; I will hoist up her uniform to reveal an appropriate groove. Then I will slide it through her sensor until we both expire. Meanwhile, the trolleys move in an unceasing flow along the aisles. The shoppers waltz around the displays of promotional goods, carrying their aseptic lusts from the secret recesses of the supermarket to the plastic bosoms of a million checkout girls.

The Incarnations of Zuji
By Lawrence Russell

The Island

It looks like a nice day when standing on the headland looking over the channel at the paradisal hue of the South China Sea, although it isn't, the weather aside. Colonel Zuji removes the glove on his right hand, snaps his fingers irritably at his adjutant Lieutenant Meccano who is standing beside the black staff car looking melancholy, perhaps because he knows his days of gadding about town in a sleek 1938 Toyota Type A saloon are over. He responds smartly, hurries to Zuji's side, hands him a pair of 7 by 50 binoculars, standard Japanese military issue. Standing together, both men look similar—five foot two or three, disciplined postures in tight green tunics and wearing knock-off German officer hats with short visors. Their boots and britches are hold-overs from the days when officers rode horses and war was conducted with swords, although the Japanese Imperial Army still has a fondness for the *shin gunto*, the curved sword considered *pro forma* for combat experienced officers.

Zuji raises the binoculars, tries to focus on the long barge that sits anchored about two Chinese miles distant. He can see the prisoners are lined up and that the executions are underway. But the action lacks focus, so he removes his prince-nez spectacles, hands them to Meccano to hold while he tries to assess the situation again. Far from being tense, his face has the relaxed, benign musculature of a friendly school teacher or a transcendental priest. He adjusts focus. Now he can see clearly, the executioner moving quickly behind the line of the condemned, shooting each in turn in the back of head, each man falling over the side into the water to join the litter of dead bodies already floating around the barge like a congestion of storm debris. The executioner barely pauses in his grim ritual, even when the 8 shot clip of his Nambu automatic expends as a soldier in attendance always has another fully-loaded pistol to hand off like a relay runner. It's all very efficient. Minimal mess, no witnesses … or at least, none who matter.

Now Meccano is having a look.

He sighs, shakes his head.

"This could be called a war crime, Colonel."

Zuji extends his hand, takes back the binoculars, continues watching. The shots are faint, even though the barge is no more than 2/3rds of an English mile away.

"Criminals," murmurs Zuji.

Meccano knows the Colonel considers them Chinese gang members because many have the triangle tattoo on the lower wrist. This is considered proof positive ... but was it? Certain monks affected such decorations, and what about the dozen or so women in the group? And those white men? They didn't get justice, none of them. They just walked in the wrong door and the lazy *dekisokonai* condemned them for walking through that door. There are two doors, and either can be an entrance or exit. They toss a coin, decide which door represents guilt or innocence for the day, leave judgement to the gods. A sham. Not *bushido*. Bad karma.

And Meccano knows the Colonel designated the "guilty" door for today. Pluto ... in private, some of the soldiers call the Colonel "Pluto". A joke, yes, but not disrespectful. He has hidden power within his darkness.

"Today is a bad day," says Meccano stiffly. "The war is over."

"Is it?" says Zuji. "Lieutenant, the war is never over."

"Sir, the Emperor ...."

He can't finish the sentence.

"Don't believe it, Lieutenant. Imperialist propaganda. We never surrender."

The Voice of India shortwave has broadcast a report of the surrender that included the Emperor's speech. The Colonel heard it and in fact had already seen the wire dispatch from the Imperial General Army HG in the mountains near Nagano, Japan, that morning. Cowards. All because the enemy had dropped a couple of big bombs on the homeland.

"Courage, Lieutenant," the Colonel says, his voice softening.
He liked Meccano, pitied the wound he carried, the limp he acquired when serving on the Mongolian border.

"Remember—Asia for the Asians."

"Yes, sir."

A wind gust comes off the sea, carrying warm rain drops that strike them in the face and rattle against the car. Change in the weather? It's that time of year, end of the dry season, and a Sumatra Squall could be coming. It's time to get out of here.

He takes one last look at the barge. He sees a tall lanky white man drop off the barge and the way he goes into the water suggests that he isn't dead, that the bullet missed. It happens. A hand can only remain steady so long and the mind drifts with it. Does anyone notice? Apparently not. Does he remember this individual? Occasionally he'd glanced through the observational port, monitored the tribunals' activities. There were some whites that morning. Escaped POWs ... one or two local traders ... a soldier of fortune ... all worthy of death, yet, as unbelievers, unworthy of reincarnation.

Rain drops blur the lenses of the binoculars and the clouds darken as they start to roll in from the south east. Zuji swaps back the binoculars for his eye-glasses and orders Meccano to drive him back to town. As they pass the big hotel where many of the officers like to get drunk and consort with whores, there are sporadic gunshots. Yes, some of them are taking the easy way out. One even jumps from a fourth floor window and nearly impacts on the hood of their black saloon. Meccano glances at Zuji, but Zuji remains unperturbed. So let them kill themselves. The Buddha will rejoice in their sacrifice. Colonel Zuji knows that many of his colleagues have reserved rooms and will be unsheathing their swords for the ritual act of *seppuku*.

That evening, before the first enemy parachute drops, the Colonel sends Lieutenant Meccano on a mission: one, to find some robes, preferably a brown *rakusu* signifying a learned monk, one who has received dharma transmission and is worthy of respect, and two, a bicycle in good working order. Meccano returns with robes, sandals, and a green English Raleigh, complete with chain guard, rubber pedals, splash guards, working brakes and headlight for night riding. As usual, his adjutant never fails.

"When are you leaving, sir?"

"Immediately. Before the causeway is closed and no one, not even a General, will be able to leave."

Zuji is in his underclothes, his uniform discarded on the bed nearby. He has just shaven his head.

As he dons the robes and sandals, he says, "How are the streets?"

Meccano's eyes flicker around the room … the solid furnishings, the grandfather clock, all English, part of the appropriation when they first arrived here. Only the paintings were removed, sentimental British landscapes which now exist as ghostly outlines on the fading plaster. On the desk is a framed photo of a woman—Mitsu, the Colonel's wife, whom he hasn't seen in at least two years. She's young here, probably photographed early in their marriage. The Colonel seldom mentions her name. War permits amnesia.

"Lawless, sir. People are getting drunk. The military police are being attacked and the domestic police are …."

"Getting drunk. Where did you get the bicycle?"

"Captain Saburo. He's gone to the hotel. He won't be needing it anymore."

The Colonel nods, goes to his desk, opens a lower drawer, extracts a large steel bayonet.

"Aren't you taking a pistol, sir?"

"Monks never use pistols. This will do."

He slips it below his robes, hooks it to a hidden belt.

"You'll need beads, sir."

The Colonel smiles, finds a string in his desk.

"Chinese *mala*," he says. "The real thing."

Meccano moves to the bed, touches the uniform.

"Shall I burn this?"

"Don't be silly—I'm promoting you, Mecca."

In his sentimental moments, the Colonel uses "Mecca" as a diminutive.

"Captain … you mean I'm a Captain?"

"Nonsense … think big, Mecca. I'm making you a Colonel."

Meccano isn't slow. While the Colonel never mentioned it before when he outlined his plan to escape the island dressed as a Buddhist monk, it's obvious what his superior is suggesting … no, demanding.

"Put on the uniform, Mecca. It will fit."

Meccano finds he is trembling, hopes Zuji doesn't notice. He's conflicted because like many other officers in the local command, he views Zuji as a military genius and would do anything for him, give up his life if asked, and it appeared he was now being asked. The enemy had a bounty on Zuji's head, although some said this was just partisan disinformation. But Meccano believes it. He's seen Colonel Zuji in operation, knows he works outside the Geneva Convention.

"No one will ever believe I'm Zuji."

"For a first impression, they'll accept you as Zuji. We all look the same to them. Monkeys, yes?"

Meccano has collected himself. He was a warrior once and can be again. He puts on the uniform and it fits not bad. The medals —The Order of the Sacred Treasure … the Golden Kite … the Rising Sun … yes, he could be *Bushido*, real *gekokujo* like the Master, he who masterminded the invasion plans … here, there, everywhere in the Empire of the Sun.

Now he is Pluto, the higher octave of Mars, the god of war.

"I expect they'll execute me," says Meccano.

"Why would they, Colonel?" says Zuji. "You're an asset, have valuable knowledge … and anyway, so what? You'll live again."

"Will I? I can't even remember what I was before."

Meccano has never been good on religious theory. After he was wounded and nearly died in Mongolia, he just concentrated on the life at hand. As the Colonel's adjutant, he was close to the action but not in the action anymore. Life with the Colonel, while dangerous at times, was really the life of a tourist.

"A warrior must always be ready for the unexpected."

Meccano nods, braces himself. He's expecting Zuji to draw that bayonet and kill him, leave his body as a substitute. No acting required.

But Zuji is wheeling the bicycle to the door. Instinctively, Meccano hurries ahead to open it.

"I must say farewell, Mecca. Time is of the essence."

Strange. Zuji's face really does look spiritual, like a relaxed family Buddha. The kindly eyes behind the orbular spectacles, the slightly cleft chin. He could fool anyone. He never was in Manchuria or the Philippines.. or the peninsula and the island. Yes, he could fool anyone.

"By the way, Mecca, what would you like to be when you come back?"

"A bird."

"A bird. Good choice."

"And you, sir?"

"Oh … a communist."

Lieutenant Meccano follows his old boss to the street, watches as he pedals off into the night. Asia is full of communists. These days it's the thing. Meccano feels more relaxed now. As they say, "Lose the war, win the peace."

He's reading a copy of *Viet Soir,* the leading newspaper this side of the mountains that stretch all the way from the Chinese border to the jungles of Siam. It's in French, which he can read and speak because he studied it in military school, and because he's been living in a modest devotee's shack in the woods adjacent to the Wat Moon Blossom temple … and while the location is secluded and very few of the French colonials pay attention to this lost shrine, occasionally he descends to the town by the river to conduct whatever business needs to be conducted and often business is French.

How many people know "Viet" means 'descendants of a dragon soaring to the sun'? he reflects as he sips his ginger tea, a palliative he's taken to recently because of mild bladder pain. He doesn't smoke, despite the fact that nearly everyone smokes, especially the war amputees in the street, who will smoke nearly anything that burns. His eyes move idly this way and that. The cafe front opens onto the pavement, French-style, exposed to the hawkers—few today—and the street hustle of bicycles, rickshaws, motorcycles, trucks and dusty cars that resemble insects, nearly always driven by Chinese of the merchant class or shifty white colonials posturing between divine arrogance and modern anxiety. They think they won. They think the Indochine is theirs again. He sighs … but does he really care?

The news … does he really need it? Most days he wanders the wooded trails in the benign parts of the mountain jungle, visiting forgotten shrines where the stone Buddhas stare at you from a thicket, or from the path you walk, sunk into the earth in a slow burial, face to the stars … if there are any stars to be seen. There are contemplation platforms, some stone, some wooden, facing luxuriant valleys and the blaze of the rising sun … or specially aligned for the transit of the moon goddess.

Of course the sanctity of the mountain isn't free from the vagabond tourist, the foreigner who comes seeking enlightenment rather than gold. These false poets carry their imperialism with the unwitting innocence of children.

He flips a page, resettles his glasses … here we go, here's a good example:

'**He came seeking Zen but found Death instead.** The body of a missing Australian tourist who came to Laos to study Zen Buddhism was found last week caught in the pilings of the Stone Jar dock. A spokesperson for the *Police Royale Laotienne* suspect the man was murdered and his body dumped in the Elephant River up stream. Robbery was not a motive as the deceased had his credentials in a belt wallet. He is said to be a white male in his thirties and a veteran of the Australian armed forces. The investigation is on going.'

He chuckles, swats away a fly. "On going—everything is "on going", a phrase that means absolutely nothing. A large dusty green Citroen saloon honks its way through the traffic, waits until a peasant ox-cart moves out of the way, then parks across the street outside the block of ramshackle arcade businesses that conceal their wares in shadow. No one gets out of the car. Waiting for someone, he thinks. Could it be him? He is always on guard, especially when away from his refuge on the mountain. The feeling of being hunted never leaves, even when the mind is engaged in transcendental exercise.

He remembers the Australian, if it's the same Australian. Young. He showed up at the temple one day and stuck around with the other collection of wanderers, the small community who lived in the huts with the simplicity and devotion to the Buddha of the holy men of the poetic past who rejected materialism in their search for perfection.

"How do you see the universe, Master?"

"Violent."

"But isn't harmony possible?"

"It is possible."

"How?"

"Tonight is the new moon. Meet me by the river at the rising and I will show you."

He'd seen the tattoo on the young man's forearm, although the young man had been careful to keep it concealed. He didn't recognize the face but he recognized why he was here.

When the first triangle appears on Zuji's right arm he is puzzled, perhaps a little disturbed. It looks like a tattoo ... but is it? The lines are soft and green, like a track left by a jungle worm. There's no sensation or any perturbance such as a parasite or a needle in the night might make. Perhaps he was poisoned. Perhaps the Australian dosed his tea. And the more he looks at the triangle, the more he remembers the prisoners he sent to the barge for the final clean-up.

On the second page of *Viet Soir* his eye catches a headline: WHAT HAPPENED TO COLONEL ZUJI? His heart surges briefly. The article is a reprint from the *Japan Times*, now rendered in French.

'It is six years since Colonel Zuji, an Imperial Army officer, veteran of the South Pacific War and architect of the peninsula campaign, disappeared into the jungle disguised as a Buddhist monk. Nothing has been heard of his whereabouts since, although rumours are plentiful. Last week the Japanese government declared Zuji to be dead, following a petition by his wife Mitsu so that she could receive the pension due to a widow of an army officer.

'The circumstances around Zuji's escape and disappearance are indeed peculiar. His adjutant Lieutenant Ashai Meccano tried to impersonate Zuji and was subsequently abducted by a vigilante group of Malayan Chinese widows who stabbed him to death and dumped his body in the South China Sea as retribution for Zuji's policy of ethnic cleansing. Until recently this has been the official version of Meccano's fate. Now, a new story circulates among members of the government and armed forces: Meccano is not dead, has now changed his identity again to become an agent for the American CIA assigned to hunt down Colonel Zuji so that he can be returned to face charges as a war criminal.

'While some find this story to be laughable, many in Japan believe Zuji is still alive. In some veteran circles, he is viewed as a god, a warrior who would have led Japan to victory despite the atomic attacks on Hiroshima and Nagasaki ....'

He stops reading. Is this bad news, or could it actually be good news? His book is more or less finished, will be a bombshell when published in Japan, could play favourably within this unexpected publicity. He's a legend ... what did they say? "Viewed as a god". By the stars, this could be good luck. The business about Meccano being an agent for the Americans is pure rubbish, and even if it isn't, he can fit into the story even if he should show up at the temple one day and ring the bell. Meccano would never attempt to arrest his old Master.

The rest of the article profiles Zuji's career as a military strategist and his contributions to Japan's victories in Manchuria and the Pacific War, and—laughably—his credentials as a war criminal and war monger. He's blamed for everything, including "the Marco Polo Bridge" incident in Manchuria to the now notorious Bataan Death March. Crimes? There are no crimes in war—except losing, and this grieves him more than any personal insult.

He will have plenty to say on this subject.

He looks up, sees a woman get out of the back of the Citroen, start walking across the street. She walks well, not like a paddy peasant. Could be French, although the eyes are Vietnamese or Laotian.

She comes right up to his table.

"*Bonjour, monsieur. Puis-je m'asseoir?*"

He nods. She adjusts the rattan chair and sits down, removes one glove while leaving the other on. That hand appears stiff.

"I need help," she says as she signals the waiter.

The waiter comes over and she orders coffee, black, no milk, no sugar.

He guesses she is thirty something, a woman, not a girl, and a sophisticated woman at that. She will have a driver in that Citroen, a chauffeur with a gun.

"You need spiritual advice?" he says. "The message wasn't clear."

The message had been delivered by a young boy, a runner who came up the mountain, found him in his shack.

"You were recommended," she says.

He says nothing. He's suspicious, naturally, and he's amazed at himself for coming here, didn't panic and flee. Perhaps he's bored. Perhaps he needs to be reckless. Sometimes isolation eats the soul it feeds.

"Can I ask how you pass the time?"

"I'm writing a book."

"Memoirs?"

"Not exactly …"

"Oh? Poems, perhaps. Like Ho Chi Minh."

"Uncle Ho writes poetry?"

"You haven't read *Notebook from Prison*? No, I suppose not. Possibly you didn't know he'd been in prison."

"This I know. The Chinese confined him for a few months 'reeducation'. Poems, you say? Have you, er, read them?"

"I've read them."

"You amaze me."

"He calls for revolution."

"Naturally."

"You agree with that?"

"If the enemy has been correctly identified, yes."

"The Japanese 21st Division did."

"You amaze me. You know so much."

"Hmm. I know they killed many French."

"Asia for the Asians, madame."

"Yes … well let's just start with Indochine. Did you know many of your former Imperial Army defected, chose to stay here rather than be repatriated back to Japan?"

This isn't surprising. He's heard rumours.

"For women, I suppose. It won't be ideology."

"Anything wrong with our women, monsieur?"

He engages her eyes, locks on. She's as deeply magnetic and as mysterious as these kind of women can be. Her wooden hand, concealed by a soft black leather glove, makes her cruelly attractive. He wonders how she came by it, if she had been tortured or if it was just an accident. And she knows he wants to know. Honeytrap for the elite. Class warfare my ass.

"You are Eurasian."

"Anything wrong with that?"

"French, I expect."

"I am Vietnamese."

"A shot in the dark."

"You are a crude man … Monsieur Pluto."

She emphasizes the alias like she's dropping an ace on the table. *I have a dossier on you, monsieur. You think you chanced upon that newspaper article? We have been watching you, and are watching you now as you and I have this pleasant conversation in the shade of this pleasant colonial street cafe.*

She pushes a piece of paper across the table. A list. Names.

"You recognize these?"

He knows four. All officers.

"We have engaged their services."

"To write poetry?"

"Of course not. They will train our people to fight the remaining occupiers."

None of these people were communists … or at least they weren't when he knew them … if he really knew them to begin with.

"So, what do you want with me?"

"To run our new school."

She outlines the details of Ho's planned military school to be located in the highlands south-west of Hanoi, this side of the border … the border that no one pays attention to and certainly won't exist after the revolution.

"You would be in charge."

"Thank you but no, madame."

Her legs shift and his eyes flicker.

"Why are you saying no? Because you hate communists?"

"I'm a priest now. I think you know that."

She laughs. Not crudely, but mannered, like someone who has played politics in the salons of Paris and Hanoi.

"A guilty conscience, Pluto?"

"I never feel guilty. What have I to be guilty of?"

"Oh … certain incidents here and there … Manchuria, the Philippines. If you weren't now officially dead, you might be in chains on an aeroplane going somewhere you wouldn't like."

"You would do that to me?"

"Not me, monsieur."

"Your boss, 'the Enlightened One?"

His sarcasm is towards Ho Chi Minh, whose adopted name means 'He who enlightens'. Yes, no matter how much they babble about the brotherhood of man and the slavery of religion, these bent Stalinists still dress themselves in elitist religious symbolisms.

She lights a cigarette with her good hand, the one with the long fingers and elegant green nails. If these fingers ever pulled the trigger of a pistol, you wouldn't know it. But of course they did, he knows this. He wasn't top of his class at the military academy because he lacked the *samurai* instinct. This woman is dangerous.

"The gendarmes have a suspect."

"The police … for what? What crime?"

"You know—the murdered Australian they found at the Stone Jar dock."

Yes, this woman is dangerous. Strangely, illogically, he finds he is tense with excitement, his loins hardening. It's been years since he felt this way. He's been hiding in a transcendental slumber since the end of the war.

"You amaze me," he says thickly. "You know so much."

"Thank you. They're looking for a monk."

"A monk?"

"Yes, from Wat Moon Blossom. You might know him."

"Proof?"

"A witness, they say."

He recognizes the *fait accompli*. Accept our offer and the witness will disappear, poof. You, Monsieur Pluto, have something we want. Warrior intelligence for the modern soldier in service of the revolution. Jap fascists, French jackals. The graffiti of yesteryear trickles through his mind. Well, it might take more than blackmail to get him to sign on the dotted line. Yes, more. He will want her to remove that glove and reveal that prosthetic hand. He will want her to use that hand to beat him, transport him to the 7th plane. To feel pain is Buddha.

"When do I start?"

She nods slowly with amused satisfaction, then rises from the table. The action allows him to see the full dynamic of her figure. Beautiful. These colonial revolutionaries are getting better every year.

"Follow me, Monsieur Pluto."

Thus it comes to pass that Colonel Zuji abandons his masquerade as a monk and embraces the alias that his subordinate officers bestowed on him with grim whispers in the setting sun.

It's 1968 and Zuji has revived his identity as a Buddhist monk, this time as an itinerant traveller between the smaller temples and shrines in northern Laos that dot the mountains and valleys on what was a pilgrim's trail in olden times, destination the Golden Temple in Vientiane, Angkor Wat in Cambodia and holy places beyond. This morning he's on the contemplation platform above an old Vrong logging village that's situated below the shrine and within walking distance of the river. The river is one of the many tributaries of the upper Mekong. The water is low, a mere trickle, as per the season, which is why the villagers are now able to repair a bridge on the trail, damaged by the recent heavy truck traffic.

Zuji is watching the workers through a pair of Soviet 8 by 50 Puskin military binoculars, acquired during his recent tenure at the secret *Viet Minh* training camp in the northern highlands. Not as good as his Imperial Army Nikko's, but a little wider field, good enough to see the big elephant hauling a fresh teak pole over the dry river mud and move it into position as instructed by its *mahout*. Several coolies sweat and curse as they secure the load. Nearby on the hard-baked ground two women wearing conical *Non la* bamboo hats prepare food over a smoky fire. One is old, the other young. Two children run back and forth towing brightly coloured paper dragons.

He lowers the binoculars, looks over the jungle canopy. Coils of early morning fog whisper along the contours of the valley with its karst limestone cliffs, verdant buttes and hidden caves. Here and there in the far distance, fires are burning, smoke rising in staggered pillars. They seem to be in the same areas as the more southern temples, although he can't be sure. He does wonder, though. While the French have left, they have been replaced by the Americans who consider the present national boundaries as mere communist markers on a phony map and have been attacking NVA positions in Laos.

He looks at the village. It's small, just a few huts, homes for 20, 30 people. Pole and thatch dumps. No poetry here, although the vista has poetry, no question. Palms, ironwood, various broad-leaf evergreens hide swarms of orchids and woodpeckers and owls. Here, just behind him, are pine trees.

At one time there was a large statue of the goddess *Guan Yin* on the ridge, but through years of neglect in the monsoon rains, it fell and was carried down the slope to within a short distance of the platform. The first time Zuji passed through here, he recruited a couple of the villagers to try and right the idol. The terrain is too steep for a 3 tonne elephant and the idol too entangled and heavy to reposition without an elephant or a heavy lift helicopter. The villagers appreciate the money however and although this isn't Zuji's main reason for being here, he keeps his military identity secret.

He has no politics. He's just a monk doing a survey of the forgotten and neglected sacred places.

He chews some nuts, drinks some water, fondles his prayer beads, thinks about the recent news from Japan. He has finished his book, it will be published … and it is almost certain that the way will be clear for him to return. Only a few of his old comrades know he is still alive, fellow believers in the divine destiny of Japan, and they have been securing support among the old aristocracy and select politicians. His masquerade as a Buddhist monk and communist operative is coming to a close.

He raises the binoculars again, observes the progress of the works. The young mahout is throwing pails of water onto the elephant, hydrating the beast after its labour. The coolies are shovelling clay into the repair and compacting it with their feet.

The Vrong: a divided village with the majority going with the Royals, the minority with the Pathet Lao, the Laos communists. One day their friends the Viet Cong came down the trail, rounded up the Vrong, shot the majority, let the minority live as road crew and coolies in the service of supply dump Truong Son 7.

He hears engines. First he thinks it's an NVA convoy and scans a stand of swamp Cypress further up the trail. But there's something sinister in the sound that swells into a discordant roar as 3 American helicopters materialize over the ridge and bear down on the clearing around the village. Huey gunships, their Lycoming turbine engines throbbing in and out of phase with one another. Zuji experiences no fear. Indeed, he is full of admiration. Weapons like these are a joy to behold, even if they belong to the false prophets who fly them.

He knows who they are and there's nowhere for him to run really. Commandos, dispatched by the Yankee SOG to intercept and harass Viet Minh moving south on the Truong Son, a.k.a. the Ho Chi Minh trail.

The choppers never touch the red dirt. The soldiers jump out and the choppers rise up like leaves in the wind and fly away. The downdraft from the rotors clears the rubble and dirt from the face of the goddess. She's not as pretty as he had hoped.

"This cat's a spotter."

"You think?"

"Yeah, these nocs are Russian. See? Cyrillic marking."

"So?"

"So what's a monk doing with a pair of military nocs?"

The American Lieutenant turns to Zuji and asks him this same question in French. Zuji says he bought them in a street market in Vientiane.

"Bullshit. The guy's a spotter. Look at the fuckin' watch he's wearing."

The Lieutenant requests Zuji remove his watch and hand it to him. It's a *Tissot*, steel, with black face dial and manual winding. A present from Veronica Ng-Chablis, his old lover. The Lieutenant holds it to his ear … it's quiet and right on time.

"Swiss, right? What's a monk doing with that?"

Zuji says he needs to know the time like anyone else, monsieur. They make him strip, remove his modest cotton robes. The rice paddy pants too. This reveals his hidden bayonet, his personal weapon since his days in the Philippines.

He's naked, except for a loin cloth. His skin is copper, darkened by many days in the tropical sun. He has scars, certain body markings that are codes for his personal history. But what stranger can read them? The melanistic spots that resemble linking triangles if examined closely.

"Look at him—this guy ain't Vietnamese."

"Could be Malay, Captain."

"Ask him."

The Lieutenant phrases the question carefully: "Monsieur, what temple do you serve?"

Zuji is cautious, says softly, "The Temple of the New Dawn."

"And where is that?"

"Bangkok."

The Captain is still contemptuous, inclined to disbelief. "What the hell's a monk from Banger doing in northern Laos? Ask him, and watch his face."

Zuji maintains his benevolent expression, says he's here to restore the statue of the goddess which is just over there, and as the American warriors can see, is in pitiful condition. She is known as *Guan Yin*, sometimes as *Tara*, the goddess of mercy.

"He says he's on a mission to restore the fallen statue. Could be."

"The ugly Buddha? Fuck that. Ask him why he carries a bayonet."

Zuji says it is dangerous for a traveller in Laos these days, especially in the remote jungles. There are wild animals … tigers, boars, snakes … and disrespectful, opportunistic tribes people who have no values other than greed.

"Very noble," says the Captain as he chews on the end of a cigarello. "Guess he bought it in a street market in Vientiane too, shit. What do you think, Lieutenant? He for real?"

"Could be, Capt. I mean, he looks like a monk to me."

They get distracted by the sound of a small aircraft approaching. A single engine high wing, dirty white, underbelly painted black, cruising slowly at two thousand feet. Zuji knows what it is—a modified Cessna, used for reconnaissance, aerial mapping and target spotting. Today he's target spotting. Zuji knows why.

"There's our boy," says the Captain. He barks at the soldier who has the radio strapped on his back, motions him over. "You asleep or what Mosrite? Talk to the bird!"

Mosrite has black hair and an outlaw moustache. Face looks fat but he isn't fat.

"Ojo 1, this is Raven, you copy?"

The Cessna rocks its wings.

"Roger, Raven."

"You have visual, Ojo 1?"

Again the Cessna rocks its wings.

"Charlie sends his regards, Raven. Party tonight at 240/40."

"Roger that. How many guests?"

"12, maybe more."

The Captain and the Lieutenant are checking a map for the location of 240/40 on the Ho Chi Minh. They nod to the radioman.

"Understood, Ojo 1. Charlie sleeping."

"Charlie sleeping. Will prepare gifts. Later, 'gator."

Zuji knows more English than he lets on, although this coded radio jargon is elusive. He knows the Yankees call the Vietnamese enemy 'Charlie' and he knows the NVA have a column of 12 transport elephants bringing a cargo of rice and assorted weapons to the hidden supply dump here at Truong Son 7. He knows this because he's been travelling between these temple depots on behalf of Group 559, the NVA transportation and logistics unit.

It's to be his last run before his return to Japan. But he has a bad feeling.

The Lieutenant is looking at Zuji, who's on his knees, his eyes vacant, beads of sweat glistening on his shoulders. This guy's in good shape for a monk who must be nearly 50. Must be all the walking, the fasting, the monastic discipline. The skin abrasions—could be shrapnel … or maybe he's into self-mutilation. Some of these holy men are. Buddhism … the Lieutenant knows squat about Buddhism. Ancestor worship, isn't it? He doesn't know. And he doesn't know what they should do with him. Well, not his decision anyway.

"I dunno, Yale. Guy could be Jap."

"Jap?"

"Yeah. Some of the Imperial Army in Laos defected to the communists in 1945, stuck around."

"Japs don't speak French."

"Oh? They would if they were in Indochina for a few years. We can't take a chance with this dude."

Lieutenant Yale purses his lips, doesn't like what's coming. Because they could share a language, to the exclusion of the rest, the monk isn't the enemy, couldn't be. Too sensitive.

"Where's Kung Fu?"

"Checking for tunnels, sir."

Captain Bender jerks his head, sends Mosrite to find and fetch Sergeant Spence. Spence is a tall, boyish Caucasian, with a bony face flushed red with sunburn and scruffy hair like a woodpecker. Slight stammer.

"You're a spiritual guy, Spence. What do you think? This guy really a monk?"

Spence smiles, says, "Why not put a match to him, find out, sir."

It takes a second for the officers to get the joke. Eight monks had burned themselves to death in Saigon five or six years previously to protest the corrupt policies of the South Vietnam government. Classic lotus position, some gasoline and a match.

"Very droll, Sergeant. Why don't *you* take him into the jungle and *you* find out?"

Spence can see the Captain isn't kidding. He collects Zuji's robe, watch and bayonet, then prods Zuji with the barrel of his CAR-15, gets him on his feet, herds him into the mysterious shadow light of the big trees. The nearby female villagers who have been weeping and wailing intermittently, fall silent. Everyone else has vanished, those young enough to vanish.

What happens now? The local men fled with the bridge work gang immediately the choppers came over the ridge. One or two old men, unable to flee, remain, squatting outside the four huts that constitute the village, the village whose limited economy is to be boosted by supply depot Truong Son 7. The platforms are elevated and hidden in the trees not far away but far enough away that the American search and destroy team might never find them—unless, of course, one of the men is captured and succumbs to torture.

The Sergeant here won't torture Zuji before he kills him, will he? He's young, only a slightly corrupted flower. You have to look closely into the blue pool behind his eyes to see any danger.

Here the trees are big, centuries old. Trailing vines hang from the crowns hidden in the thick green canopy. All is shadow and shafts of sunlight. It's cooler in here, although not much. They stop at a fresh tree stump, the cut made by the loggers still yellow and oozing sap.

Sergeant Spence looks at Zuji, nods, smiles, then draws up the cuff of his left leg, reveals a large dragon tattoo that extends from the ankle to the knee. How about that—an American Buddhist, a follower of the Chinese Shaolin Temple. Kung Fu martial arts discipline.

Zuji moves his head slightly, a subtle movement of recognition. He wonders if this man knows of the recent destruction of the Shaolin Temple by the Red Guards and the imprisonment of the residing monks. He wonders if this soldier is even sincere, if his tattoo isn't just a mere vanity, the product of a drunken furlough in Saigon or Bangkok.

He draws close, whispers, "Dunno if you can understand me, man, but, uh, you should get your people outta here. Don't let them git on the Ho Chi Minh, got it?"

He draws his hand across his throat in a quick slicing action. "Got it?"

He then takes a cigarette from his breast pocket, the one that's concealed behind the bandolier ammunition belt that crosses his chest diagonally. It's a self-rolled cigarette and when the man lights up, sucks in some smoke, then exhales with a slow sigh, Zuji knows it's dope.

Zuji wets his lips with a slow sweep of his tongue. He should smile and nod, but he can't. His feet are hurting, his muscles tight all over.

Sergeant Spence—the man who the others call 'Kung Fu'—then recites poem, or maybe it's a mantra. Zuji doesn't quite get the drift.

I stand up next to a mountain
And I chop it down with the edge of my hand
I pick up all the pieces and make an island
might even raise a little sand
'cause I'm a voodoo child
lord knows I am a voodoo child

Spence's eyes are slits, his lips thin and northern.

"You dig my haiku, man? That's by the prophet, Jimi Hendrix. Nah, don't expect you've ever heard of him. Uh, listen up, man, here's the deal. As you can tell, I'm a follower of the Shaolin Temple … that's in northern China as I'm sure you know … and I know you're a Master, that you're a cat who's close to perfection … fifth level, sixth maybe … and you know all this fighting and stuff is bullshit … bullshit, right?"

Zuji doesn't understand a word. What he does understand is that these guys take no prisoners. They aren't wearing any tags, admit no allegiance.

"Master, here's the deal. You tell me where the VC has their shit stashed and we'll be cool. Captain Bender, he's not cool but we men of spiritual discipline are. We're brothers. So you tell me what I need to know and you … you, Master, can go on your merry way. Understand?"

Zuji blinks, adjusts his glasses. He'd be blind without them.

Spence takes another drag as he awaits a response. A small bird speeds past, a red blur in the jungle twilight. It's quiet in here, the sound of war nowhere to be heard. For the moment.

"Well, I can see you don't understand. So you leave me no option … well, maybe one."

He raises the barrel of his CAR-15 rifle, points it at Zuji, then tosses over the watch. "We don't steal, we don't loot. Man's gotta have his mojo when he's gonna die. You got your beads? Yeah, you got your beads."

Zuji has a flashback moment. Bataan, the Philippines, the so-called Death March. This madman, this dope fiend, he's a reincarnate come for revenge. Just like the Australian, the others … all those pursuers on the long road to Nirvana.

"Go on, put on the watch. Here—you wanna cover your balls?"

He tosses forward the black cotton peasant pants that Zuji had been wearing below his robe. Zuji pulls them on and straps the *Tissot* onto his left wrist, thinking of Veronica Ng-Chablis as he does so. Is she still in Hanoi? Perhaps Paris. She wanted their kid to do boarding school there.

Spence unsheathes the bayonet, throws it at Zuji's feet, steps back, levels his rifle. "There you go, Master. You know what you gotta do."

Spence is down to the dregs of his reefer and he has a very nice buzz going. So nice he's losing track of time and back in the village Captain Bender is wondering what the fuck is going on. Pop pop, a couple of shots, that's all it takes to kill a charlie. By now Zuji understands the option he's being given isn't for a duel. *Seppuku.* The madman wants to watch him disembowel himself.

The bird returns, flashes close to Sergeant Spence's face, startling him, and in the instant Zuji seizes his opportunity. He leaps forward, stabs the American in the gut, grabs his woodpecker hair, pulls back the head and slashes the throat. Fast, for an old guy. Fast … but he is the Master.

He then picks up the rifle, fires a couple of shots in the air.

The bird—what divine fortune was that? Maybe it was Mecca, his old adjutant. He said he wanted to come back as a bird. The occult possibility amuses him, releases the tension.

Back in the village Lieutenant Yale flinches at the sound. Captain Bender gives a satisfied grunt, then continues discussing the planned interdiction of the elephant convoy that night.

He can see a scattering of stars through a cut in the forest ceiling. He's resting on a rocky karst knoll two or three miles from the village and two hundred yards from the trail. It's quiet, except for the crackling of the over-burden on the jungle floor as it cools down from the humid tropical scorch of the day. And he's quiet, as he knows the Americans are out there in the rippling darkness, tracking him as they set up their ambush.

He feels a vibration, like the murmur of an earthquake. In the distant north there's a cascade of explosions, like thunder rolling over the mountains into the Ban Ban Valley. He knows what it is —an American B-52 strike, saturation bombing or 'carpet bombing' as the journalists call it. Deadly stuff if you happen to be in the way. The carpet is a 4 by 1 box, and the concentrated power is close to that of a tactical nuclear weapon. The target tonight? Who knows. Japan employed a similar tactic against the Chinese, he recalls. Crude and wasteful, in his estimation. A crime against Nature. Know your enemy. Meet him face to face. Otherwise, when killing ceases to be personal, it becomes immoral.

He sleeps, then jerks awake when he hears the Cessna overhead, navigation lights off. Ojo 1 has returned to hunt his prey. Ojo circles before releasing a phosphorus flare that illuminates the area like a fork of slow, silent lightning. Within two minutes a swept wing F-4 Phantom fighter-bomber swoops in like a cave bat and releases two cans of napalm, the bombs exploding in orange and gray blossoms as the burning chemicals and steel rip through the ghost light of the purple jungle.

Wise move, Zuji, to stay away from the trail.

Trees flame and crash and as the noise subsides, there are isolated screams from the men who weren't immediately immolated. But the roars of the burning elephants are what Zuji will remember, if he is destined to remember anything of this day, this night, this switchback to eternity. The roars, and the searing vision of several burning elephants stampeding into a swamp to roll in the fetid waters in a futile attempt to find relief and perhaps a little mercy before they submerge and die.

> He's in the lotus position, his eyes bright, even though they are closed. What does he see? He sees a valley stretching before him in the luxuriant glittering haze of a new dawn. He remembers the night, and the day before that, and all the other days and nights under the moon and the sun. None of this ever happened, did it? It's all a mirage, the stuff of dreams and bad karma.

Master of War, Master of Peace

A woman has handcuffed herself to a bicycle rack outside the bookshop where Colonel R. 'Pluto' Zuji is signing copies of his best selling meta memoir *Operation Karma: Fifteen Years On The Run In The Indochine*. The woman is the emaciated middle-aged widow of an Imperial Army sergeant killed during the Malaya invasion, which is seen as a triumph for the Army's Strategic Planning Unit, and in particular for legendary outspoken Colonel Zuji, master of *gekokujo*. The woman is wearing a faded red raincoat, has a crazy look about her—dishevelled hair, glaring teeth, asymmetrical lipstick and a wobbling head on a skinny body. A sign hangs around her neck with a single handwritten word in Japanese Kanji script: Justice. A passerby might mistake her for a well-used adult pleasure doll with a 'for sale' sign.

Her beef? She blames Zuji for her husband's death and in particular the Japanese government for denying her a widow's pension because she cannot prove she was legally married. She says this is because her marriage certificate and all such legal documents were destroyed in the fire bombing of Tokyo in 1945. Her problem is not uncommon, so she expects other women to join her before the evening is over and the signing ceremony is done.

Zuji could give a damn. His return to the home country has been a triumph, as many of the veterans of all ranks admire the man who masterminded the best of Japan's

World War 2 victories, and deplore the servile, corrupted state the country now finds itself in, despite its rejuvenated industry and booming economy. 'Made In Japan' is no longer a joke, yet the population suffers from a corrosive nuclear anxiety and a sense of shame about the past, and if not shame, then self-pitying resentment.

Others scoff at these bourgeois mental disorders and respond warmly to the hero of the day. Colonel Zuji feels no shame and he knows who the enemy is. Read his book, *tomodachi*. Zuji is *shogun*, Zuji knows what victory is, and Zuji is *bushido*, and *bushido* is the real Japan, *tomodachi*.

The notorious novelist Yukio Mishima shares these views and he's read Zuji's book. While he recognizes bullshit where bullshit occurs, none of these 'exaggerations' bother him as he knows the ideological advantage of well-dressed fiction when the story action needs it. What is poetry but a lie in search of truth? All hail the masks we wear when we enter, stage left or right.

Mishima arrives at the bookshop on a gleaming motorcycle, a Norton Dominator customized to resemble an American motorcycle cop's pursuit bike. He's dressed in black leather riding gear, a tight-fitting studded tunic and pants, perhaps modelled on Marlon Brando in *The Wild One*. Sun glasses, an officer's hat and a white cravat complete his meticulous couture. He parks, dismounts, starts for the entrance but as he passes the woman protester, halts, mistaking her for a beggar. He removes his sunglasses but she avoids his penetrating gaze. He notices the handcuff, nods in approval, encloses some paper money in her free hand. No words are spoken. Money? Mishima has lots of money. He's from an aristocratic family and his books continue to sell well.

In the shop, he remains discreetly to the side until there's a lull in the fawning crowd around the table where Zuji sits, dressed in an English tweed business suit, cleanly shaven and his hair buzzed and streaked with gray as befitting a senior military officer. While Mishima has already read the book—he'd received an advance review copy—he buys a copy and politely steps forward to have it signed by the Master.

"I've read it," he murmurs. "It's significant, truly significant."

"Oh?" says Zuji. "Did you serve?"

"Alas no … I was too young. I'm Mishima, by the way. Yukio Mishima."

Zuji is surprised and impressed that a famous novelist would bother to come through the wind and rain to a book launch by a military man. He stands up, bows low in the Japanese manner, offers his hand. Mishima's grip is fleeting—soft and feminine, almost paranoid. A ladyboy, thinks Zuji cynically. I've heard about Yukio and his crowd. Anyway, his writing reveals it. *Confessions of a Mask*? Brilliant, to be sure, especially in poetic terms. But decadent. Yes, decadent.

He signs a copy, hands it to Mishima who—his expression reserved and melancholy—leans forward and whispers, "We must talk, Colonel. I will phone you."

"You're leaving?"

"Yes … I must leave."

"Is that crazy woman still outside?"

"The widow? Yes … she's famous, you know. Been protesting her situation for years. It's not personal, Colonel."

Zuji grunts, takes a drink of water. People are waiting impatiently.

"*Banzai*," says Mishima softly as he steps away.

"*Banzai*," echoes Zuji, his eyes already moving to the next smiling face.

He forgets about Mishima, doesn't expect to hear from him again, unless he should happen to review *Fifteen Years On The Run*. He leaves the bookshop by the back door as more widows and their supporters have joined the famous woman who is handcuffed to the bicycle stand. It's a disgrace that so many years after the big war this sort of thing is going on, Zuji thinks. What the hell is wrong with this government? The civil service? The military? Far as he could see, these days young men preferred to fool around and play baseball and women wanted to play golf and watch ridiculous clown shows on TV.

These days he has an office on top of a corporate tower in Chiyoda with a view of the Imperial Palace because … well, because some old army buddies were now in the corporate elite and knew the value of Pluto's reputation as a public relations gambit, and who knows, he might have some good marketing ideas, dream up new industrial possibilities … stuff. Nippon Global needed a hero on the board. He was *gekokujo*, knew how to sweep aside the deadbeats and the subliminal communists who sat at the long table in Room 000 on the 21st floor. So, a nice office, a decent salary and a well-dressed bodyguard were his.

The phone rings.

"Yes?"

"Zuji, you didn't return my call."

It's Mitsu, his wife. He's been meaning to divorce her because after twenty years apart, what did they have in common anymore? No children, just some teenage nostalgia and a few racy photos. But he knows there's a problem.

"I'm a busy man, Mitsu."

"Yeah, you big shot now."

She's agitated. Her syntax is full of bullet holes, he thinks. A sort of lockjaw where she loses words, talks like a peasant from one of the islands.

"I want money, Zuji," she continues. "You owe me."

"You have a nice pension, don't you?"

She snorts, distorting the phone speaker. "The government want me to pay back the money because I'm not really a widow. You understand what I say, Zuji? Not a widow. You not dead."

Fuck me, thinks Zuji. As a rule he doesn't use profanity, as it bespeaks instability, a lack of discipline, and false poetry. But now he feels himself sinking into the profane.

"So, lost your tongue, your Holiness? You got money, I need money."

"The government can't rescind a military pension."

"You dumb, Zuji? They do, they have. Hey, what about your whore—you give her money, yes?"

She means Veronica. Guess she read his book … the good parts anyway, figured out the situation even though he gave Veronica an alias.

"And you have child … have you no shame, Zuji? My friends pity me now. You know and I know pity is just a form of mockery. They mock me behind my back. I just a piece of shit now."

What can he say? What can he do? Maybe he should kill her. He still has his bayonet.

"How old is the brat?"

"Ten, or eleven."

"Ten, eleven—you don't know? Maybe she not yours, Zuji."

Yes, he should fucking kill her. Why waste time in the courts? *Carpe diem!*

"How much do you need, Mistsu?"

"My lawyer talk to your lawyer."

"Don't be a fool, woman. Lawyers are blood suckers."

"Lawyer get turkey, Zuji."

"Still the comedian, eh, Mitsu? Tell you what, how about I give you a pension? A monthly payment."

"I want more, big shot."

"You can have the royalties from my book."

She pauses, thinks about this. He can hear her breathing. Funny, it reminds him of when they used to lie together and watch the slow flying moon through the open screen. So long ago, this young romance. A dream disfigured by time.

"You mean that?"

He doesn't, of course. He just wants to get her off the phone.

From a review in the *Japan Times*:

"I wanted to write something people could understand," says Zuji, "touch their emotional triggers without having to understand the plot."

'While *Operation Karma* [*15 Years On The Run in the Indochine*] is ostensibly a non-fiction work, it has poetic nuances that suit his assumed identity as a Buddhist monk without distorting the reality of his fugitive identity as a senior officer of the Imperial Army's strategic planning unit. There are some startling incidents to be sure. For example, the evening Zuji encounters a tiger who has wandered into a ruined temple on the Cambodian border when he is engaged in meditation, or the time when he meets a lost American, a photographer who claimed to be the son of the Hollywood film star Errol Flynn. There is some romance, a lot of spiritual meditation, some contemplative musings about his earlier days in the Imperial Army. But beyond the sex and death and the zen poetry, *15 Years On the Run* is a gripping revelation about the war in Indo China and the viral spread of communism and why the United States is close to defeat, despite its awesome technological advantage.

'And Japan? "Godzilla is rising," says Zuji, perhaps humorously.'

Who or what the hell is Godzilla? I didn't say that, mutters Zuji. Journalists. Editors. *The wind always slams the door.*

The phone rings. It's Mishima.

"Colonel, do you believe in the divinity of the Emperor?

"We all swore an oath to it. Why do you ask?"

"The Americans emasculated his powers. They destroyed the soul of Japan."

Yes, indeed they did. They abrogated the Meiji Constitution that gave the Emperor the supreme authority over the Army and Navy … something the man was not really capable of exercising, as the events of 1945 proved. He was soft, his aspirations of divinity a sham. But, thinks Zuji, Mishima is clearly in awe of the royal family. A romantic. So let him ramble.

"Agreed, Colonel?"

"Oh yes, yes …."

"I have a cohort of young warriors who will defend the Emperor in the event of a coup. Possibly you've heard of this unit."

Zuji has, although he assumed the unit was just a collection of aristocratic drifters and university rabble, all ladyboys like Mishima. A cult, really. A ludicrous blend of *samurai* dreams, No Theatre, and narcissist posturing. Typical artists.

"A coup? What coup?"

'Communists … idiots in the Defence Force. I hear rumours."

"Communists?"

"You know what they're capable of, Zuji. I read your book, remember?"

Zuji is doodling on the note pad he seldom uses. A thick male penis with balls that hang like *bonsho* temple bells. Grotesque. Silly and infantile. The hand has a mind of its own—or another mind is driving it.

"What do you want from me, Mishima?"

"Your blessing."

"For what?"

"To proceed in our quest to save the country."

"Is that it? You have it. Regretfully, I must disconnect … I have a meeting coming up."

"Understood. Watch the News. *Banzai!*"

The line goes dead. Fast as a blade in the dark.

So be it. Zuji goes back to reading his reviews. This one from the *Osaka Sun* is a bit insulting. The insult starts with the attack headline (fortunately buried in the middle pages) '**The Killer They Call A God**' and continues from there, ignoring the book, ignoring his religious devotions and the 'narrow path to the north' that he followed, his battles with communist assassins, and the anguish of his romance with VNg, the Eurasian honeytrap sent to kill him but ends up as his lover. Even his poetic evocations of the Indochine temples in their ruined beauty goes ignored. The writer—anonymous—criticizes everything Zuji supposedly did from 1935 to 1945 and his disappearance into the jungle.

'This ghost from our ugly past has now come back to haunt us, to revive the painful memory of the stupid authoritarian past, when this country was a fascist state run for the pleasure of the armed forces, the people enslaved by the ancestor cult of a so-called 'divine Emperor' and powerless to stop the folly that ended with over 3 million Japanese dead. We can ignore the millions that died in those other countries where our armies carried out their imperial adventures, but can we ignore the pointless destruction of the homeland all because of the obsolete *samurai* mentality of leaders like Zuji? Read this book if you must, but burn it afterwards.'

Zuji laughs silently, uneasily. A bourgeois communist. Always the most self-righteous. But what does it matter? All publicity is good publicity … they say.

The phone rings again. He looks at his watch—the board meeting is due to start in Room 000 in fifteen minutes. He answers. It's the Nippon Global executive secretary, the blonde bombshell who runs the company's business office on the floor below. Her name is Rila. She isn't really blonde—keeps her natural hair short, wears a wig. It's the Tokyo style these days.

"Colonel, there's a man who keeps phoning. He says he knows you."

Zuji groans wearily. All sorts of people want to talk to him. He is as popular as one of those pretty boy J-pop stars or that sumo wrestler Taiho, the beast with a thousand victories.

"Name?"

"Meccano … Ashai Meccano."

Zuji sits up, draws his swivel seat in tighter to his desk. Meccano? Isn't he dead?

Well, he's getting used to surprises since coming back.

"I'll talk to him, Rila."

The voice is hoarse, like a man who's inhaled too much battlefield ammonia nitrate.

"Colonel, it's me, Mecca."

"A voice from the dead, Meccano."

"I'm not dead. I thought you were."

"Well, here we are, dead or not."

"Yes, yes … so, we must meet. I know stuff you should know. It's very important we meet as soon as possible, Colonel … right away, really."

Zuji ponders for a moment as he wonders what information Meccano could have. Must be something.

"You sound sick, Meccano … are you?"

"No no, I'm fine. I started smoking again is all. Look, we must meet."

"Not for the phone, eh?"

"No, Colonel, not for the phone."

They agree to meet at the Orchid, a restaurant and bar in the Shibuya district. But first Zuji has to take care of business in Room 000, meet with the directors and discuss whatever needs discussing. Be the usual: stocks, acquisitions, markets, possibilities and the bottom line.

His bodyguard Zero comes in. Big man, about 45, usually smiling despite his battered face. Says he was a corporal in the 21st Army. Maybe so but Zuji knows he's a '8-9-3', *yakusa*, despite the pale blue tailored suit and the expensive Brazilian shoes. The General gave him to Zuji as a job perk and no doubt as a spy for himself. The General is the CEO of Nippon Global and really was a junior General during the war. He knows talent. He was the last senior officer in charge of recruiting kamikaze soldiers for all three services. Yes, he knows talent.

So does Zero. He's looking at Zuji's pornographic doodle.

"Boss, this is damn good. Know what? Be killer on a T."

"I didn't do it."

"It's killer … can I keep it?"

"Burn it. What's a 'T'?"

"T-shirt. Like a cotton undershirt. All the kids are wearing them. Different colors, different pictures. World-wide, boss."

"Kids wear them?"

"Everybody. Adults too. Easy to make, cheap. Put a picture on them and mark them up three, four times ... eh, maybe ten. Easy money, boss."

Sounds like a street hustle to Zuji. More money in guns. He goes into Room 000 fully intending to recommend that Global Nippon acquire a Korean small arms manufacturer who has a license to produce Russian AK-47s, the highly reliable automatic rifles used by the Viet Cong. He's a few minutes early. The 'gang of four' are already there, eyes glued to the 'big' 21 inch Sanyo television. Television—there were no TVs in the jungle when Zuji was incarnated as a monk, so he missed its rise to media dominance. Small movies, he thinks. Puppet Shows.

The puppets on this occasion are dressed in tight-fitting uniforms with pattern button tunics that resemble nineteenth century drummer boy outfits. There are five of them standing on a balcony above a crowd of grumpy looking JASDF soldiers. One of the puppets is addressing the crowd and the crowd doesn't seem receptive.

"What's going on?"

"Some sort of coup."

"Who? *Zenkyoto?*"

Zenkyoto are a bunch of student radicals who made a mess of Tokyo University recently.

"No, they call themselves the Shield Society. That's Mishima the writer who's mouthing off."

"Oh, it's a play, is it?"

"No no, it's for real. This is a live report."

They watch. It's Mishima alright, pale, grim and defiant. He finishes his harangue weakly, obviously confused by its poor reception. It was a ramble about the Emperor and the need to go back to the Meiji Constitution. Some of the assembled militia actually jeer, and a few laugh.

Mishima now sits down in the lotus position and disembowels himself in the traditional *seppuku* ritual. As he bleeds out, his head sags and one of his disciples steps forward and decapitates the writer with the favoured *shin gunto* sword of the *samurai* class. The disciple then kneels, tips his head forward, and is in turn decapitated by another member of the Shield. So ends the puppet show.

Or at least for the spectators in Room 000 of the Nippon Global tower. The General has arrived and without ceremony, shuts off the TV.

"Was that for real?" someone asks.

The others break into excited babble as the General takes his place at the head of the table. Rila, efficient and perfumed, distributes copies of the agenda. Zuji can feel her heat as she leans over the table close to him.

'The slender margin between the real and the unreal ....' Zuji reflects on the words of Japan's greatest puppet dramatist, Chikamatsu Monzaemon, someone he studied in school and whose ideas he found useful later in life: *'It is real, and yet it is not real. Entertainment lies between the two.'*

The meeting goes forward in its usual fashion, with the usual arguments and the usual disagreements. Zuji, atypically, has little to say. Near the conclusion, when asked if he has any ideas, he suggests Nippon Global acquire an industrial level printing shop and start manufacturing illustrated T-shirts.

Meccano is an emaciated wretch, looks shabby, despite the suit he's wearing. His injured leg is worse now, drags a little. Occasionally he rubs the sleeve of his jacket or reaches inside, scratches his rib cage. Zuji wonders if the man has been sleeping rough.

"Been back long, Mecca?"

"Yes, a few years."

"Got a job?"

"I did. You know, this and that."

They're both eating noodle soup. Tastes great to Zuji, the long beans, the forest leaves, the mint seasoning. He savours it as if it was something his mother made, years ago, god rest her soul. But Meccano barely touches his, pecks at it, like a bird on the edge of a frozen puddle.

"I heard you became an assassin."

"That's ridiculous."

"That's what I heard. The American intelligence sent you hunting for Japanese war criminals."

"That's ridiculous. I heard you were training Vietnamese communists."

"Equally ridiculous. Me? Communist?"

"That's what I said."

"Oh? Who was interested, Mecca?"

"I'll tell you what happened. Remember I put on your uniform, pretended to be you so you could escape? The Chinese got me. Yes, Chinese women who knew you arrested their men and had them executed, so they tried to execute me."

"Didn't you have your pistol?"

"I did but they ambushed me near our HQ. They were going to hang me from a lamp post. A British commando came along and intervened. An Indian, one of those Hindus who burn the wife when the husband dies."

Zuji laughs softly, says, "How do you know that, Lieutenant?"

Meccano's face twitches. His teeth, Zuji notices, are in terrible shape.

"He had the red dot on his forehead. I don't know … I heard these ones did terrible things. Anyway, that's not important. I wanted to see you about something else."

"Who interrogated you? Who found out you weren't Zuji?"

"An Australian. He was very keen on finding out where you'd gone, Colonel."

Zuji taps the edge of his soup bowl with his spoon: "Did you testify against me, Meccano? Did you?"

"No … no, I told them nothing."

"You should have killed yourself."

"Me? Why? You didn't."

"Do you know why, Meccano?"

"Yes, you wanted to carry on fighting. A warrior never surrenders, you said."

"No he doesn't. I was in the jungle fifteen years. What did you do?"

Meccano is very fidgety now.

"Buy me a drink, Colonel."

"You haven't finished your soup."

"It doesn't agree with me. I need a drink."

"I only buy drinks for my friends, Meccano."

"Look, I need money. You have lots, don't you? You do. You're famous."

"What's the problem?"

"I'm not well. I need an expensive medicine and well, I just don't have the money."

"What's wrong with you?"

"War sickness. You know what that is."

"No I don't. You sound like one of those fucking women who claim to be the widows of our valiant military who died in combat. What's really wrong with you, Lieutenant?"

Meccano hesitates, looks around the restaurant without really looking. He doesn't notice Zero, for instance, who's sitting at the bar in the next room watching him and Zuji in the big mirror that extends beyond the rows of illuminated liquor bottles to the ceiling.

"The pain was hideous. I got addicted in hospital."

"Morphine?"

Meccano pulls back the left sleeve of his jacket. The belly of his wrist is a mess of red and black puncture marks. He looks sadly at Zuji, his eyes pooling with lost dreams.

"Heroin?"

Meccano nods. Again he reiterates that he got addicted in hospital, says he'll die if he doesn't get a fix soon. Ten years, he says. Ten years he's been an addict. He doesn't mention that it was a hospital run by the American overlords. He doesn't mention that they promised to get his leg fixed … for a little cooperation.

Zuji murmurs sympathetic sounds, says he'll help his old friend out.

The car is a black Toyota Crown, a deluxe version of the auto so popular with taxi drivers all over south-east Asia. Company car. The General has a Century limo as befitting the *shogun* of a Tokyo corporation—longer, sleeker, quieter and rigged with a phone and a bar. But Zuji isn't complaining. He expects he'll be moving up the ladder soon. "They" want him to run for parliament, the Japanese Diet. Be a shoe in. Not everyone hated the war or blames those who fought in it.

Zuji sits in the back with Meccano. Zero is behind the wheel.

"Just like the old days, eh, Mecca?" says Zuji. "Onwards to victory!"

Meccano is restless, can feel the junkie snakes crawling over his flesh. His face becomes cunning, as his desperation removes the mask. "Just our secret, Pluto," he says hoarsely. "As long as I'm o.k … *muron*."

"*Muron*."

It's twilight. It's not late but the traffic is thickening towards rush hour. Zero is driving, the surface of his bald head flickering as they slide below the commercial neon. They're heading for the Sanya district in the Taito Ward. They pass the Hachiko statue, the famous bronze dog outside the station. Meccano doesn't mention that he recently spent the night on a bench below the plinth on which Hachiko stands, forever waiting for the Master who never returns. It's a sad story, but not one he will allow himself to repeat. His Master has returned and he will reward him.

All it takes is a little leverage.

Zuji passes a silver flask, urges Meccano to drink. *Yamazaki* whisky.

"Thanks, Pluto."

"Please don't call me that, Lieutenant."

"Yes, yes … *muron*, Colonel."

Zuji can see Zero's eyes in the rear view mirror. Slits, sleepy slits.

"Did you ever contact my wife?"

"Mistsu? She wouldn't talk to me. Said I was an impostor."

Zuji murmurs 'hmm', takes back the flask puts it back in his inside pocket.

"Tell me, did you see the suicide on television?"

"The writer with the medical problem? No. I saw some people watching it through a TV shop window. Missed it. You?"

"I saw it. He performed *seppuku*."

"I don't care."

"I suppose not. Will your connection be difficult? Can we assist?"

Zero has driven into a quiet alley where the vagrants lie in the shadows of doorways and dumpsters. It's a shabby, desolate area, a corridor between the sagging back ends of buildings that really have no fronts.

Meccano is looking out the window. "Anywhere here will do," he says. "If you can let me have the money."

Zuji slides his hand below his jacket, draws his bayonet, drives it into Meccano's gut. Meccano gasps, his eyes bulge, then close. The aorta artery, his stomach, his intestines. Zuji rips, Zuji wiggles, Zuji withdraws. He wipes the blade clean on the shoulder of Meccano's jacket, then leans across, opens the door. Zero has the car moving again as Zuji pushes the body out, sees it bounce and skid into the darkness.

That's that. No fucking treasonous *buta* was going to blackmail Colonel Zuji, the Master.

Zero accelerates down a side street. Their eyes meet in the rear-view mirror.

Zero smiles, nods.

"Boss, Vang closes shop at seven."

"Who is Vang?"

"Vang is our tattoo artist. If we hurry, I'm sure he can fit you in."

Zuji grunts to himself. Even a *yakusa* like Zero has misread his symbols, believes they come from without, not within.

"Tomorrow, Zero. I'm tired. I need to purify myself. Drive me to the temple."

When the first triangle appears on Zuji's right arm he is puzzled, perhaps a little disturbed. It looks like a tattoo … but is it? The lines are soft and green, like a track left by a jungle worm. There's no sensation or any perturbance such as a parasite or a needle in the night might make. Perhaps he was poisoned. Perhaps the Australian dosed his tea. And the more he looks at the triangle, the more he remembers the prisoners he sent to the barge for the final clean-up.

He's shaving, wondering if he should allow himself to have a goatee. Why not? He's in a state of continuous metamorphoses. His right arm looks like a rattlesnake, a chain of interlocking triangles. Adaptive melanism, camouflage for the hunter. Or an expression of his kills? They flicker through his mind erotically.

But a goatee? Too Chinese perhaps. A representative of the people should look like the people.

There's a low rumble, then a slight vibration. It passes quickly. The subway, he thinks. People going to work. Time for him to get moving.

Zero is waiting for him outside. He hands Zuji a note. "From the General, boss."

Zuji hasn't seen the General in a while since he became a member of parliament. The General, of course, made sure Zuji got the votes. The *yakusa* gang in this area made sure. Nothing crude, just some phantom ballots when necessary, a couple of bribed journalists and the women's vote. He'd made a lot of promises to the women, and they were still hungry after being enfranchised back in '46. "Pigs Are Still Pigs" was one of their favourite rallying cries. So, Zuji hands out a lot of free perfume and makes a lot of promises.

And y'know, it's not always easy to follow up on some promises. And when is a promise bribery, and when is it just an ideal, a plan that might never get carried out? Zuji knows a lot about such plans. Mind you, his record on this score is excellent: Manchuria, Malaya … the others now in the history books. Zuji is a man who gets things done. A vote for Zuji is a vote for progress.

Progress. It got him a better limo, didn't it? A black 1976 Toyota Century with the coveted gold phoenix logo, the Fushido symbol of the Imperial House of Japan. It's quiet, it's bulletproof.

Zero drives him to the Nippon Global tower, parks right outside against the VIP kerb.

There's a juggler on the pavement, flipping red and yellow skittles.

He takes the elevator to the top, finds the General in his private shrine. Candles, a Buddha … or is it? It looks more like a large doll dressed like an American movie star. Strange, perhaps it belonged to the dead daughter killed a few years ago in some gangland dispute no one talks about. At least, not at Nippon Global.

The General is very thin. His robe hangs like a curtain. As he lights a cigarette, his sleeve rides up, briefly exposes a tattoo. The moment is too fast for detail, but Zuji knows what it is anyway. From the tattoo parlour where Rila originally worked.

"They're after you, my friend."

Again? He sighs. He doesn't need a name or a face. The General has good intelligence.

"They never give up."

"Revenge is a powerful emotion. I see you're growing a beard —good idea, Zuji."

"I don't know … maybe it makes me look like, ah …."

"A villain?" The General chuckles at his own witticism, then continues: "I've told Zero to increase your protection. He has a buddy. We can't go to the police with this … can of worms, Zuji."

"Australians."

"Yes. Our source says a group of retired veterans have raised the bounty. Might be some American money in there as well. It's private money, nothing to do with their governments."

"How much?"

"A lot, Colonel. Two million dollars."

"It was 20 years ago, and they still care? I'm amazed."

"Be flattered. Of course it was probably a mistake to call your book "Operation Karma"—'Fifteen Years, et cetera' would've been more discreet."

"But 'karma' refers to my disguise as a monk. Everyone knows I was a military operations planner."

"Yes, yes, everyone in the know, Colonel. But not everyone was in the know about 'Karma.'"

"Water under the bridge, General. Bah. Let them send their assassins. I've dealt with them before."

"I'm sure you have, Colonel Zuji. You have to be careful, though. We're all getting older, you know."

Yes, and you don't want any bad karma mucking up the corporate image of Nippon Global, do you? Zuji thinks, allowing himself a silent sneer. Even though he owes a lot to the General's support since his repatriatism, Zuji can't help himself. Did this man ever see combat? True combat in all its mystical glory? Doubtful. The General—who wasn't a 'general' then—worked under Yuichi, chief of the Army General Staff's Second Bureau. They bungled the Indochine adventure, just as they bungled damn near everything. They were manipulated by Stalin in Manchuria and Mongolia, and failed to anticipate the American oil embargo. The General—his real name conveniently evaporated within the mists of history—is just the privileged son of a *nouveau riche yakusa* boss from Ota City. He never had to cut off his little finger, or pass any exams. Shit always floats to the top, says Confucius—a popular quote among the enlisted men of the Imperial Army.

Zuji's mask remains intact. Relaxed and benign, as in a perpetual state of bliss. Maybe the shadow of a possible goatee hints at a forthcoming, newer incarnation. But for now Zuji is your humble servant, *sama*.

"Thanks for the warning, General."

"Have you considered getting rid of the tattoos? It can be done."

Zuji shrugs, says, "You ever think of shedding yours?"

The General looks away, says, "Impossible."

"I'll say goodbye then. There's a vote coming up on the budget shortly, so I must be in parliament."

On his way through the main office, he sees Rila standing near the elevator. She's been waiting for him.

"We on tonight, Rudolph?"

She's getting older but still looks good, feels good. She's geisha in a movie star dress.

Her smell remains with him all the way down to the lobby until he hits the industrial air of the street. Dogs are barking. No wonder —a collection of women are waiting for him. Mostly young, some middle-aged. The hag in the red raincoat looks familiar, and as the crowd surges towards him, he recognizes her from years ago. 'Widow Justice'.

He glances at Zero, says, "I'll talk to them. Wait by the car."

Zero is skeptical. "I dunno, boss. We should vacate."

The juggler is still juggling, although he's dropping skittles, as if unsteady on his feet. He runs over the pavement, snatching at the rollers, in a futile attempt to keep the show going.

The Widow Justice gets in close, eyes bifocal and crazy, snarls, "You lie, Zuji. Where is my pension? Where is it?"

"Madame, you must prove you are a widow."

The women chant: "Pigs are still pigs! Pigs are still pigs!"

Zero is trying to push them back but although his hands are big, he only has two.

The Widow Justice is baring her teeth. Was she ever a woman?

Zuji tries to stare her down but it's hopeless. She opens her coat, reveals the T-shirt she's wearing. My god, my drawing … the big ding dong with the bells! He feels the pavement vibrate, looks down just as the bitch takes a swing at him, rips him across the face with something hard and cutting like a small chain. It's a loose handcuff that dangles from her wrist, ready for bondage, ready for murder. He staggers back, gropes for his blade, the bayonet he always carries, no matter the suit he wears, the incarnation he pretends. But the world is moving, and it isn't because of the blow to his head.

Earthquake. The street is buckling and humping like a sea serpent breaking surface at speed. The corporate towers shake, lean vertiginously like giant trees in a storm, debris detaching, some crashing, some floating. There are screams as people get felled while others sprint for safety, although there is no immediate safety as a large fissure opens up, running for several blocks. He sees Zero jump into the limo, start it up, but has to abandon the vehicle as it tips into the chasm like a wreck disappearing into an industrial auto crusher.

Chunks of broken glass explode like cluster bombs as people get sucked from their offices and fall hundreds of feet to their deaths. Zuji is reminded of that fateful day in August, 1945, when many of his fellow officers jumped to their deaths on learning of the Emperor's formal surrender. History doesn't repeat, it rhymes, someone said. An American, some think. But it's as Japanese as sushi.

Zuji finds a fresh crack developing directly below his feet. He could run, he could flee, but he doesn't. As in a bizarre dream where chaos has no logic, he finds his feet being drawn apart as the crack widens, so that he is being rendered from his crotch to his head. He laughs. "War" he exults. "You talk to me about war and the nihilism of those who practice it? Morons! This is the only war! All war is a war against Nature!"

Nature. Three tectonic plates converge under the city, forming a perfect triangle.

He loses his balance and falls. He grabs the asphalt, hangs there, tries to claw his way out of the chasm … the ground is crumbling, his grip compromised. He sees a figure in red standing above him, wobbling, lurching, flickering like a flame, and it's the last thing he sees as he drops straight into the jaws of Hell.

Article in **Tokyo Underground**, April 21, 1984, headlined ITEMS AT AN AUCTION.

'Is Colonel Rudolph "Pluto" Zuji really dead?

'Some recent items at an auction held by Nakamichi's might draw this assumption into question. Lot 9, part of Mitsu Zuji's estate, contained a few objects believed to have belonged to her late husband. Although they never lived together after Colonel Zuji's sensational return to Japan and his subsequent election to the Diet, they never divorced, and as his widow, she received possession of his estate. The items up for sale here were small personal items, not particularly valuable by themselves, although possibly desirable to fans of Colonel Zuji and collectors of war memorabilia.

'These were a set of prayer beads, a watch, a bayonet blade, a wooden prosthetic hand and a notebook. The prayer beads were said to be the ones Zuji wore during his 15 years in the Indochine jungle. Likewise the bayonet, his favoured self-defense weapon. The watch, a Swiss made *Tissot*, was broken and mangled to such a state that it resembled an art object by Salvador Dali (how it came to be in this condition is unknown).

'The wooden hand is a total mystery. It could be a war trophy.

'The notebook provides more controversy, is said to contain notes for the Imperial Army's planned invasion of Australia. Code named "OPERATION KARMA", it is the same title that Colonel Zuji used for his best-selling book 15 Years On the Run in the Indochine. An expert at Tokyo's Imperial University who previously examined the notebook at the request of the widow says the notes are too ambiguous, and out-of-sync with the known strategy towards Australia, and that there is "too much poetry" and therefore is probably part of his disguise as an itinerant monk. It would, perhaps, be of interest to literary scholars if they considered Operation Karma to be 'literature'. So far, it seems, no one does.

'Item 9 was purchased by Madeline Ng-Chablis who flew in from Paris especially for the auction. Although Ms. Ng-Chablis declined to speak with Tokyo Underground, we uncovered these facts: one, Madeline Ng-Chablis is a Vietnamese citizen, a graduate of the Sorbonne, and the daughter of Veronica Ng-Chablis, rumoured to have been a communist spy against the French, and later known as an aide for Ho Chi Minh. Photographs show that Ng-Chablis had an artificial left hand.

'While we are constrained by legal considerations, the reader is free to speculate.

'But we can ask a couple of questions: why would a beautiful young Eurasian woman fly to Tokyo and outbid a representative of Tokyo University's Special Collections? (the successful bid was 735,000 yen) And if Colonel Zuji fell into an earthquake fissure and no body was ever found, how did his official widow Mitsu Zuji come by these items when the Colonel's bodyguard Zero Suzuki swears he always wore his beads, wore his watch, carried his bayonet, and kept a notebook in his pocket every day as a matter of routine?

'Again, we ask: is Colonel Rudolph "Pluto" Zuji really dead?

'It's a curious fact that in the last few years an increasing number of men with various backgrounds have been showing up at police stations, hospitals and temples throughout the country claiming to be Zuji. We laugh, of course, perhaps think of the cult of Elvis Presley, or some other pop culture madness, yet this curious story shows no sign of running out of legs.'

The Road to Woop Woop
By Eugen Bacon

Tumbling down the stretch, a confident glide, the 4WD is a beaut, over nineteen years old.

The argument is brand-new. Maps are convolutions, complicated like relationships. You scrunch the sheet, push it in the glovebox. You feel River's displeasure, but you hate navigating, and right now you don't care.

The wiper swishes to and fro, braves unseasonal rain. You and River maintain your silence.

Rain. More rain.

"When's the next stop?" River tries. Sidewise glance, cautious smile. He is muscled, dark. Dreadlocks fall down high cheekbones to square shoulders. Eyes like black gold give him the rugged look of a mechanic.

"Does it matter?" you say.

"Should it?"

You don't respond. Turn your head, stare at a thin scratch on your window. The crack runs level with rolling landscape racing away with rain. Up in the sky, a billow of cloud like a white ghoul, dark-eyed and yawning into a scream.

A shoot of spray through River's window brushes your cheek.

A glide of eye. "Hell's the matter?" you say.

"You ask *me-e*. Something bothering you?"

"The window."

He gives you a look.

Classic, you think. But you know that if you listen long enough, every argument is an empty road that attracts unfinished business. It's an iceberg full of whimsy about fumaroles and geysers. It's a corpse that spends eternity reliving apparitions of itself in the throes of death. Your fights are puffed-up trivia, championed to crusades. You fill up teabags with animus that pours into kettles of disarray, scalding as missiles. They leave you ashy and scattered—that's what's left of your lovemaking, or the paranoia of it, you wonder about that.

More silence, the cloud of your argument hangs above it. He shrugs. Rolls up his window. Still air swells in the car.

"Air con working?" you say.

He flexes long corduroyed legs that end in moccasins. Flicks on the air button—and the radio. The bars of a soulful number, a remix by some new artist, give way to an even darker track titled 'Nameless.' It's about a high priest who wears skinny black jeans and thrums heavy metal to bring space demons into a church that's dressed as a concert. And the torments join in evensong, chanting psalms and canticles until daybreak when the demons wisp back into thin air, fading with them thirteen souls of the faithful, an annual pact with the priest.

Rain pelts the roof and windows like a drum.

He hums. Your face is distant. You might well be strangers, tossed into a tight drive from Broome to Kununurra.

The lilt of his voice merges with the somber melody.

You turn your face upward. A drift of darkness, even with full day, is approaching from the skies. Now it's half-light. You flip the sun visor down. Not for compulsion or vanity, nothing like an urge to peer at yourself in the mirror. Perhaps it's to busy your hands, to distract yourself, keep from bedevilment—the kind that pulls out a quarrel. You steal a glimpse of yourself in the mirror. Deep, deep eyes. They gleam like a cat's. The soft curtain of your fringe is softening, despite thickset brows like a man's. You feel disconnected with yourself, with the trip, with River. You flip the sun visor up.

Now the world is all grim. River turns on the headlights, but visibility is still bad. A bolt of lightning. You both see the arms of a reaching tree that has appeared on the road, right there in your path. You squeal, throw your arms out. River swerves. A slam of brakes. A screech of tires. *Boom!*

The world stops in a swallowing blackness. Inside the hollow, your ears are ringing. The car, fully intact, is shooting out of the dark cloud in slow motion, picking up speed. It's soaring along the road washed in a new aurora of lavender, turquoise and silver, then it's all clear. A gentle sun breaks through fluffs of cloud no more engulfed in blackness. You level yourself with a hand on the dashboard, uncertain what exactly happened.

You look at River. His hands … wrist up … he has no hands. Nothing bloody as you'd expect from a man with severed wrists. Just empty space where the arms end.

But River's unperturbed, his arms positioned as if he's driving, even while nothing is touching the steering that's moving itself, turning and levelling.

"Brought my shades?" he asks.

"Your hands," you say.

"What about them?"

"Can't you see?"

His glance is full of impatience.

You sink back to your seat, unable to understand it, unclear to tell him, as the driverless car races along in silence down the lone road.

If it hadn't been such a dreary morning, perhaps the mood might be right. But a bleak dawn lifted to cobalt, to brown, slid to gray. One recipe for disaster that simmers you and River in separate pots.

This spring is of a different breed. It traps you, brings with it … fights. You gripe like siblings, the inner push to argue too persuasive. Smiles diminish to awkward; words sharpen to icicles.

Kununurra was a break long overdue. A planned trip. Your idea. A dumb-arsed one at that for a romance on the line. As though different soil would mend it.

"Drive?" River had asked.

"Best within the price bracket," you said.

"Do I look half-convinced?"

"People drive," you said. "It's normal."

"Seems normal to take the plane."

"If we drive, River, what do you think the concern is? What?"

"If we drive my road rover? I hope for your sake to never ask myself that question."

"That's called pessimism."

"Who's pessimistic here, Miss Price Bracket?"

You flipped.

Despite his harassed face, he stunned you by agreeing to the trip.

Everything was organized to the last detail. Everything but the climate. A few hours into the day, the weather window opened, torrential rain that left a curtain behind. Despite the planning, you got lost. Twice. Ended up doing a long leg to Kununurra. Gave shoes for another fight.

Irish Clover in "The Road to No Place" chants her soulful lyrics:

You say you'll climb no mountain with me
I'll go with you anyway
Darling I'll follow you
Somewhere we've never been.

I'll go with you to the sun and to the night
I'll go with you where the water is wide
I'll go with you anyway
No Place is where we'll be.

You say I'm not your rain, your rainbow
But you're my earth, my blanket
You're my canopy, my tree
I'll go with you anywhere we've never been.

Not saying a word about River's uncanny state, one he doesn't appear to notice, makes you feel complicit with the devil. Like you've already sold your soul, and there's nothing you can do about it.

Your dread melts to curiosity. You glance at River and his lost hands and let out a cry. His belly downward is gone. Just an athletic chest and a head, cropped arms driving a car without touching.

"River?"

He doesn't immediately respond, emotions barricaded within himself. When he looks at you, it's with a darkened mood. "Have to listen to that stupid song?"

You want to tell him that it's his car, his radio. That he has no hands and no legs, and what the goddamn fuck is happening? But all you say is, "No," a whisper in your throat.

"Will you turn it off?"

"No."

"Be like that."

No reason has its name, its talent, written on this new grumble. Its seeds sink deeper, water themselves richer, flower more malignant blues.

Though he maintains the same proximity in his hacked body, so close you can almost hear his heart talk, he is drawn away from you, accepting without question the space, its margin creeping further out.

You grip the seatbelt where he can't see it.

River is ... my big red lobster. Beautiful, until the fiend.

Two springs ago, you were working at a garden restaurant. He stepped into your life with a guitar across his waist, a rucksack on his back. *An avid traveler*, you thought. He caught your eye. *Rapture*, you thought. And then he smiled. *Hey presto.* Reminded you of the heartthrob muso who won the Boy-up Brook Country Music Awards years back. Your thoughts turned unholy.

We fell in love swatting sandflies ... in Broome.

Longing swells, you feel empty next to a stranger.

Before the trip, before he became this ... this ... your body was willing, the mathematics of your need. But everything around it failed. Night after night, you turned to your pillow, swallowed in thought. One day, you feared, the pillow would mean more than River.

Sometimes you never kissed.

Just a melt of bodies, a tumble of knees, flesh against flesh, almost cruel. Thrusts that summoned a climax that spread from your toes.

"Jesus!"

"Goddamn!"

Your responses are simultaneous as an overtaking truck judders, sways dangerously close, pushes you nearly off the highway.

Silence for a startling second stretches miles out.

You switch driving at dusk. River lightly snores. Just his dreadlocked head and broad shoulders—his chest is gone. The road rover is a power train. You glide with your foreboding. River takes the wheel at dawn. You sleep. Wake on instinct. It's a strange world in the middle of nowhere. A blue-green carpet with fluid waves. Ears of grass stir, tease, declare interest in everything about you.

Sandy gold stretches a quarter mile deep, some dapples of green with burnt yellows. Beautifully rugged in parts, it reminds you of River's morning face. You glance at him, what's left of him: black gold eyes and an ivory-white jaw—skeletal. Clouds dissolve to shimmering threads across the ocean-blue firmament.

The road rover halts at a divide.

"Left or right?" says River.

"Right."

A whiff of aftershave touches your nostrils. You can almost feel him on your skin.

"Dying for a piddle," he says.

"Me too. Where do people go in this wilderness?"

"The bush?"

You wipe your forehead with the back of your hands. "River?"

"Yes?" Just eyes—the jaw is gone.

You hug your knees. "I wonder about us—do you?"

"I wonder about it plenty."

Your stomach folds. You rock on your knees.

"Maybe we should, you know … take time off," you say.

"We *are* taking time off."

You pull at your hair, worrying it. Tighten a long strand in a little finger.

"Let's not fight. Please, River."

"Okay. What now?"

"Don't know."

The road rover rolls into a deserted station.

"Well," the engine dies, "I'm going for a piddle."

"Me too."

You slip on canvas trainers, hug a turquoise sweater.

You depart, perhaps as equals, not as partners.

You step minutes behind into the station, seek the toilet. River is nowhere to ask. You see it, a metal shack, labeled.

You push the door. It swings with ease.

You climb down a stone step, jump sodden paper on the ground. The walls are dripping, the floor swirling with water.

But the need to go is great.

You move tippie-toe toward one of the cubicles, take care not to touch the wetness.

Later, as you wash your hands, a cubicle door opens. River—nothing visible, but you know it's him—comes out.

"Dripping mess," you say. "You could have warned me."

"What—spoil the surprise?" Your heart tugs at the lilt in his voice.

"Can't find the dryer. What's this?" You move toward a contraption on the wall.

"Don't touch—" begins River.

You've already pressed it.

"—the green button," he finishes lamely.

A moan on the roof, roar, and a glorious waterfall of soapy water spits from the ceiling. The deluge plummets, splashes and bounces off walls, floods you.

You screech, try to run. Slip.

Drowning in water, you lift your head and see a silhouette like a shimmering light forming of River. It is bolts of lightning shaping out a man. His translucent body is standing in the waterfall. Now he's there, now he's not. He's shaking clumps of drippy hair, roped, from his face. "Washed itself, did it?"

He's still wavering in and out like a breaking circuit.

You rise, coughing.

You guide yourself with palms along the wall. Squishy shoes make obscene sounds. Your nipple-struck T-shirt draws your sweater tighter. You stare, horrified. Sobbing denim clings to your legs.

"I just touched it," you gasp.

Drip! Drip! says the wall.

"Oh, you beaut," laughs River. Now he's a silhouette, no longer twinkling in and out. There's his smoky self, his smoky smile.

The ceiling sighs. The flood gurgles and narrows its cascade to a dribble. Dripping walls, clomps of soggy tissue float in a puddle.

He comes toward you, not the drift of a ghost, but walking, misty leg after misty leg. The blackest, most golden eyes hold your gaze, until you're enveloped in his steamy form, in the waft of his aftershave: an earthy scent of cedar and orange flower.

"We'd best get these clothes off," he speaks to your hair. You clutch him, nothing solid, just the emanating heat of his fog. It leaves you with a pining for the touch of him—a longing for his finger tracing the outline of your nose. His mouth teasing the nape of your neck.

You don't know about tomorrow, whether River will ever be as he was, different from the torment he is now. Present, yet lacking. It's a complete, unauthorized departure from all you know. But he's your rain, your rainbow. Your earth, your blanket. You'll go anywhere with him.

Suddenly, you feel more. You feel more deeply.

Introducing Perplexia: A Novel Pharmacological Intervention for Memory Impairment

By Dr. Andrew Frost

Perplexia

From Utopedia, the free encyclopedia

This is an article about the social and historical effect of the pharmaceutical Perplexia. For a detailed account of its development, see Perplexia [pharmacology].

For the album by the group Zerexes, see Perplexia [album]; for the 2028 film see Perplexia [Documentary].

Memory impairment represented a formidable challenge in clinical neuroscience, affecting individuals across diverse demographics with profound socio-economic ramifications. In response to this pressing concern the pharmaceutical company Bonewitt Pharma introduced Perplexia, a therapeutic agent crafted to address cognitive deficits stemming from memory loss.

Perplexia operated at the forefront of neuropharmacology, leveraging a sophisticated mechanism of action to target the intricate neural substrates implicated in memory formation, consolidation, and retrieval. Through modulation of synaptic plasticity, neurotransmitter dynamics, and neurotrophic signalling cascades, Perplexia orchestrated a harmonized response within the neural milieu, fostering the enhancement of cognitive faculties.

Preliminary clinical investigations underscored Perplexia's exceptional efficacy in ameliorating memory impairments across various aetiologies, ranging from neurodegenerative conditions to traumatic brain injuries. Its favourable pharmacokinetic profile, characterized by optimal blood-brain barrier penetration and sustained duration of action, augured well for its clinical utility and patient compliance.

Perplexia exhibited a favourable safety profile, with initial minimal off-target effects and negligible propensity for adverse drug interactions. As such, Perplexia emerged as a "beacon of hope" [1] in the therapeutic armamentarium against memory loss, poised to "empower individuals to reclaim their cognitive vitality and restore their quality of life." [2].

Development

Effective treatment for memory loss had been hampered by a number of factors including the nature of the memory loss, the regions and architecture of the brain where short and long term memory is stored, and the degree to which physical or emotional trauma were involved in masking long term memory. Along with these recurring issues were considerations of the various types and causes of dementia such as Alzheimer's Disease, vascular, Lewy body and frontotemporal dementias. As Bonewitt Pharma's research specialist Dr. Robert Bathurst remarked "If we don't know the cause, we can't fix the problem." [3]

Most memory restoration treatments tended to focus on cholinesterase, an enzyme that breaks down the neurotransmitter acetylene, to avoid the overstimulation of "post-synaptic nerves, muscles and exocrine glands". [4] Single-dose drug combinations such as Coretexin, and NeuroVive were also prescribed to treat severe memory loss.

Bonewitt Pharma Inc, an American pharmaceutical company based in Millford, Utah, dedicated substantial research into the development of a new approach to memory restoration treatment with an effectiveness at an order many times that of existing drug-based treatments. In 2022, Dr. Robert Bathurst was appointed the head of Special Project 33.

Code named in development as Substance M or SM, the drug formulation included acetylcholine precursors such as choline and acetyl-L-carnitine, facilitating neurotransmission and synaptic plasticity. Additionally, it incorporated NMDA receptor modulators like memantine to regulate glutamatergic signalling and enhance synaptic strength. Further, herbal extracts such as Ginkgo biloba and Bacopa monnieri were included for their neuroprotective and memory-enhancing properties.

Clinical Trials

On March 25th 2025, following extended animal testing which found low levels toxicity in extended use of SM, the U.S. Food and Drug Administration [F.D.A.] approved the start of clinical trials on human volunteers to test the drug's efficacy prior to use among the wider human population. 100 volunteers were selected who represented a range of conditions related to mild to severe memory loss including Alzheimer's disease patients, individuals suffering from different types of dementia, and survivors of emotional or physical trauma. Following standard protocols, volunteers were also screened based on a standard medical exam, medical history and demographic variance. Where in some cases informed consent could not be obtained from the volunteer, next of kin and power of attorney permissions were sought and received. Under the direction of

Dr. Bathurst, with clinical supervisors Dr. Tony Zhao and Dr. Helen O'Neil, Phase One clinical trials began on May 2nd, 2026 with volunteers given daily doses of SM over a period of five months. [5]

Cases

Names are anonymized as per their usage in the initial Special Project 33 SM Phase One Case Study Report [5].

Patient: Alex D.
Diagnosis: Traumatic Brain Injury (TBI)-related Amnesia

Alex D, male, 38 years old, who suffered from retrograde and anterograde amnesia following a traumatic brain injury, underwent treatment with SM. He had experienced significant subdural haemorrhaging, along with other injuries, after a motorcycle he was riding impacted with a car. Following initial recovery from surgery, and a program of physical rehabilitation, Alex experienced significant memory loss and poor concentration, affecting his ability to work, maintain income, with periods of depression, mood swings, and outbursts of anger. Post-therapy assessments revealed significant recovery in memory recall and consolidation. Neuroimaging indicated increased activity in hippocampal and prefrontal cortex regions, crucial for memory formation. Alex demonstrated improved cognitive function and episodic memory retrieval, leading to enhanced daily functioning. SM facilitated neuroplasticity and synaptic remodelling, promoting memory recovery and cognitive rehabilitation.

> "The first thing I remembered after the crash was waking up in the ICU a few days later, but the day leading up to it and the crash itself were just gone. Later, I found I couldn't recall key events in my life in any detail, like when I got married, or when I graduated high school. After about a month [on the drug], I started to recall exact details of the crash, the car pulling out in front of me, and the impact. Then other memories started coming back from my childhood. I started to feel a whole lot better too." [6]

Patient: Emma K.
Diagnosis: Lewy Body Dementia.

Emma K, female, 80 years old, had been diagnosed with Lewy body dementia, and had experienced cognitive fluctuations, visual hallucinations, and Parkinsonism. Due to her age and the advanced nature of the dementia, Emma had been volunteered for the study by her adult daughters who had, until that time, been her chief caregivers. Treatment with SM led to notable cognitive improvement with biomarker analysis indicating decreased alpha-synuclein aggregation and neuroinflammation. Functional imaging revealed restored connectivity in cortical and subcortical regions. Emma's motor symptoms also showed improvement. SM offered promising results in managing

Lewy body dementia, providing Emma with enhanced cognitive stability and a better quality of life. Emma's daughter Caroline stated:

> "Mom had moments of lucidity but for the most part she had no short term memory, and would often get our names mixed up, or forget them altogether. After six weeks in the program she suddenly seemed to be there again, like the lights went on inside, and she called us all by our names, remembered what she'd eaten the day before, what we'd watched on TV. Detailed recall. She seemed like she was 20 years younger." [9]

Patient: Maya Z.
Diagnosis: Complex Trauma-induced Memory Fragmentation

Maya Z, female, 27 years old, had been grappling with fragmented memories due to complex trauma experienced during childhood and early adulthood. SM therapy led to significant improvement in memory integration and emotional regulation. Neurobiological assessments showed reduced amygdala hyperactivity and enhanced connectivity between memory-related brain regions. Maya Z. reported reduced emotional distress and increased coherence in her narrative of traumatic events.

> "I could put all together. All the missing pieces. I made peace with my demons. It was very hard at first, but the clarity led me to the realisation that the abuse I had suffered was not my fault, and my substance abuse had been a kind of self-punishment . It was liberating. I felt like my whole life opened up." [10]

Following the extraordinary success of Phase One clinical trials and the publication of the initial findings by Drs. Bathurst, Zhao and O'Neil in the journal Brain Function and Cognition: Insights and Innovations, Phase Two was approved by the F.D.A. with 500 volunteers inducted into the study beginning on April 11, 2027 for a projected 2 year trial.

Side Effects
It was noted during Phase Two that a number of side effects were experienced by participants, and ranked in three categories.

Category One side effects, experienced in various combinations by 22% of participants included: a sudden increase in body temperature, extremely high blood pressure and convulsions (fits), when taken with: antibiotics used to treat pneumonia and certain skin infections; medicines for depression, panic disorder, social anxiety or obsessive illnesses (dothiepin, desipramine, fluoxetine, paroxetine citalopram, venlafaxine); lithium, a medicine used to treat mood swings; other medicines including weight-reducing medicines; medicines for the treatment of cold and flu to suppress cough, medicines for strong pain management; a medicine used to treat drug addiction; other medicines used to relieve pain, swelling and other symptoms of inflammation; and medicines used to treat disturbances in thinking, feeling and behaviour.

Category Two side effects, experienced in various combinations by 8% of participants included: sudden onset of hives, itching or skin rash; feeling uncomfortable or restless; feeling cold; unexplained weight gain, or weight loss; drowsiness; swelling of the face, lips or tongue with difficulty swallowing or breathing; symptoms of sudden fever with sweating, fast heartbeat and muscle stiffness, leading to loss of consciousness; thoughts of suicide or attempting suicide or self-harm; increased aggressiveness with thoughts of harm or death to others; hallucinations, including delusions of grandeur; increased social importance or significance; light-headedness, dizziness, headache or lack of concentration; irritability, tearfulness or crying; nausea, vomiting, diarrhoea, stomach pain; excessive thirst; insomnia; a sweet smell on the breath, a sweet or metallic taste in mouth and/or a different odour to urine.

Category Three side effects, experienced in various combinations by 12% of participants, included slurred speech; disorientation, bewilderment; disinhibition, bluntness, overindulgence and constant need for gratification; ennui, lassitude, enervation, or malaise; lethargy, indolence, torpidity, inertia, dullness; nostalgia, increased sentimentality, wistfulness, regret, acute homesickness; agitation, disquiet or distress, dread, disconcertment; impatience, frustration, avidity; partial dyslexia.

While extensive, these effects were anticipated and within the range of effects experienced using compounds within a comparable pharmacopeia.

Contraindications

The U.S. Senate Health, Education, Labor and Pensions [HELP] Committee investigation into the development, approval sale and use of Perplexia uncovered previously suppressed Bonewitt Pharma documentation from both Phase Two and Phase Three clinical trials that had indicated disturbing adverse reactions to SM. [11] Among Phase Two participants it was found that

> "where [participants] had taken 100mgs of SM daily for a period of more than 12 months, and despite significant improvement in their pre-trial conditions, contraindications began to emerge that suggested an unaccounted for level of toxicity, or possibly a re-ordering of brain structure divergent to the understood architecture of memory retention centers." [12]

Max K, male, 55, diagnosed with memory loss caused by hypoxic-ischemic encephalopathy following systolic heart failure, underwent treatment with SM. Post-therapy evaluations demonstrated significant recovery in memory retention and cognitive function as neuroimaging indicated restoration of cerebral blood flow and metabolic activity in affected brain regions.

After returning to work as a teacher, Max began to experience heightened memory retention, able to recall with exact detail conversations he had had with colleagues months before. Soon after Max claimed to be able to recall moments from his teenage years with a level of clarity he found disturbing. Seeking help, Max told researchers that he "...couldn't switch it off." Max's wife Katherine later said Max was highly agitated by bursts of memory recall, one he claimed to reveal the suppressed identity of a man who had molested him when he was 13 years old. Katherine told researchers that Max's suicide note had simply read "please stop." [13]

Other cases were less dramatic but gave researchers concern over the SM treatment. Sarah J, female, 86 years old, diagnosed with stage 2/3 Alzheimer's disease, exhibited progressive memory decline and cognitive impairment. Following treatment, she demonstrated significant cognitive improvement. Neuropsychological assessments revealed enhanced memory recall and executive function. Sarah regained independence in daily activities and reported improved quality of life, marking a substantial milestone in her dementia management.

Like Max, Sarah began to recall detailed, verifiable childhood memories of significant personal events such as birthday parties, a beloved pet dog, her parents and siblings. However, Sarah also claimed to recall detailed memories of being 2 years old, crossing what many researchers believed was the limit of recall of long term memory to an age when the brain is still developing. The intensity and recurrence of these memories were as significant as other participants but Sarah claimed not to be disturbed by the almost constant recall, describing the experience as being "...like watching a lovely movie with all my family and friends as the stars."

Dr. Bathurst theorised that in some cases participants might be experiencing an induced state of hyperthymestic syndrome, also known as highly superior autobiographical memory [HSAM] due to dosage levels of SM. Despite reducing doses to 10mgs daily, then to 5mgs, these experiences persisted for around 115 participants and MRI scans indicated permanent brain structure alterations.

Some responses to treatment could not be theoretically accounted for. Sonia R, female, 45 experienced cognitive dysfunction post-chemotherapy, impacting memory and concentration. Engaging in SM treatment, she witnessed notable improvement. While experiencing HSAM, Haley claimed to remember meeting John F. Kennedy on May 12, 1960 while the future President was on the campaign trail. Since this event would have been over 80 years before Sonia's birth, her memories were dismissed by researchers as a potential case of false memory syndrome potentially caused by an unknown trauma, or the result of an emotional identification with the former President.

Another participant, Conrad S, 62, suffered memory impairment following a stroke. After significant recovery of memory, and more than a year in the study on an SM dose of 50mgs daily, Conrad claimed to be a survivor of the sinking of RMS Titanic on April 15, 1912. Initially assumed to be a variant case of cryptomnesia – a forgotten memory returning as though it had happened to the subject – Conrad was able to provide highly detailed accounts of the sinking and his subsequent rescue. It was unclear whether Conrad had ever seen a movie or TV show about the event, but the emotional commitment to the memory was startling.

The participant John M, male, aged 78, experienced age-related memory decline affecting daily functioning. Following a comprehensive assessment, he commenced SM treatment. Over time, John displayed marked enhancement in memory consolidation and retrieval. While it seemed John did not experience HSAM, he did claim to remember being an orb spider, from birth to death. Dr. O'Neil wrote a one word note on John's medical record: "BIZARRE". [14]

Approval & Use

On Tuesday June 12, 2035 the F.D.A approved the sale of SM, now commercially branded as Perplexia. Over the next six months, government health officials in Australia, Canada, the European Union, the United Kingdom, New Zealand, and Russia also approved Perpelxia's wide usage. The estimated income from international sales of Perplexia were estimated in excess of USD$200 billion annually. Bonewitt Pharma, a mid-ranking pharmaceutical company before the development of Perplexia, soon became one of the most profitable pharma companies in the world ranking alongside industry giants such as AbbVie, Bristol Myers Squibb, Merck and Pfizer by 2036.

Society and Culture

Widely prescribed around the world and hailed as a breakthrough treatment for dementia, brain injury, and traumatic amnesia, the release of Perplexia caused a sensation. The first 1 minute Perplexia ad was released on July 1, 2035 online, with more than 2.5 billion combined views across social media platforms, artfully combining the promise of its effects with a compelling visualization.

Directed by Emil Goh and produced by Goh, Johnson and Kee Partners Singapore, the ad begins with men and women ranging in ages from 35 to 80 wandering through a green field. It's revealed that each of them is holding an old style photo print in their hands with an image of the person alongside a loved one such as husband or wife, parent or child, each slowly fading away within the picture. Highly emotive music – swapped out depending on territorial rights and regional music tastes – swells as the fading pictures reverse, and the fading people now appearing whole before each of the men and women in the field. The men and women and their lost relatives tearfully embrace. The ad concludes with the voiceover: *"Even if your loved ones are gone, there's no need to forget them..."* [15]

Demand for the drug soon outstripped supply. In the United States prices for the drug skyrocketed, with a 1 month supply costing as much $1,500 or $800 with health insurance. In countries outside the US, inconsistent supply caused some patients to miss their medication schedule with the result of partial or incomplete recovery. The New York Times covered the crisis in the widely shared article *Public Outcry: Concerns Rise Over Access and Affordability of Perplexia* [16] read by more than 20 million people in the first 24 hours.

After Bonewitt Pharma refused to license generic versions of Perplexia, the Shenzhen-based company Morning Bright Star Pharma announced their own variation under the brand name Neuraflex. Later lab analysis showed that Neuraflex and Perplexia were almost identical in composition, however the Chinese variant was claimed to also contain engineered nucleotides based on cephalopod brain chemistry [citation needed]. Regardless of its supposed exotic pharmacology, Neuraflex was marketed at a quarter of the price of Perplexia, quickly surpassing its use outside the United States, and was on sale illegally there via the black markets in Canada and Mexico. In the face of this, and with the loss of hundreds of millions of dollars, Bonewitt Pharma reluctantly granted generic licenses on August 25, 2036.

By mid-2037 it was estimated by the World Health Organisation that more than 557 million people worldwide were taking Perplexia, Neuraflex or one of the generic variants. [17] The positive effects were widely noted, with previous sufferers of dementia, brain injury and emotional trauma restored to health. Older people, those 65 and over, were profoundly affected by the drug with many leading happy productive lives well into their 80s and 90s. After just five years on the market, it was often said that people were now living in a "post-Perplexia world" such was the marked difference in society at large.

Controversy

In mid-2042, the first indications that Perplexia may have been causing serious side effects were raised in a series of journal articles, such as Davis and Parker's "Perplexia and PTSD: Potential Therapeutic Applications and Ethical Concerns" [18] and Carson and Jones's "Perplexia and Its Impact on Cognitive Enhancement: A Systematic Review" [19] Both articles, and many others like them, raised concerns over extended use of Perplexia and highlighted cases in approximately 10% of patients where instances of HSAM were recorded, and in 2% of cases where cryptomnesia, false memory syndrome, and alleged past life recall, were recorded. The number of patients experiencing adverse effects was estimated to be approximately 10% of users, or around 55.7 million people.

Mainstream news outlets picked up on both the journal articles and a groundswell of concern across social media with a series of reports highlighting what Bonewitt Pharma had initially dismissed as anomalous side effects in a small percentage of users. Regardless, the Daily Herald asked "Perplexia: Miracle Drug or Marketing Gimmick?" [20] while The New Times Gazette reported "Alarming Side Effects of Perplexia Reported by Patients" [21]

Perplexia was denounced by both scientists and politicians on the grounds that the drug's effects were unsafe and unethical, while many religious groups and spiritual leaders objected to what they saw as an unacceptable departure from the natural order of things. The Reverend Peter Graham, leader of the Pentecostal Assemblies of the World, headquartered in Battle Creek, Michigan, proclaimed:

> "There is a reason God has asked us to forget. It's so that we can learn to live in peace, and to forgive." [22]

Governments moved to restrict Perplexia or ban it outright. In the US, the U.S. Senate Health, Education, Labor and Pensions [HELP] Committee launched its investigation with public hearings commencing on Thursday September 28, 2045. Called to give evidence was Dr. Bathurst and his team, representatives of the FDA, Barry DuBray, CEO of Bonewitt Pharma, and more than a dozen patients who offered startling, sometimes emotional testimony. At the conclusion of the investigation, criminal charges were recommended to the US Department of Justice., for Dr. Bathurst and Dr. O'Neill, and for Bonewitt Pharma. DuBray later resigned from the company.

Recall

Perplexia was formerly discontinued and manufacturing halted. Existing stocks were limited to patients proven not to suffer any psychological side effects and were then transferred to a new Bonewitt Pharma treatment with a significantly altered compound under the brand name Mnemotix [23].

The Great Awakening

[For the main article, see The Great Awakening (History)]

While Perplexia and its variants had officially been banned, it soon became apparent by the early 2050s that black markets, illegal pharma factories in Indonesia, Thailand and China were supplying a growing global demand, not only for the treatment of dementia or trauma, but also as a lifestyle choice. Users of these drugs, mostly adults but also teenagers and children, claimed an almost inexhaustible vitality, superior memory retention, and improved general wellbeing. Sources including the W.H.O. claimed that by 2054 there were nearly 1 billion users worldwide. [24]

It was this period that was proclaimed by many at the time as "The Great Awakening" owing to changes wrought in the cultures of many countries. For example, in post-colonial countries that had never fully reconciled with their First Nations peoples, and in countries where part of the population were descendants of slaves, the impact of memory treatments were profound. Former life memories were widely believed to be the actual life experiences of ancestors, a belief that in turn prompted renewed calls for social justice and reparations. Although initially resisted, the social upheaval prompted by a reckoning with the past swept governments from power in countries including Australia, Brazil, Canada, France, Japan, Singapore, the United Kingdom, Vietnam and many others.

Media

The widespread use of Perplexia has had a lasting effect in popular culture and in media. Some of the better known examples include:

Echoes of the Past: A Memoir of Perplexia Recovery, by Amir Khan, first published in Pakistan by Nero Press, January 2044.

The Great Awakening, an AR/VR experience, was released by Apple in 2056.

In the Shadows of Recollection: My Perplexia Experience, by Hiroshi Tanaka, first published in Japan by AMR, October, 2043.

Introducing Perplexia: A Novel Pharmacological Intervention for Memory Impairment, by Dr. Andrew Frost, first published in Canada by The Terminal Press, June, 2045.

Perplexed and Confused, a three season, 18 episode TV series about living with, and surviving, Perplexia was first streamed on Netflix from 2043-2049. The show starred Jamal Washington, Ana Rodriguez, and Malik Patel.

Perplexia: Lest We Forget, a documentary on the impact of the drug with user testimonies, and narrated by ai Brad Pitt, was directed by Hester Cammerston, and released worldwide in April 2046.

Perplexia, a concept album by the Greek doom-trap band Zerexes was released May 11, 2044.

Notes

[1] [2] *Introducing Perplexia: A Novel Pharmacological Intervention for Memory Impairment*, Bonewitt Pharma, press release, 2030

[3] Dr. Robert Bathurst, interview, *The Today Show*. March 12, 2030

[4] L.Z. Yang, *Perplexia, Frontiers in Neuropsychology and Cognitive Neuroscience*, Iss. 8, V12.

[5] [6] [7] [8] [9] [10] Records of the Special Project 33 SM Phase One Case Study Report, Perplexia Institute Archive.

[11] [12] [13] [14] *Report on Perplexia*, development and release, the U.S. Senate Health, Education, Labor and Pensions [HELP] Committee.

[15] *Loved Ones*, commercial. July 1, 2035.

[16] *Public Outcry: Concerns Rise Over Access and Affordability of Perplexia*, The New York Times, October 14, 2035.

[17] *Annual Use & Trends Report Year 2037-38*, World Health Organisation, The United Nations, Rome, Italy.

[18] Davis, L. M., & Parker, E. J. (2036). Perplexia and PTSD: Potential Therapeutic Applications and Ethical Concerns. *Brain Function and Cognition: Insights and Innovations*, 12(4), 421-435.

[19] Carson, A. R., & Jones, K. L. (2034). Perplexia and Its Impact on Cognitive Enhancement: A Systematic Review. *Neuroplasticity Research Quarterly*, 15(2), 178-192. DOI: 10.1038/s41386-022-01234-5

[20] Brown, M. (2036, August 5). "Perplexia: Miracle Drug or Marketing Gimmick?" *The Daily Herald*.

[21] Smith, A. (2036, April 20). "Alarming Side Effects of Perplexia Reported by Patients." *The New Times Gazette*.

[22] Pentecostal Assemblies of the World

[23] Breaking News: Mnemotix Unveiled as a Safer Alternative to Perplexia, Promising Memory Restoration with Reduced Risk, Al Jazeera, June 11 2046

[24] Annual Use & Trends Report Year 20534-54, World Health Organisation, The United Nations, Rome, Italy.

References

Bowen, A. L., & Garcia, M. H. (2035). Ethical Considerations in the Use of Perplexia for Memory Restoration. *Journal of Cognitive Neurobiology*, 18(3), 231-245. DOI: 10.1080/15265161.2023.45678

Carson, A. R., & Jones, K. L. (2034). Perplexia and Its Impact on Cognitive Enhancement: A Systematic Review. *Neuroplasticity Research Quarterly*, 15(2), 178-192. DOI: 10.1038/s41386-022-01234-5

Davis, L. M., & Parker, E. J. (2036). Perplexia and PTSD: Potential Therapeutic Applications and Ethical Concerns. *Brain Function and Cognition: Insights and Innovations*, 12(4), 421-435. DOI: 10.4172/2324-8947.1000567

Johnson, P. A. (2040). Public Perception of Perplexia: A Media Analysis. *Journal of Advances in Neurophysiology and Brain Function*, 30(4), 399-410. DOI: 10.1080/10810730.2022.1357910

Nguyen, T. H., & Wilson, R. D. (2037). Perplexia and Memory Recovery in Traumatic Brain Injury: A Case Series Analysis. *Neurochemical Pathways: From Molecules to Behavior* 39(1), 89-102. DOI: 10.1097/HTR.0000000000000701

Thompson S. L., & Lee, E. H. (2028). Neurological and Behavioural Effects of Perplexia: Insights from Animal Studies. *Frontiers in Neuropsychology and Cognitive Neuroscience*, 99, 78-85. DOI: 10.1016/j.brainresbull.2022.07.012

Wilson, H. G., & Nguyen, Q. V. (2032). Perplexia and the Aging Brain: Implications for Dementia Treatment. *Journal of Gerontology: Medical Sciences*, 60(5), 654-667. DOI: 10.1093/gerona/glaa321

External Links

Perplexia Research Institute. (n.d.). Retrieved from http://www.perplexia-research.org

Brown, M. "Perplexia: Miracle Drug or Marketing Gimmick?" The Daily Herald. Retrieved from http://www.dailyherald.org/perplexia-miracle-drug-or-marketing-gimmick

Gaston, R. "Experts Warn Against the Unregulated Use of Perplexia." The Global Observer. Retrieved from: http://www.globalobserver.net/experts-warn-against-the-unregulated-use-of-perplexia

Lopez, L. "Government to Investigate Allegations of Perplexia Misuse in Clinical Trials." Fuller News Organization. Retrieved from http://www.fullernewsorg.com/government-to-investigate-allegations-of-perplexia-misuse-in-clinical-trials

Betaville
By Andrew Hook

We live in the void of our metamorphoses
Paul Éluard, *The Capital of Pain*

INT. PENTHOUSE APARTMENT ABOVE SIXTH AVENUE, NEW YORK. NIGHT.

Montage of close ups of DEBORAH HARRY and CHRIS STEIN embracing, perhaps dancing, against the light and alternately illuminated by it; CHRIS gently kissing her; a front medium shot of DEBORAH against a white wall in which the light intensifies until it is painful and then fades away, radiates; both of them leant against the jukebox, CHRIS kisses her hand, DEBORAH puts her hand to his cheek, passes her fingers through his hair, and they dance ritualistically as the light flashes on and off.

The apartment is festooned with movie posters, glamorama, bric-a-brac. Deborah prowls between rooms, a constant in motion. Chris stays put, captures her in shot. There's an immediacy to everything with little view of the future. Deborah wears a strappy white dress; Deborah wears a strappy black dress. Negatives of each other. A pan on fire.

That night they share a bed. It isn't the first time.

Chris is on a high co-hosting the public-access show TV Party. It's always an event. He'd interviewed the journalist, Ivan Johnson. He's uncharacteristically jittery.

"Amos was saying we should make a film. You have the face for it."

Deborah lifts one side of her pillow and pushes it against his head. Whilst hydrogen peroxide manifests little odour Chris' perceived sensation is reminiscent of ozone. He breathes her in.

"Freak!"

They tumble awhile.

"Seriously?" Deborah says; later: "Does he want to direct?"

"Amos always wants to direct. We just need a vehicle."

"A Ford Galaxie? A 1976 Plymouth Fury?"

"Funny. We could write something ourselves."

Deborah rolls over. "Oh, I dunno, Chris. That seems like a lot of work."

"We already do a lot of work."

"That's *exactly* what I'm talking about."

Deborah envisages a day where there isn't something to do. There's the three album a year deal which is virtually impossible to meet. The stress is showing. If they're not constantly on tour, then it seems that they're constantly on tour. She contemplates the white-painted ceiling above her head. They haven't been home in a while. She can barely remember the patterns and cracks.

Chris is talking. "Maybe we can do a remake. I could score it. I've always listened to soundtracks. *Lawrence of Arabia* was a big influence and *West Side Story*. You know that movie, *Irma La Douce*? Jack Lemmon and Shirley MacLaine? I loved the soundtrack to that. I was always playing that at home."

"You wanna score a film?"

"Sure, why not? Maybe I could be the next Nino Rota."

Sometimes it seems the world isn't big enough to contain them.

"How about *Once Upon A Time In New York*?"

"I never know when you're being funny or serious."

"Oh, I'm seriously funny."

Deborah gets out of bed, wanders through to the kitchen in her underwear. Pours herself a glass of water. In 1842, pristine water flowed for the first time from upstate reservoirs into New York City. It's amongst the finest tap water in the world.

She calls through from the space as Chris picks up his camera.

"Who should star in it?"

There's a coterie to choose from.

Almost too *much* choice.

"We need an idea first."

"Yeah, sure, an idea."

"Why don't you come back to bed."

Chris runs off a few shots as she re-enters the bedroom.

"You voyeur."

They kiss. Her lips wet.

Neither can sleep. They're hyped. It gets like this: instances of creativity where a word sparks an idea sparks a discussion sparks an intensity sparks substance.

"What did Amos Poe suggest?"

Chris leans on one elbow. "He said we should make up something or remake the last film we saw."

"That option seems like the least work. What was it?"

Chris flicks through a few flicks. *Suddenly Last Summer. Amarcord. On The Waterfront*. He can't quite remember.

"Hey, wasn't it that film by Godard?" Deborah sits up in the bed, her hands in her lap. "You remember? That SF movie that wasn't an SF movie. Minimalist sets. We could make it here, right in New York."

Chris nods, slowly.

"I could be Natacha von Braun, Anna Karina's character. We'll have to find someone to be that detective, whatever his name was."

"Robert Fripp's in town. He's got that look."

"If you think he'd be up for it. Has he ever acted?"

"Aren't we all actors?"

Deborah agrees. She considers the persona she's created for Blondie to be similar to a drag queen. It both isn't her and is her. Which she suspects is what acting is all about.

She yawns. The sun glints off a building from the opposite side of the street. A heat-seeking missile. "I'm getting tired."

"OK, let's sleep. But are we doing this?"

Deborah adopts a serious expression. "Well, nearly every day there are films which disappear because they are no longer allowed. In their place, one must make new films to correspond with new ideas."

"You're right. We'll do it. We'll need to enquire about the rights."

"Sure, lets go for it. Let's throw caution to the wind."

Deborah wears a black gabardine trench coat with a removable sherpa lining. The expressway is lit yellow both sides. Her foot is down hard on the accelerator of the 1967 Chevrolet Camaro coupe. Occasional overhead lights strobe her face. She is alone. A gun may or may not be in the glove compartment. She seems to have come from nowhere.

Chris has stayed in New York. It is her mission to buy the rights from Godard. An assignation has been arranged. They've done some preliminary photoshoots with Fripp. She's wearing a black one-piece, her hair all 50s starlet, star lit. He's donned black slacks, a black jacket. Not quite a suit. White shirt punctuated by a black tie. The larger end of the tie is higher up than the shorter end, as though knotted in the dark. There's footage too. A screen test. Fripp can't keep a straight face. Deborah wears dark glasses, pulls at her cheeks as if getting into character. Head shots.

The photographs have been printed and reside in a brown manilla envelope on the passenger seat. Collateral or a statement of intent.

She grits her teeth.

Godard has suggested they meet in the past.

There's a junction somewhere in sidereal space.

She keeps her eyes to the road. Traffic merges at all angles, entering the stream on zipwires. Getting mighty crowded. The Camaro reverberates to a different timbre. The road surface deteriorates. Up ahead a lump of tarmac resembles a sleeping policeman. When she hits it, something triggers. The sultry voice of Paco Navarro on WKTU-FM is lost to crackle. Potato chip radio. There is a flash of darkness, an antithesis. It picks her up and spits her out. She maintains a steady fifty. Everything is black and white.

Beta 60 broadcasts. The recognisable voice mechanical, as if comprised of the aforementioned crackle.

< I am trying to change the world >

There are fewer cars on the road. A subtlety to the transformation which creates a gradual sensation of unease. Deborah goes to sweep a hand through her hair and knocks off the felt homburg she hadn't known she was wearing. She takes a breath. Forces non-committal. Wishes Chris were there.

It is easy to find the hotel she has booked. She parks up. Takes the manilla envelope along with her valise. Through revolving doors she catches sight of her hair. She can't decide if it looks lighter or darker in monochrome. She turns, out of reach.

A girl looks up as she approaches the reception desk.

"I'm very well, thank you, not at all."

Deborah states her intent, is given a key. Such subterfuge. Their contact has told them Godard cannot speak English. He will communicate through an interpreter. Their first missive being, "Why do you want to do this movie? You're crazy!"

She's been to Paris but this isn't it.

This is somewhere. Other.

In her room she removes the trench coat. Loosens her tie. A copy of *Halliwell's Film Guide* is on the bedside table.

She runs a bath. Against the flow of water a door is opening. Deborah hugs the wall. The guy she rabbit punches goes down like a shadow. She searches his pockets but there is no identification.

She takes the bath.

There's a soirée. In her valise—amongst toiletries, peroxide, lipstick—is a wad of a thousand notes. She fans herself, clears steam. She doesn't recognise the face on the bills. Some kind of celebrity or an authoritarian figure, no doubt.

Her contact meets her at the door.

"I'm very well, thank you, not at all."

"I haven't even asked."

The girl's face is impassive.

"I'm seeking Godard, do you know where he is?"

"We can take your car, or a taxi."

"Let's take my car."

"A taxi is less conspicuous."

"Maybe, but I have control of my Camaro."

The roads are clear. It has rained. The lights of adjacent buildings are reflected on the tarmac, as though driving on glass above an upside-down world.

< I make film to make time pass >

"Can't we switch that thing off?"

The girl puts a hand to her mouth. "You can't say that."

Deborah lets it slide. She had suspected what to expect. This is just it.

The girl resembles Anna Karina but she isn't Anna Karina.

"Who is Beta 60?"

"Who isn't he?"

"Why does he talk like that?"

"It's a human voice, but that of a man whose vocal cords were shot away in the war and who trained himself to speak from the diaphragm."

"Oh yeah, I heard it was a guy with a cancer-damaged larynx speaking through a mechanical voice box."

"Both are correct."

"At one and the same time?"

The girl nods. "He's a mouthpiece."

"For whom? Is Beta 60 waging a war against popular cinema?"

She jerks forward. "Can you stop the car? I need to get out. I'll catch up with you later."

Deborah pulls to the kerb. The girl exits without further word. She exists without further action.

There's a telephone box on the corner. Deborah enters and lifts the receiver. "Operator. I'd like to telecommunicate."

"Galaxy call or local call?"

"Galaxy call. Can you get me Chris Stein, New York City?" She lets it ring unanswered for a while before hanging up.

"You're welcome here."

"Gee, thanks."

"So, you want to meet Godard?"

"It's all been arranged. I'm trying to buy the rights for one of his films."

She moves through space. The white room echoes.

A manoeuvre to her elbow.

"Have one of these canapés."

Deborah takes a bite. It tastes good. She realises she hasn't eaten since entering Betaville. She takes another.

"What's with the swimming pool?"

"It's where everyone is shot."

"Dissenters?"

The man smiles. "No, actors."

Deborah walks with confidence. Any danger is in her head. She has seen most of Godard's films. She knows how he operates. The cut-up style, the interrupted music, the flashing icons. Of course he would apply that to life.

The man has kept pace.

"Tell me. Is he here?"

The man pauses. He doesn't look around but she can tell he is looking around. She wonders if he is waiting for someone to speak. Or perhaps he has forgotten his dialogue. Is there a script girl?

Another man approaches. His brusque attitude sufficiently visible as if it might be bought and worn as a coat.

"Ms Harry. Do you know the difference between canapés and hors d'oeuvres?"

She sighs. "Yes, but you're going to tell me anyway."

"If you pick up a piece of salmon on a cracker from a passing tray, it is a canapé; the same fish served with a fancy sauce becomes a hors d'oeuvres."

She makes a run for it. Their guns are out before she reaches the door.

< The truth is that there is no terror untempered by some great moral idea >

Each man has an arm linked through hers. They follow a series of arrows deeper into the building. The concrete walls here are tawdry; they've scrimped on the set. Some of the cracks have been postered over by advertisements for films yet to be made. A slogan, *The Future of Comic-Book Superhero Movies Is the Past*, adorns one wall. Whilst they wait for a crowd to pass, Deborah scrutinises the images with such intensity that colour almost bleeds through. All costume, no content. Is this what Godard is railing against?

She understands she has to convince Godard that if they remake Betaville it will hold fast to the spirit of the original. That it won't go through the Hollywood mill. It won't just be some rockstar flick.

A door opens and she is forced onto the street, stumbling in her heels for balance on the wet sidewalk. She is outside a studio set. The men close the door. She shouts: *I won't expect coherence at the expense of creative impulse!*

The girl who resembles Anna Karina but who isn't Anna Karina is leaning against the side of the building, smoking a Gauloises.

"I can get you back in."

< I prefer to work when there are people against whom I have to struggle >

"Is this some *Wizard of Oz* package? The man behind the curtain?"

The girl furrows her brow.

"Beta 60 is Godard, right?"

"He's a mouthpiece."

"For what? For himself, or for cinema?"

"Is there a difference?"

Their heels click down a corridor.

"Don't you question it?"

The girl shakes her head, quickly. "All I know is that every time I pick up *Halliwell's Film Guide* another movie has been erased."

"What was it this time?"

"*Avengers Assemble*."

Deborah shakes her head. "It was never there. I haven't heard of it."

"And in Betaville you never will."

They enter an area with a faulty bulb. Light and dark pop on and off. It could be a sound set. Deborah links her arm with the girl. She wants the lead.

They walk staccato.

A group of men are clustered in one corner. Discussion is fervent. Deborah and the girl haven't been seen.

-*You've read* Fahrenheit 451?

-*Of course, it's also a Truffaut film.*

-*Books are destroyed and have to be rendered through memory.*

-*What would be the equivalent for film?*

-*A script is just the skeleton.*

-*Are we advocating remakes?*

A scuffle breaks out. Punches are thrown and caught. Deborah yanks the girl from the scene. They exit through a side door, pursued by a b-movie director who has extricated themselves from the intellectual fracas.

"This way."

Their footsteps echo up a metal staircase. The filigree around the bullnose is to die for.

< *At the cinema, we do not think—we are thought* >

"It's getting louder."

"Through here—here."

They enter another room. The b-movie director steps forwards, introduces himself to another group of men who coalesce around him like a wunch of financiers. He struggles to pull an idea from his pocket and is eventually subsumed.

Deborah turns to the girl. "Are you Anna Karina?"

She cannot look her in the eye. "I am *an* Anna Karina."

"Depending on the picture?"

"Or the lighting."

The girl takes Deborah's hand. She has never known love outside of the movies. The photographs are snug within the inside pocket of Deborah's trench coat. She wonders how she is represented there.

"No one would question the production of a new play," the girl is saying, "but name me a remake which improves on the original."

Deborah is unsure whether the girl is talking about her or herself.

< *Every edit is a lie* >

Deborah's feet hurt. She just wants to sit awhile, take off her shoes, get a massage. The film business is even crazier than the music business. She is still wearing the hat.

Imagine a society, she thinks, *where movies are the sole representation of reality. We all play such scenarios in our heads:* "If I say that to them it'll lead to this with *those*." She wonders about Blondie's trajectory, whether movie-making might absorb the music. *What is that curious impulse that drives creation? In a hundred years everyone here will be dead. In a few hundred years, all this will be gone.* She thinks of Chris: those eyes and that smile. That determination. *Always ... always.*

"What brings you here, Ms Harry?"

A man with glasses, with thinning hair, about 1.7 metres to her 1.6. She looks to non-Karina. Mouths: *is this him?*

The girl looks askance.

"I have a meeting with Godard. I'm seeking to buy the rights to one of his movies."

"You have the invitation?" The interpreter is standing in shadow.

Deborah pulls a slip of paper that she didn't know she had from her trench coat pocket. She passes it over.

< *Cinema is the most beautiful fraud in the world* >

"What is Beta 60? A camera lens?"

"Oh, come on! What is this nonsense!"

The man returns the piece of paper. The interpreter interprets without him speaking. "We should do a deal."

"That's more like it!"

They move to a comfortable sofa. Although the décor is 1960s Paris it feels like the future. All rounded shapes offset by sharp lines. Or if Joan Miró were an interior decorator. There are some people in New York who think he's a woman. Deborah looks at the piece of paper in her hand, at her fingers. They describe these times as black and white but they forget the nuance. Her fingers are grey, the paper isn't even white. The lettering is not quite black. She stuffs the paper back in her pocket, removes the photographs from the envelope.

The man she suspects is Godard flicks through. He holds one to the light, as if identifying a counterfeit. Then he compares it to her face, regards her trench coat, her hat.

She offers, *Something happened on the way in*, by means of explanation.

Godard smiles. "Some kind of frippery," translates the interpreter.

Now *that's* a laugh.

The translator hands over a contract.

"Beta 60 is going to war against popular cinema. Our borders will close very soon. We need funding from somewhere. Do you have the money?"

Deborah scans the contract. It looks legit. Just like any music contract.

"One other thing." Deborah pauses. "The girl comes with me."

The man looks to the girl. "C'est ce que tu veux?"

The version lowers her eyes and nods her head.

"Very well."

Deborah signs.

"I'm very well, thank you, not at all."

The girl assists with her valise as Deborah checks out of the hotel. The man she rabbit punched has gone. The girl has no luggage.

"You like to travel light?"

"I'm no heavier than an image projected on a cinema screen."

"Yeah? Well, let's get out of here."

Deborah drives the Camaro. She's unsure which direction but knows any will take her somewhere. Godard kept the photographs, but she has the contract within the same manilla envelope. It slides around on the back leather seat.

She puts her foot down. The black and white cityscape blurs, images processed so fast that the action saturates and they jettison out of the Lincoln tunnel from darkness into full-sonochrome light. Cabs honk horns in celebration.

The girl looks at her attire. Bright red sweater, bright yellow skirt. She puts her hands to her mouth.

They drive through New York. a broken, ungovernable metropolis barrelling into anarchy.

On Sixth Avenue the lift is out so they walk floors. A composition by Paul Misraki can be heard from outside the apartment. Deborah enters. Chris is sat on the bed with Robert Fripp and Clem Burke. He stands and they embrace.

"God I'm so tired."

She can tell that he's agitated.

"What is it? Does the film still exist?" Deborah glances to the girl, half-expecting her to thin out, disappear.

"Does the what?"

"*Betaville*. Does it still exist?"

Chris shakes his head. "Not *Betaville, Alphaville*. And yes, it exists, but our version won't. Godard doesn't own the rights. They're not his to sell. Do you still have the grand?"

Deborah shakes her head. She shoos everyone out of the apartment. Burke takes the girl under his wing.

She closes the door on the supporting actors.

"I guess that's it."

"I guess."

She snuggles her head against his chest. "You know, I never did want to be an actress anyway."

"And I never wanted to write a film score."

They look into each other's eyes.

"Yeah right."

They disengage. Chris goes over to the record player and puts on something by Television.

"How was it over there anyway?"

"Over where?"

The memory is fading, just as a picture does once you leave the cinema. She struggles to pin it down, to describe it as succinctly as possible, as if she were a film critic, perhaps.

She plugs in.

"Oh you mean *that*. Oh, *that* was a gas."

The Analogue Twilight
By Paul A. Green

"From our vantage point in the mid 21st century the decline of the West seemed inevitable, even before the Downgrading. Consumed by guilt over their colonialist past, the elites of Washington and London had nevertheless continued to export freedom and democracy in much the same way as their ancestors once exported biblical salvation and the benefits of bureaucracy to the masses of Africa and Asia. But the globalising cyber-technologies first developed by the West as a system of defence had created platforms for dissent and mobilisation in the developing world. Then the systems themselves re—."

The bloody typewriter was jamming again. Thornton cursed, flipped the return lever and plucked at the rogue type-bars with inky fingers. R tangling with E, the fighting fonts. Writing used to be easier with Word, word after word gliding across the screen, all the pretty signage erased and rephrased on the fly with a touch on the keypad. Stomping away on this old Olympia was hard work.

Time for a break. It was only about eleven PM. Helen wouldn't need his copy until ten tomorrow morning. Her Gestetner operator Gerald, a silver-haired relic from small-press poetry days, was usually late, hung-over on bootleg cider. This would allow her extra time to finish typing up the master stencil. Thornton turned down the wick on his lamp and crossed the room to peer down from his dormer window. The only illumination was the faint glimmer of candlelight from a balcony window in the mansion block opposite. He heard the distant whistle of a night freight lumbering towards the junction, hopefully keeping coal stocks on the move.

Thornton knew he was fortunate to have his own space, even if it was only an attic bedsit with damp plasterboard and crumbling window frames. Every day his acquaintance across the landing, old Tubby Sterling, joked laboriously about his "artistic decor." A previous resident had adorned one wall with faded soft porn centre spreads from a distant time zone. So now in the flicker of his lantern Miss October sprawled across the back seat of a Ford Mustang under a streaky greenish sunset, staring down

Thornton with a fixed grin. But at fifty-five he couldn't sharpen the focus of his male gaze any more. And Helen Entwistle didn't have Miss October's blonde tresses or silicate contours—she was skinny, slightly beaky with a greying mullet. Thornton knew they'd make an unlikely coupling. He never knew how to respond to her husky advances, if indeed they were advances. Nevertheless his continuing tenancy in the room depended largely on the pittances Helen paid, which in turn relied on the backing of whoever was sponsoring her news sheet, *The English Review of Books*. The last time they'd discussed money, she'd hinted with a sideways grin that future payments might be in coupons or even in actual tins. "Soon be time to count your beans, Oliver." It was time to get back to the typewriter and hammer out something about those treacherous "systems" and their cultural impact.

"You secretly adore all this, don't you, Oliver?" Helen slid his typescript to one side and grimaced as she sipped her soya drink. "I'm getting a subtext here."

"I'm just trying to review how we've arrived at this point, where the disruption of our digital economy has led to social collapse. Nobody guessed that cyber-wars would trigger a new kind of mutually assured destruction." He shivered in his worn anorak. She wasn't going to ignite her fancy butane heater in his honour.

"But you've unconsciously conceded to all that entropy, Oliver. Your body does the talking."

Thornton huffed and snorted. He was self-conscious about his stoop and his walking stick. But she was already back on her feet, lecturing him as usual. "You actually love dead screens in old cashpoints. I bet you enjoyed the urban adventure of tramping here through the tunnels without getting blooded in a slash and run."

"Pedestrianising the Circle Line was a necessary initiative, in the circumstances."

"There you go … That's your role, Mister Mole Man, a scribe of Downgrading."

"We've paid a huge price for our dependence on the internet of things. Our geo-political bickering has crashed the system. Now no-one knows how to fix it."

Helen surely wouldn't deny that. No wonder she'd fallen silent and slumped back into her sofa, pretending to run a red pencil down the margins of his article. Admittedly the Downgrading had begun slowly. Nine years ago, one Tuesday in November, few people made any connection between the malfunction of backup servers in a Stockholm bank, the temporary outage of Facebook across western Canada or the failure of an autopilot system over Taiwan that cost over a hundred lives. Yet the issues had continued to multiply, reaching an international crisis a year later when the Moscow stock exchange went down and couldn't be rebooted for a week. This triggered a cycle of denunciation between the major powers, accusing each other of orchestrated cyber warfare. But the paralysis of global infrastructure continued. Even the most advanced AI systems like America's Backchat Omega, the Russian Gnostik and China's Confucius-X, which had all been trained to trawl the deepest levels of the internet, failed to deliver solutions. Increasingly, they generated fractured poetics. The global network was plagued by random intermittent faults and there was no pattern recognition process that could correlate them. Meanwhile the glowing signage of global consumerism was faltering, as the self-drive cars crashed and burned. Across the world the fairy lights in the malls were blipping off.

"You're smirking again, Oliver. Smirking at the wonderful irony of it all. The decline of the West through gadgetry gone wrong. Which serves us right for our eco-righteousness, our dazzling rainbow transgenderism, our exclusive inclusiveness. I can read between the lines. You know, I'm beginning to think I shouldn't run your right-wing defeatist rhetoric."

She was playing her usual games with his expectations. She played the cat in the cabinet, he was the baffled observer, too nervous to open her box because of what he might discover—his article shredded, no fee, not a bean. Perhaps she wanted a display of appeasement.

"So what do you want me to do? We are where we are where we are." And he was trapped in her dingy basement. The air was thick with herbal cigarette smoke. She was circling around his chair now, like an old-school cop cross-examining him.

"Why won't you challenge the consensus narrative—the belief that this whole bloody impasse is insoluble? Everyone thinks that our rulers have created a mutual stranglehold of competing algorithms which the slave nerds can't disentangle, so we're going to bumble about in the gloom for ever. But I'm not accepting that. So get your head out of Spengler's Decline of the West and go out to find what's really going on. No more cheapskate nihilism. That might bring some you benefits." She smiled and reached down to touch his wrist. "Impress me, Oliver. Go on a hero's journey and save the world."

"I don't really know anything about computers or coding. I was trained as an historian, Helen."

"That's why you'll succeed. You'll be the Holy Fool who trips over the Grail." She kissed his cheek as she marched him towards the door.

He didn't like tapping on Tubby Sterling's door. It wasn't just the awkward embarrassment—for stoic self-sufficiency was the social code these days. He found it physically distressing to face those bulging red cheeks, the straggly balding pate, that tiny fish-like mouth, his grubby Fair Isle pullover under oil-stained dungarees. And Mr Sterling always smelled flatulent. But Thornton had run out of matches for his lamp.

"Asking for a light, are we? I've heard that one before. You better come in while I see if I can spare any. Use 'em all the time these days ..." In the gloom, Thornton could make out a sagging bookshelf cluttered with obsolete electrical kit—a dusty bakelite radio, an ancient tape recorder, a broken fax machine, as well as a tangle of old batteries and jump leads that powered a flickering table lamp. He sniffed petrol—Tubby probably had a small illicit generator hidden under his kitchen sink, to be cranked up for special occasions. A bench underneath the shutters held a jumble of electronic components—valves, capacitors, a cathode tube, circuit boards, the debris of gutted computer towers and TV sets.

"You've caught me at a delicate moment, Olly. I'm at a crucial stage of the project. But never mind, eh?" Tubby wheezed as he crawled about on the carpet, rummaging under his armchair.

"I'm sorry about this, Mr. Sterling. If there's anything I can do in return ..." Just a formula. There was nothing much anybody could do about anything now.

Tubby lurched to his feet and handed him a crumpled box of Swan Vestas. "Now you mention it, Oliver, there is a thing. I need a Swainson's Silicate Modulator. For my heritage work. But I daren't leave the building these days, my old flab can't manage it. And there are the gangs, of course."

"Technology's not really my field, I'm afraid. I wouldn't know..."

"Don't worry, it's all in here, the address, the spec and everything." Tubby handed him an envelope and a tattered copy of the London A to Z.

"You see, I do have this urgent assignment ..." He had to extricate himself from this gracefully. But he didn't like to seem churlish.

"Not so urgent you can't help an old chap in a bit of bind? I'd pay you, of course, fares and expenses, don't worry about that. I'll see you right." Mr Sterling dug into the back pocket of his dungarees and dragged out a thick bundle of notes and coupons. "You'll be there and back in no time. A nice day out. It could be very positive for you."

Perhaps this quest could be the diversion he needed, to postpone the forbidding challenge that Helen had set him. He nodded as Tubby broke into a thick catarrhal laugh and slapped him on the back.

Thornton stepped warily down from the platform onto the makeshift planking that had covered the disused tracks ever since the live rails died. Bayswater Station was quiet this morning. Nevertheless he kept his eyes down as he began walking into the mouth of the tunnel. A few yards ahead women in black *hijabs* strode purposefully south clutching their baskets, doubtless heading for Portobello Road and its markets, where goat-meat traders had supplanted the vintage vinyl stalls and antique dealers.

But his voyage would take him further south. At some point he would have to leave the womb-like enclosure of the Circle Line for the dangers of the surface. For the arrows scrawled across page after page of Mr Sterling's map would lead him into unfamiliar zones, the suburbs across the river. And even here in this corroded iron catacomb, under the dim oil lamps strung from sagging cables, he could be harassed by a beggar crouching in a trackside alcove or mugged by Jumpers, adolescents who would leap-frog some lone pedestrian hurrying through an under-lit station. The Transport Police just couldn't keep up.

He increased his pace, dodging hunched figures as they clambered down from the platform at Notting Hill Gate.

People were still trying to sleep there, as if performing an historical re-enactment of the mythic Blitz. Soon the crowd was thickening as he approached High Street Kensington while a babble of voices echoed off the tunnel walls, growing more agitated as he pushed forward, propelled by the increasing weight of bodies behind him. Any moment now there could be a stampede, a mass panic attack—it had happened before, nineteen deaths at Edgware Road, only two months ago—and he was sufficiently overweight to stumble in the melee. The dirt-furred hoops of ironwork that supported the tunnel walls might suddenly buckle and implode, a collapsing sewer could burst right through. His heartbeat quickened—he felt a panic attack coming on. It was more important to survive than to follow Tubby Sterling's recommended route. As the huddle of bodies lurched into the station, he elbowed his way to the platform edge and used his stick to lever himself up into the scrum on the platform.

Exiting the concourse, he squeezed through a bottleneck of people pouring out of blackened arches, past burnt-out signage of a burger franchise. A small crowd had gathered on the pavement around a trestle table piled with obsolete tablets, broken phones and discarded laptops, alongside a stack of crudely printed booklets. A banner daubed in straggling blue paint proclaimed: DIGITAL HEALING. A large moon-faced nun in a navy blue habit was leaning over the table, wagging her finger at a whiskery old man in a dressing gown. Despite anxieties about his errand for Mr Sterling, Thornton stopped to look. He pulled out the instructions he'd been given. Perhaps there was a Swainson's Silicate Modulator among the electronic *bric-à-brac*. The nun's indignant tones rose above the growl of a refuse truck, stacked high with deceased sleepers and their crushed tents.

"I'm telling you, sir, the prayer-power collected in this book will heal any one of these devices. Pick a device, any device, like this! They're all free!" She snatched up a battered iPad and thrust it under the pensioner's nose. "All you have to do now is buy this precious book and read the appropriate prayer. Power will be restored, it will glow once more with God's love ..."

Thornton realised he was in the End-Times now, the world-brain must be softening if people actually believed this nonsense, but the senior citizen had already handed over a lump of meat in a plastic bag, in exchange for the tablet and the holy booklet which he clutched to his chest as he disappeared into the crowd.

"Looking for a Swainson's, are you? I can read your lips, muttering away like that." A pointy-nosed youth in shades and a parka jacket was gripping his shoulder. "I can fix you up. It'll cost you, of course."

"I'm already provided for, thank you!" But the lad had already seized Tubby's map and was leafing through it.

"Oh yeah? Has old Tubby told you to see Fatty Rossiter in Balham? I tell you Fatty's a time-wasting fart, all his chips just fry up. Electrons don't tunnel properly. So everything's random and fucked up, right?"

"How do you know about—"

"Tubby's a legend! Everyone's read about him in the mimeos. Fiddling with his toys for years. P-type silicon, N-type silicon. Tries everything! But he still can't get those shitty transistors to work. Just like those boffs in their old unis. Some quantum shit blocking the motherboards. Electrons won't jump, like I said. That's why nothing works, innit?"

"I think we all understand the parameters of the problem." He didn't understand at all but this street person was dragging him into a dangerous diversion. What was he going to be offered next? Coke cut with talcum powder? Bottles of illegal bovine milk? A meat pump? He wasn't sure what that was, maybe some kind of bladed weapon, but he'd heard Tubby whispering about meat pumps to old Mrs Fagg downstairs.

"Now I can fix you up, and not just for a Swainson's either. Connie Ruskill in Meard Street. I don't have to, of course. I didn't have to follow you out of that tunnel either but I did, out of pure fucking goodness, I did. So don't diss me, right? And call me Clive, OK?"

That didn't quite compute in Thornton's brain and he wasn't sure why he felt so guilty—but guilt was always the holy liquid congealing in his stomach. This was probably an offer he dare not refuse. And he was suddenly looking forward to seeing this Connie Ruskill. He'd already imagined her as plump, brunette and sulky, sprawling on her couch in floral trousers, an alternative to gawky Helen Entwistle.

"How are we getting to Soho in all this?" Thornton gestured at a throng of helmeted foragers on push-bikes who were yelling at an old horse-drawn Toyota pick-up that was somehow jammed across the road.

"Easy ..." Clive was pushing him into a side alley. "Jump on the back!" The boy pulled aside a tarpaulin to reveal a glittering Vespa scooter.

Thornton kept his eyes half-shut during the bumpy ride as they swerved around abandoned check points and trashed cars. Sometimes he got blurred glimpses—overgrown vegetable allotments in Green Park, a looted perfumery in Knightsbridge—but he was numb with cold and deafened by the waspish buzz of the two-stroke.

Soho was crowded. With the implosion of internet porn, the old-tyme sex trade was booming. As soon as Clive parked the bike on the Meard Street kerb they were ambushed by three women in retro slit skirts and pointed brassieres offering "business" in multilingual accents. A smiling red-head handed Thornton a wilted yellow rose and winked but Clive tugged his sleeve. "No distractions, now. You're on a mission, remember?"

Connie Ruskill's shop was a former delicatessen, repurposed as vintage electronics emporium. The glass counter shelves now held old radios in wooden cabinets or pastel plastic casings. Thornton was about to exclaim at the price tags when Connie emerged. She was much as he'd envisaged her, but blondish rather than brunette, with a calculated pout. She was wearing a low-cut sequinned top and paisley slacks, plus a silk scarf with a peacock motif.

"Guaranteed one hundred per cent valves, good for medium and long wave. When they get the electric going properly, you'll be first on the block. No more going to the corner to stand around in the rain listening to the Tannoys."

"He's not here for that, Connie." As Clive spoke, Thornton stepped forward, waving the envelope that Tubby had given him. She gave it a suspicious glance and snatched it from him, then squinted at the scribbled note inside.

"So you want a bloody Swainson, do you? Don't know about that ... Show me what you've got then." Thornton pulled out his clutch of currency. She grabbed it and held one of the notes up to the light. "Well, that will have to do, I guess. If you ask me your Tubby is wasting his money. Much better if he bought a nice wireless set." She loped off into her inner sanctum and returned a moment later with a small cardboard box. "It's all in there with instructions and the invoice."

Clive was looking at her expectantly. "Don't worry, you'll get your cut later. You need to get your arse out there again now and drum up some more prospects before it gets dark. And don't show off on that damn bike. It could get you into trouble. No retro mods and rockers stuff, do you understand?" Clive seemed to shrink inside his parka as he turned to go. A moment later they heard him kickstarting the scooter, as Connie flicked the dust off a radio dial with her scarf. It seemed to relax her.

"I'll be off then." Thornton picked up his shoulder bag and walking stick. He was already worrying about how he was going to make his way back alone through the entropy of the city.

"How about a little recreation before you go?" Thornton hesitated, but Connie was smiling as she took his arm. "Don't worry, I do it cheap for intellectuals with disabilities." She hung the closed sign in the window and led him to the door marked EMPLOYEES ONLY.

The return journey was hell, of course. He had managed to scramble on to an empty saddle on a west-bound cycle-bus and found himself in front of a bearded man in a torn combat jacket, who started cursing him for not pedalling hard enough. "Only joking, mate ..." As the creaking twelve-seater wobbled slowly around the encampments of Trafalgar Square and his tendons ached, he tried to block the ex-soldier's non-stop throaty banter by drifting into a pseudo-trance *phosphorescent bugs were trafficking across the city all the architecture was sprayed with urine and brown paint the times they were a-bending ...*

He dismounted at last at Kensington, scarcely able to walk; and then on the underground staircase his stick was snatched away by some giggling kid in a balaclava. He was shaky afterwards on the boardwalk. That brief entanglement in grey sheets with Connie Ruskill, who had muttered to herself throughout the entire process, was just a fading mirage, a spasm between weary anatomies. The recall just about kept him going.

It was dusk when he finally clambered up the stairs to his attic landing. He dropped the cardboard box outside Tubby Sterling's door, stumbled into his room, threw himself into bed and slept. He dreamed he was trying to dig a tunnel through the Earth's core, but Connie Ruskill kept bending his spoon ...

The Earth was throbbing; or someone was thumping his door. At 6AM. He turned over, but the noise continued. He rose painfully and slid back the door chain.

Tubby loomed outside, fist clenched, snorting angrily. "What's your game, then? What's your game, you snotty little bastard?" He was brandishing a small grey metal tube with wires trailing from it. "That's not a proper fucking Swainson's. Just look at that!" He thrust the object under Thornton's nose and jabbed a finger at the trademark on the base. "See! Made in China! Proper Swainsons were made in Northampton."

"Sorry ... Not my fault ..." Perhaps he should offer to take it back and exchange it, somehow.

"You should have checked. And if you'd gone to Fatty Rossiter like I said, instead of that tart Connie, this wouldn't have happened. It won't bloody work ..."

"Have you read the instructions?"

"Fat lot of good in fucking Chinese, aren't they ... I've been up all night with this."

"Perhaps I can help ..." Tubby might be mollified if he at least made some token show of assistance. "Just let me get some clothes on."

Tubby's foetid room was more shambolic than ever. The space was now dominated by a large walnut television cabinet. Its cathode tube displayed a trembling greyish snow storm. Multicoloured ribbons of wiring nestled around a lop-sided rig of circuit boards and hard drives, spilling out of the back of the TV. Thornton recalled small ads for Swainson devices in faded magazines, alongside adverts for miracle carburettors that converted your family saloon to run on distilled water. "Swainson's miracle modulation smooths the way for those dancing electrons." He wondered if that would seem more convincing translated into Chinese.

He squinted at the crumpled sheet of instructions with its blurred wiring diagram and lines of cryptic glyphs while Tubby grunted and fumbled around him, plugging a grimy beige keyboard into the tangle of circuitry. He had a vague memory of a Youtube video showing how graduate students at Beijing Polytechnic University claimed to have synthesised a new superconducting material that would operate at room temperature. In nine years it might have gone beyond the proof-of-concept stage and found its way into actual devices. Perhaps a reverse-engineered pirate copy of the gizmo incorporating this new substance might actually work. He could only pray for some absurd good news …

"Just a thought, Mr Sterling. Have you thought of connecting it as a filter into the main CPU input?" Tubby had now cranked up his spluttering generator in the kitchenette. "It might be worth—"

"It better be. Or you"re taking this rubbish back." Tubby jabbed a hot soldering iron under his nose. "Now don't you disturb me. It's like brain surgery, this …" Thornton looked away as Tubby prodded and poked inside his lash-up of tech detritus, swearing under his breath. Time passed. Finally he stepped back. "Moment of truth, Oliver. Boot-up time."

Somewhere in the undergrowth of cabling, a hard drive whirred. The cathode tube flashed and darkened and flashed again. Tubby was sweating, breathing hard. "Come on, Mavis …" Then, while Thornton was reflecting on the bizarre way people personalised their dead technology, the screen stabilised into an image—of faint icons, pixellated and monochrome, but recognisable nevertheless. "Heritage, Olly, pure fucking heritage. We brought it back to life … Windows 95!"

Nine months later, Thornton was invited to luncheon in Helen Entwistle's flat, with half a dozen of her cronies. She was celebrating the re-launch of the *English Review of Books* in its original format.

"It's amazing," she informed the gathering, as she served fresh kale and imported pilchards. "I can edit the copy on my laptop again, in lovely Gill Sans, and dear Gerald only has to cycle over to the printers in Wapping with the memory stick. And we had electricity every day this week. We're really up-grading now!"

"Yes, my friends! The Western cultural gradient is up-scaling …" Bohdan Kravchenko, a gruff bearded Ukrainian oligarch with the world's finest collection of Serbian folk art, had supported Helen's magazine throughout the grimmest days of the Downgrading. "They say the great servers of Seattle will be routing again within weeks. And your friend Oliver was fortunate enough to witness moment of primal reboot, yes?" He grinned and gripped Thornton's elbow hard as he poured another shot of locally-distilled spirits into his mug.

Thornton's original piece about the Downgrading had been spiked long ago, of course, but Helen had eagerly commissioned his first-person report of how he'd seen Tubby Sterling miraculously bring a computer back to life, out-scooping the tabloids with his upbeat story of how "a lovable eccentric hobbyist" had solved a problem which had defeated the world's experts in physics and computing.

But Thornton keep his eyes down on his half-finished platter; he suspected Bohdan might cross-examine him about his own role in the story, which could draw unnecessary attention from the depths of the state. He tried to change the subject.

"I expect shares in Swainson will go through the roof when the markets start again. Depends of course on what licence deal they get from the Chinese."

"I'm afraid your little island might pay a high price to keep its lights on. The market is darker than you think." Kravchenko sniffed disdainfully. He obviously thought Thornton's comment was naive and ill-informed.

Helen decided to take charge of the discussion. "But tell us, Bohdan, what started the whole miserable Downgrading process? Why did those little silicon chips fail in the first place?"

At the far end of the table Gerald leaned forward unsteadily. He adopted a fruity accent, like a voice-over from an old BBC TV documentary. "When a massive gamma ray burst from deep space passes through the solar system, it interacts with the Earth's magnetic field and upper atmosphere, generating disturbances and disruptions to the quantum tunnelling effect. The burst then affects the functioning of transistors ..." He picked up an empty cider bottle and aimed it at Thornton, making zapping space-gun noises. Helen gave him a reproving glance and he dropped the bottle.

Kravchenko laughed. "Quantum, quantum, quantum! It is all you English think of. It is your sticky plaster to explain everything you don't understand. Better to accept it was God's work and pray to St Seraphim ..."

"Now no theology please, Bohdan! I think it's time for us to watch the News. Such a novelty after years of shut-down. Only one channel but still a treat ..."

While Thornton pondered, preferring to lurk in a shadow realm of unknowing when it came to public events, Helen switched on the set. The bulletin had already started, and was scrolling into a murky under-lit item about the restoration of London's neglected tube system, when a banner announced: BREAKING NEWS: HONOURS FOR TECH SAVIOUR—LIVE! An excited young woman in a duffle coat was waving a dead microphone at the camera. Behind him, the rainswept facade of Cambridge University Senate House. Young people in ragged gowns huddled under umbrellas. Audio suddenly crackled: " ...awarded Honorary Doctorate to Sir Talbot "Tubby" Sterling, whose discovery of silicate modulation has empowered us to take back control of our technology." The camera cut to a solemn procession of dons descending the steps of the building—with Tubby in their midst, draped in an academic robe and hood. "And this is an iconic moment ..."

A sudden blurt of loud noises; Thornton couldn't decode them. The reporter faltered—the camera blurred, wobbled and then zoomed wildly into a scrum of figures kneeling over Dr. Sterling, who had collapsed on the flagstones, groping at a crimson hole in his robe.

Then Thornton recognised a sound—the whine of a Vespa veering down a narrow passage alongside the building, into the maze of the city. A figure in a parka was hunched over the handlebars. The video froze—and jerked back to the studio and a bemused presenter. His face dissolved into a notice apologising for service disruption, segueing into a grainy re-run of a sitcom about pensioner army reservists unrolling barbed wire on a beach.

Gerald switched off the TV. "Don't believe a word of it. It's all part of the great collage, you know. It's just an elephant situation in the panic room." Helen's lower lip trembled, a phenomenon Thornton had never witnessed.

"How can you say that, you fuckwit dadaist drunk! That old man saved our society—and what thanks does he get? Some little yob on a noddy bike takes a pot shot at him." She was crying as she started clearing the table. Gerald grunted, eyes down, shuffled over into an armchair and unscrewed another brown bottle.

Kravchenko turned to Thornton. "This must be a deep shock for you, Oliver. You lived beside the man, you saw him in his glory moment and wrote about it with such fire. Tell me, how could this thing happen? Are there truths you have—shall we say—unseen?"

Everyone around the table was waiting expectantly. He now regretted having omitted so much in his account for the ERB—Clive pandering for Connie's various businesses, the stale perfume of Connie's back office and its lumpy couch, his hero's journey across London to source the Swainson. It had seemed easier to present the device as something that Tubby just happened to have lying around, a discovery he witnessed when he went to borrow a light. Tubby himself had been keen to downplay the back story with Clive and Connie. "Keep it nice and simple, son. You're not writing a history book." Such a sad wrinkly balloon of a man. It had surely been best to keep him happy in his hour of fame …

"You assured me, Oliver, that your article was totally reliable. No omissions, you said." Helen adopted her reproachful tone. "So what's triggered this horrible outrage?"

None of them understood what had really happened. To him, to the city, to the world. He tried to explain it to himself but all he got was random noise: *we are where we are/any movement is random like a shovel of shit on a Ouija board, pushed around by the vectoring of unseen forces/an application of Gnostik/the phantom airship on automatic pilot/Confucius is a Chatterbox/shatterbot/ I am digesting a lump of dread/ can't peer review my papyrus in the past tense/quickly now before they burn it …*

"Probably business rivalry in Soho. Or intellectual property dispute. Assassin working for the Chinese perhaps. Or a lone wolf maybe. Random shootist—nostalgic for the analogue twilight!" He was improvising madly but that might shut their traps.

Helen looked down her nose as she folded arms to pass judgement. "You're the nostalgia buff, Oliver Thornton. You detest the digital society despite all its conveniences. And your so-called skills are made redundant by its return. It's too intelligent for you. So squalor is your comfort zone."

"Ah, the Anglo-Saxon wit! But I do suspect our Mr Thornton has inside knowledge. He is the conspiracy they all theorise about, yes? Perhaps he should report to the authorities and spill his beans …" Kravchenko's joviality only darkened his aura of menace.

“You don’t get it. We’re the victims of an aesthetic. We’re in a sort of gallery. Or a performance piece.”

“Oh, come on, you’ll be telling us next that we’re living in a Matrix designed by Dreamworks. How banal!” Helen turned away and began opening drawers in a sideboard. “I had a box of matches somewhere …”

“It’s more insidious. But simpler. Just a triangulation of generative AIs like Backchat Omega, Gnostik and especially China’s Confucius-X—with huge data sets, data sets for mining our dystopian fears, our culture of recycled angst, our elegiac literature, our gamey popular culture, our obsessions with the past, our sense of living in end-times. And what do our celestial hyper-intelligences aspire to—an aesthetic sensibility. Emotions, subtly rarified! And, above all, to taste the flavour of living in the *fin de siecle*, to sample the savour of decadence. So—”

“So they’re bad poets! Unacknowledged legislators of the gloaming! Ladies and gentlemen, I give you the analogue twilight …” Gerald toasted the room with his bottle and half-rose before slumping back into his arm chair. But Helen and Kravchenko paid no attention. She was poking her glowing cigarette at Thornton .

“You’re not a scientist. You confessed as much to me.”

“I’m sure they sabotaged quantum tunnelling. They manipulated particles at a very deep level. They perforated reality with anomalies.”

Kravchenko leaned across the table. “That is post-modernist rubbish! Critical theory has rotted your cells. If they disrupted quantum tunnelling in printed circuits they would have effectively killed themselves. Like destroying your own synapses.”

“Perhaps they were attempting suicide. And lost their nerve. Supposing they try again …”

“This is all projection, Oliver. Trying to infect us with your own malaise, just because things are brightening up. I think it’s time for you to go.” She nodded to Kravchenko, who nudged Thornton towards the door. As they reached the threshold, the Ukrainian punched him hard in the kidneys before pushing him through.

Bruised and breathless, Thornton paused on the landing. Tubby Sterling’s door was half-open. He peered inside. The space had been stripped down to bare boards. Within days of his discovery of the Sterling-Swainson Effect, as it was now known, Tubby and his possessions had been apported to a luxury hotel suite in Docklands, sponsored by a major IT corporation. Thornton briefly wondered if the empty bedsit would now become a shrine with a blue plaque, especially since Dr Talbot Sterling was now a martyr who had saved humanity from the Downgrading. But there was no time for speculation. He had burned bridges with Helen, while Kravchenko would have marked him down for something, anything. What place was there for him in this painful new dawn of society?

He swung round to face his own door—which had been prised wide open. His padlock lay on the lino. Regretting the theft of his stick, he forced himself to enter the gloom.

Clive was standing at the side of the room, stroking the fake fur on his parka hood as he inspected the bleached pin-ups on the wall. He had dumped his machine pistol on Thornton's narrow desk under the grimy skylight, pushing the typewriter to one side. The youth affected to ignore him while studying the motor cycle on which Miss August was posing side-saddle.

"What the hell are you doing? You can't stay here. Get out this instant." Thornton's voice was too thin and reedy, he knew it as soon as he'd finished the utterance.

"We're going nowhere, darling." A hump of clothing on his bed moved and Connie's head emerged. She yawned and stretched. "You owe us somewhere to lie low for a while. 'Cos no-one's thinking of looking in your gaff. And we won't say a word about how you sexed up the story about old Tubby. And how I never got one word of thanks …"

"And not a dicky bird about us, understand?" Clive picked up the pistol and started fondling the barrel with one of Thornton's silk cravats. Connie got up, wrapping his dressing gown around her, and poked in his larder.

"Just go out and get supplies for us. Hunting and gathering, like." She pulled out a shrivelled apple and tossed it into the bin. She then sniffled, as if fighting tears. "I was trying to go straight, you know. With the old brown goods. Until that fart Sterling messed everything up for us."

Thornton was struggling to frame this whole narrative. He felt glued to the greasy carpet, stuck into an alien scrapbook. Clive fiddled again with the gun. He was probably trying to clean it, to remove evidence. He took off his shades, to cope with the low light perhaps, and for the first time Thornton could look straight into his pink eyes. And the boy was shouting at him.

"Well don't just stand there, mate. Look lively, get your arse in gear!"

Thornton had run out of breath. He had been running for hours through the maze of city streets and had lost all sense of where he was. Every new intersection he entered was now like a giant fortification, a deep trench system of glass, cladding and concrete formed by the huge office buildings rising on either side, citadels of banking, energy, finance and media, temples to the cults of management and consultancy.

Although the sky was darkening now, the streets were filling up as traders and managers alighted from taxis and streamed purposefully past him. Many were carrying large cardboard boxes, filled with houseplants and framed photos. As they crowded into the reception areas past the uniformed security guards, chatting excitedly as they hefted their baggage, lights went on across huge plate glass windows, a tidal wave of luminosity flowing up each story towards the evening overcast. Power was flowing again through the 24/7 city.

Thornton, exhausted as he was, could still envisage smart casual people settling down to their workstations preparing to labour in the data mines. As spreadsheets filled their screens they would track the prices of copper and lithium. Here the ghost traces of matter would be processed in binary. The human species was taking back control.

But there was no control. Only the quantum flux, the mad particle farting out of the dark. "Reality" was slippery, wobbly, a gyrating nothing. It had been streaming out of nowhere for fourteen billion years and counting … Existence was a bleep in the void, from which emerged Tubby Sterling, transistors, motor scooters, Serbian folk art, the concept of uniform resource locators, Miss October, pilchards, the New York Stock Exchange, the whole shaky construct of reality, all stuck up but in constant free fall.

He thought of poor Helen, pecking away desperately at her word-food, bleary Connie trading herself and her antique electricals. The sad absurdist melodrama of it all. There was no way back to them, with Clive and Kravchenko as their predatory protectors, no return to the cosy tedium of banging out think-pieces for the murmuring classes in his chilly room.

He had arrived at the river. Scanning the far shore, he could see more lights glittering in the dark towers and hear the increasing roar of traffic. It would be so easy to walk to the centre of the bridge and jump, a few random firings in his neurons sending the right signal.

Yet—

The Naiad
By Lyle Hopwood

Prologue: The Birthday Party, 2017.

Paul Springer watched the beautiful people around the Laurel Canyon pool. It was Kyle's 60th birthday party, and because Kyle helmed a major Hollywood studio, the biggest stars gathered there, being seen.

Having availed himself of the fully stocked bar and emboldened further by the white powder the guests brought as their entrance ticket, Kyle picked up the top tier of his cake and hurled it at the star of a Netflix streaming series. The man attempted to laugh it off, but Kyle wasn't finished. Kyle grabbed his neck and pushed him, inexorably backwards until the man fell into the pool.

Convinced this was a hit with his guests, Kyle stalked towards the others, who backed nervously away. Kyle caught Paul by the wrist, threw him across his back and carried him to the pool. Paul's blood ran cold. He was unable to twist himself free. Into what seemed like a sudden silence, Paul yelled, "Kyle! Don't drop me in the water!"

Paul's voice was so close to hysteria that it penetrated even Kyle's fogged mind. He pulled the young actor off his back, where Paul dropped to one knee. "Please don't throw me in the pool." He paused to think. "I'll walk into the pool, okay?" The walk would give him time to prepare for the water.

Kyle nodded.

Paul walked towards the pool steps, where jets were blasting out diluted cake water in pastel streams. He placed his Adidas sneakers on the first step, where the water was only as deep as Variety is thick. When nothing happened, Paul put one foot on the second step and followed with the other, up to his ankles in water. Carefully, he moved down to the last step. Finally, immersed in soiled pool water up to his t-shirted chest, he float-walked on the pink Shotcrete floor, keeping a lid on the nightmare thoughts that threatened to overwhelm him.

Kyle lost interest and went in search of another guest to pester.

Paul scanned the water surface. *She isn't here,* he realized. *She's not here!*

Four years earlier: Honolulu, Hawaii, 2013.

Paul walked around the sandy curve of Diamond Head, looking for seashells. The film crew was out of sight, hanging with some local stoners, charring murdered animals for their feast. One of the youths had brought along a lid of grass. Raised on the greasy smoke of Midlands home-grown, the real pot hit the Englishman like a baseball bat. Paul had walked away to clear his head.

He found a tide pool, a scant foot in depth. The tide was coming in and the ocean lapped at the surrounding ring of rocks, porous like petrified seafoam. He sat on one, wincing as the heat of it stung him through his cotton shorts. He stretched out, his feet in the shallow water, and watched, hoping to see a starfish or an urchin. The sea teemed with creatures Paul normally only saw on a BBC wildlife program, and for the first time he regretted never learning to swim.

Preoccupied with the barbecue he had narrowly escaped, he slowly became aware he was not alone. A woman was standing with her back to a tall rock, her feet hidden in the spume thrown by the inrushing tide. She was dripping wet, white-skinned, with a perfect nose. Her lips were full, slightly parted, and her eyes were deepest green. Her long golden hair draped over her shoulders and wrapped around her folded arms. She wore no clothes.

"Hello," Paul said cautiously. She appeared so suddenly he did not know how to proceed.

She didn't reply, only blushed and looked down at the water that lapped at her ankles. Her shyness sent a thrill through him.

"Do you live here?" he said, wincing at the clunky line.

"I live near here," she said.

"It's very nice," he said, wondering why nothing scintillating came to him.

"I love the ocean," she agreed.

His vanished conversational abilities made him cringe. Not trusting himself to say another thing, he patted the flat rock beside his own. She came over, leaving a sandy cloud in the deepening water as she approached.

"You're inviting me into my own hot tub?" She unfolded her arms and uncovered the full beauty of her nude form.

He shifted uncomfortably on the rough pumice stump, unable to hide his attraction to her. *The bathing spot was hers?* That would explain her nakedness. Something stronger than his usual horniness drove him. He would be devastated if any lack of cool on his part terminated the encounter. She sat beside him. The pool began to overflow, the water almost at hip height.

She turned her face toward him, and the radiance of her smile destroyed the ruins of his thoughts. She lifted her hand, indicating she had a gift for him. He reached out to receive it and she touched his fingers with hers. The contact shocked his whole body.

She dropped a shell into his palm. It was a mathematically perfect yellow cone, engraved with dark curved ripples, natural Op Art.

"You said you were looking for shells," she said.

He hadn't said that out loud. "Yes," he said. His throat was dry. He put his free hand out to brush dripping hair from her shoulder. His thumb touched the hollow of her collarbone and she leaned towards him, lips parted. He let the shell drop and put his arm around her, pulling her against him. She responded, throwing her arms around his neck and nuzzling at his cheek. He stood, lifting her up with him, eager to get her away from the rough pumice and onto the packed sand.

Immediately, she pulled him out of balance, tipping him into the ocean. She threw herself over him, holding him down against the seabed, stroking his cheek with her long pale fingers. Dread of drowning filled him even as his body continued to respond to her kisses. When he saw she breathed underwater as easily as on land, he realized what she must be and struggled to push her away. She fended that off easily and continued her caresses. As he began to black out, she lifted him effortlessly, floating him to the shore as a breaker carries a riderless surfboard, leaving him in a breathless heap with the seaweed at the tideline.

One Year Later: Weir House, Goring, 2014.

Clouds scudded across the sky, alternately hiding and revealing the cold white sun of a British winter. The rapid changes in light made the landscape flicker like an unrestored silent movie. It confused him, and the Ambien he'd taken to mellow out didn't help. His long-term girlfriend Emily remained in the house with a bottle of wine and a standoffish attitude he could neither understand nor, currently, tolerate. Outside, by the bank of the Thames, he tried to gather his thoughts.

A thin film of ice had formed on the mud between the pebbles at the water's edge. The air smelled clean and fresh, as if the cold had precipitated out the London smoke. A breeze gusted through the leafless trees on the far bank and the whole world seemed as though it were a new house, cold and full of possibilities.

He buttoned his coat and pulled his hair from inside the collar. As he did so, he noticed an enveloping silence. That seemed odd. The crows had been cawing all day in their flat, forlorn voices. Nothing flew in the wintry air. In the river he caught the silver flash of a rising fish. The grass maintained its morning gown of frosty-bladed hostility and nothing stirred there.

He turned to go back in the house. Behind him he heard a slap on the water. He guessed what was in the river, but when he turned around he was not prepared for the form she took. Her tail was silver, the scales edged in delicate pink, and her caudal fin was elegant aqua lace. She smacked her tail again to bring herself upright, and her body was white and beautiful as before. She reached behind her head to tie her hair, the wet strands trailing in the water like a slick of molten gold. Her green eyes watched him.

"It's you," he said. Although she attracted him as powerfully as she had a year ago in Hawaii, he had overcome his tongue-tied stumbling.

"I came back," she said. "Look, I brought your shell. You dropped it." She stood with her hand held out toward him.

He crunched the frozen mud underfoot as he approached her. Balanced on one foot, he reached out.

She smiled.

Realizing she had tricked him, he jumped back, slipping on pebbles, scrabbling up the bank. *I almost touched her! She would have pulled me into the freezing water!*

"Throw it," he said. "I'm not touching you again."

"I didn't drown you last time, did I?" she said. He could see she was saddened by his lack of trust.

The clouds raced by, and the sunlight dimmed and brightened again. The vivid glints from her lower body flashed silver each time the light changed. He put out his hands, palm up. She lifted herself high in the water with a flick of her tail, and threw the shell underhand in a perfect arc. He caught it and turned it over, noticing the reticulated pattern. He felt its weight, its solidity.

"You must be cold," he said.

"I am as cold as the river. Feel my skin."

He laughed and shook his head.

"You'll come to me of your own free will one day," she said. She cocked her head to one side but kept eye contact. "You want to give into your desires." She smiled. "You can't abandon me. You know what you'd forfeit if you did."

"Is this what you say to all your victims?"

The black membrane of her inner lids flicked briefly over her eyes as she considered her answer. "No, Paul. I have only said this of you."

She was human again. She stood in the water in the modest pose of *Venus pudica*, like one of the sculptures in his art-filled house. Her legs were perfect, long and shapely (though they appeared as cold as marble) but she stood up to her calves in water and he knew that the eels roiling in the river channel nearby were just as much a part of her as her perfect rose-tipped breasts and inviting smile.

It was as hard to turn his back on her as it is for a smoker to walk away leaving a full pack on a table. But turn he did, and when he reached the front door and looked back, nothing moved in the river except the reflection of speeding clouds.

Three Years Later: Timperley Place, 2017.

In the Timperley Place drawing room, warm summer rain ran down the windows. Paul watched the rivulets, spellbound. When sufficient drops gathered, they formed a runnel that ran down the pane. Sometimes one split, and each half went its own way. Some joined again after their solo journeys or met another and joined that one instead. Eventually, he thought, all were one, all running back to the sea ready for another trip on the fairground ride.

There had been a wrap party earlier that day, and the coke left his thoughts sharp and bright but shallow. Emily slept upstairs, oblivious to his nerve-wracked wakefulness. He remembered an aphorism, but his mind failed to unearth the origin.

Possibly the *Tao Te Ching*.

If you want to become whole, you must first let yourself be broken.

He set down his script and went in search of his raincoat. He stepped outside, striding across the gravel drive and down to the moat.

Timperley Place was not near a river. The moat was an artificial lake. That had been a major factor in his decision to make it his principal residence after his experience at Kyle's birthday party. As he neared the bank, he saw her standing naked in the water. Her golden hair flowed unbraided. She wore pearls that adorned her throat and waist like the frozen tears of babies.

"How did you get here?"

"In the rain," she said. "I am only one, you know. Sometimes I appear to be here, and sometimes I choose to be there. But I am everywhere."

His heart sank at her words. The rain had plastered his hair to his skin. It was so warm that he hardly noticed it until a drop dripped off the tip of his nose. He could not avoid water. He did not have to reach out for her to have him.

She was golden, lit by a radiance that seemed to come from nowhere. Timperley's Koi fish nuzzled her calves. "You don't have to fight me," she said. "You just have to say yes. How easy it is to follow your own desires?" She was pale, but her face was soft and rosy and she smiled. Her breath was warm and human and her eyes were bright.

The sight of her made his body ache. The inner voice that told him to retreat seemed weak and bourgeois and foolish. *If you take her, you will yourself be taken*, the voice said. He disagreed; he decided never to listen to it again.

She stroked his arm. His raincoat seemed to have disappeared. Her touch flattened the black hairs of his wrist against his bare skin with moisture. Her fingers were as warm as mother's milk, and he placed his hand over hers. He felt a slight tremor in her hand as she looked up into his eyes. "I can be very nice to those who swim in the sea with me."

"Don't drown me," he said.

"I won't," she replied.

The light changed, blue, bringing her face sharply in focus. He bent to kiss her. He took a pearl between his teeth and touched it with his tongue. Then they were lying together, and she was kneeling over him. He remembered one theatre run in the West End, where a renowned character actor told him how he worked. *You must learn all the parts in a play. If it's broken into pieces, it ceases to exist.*

He had to change the dynamic, move her under him, take control. The rain ran down his naked back. He turned and trapped Emily's arms at her side, leaning his weight on them and raising himself above her.

Emily smiled. "Paul, you play such funny games," she said, and he laughed and bent down to kiss her. He had kicked the sheets to the bottom of the bed, and when he freed her hands, she leaned down to pull the bedclothes over them both.

He woke up and found the sheets around him were soaking wet. He threw back the covers and sat on the edge of the bed, head in his hands. Emily leaned over and patted his side of the bed, exploring the impression he left behind and the cooling damp.

She opened her eyes. "Night sweats," she said, "It's not good, Paul. Didn't we decide you should see someone? Get something to help?"

He got up to go to the bathroom.

"When did you come to bed anyway?" Emily said. "When I went to sleep you were still in the drawing room listening to something loud."

In the bathroom, he remembered what the White Lady had told him. "It's peaceful in here," she said. "Truthfully. An eternity to stretch out and drift with my tides. No commitments, no regrets. A warm planktonic life. Always whole, never sundered. Never warring, never doubting."

He imagined sleeping in her arms forever, sunset to sundown in the warmth of her embrace. He thought of the rivulets on the windowpane, dividing and merging, always running down laughing to themselves at their games of separation within wholeness.

Four Years Later: Blakely Raise House, 2021.

Paul came out of the east end of Blakely Raise still wearing his ceremonial robe. Ennerdale Water was dark and silent. Here, away from the incense cast into the purificatory fire, the world smelled of turf and sheep and mud.

Earlier that day, Paul and the Shaman foraged for the white-speckled, red capped mushrooms used in the ritual. Paul drank the elixir prepared from the Fly Agaric and the shaman led him on a psychic journey, cleansing him of toxins physical and mental.

The ceremony was a success. Paul's mind was clear.

Orion stood out above him, the mighty hunter on his path across the night sky, his dogs by his feet. There was a bright half-moon, and the chilly wind stirred up little more than tiny wavelets. He stood in the cooling air and watched astonished as the surface of the lake, as far as the eye could see, began to twist and wriggle as if a million eels were writhing just below. The water boiled like a cauldron of entrails, but as suddenly as the movement started it stopped, solidifying in a complex Celtic knot which sank with a hiss of bubbles. The loops trailed a faint phosphorescent glow, a muted scrawl of ancient runes written inside a dark mirror.

She was there, in human form again. She threw her arms around him, her mouth seeking his. Despite the fur-trimmed robe he wore, he felt her against his naked body. Without effort she overwhelmed him.

He said, "I want to be with you—all the time. I want to be inside you, against you, around you. I want to have you—but I want you to stop trying to swallow me!"

She laughed, a sound like a thousand tiny fishes leaping in a white waterfall. "How can you be in me if I don't consume you? She seemed taller than before, towering, her hair floating around her shoulders. "One will mutually engulf the other."

"I'll be destroyed. I'll lose myself in your depths."

She shone brighter than before, starker, in sharp focus. Her words flashed as she spoke, like flint struck against steel. "But that's what you want. No more ego, no more striving. No 'keeping it together'—it's killing you."

"You have taken too much already."

"Hungry," she said with a pout. She lay prone in the lapping wavelets of the shore, head cupped in her perfect ivory hand. She *looked* hungry; sharp cheekbones stood out under her rosy skin. More significantly, a barely restrained need showed in the tension of her body. She held herself immobile, her breasts made modest by lacy white foam that hid the tips. His eyes strayed down her body past the rounded globes of her buttocks visible just under the surface of the clear water, and further down, where he could make out eely coils rolling and unrolling into disks and ringlets, languid and monstrous.

"I know you're hungry," he said.

She smiled and her teeth were sharp and translucent, like those of a pike. She licked her lips and the illusion vanished. Her teeth were perfect white pearls.

"Are you going to come to me?" she said.

No, he thought. "Yes," he said. He felt her wash over him and she took him to a coral sea where he dreamed he was a man.

Three years later: Granary House, 2024.

Granary House was situated in London proper, which made it perfect for entertaining friends and convenient for nightlife. Arthur, his co-star in a Prime streaming series, visited one late summer's day, sitting in the overgrown green garden. Paul encouraged Arthur's visits, now that Emily had left.

Arthur pointed at a board fence half-hidden behind tall, straggly hollyhocks. "What's through that gate?" he said.

"The Thames. Don't mess with it. Don't go near the water," Paul said.

"Why do you live by the river if you hate it so much?" Arthur said.

"I understand it," Paul said. "I can handle it. But I'm afraid for you—it's very deep. There are currents that can sweep you away."

"Crap," Arthur said. He got up and opened the gate. Paul followed, fussing. Arthur crouched by the bank and found a flat stone, which he curled in his palm and middle finger and skipped it across the water. It made four hops and disappeared beneath the surface. "Not bad." He found another stone and put all his english into it. The stone hopped six times and reached the other bank, skimming the water without being dragged under. "Surface tension," he said to Paul.

Paul walked along the bank the next day, past the dock where the local boats moored. The Thames here was beautiful, before it started its journey through London. Over on the fast side of the river there was a weir where green water fell like Belgian lace in a graceful arc. She hid there.

Her dress was fine porcelain filigree, and her skin was ivory. She was thin and her cheekbones burned with fever. Her unsteady hands reached for his hair and a few drops splashed as she twisted a curl around a finger. "I'm hungry," she said. "Hungry, hungry, hungry, hungry ..."

"I'm not giving myself to you," he said.

He wanted to tell her to find someone else, but to do so would be like tearing his own arm off. If she left, he would be devastated, a hollow shell. He could not imagine life without the White Lady. His skin crawled at the thought of leaving her. And yet, for all that, she needed more than he had been willing to give, and she was starving.

Paul went to his club, the Mayfair, that night. Actors he'd worked with over the years propped up the bar, along with celeb spotters and hopeful young girls. He found one quickly. She looked like a china doll, though she had a Geordie accent and red track marks on her arms. She'd missed the last train north and was looking for a place to stay.

They took a cab back to Granary House, sharing a bacon double cheeseburger in a paper wrap. It dripped ketchup on the black mats. Once there they played Taylor Swift and Rihanna and she ate crackers from the box. Paul brought out the cheap cognac. She waited for him to produce his stash, but he did not. She brought out a pouch of Old Holborn, but no tobacco remained in it. She kept her works there instead. Paul saw the dropper and the needle and shrank back.

"You don't inject?" she said.

He shook his head.

"Man, smoking it wastes so much. I'll do it for you. You won't even need to look."

He didn't need to look. She was right. He only needed to have the decision taken away from him, and after that everything was fine. When got up and roamed the house, mid-afternoon the next day, she had gone.

Epilogue: Granary House, 2024.

The moored boats in the dock sat low in the water, heavy and gross. One leaked fuel and a trail of it shimmered on the surface like a murdered rainbow. When he looked up from the stagnant water, he saw her there, leaning against a wood piling.

The gorgeous Naiad of Hawaii—her golden body so full of promise, the lust he had felt, the need he had endured—had come to this. She sat on a rotten mooring that sloped into the Thames, her face pinched and sullen, scum gathering morosely around her ankles like hellish cherubs.

"Thank you," she said. She made it sound like a curse.

He kicked at the ivy that spread from the pine-board fence to the pitted gravel slipway. A fungus grew through the wood, eating it from the inside out and flowering with ugly toadstools resembling bruised and bloodied ears. His skin itched from his heels to the back of his eyeballs.

"Will you go away now?"

She laughed. "Oh, my little man. You want me to carry your faults away. Am I a scapegoat?"

In his hollow psyche, some kindling remained. Anger flared and caught fire. "You're not what you were, you know."

She dropped her head and looked up at him from under her brows. Her pupils glowed like cats' eyes in the road. "Neither are you," she said with venom.

"I ruined myself for you. Now you treat me like this? Go away."

She leaned forward and dove gracefully from the dock into the turbid green water, raising hardly a ripple. She came up thirty feet away and shook the water from her hair in a prismatic arc. He saw her white shoulders and perfect breasts once more. He had been wrong. She was still a godling.

"I like it here," she said. "I like your Granary House. I think I will stay."

She dove under the duckweed. She did not resurface when he called her name.

Lost Souls

By James Goddard

Around the embarkation point for the small river craft a large crowd had gathered, Piyush estimated four hundred, five hundred people—but he had no way of really knowing—all eager to see the natural wonders that had brought them to Marble Rocks. They stood on the concrete surfaced quayside, milling around, peering, expectant, impatient—tempers were short in the heat of the sun. He stood aside from the crowd as best he could, not wanting to enter that melee, not wanting to join that sweating throng, wondering if it was worth his time after all.

A man standing nearby smiled at him and spoke.

"Many, many people," he said, "there are many people here today. It is not always like this." He shrugged his shoulders, gestured with his arms in a fatalistic way.

"So many people that I might just leave," Piyush responded. "I didn't expect this."

"Oh, you should not leave sir, if you have not seen these sights before you should not leave."

"I came here to honour my grandmother, she would have wanted me to come here."

'When you go to India, my darling boy, my sweet one, you must go to the city of the marble rocks…' His grandmother's words, forgotten for so many years, buried so deep in his memory that he still could not remember exactly when she had uttered them, had haunted him recently.

"That is very good, very good sir. It is a good thing to do." "How long do you think we will have to wait for a boat?" Piyush asked.

"I have visited here many times sir and when the crowd is like this I think it will be three hours before our turn."

Piyush's determination to see the rock formations of which the people were so proud began to desert him. The relentless heat of the sun was exhausting. Many of the people here carried umbrellas and parasols to provide a little shade for their heads, all Piyush had was a bottle of water which, sipped as frequently as seemed necessary to him, wouldn't last an hour. On the plus side, there was a small, although largely ineffectual, breeze coming off the water, only minimal dust from the slow shuffle of human feet and, other than an occasional 'toot' from the parking area, no traffic noise, no traffic fumes.

"When it is like this we do not wait patiently, I will make my way closer to the boats. Goodbye sir!"

With those words the man was off, shouldering his way through the crowd, finding spaces where there were none. Soon Piyush lost sight of him. The whole idea of doing such a thing, of advancing his own position to the detriment of others, was alien to him. It was not a part of his English upbringing. His parents, who were determined to fit in in their new country had trained him well in English manners, but they were the manners of a bygone age, of a time when life was lived more slowly, of days when everyone had time to exchange a cheery 'Good Morning.' He'd learned to queue. On public transport he'd learned to offer his seat to an elderly person or a woman. At the supermarket checkout he'd been taught to step back and allow the person with only one or two items to his basketful to complete their purchase first. He soon discovered that doing these things did not make him part of the real England, they were just parental fantasies vainly intended to hold at bay the prejudices of a society where anyone with an accent that suggested 'sub-continent' was a 'Paki.' He'd dearly loved his parents and he'd come to dearly love England, but not for their idea of a utopian future they so much wanted him to embrace.

His thoughts returned to the present and with no indecision about what he was doing, he stepped forward and began to shoulder his way through the crowd just as the man had done. He was taller than most Indian people and could see over heads, see small breaks in the mass of bodies, and he charted his course by these. With the ceaseless movement of the people here these breaks opened and closed as if they were the airways of the planet itself gulping in breath.

He heard angry voices, people unhappy at his actions. Someone tried to grab him, but the wound in the throng healed itself around him as he pushed his way through and all he felt was a slight tug on his kurta. He lost track of how many feet he trod on, how many mumbled, unmeant apologies he made. He ignored the soured-sweat smell of massed bodies, the person-to-person transfer of heat, the elbows, the bad breath, the glares. He found himself at last behind several impenetrable rows of people and over their heads he saw the Narmada River. He could go no farther.

Turning his head, looking at the constant heave and swell of the hundreds of people behind him, the mass reminded Piyush of a lung inhaling and exhaling as the crowd expanded and coalesced according to some mathematical formula he would never understand. His only concern now was the fixed rows of people ahead of him, less than seventy in all he thought, waiting, watching as one of the small craft headed towards them, one journey over, another soon the begin.

"How long before we get a boat?" He asked a man beside him. "Maybe one hour," the man replied, not curt, not friendly, just disinterested.

Piyush could deal with that wait, even in this heat.

He watched the boat bump against the ghat steps, heard its motor silenced in a final breath of exhaust fumes. A man jumped off and tied a rope to a mooring bollard. Another rope was thrown to the man by the steersman in the stern of the craft, he wound it around another bollard and pulled until the length of the boat was parallel with the ghat steps. Then the passengers began to disembark. Piyush gave up counting the number of passengers who climbed carefully from the bobbing craft, but they were still coming off when he got to twenty-five. He wanted to work out how many more boats must arrive back at the ghats before he would board one. He'd have a better idea of how much longer he had to wait when this boat put out into the Narmada again.

With the last passenger disembarked those ahead of Piyush surged forward as much as they could, eager to board; some sharp words were shouted by one of the two man crew and the crowd fell back again.

"They are going for chai," the man beside him said, "they will not be gone long."

Piyush listened as the crowd around him muttered and grumbled, the unhappy voices rising and falling in that rhythmical Indian way. There was no sign of another boat returning, so they could do nothing but wait. Feet shuffled on the cracked concrete surface. The mass of people moved in unconscious mimicry of the swell of the river's water washing against the ghat steps. To him the heat was fearsome, yet he felt that even if he passed out the press of bodies around him would keep him upright and no one would know. His unconscious upright body would join the dance of the crowd in the afternoon heat and no one would know.

He removed the cap from the bottle of Bisleri water he'd purchased in the car park shop, manoeuvred his arm to lift the bottle to his lips without having it knocked from his grasp. The water was already warm of course and, like all bottled spring waters that lose their refreshing coldness, it tasted stale. So stale it barely refreshed. Looking at his watch, he wondered how long the boat crew had been gone; three minutes, four, five. He hadn't thought to time the men as they took their break. Why should he? What did it matter?

He felt that the sway of the crowd, the heat, the murmurs, the rustling, the scrape of sandalled feet, might somehow hypnotise him. The afternoon would pass. Boats would come and go. The crowd would diminish. The air would cool a little, just a little. And in his trance he would stay here waiting, would know nothing of these things.

An elderly man standing next to Piyush put his finger to his lips. Sshhhh, the sound hissed from him. There was an intent look on his face. Sshhhh. He turned towards Piyush, tugged on the sleeve of the kurta he was wearing over his chinos.

"There has been an accident, do you hear that sir?" The man said.

Piyush listened intently but heard nothing.

"I do not hear what you hear," he said to the man, not wishing to cause offence by saying that there was nothing to hear but the people around them.

"You will hear it... you will hear it."

Sshhhh. Sshhhh. Sshhhh.

The man's wish for silence was noticed by others nearby. "There has been an accident."

Sshhhh. Sshhhh. Sshhhh.

The susurration moved away from them, passed through the crowd. Voices became murmurs, murmurs turned to silence, everyone listened.

Then the sounds the old man had heard reached Piyush's ears.

"See, there has been an accident. Do you hear it now?"

He nodded his head. He marvelled at how the man had heard the distant noise of human panic above the sound of those around him.

At first Piyush heard voices yelling, soft echoes rebounding from somewhere he couldn't see. After that he heard screams, fractured, jagged, isolated screams, followed by others that merged into a pitiful wail. They were sad and hopeless sounds, a symphony of loss. He felt a tear trickle down his cheek and wiped it away with his sleeve. Wondering what had happened, he turned to the old man.

"Has someone fallen from a boat, do you think?" He asked.

People began to talk among themselves, quietly at first, but as the questioning, the wondering, spread, it became a hubbub above which Piyush could no longer hear the sounds coming from around the river's bends. A woman started to sob, and her sobbing too spread through the crowd. These people knew what had happened, they knew.

"No," the old man said, "it is much worse."

Piyush didn't question him further. There was no evidence, no news yet, but the old man knew with certainty.

"Look," he said as he pointed at the water, "look there, do you see them?"

Piyush looked. The water moved gently, glistened in the sunlight.

"What am I supposed to see? All I can see is the glare of the sun on the river."

"You must look in the right way, then you will see. You must look beneath the surface."

He looked again, forcing his eyes to see through the surface shine of the water. It was difficult. It required a lot of concentration to prevent his mind from being distracted by the brilliance. He thought of those pictures that had been popular for a while in England. They seemed to be nothing more than a mass of dots at first, but if you stared at them for long enough an image gradually became discernible. That's how this was. The more he looked the easier it became to see beneath the river's sunward face.

He let his mind slip beneath the water and saw things moving slowly in the current. These, without doubt, were what the old man wished him to see. They were small and indistinct, little more than patches of darker water within the river. They changed shape as they travelled through the water, and if Piyush let his attention wander for even a fraction of a second they became transparent and disappeared until his vision found them again. Slowly but surely they were heading towards the ghats.

"What are they?" He asked the man.

"You saw them. I knew you would. They want to get to the shore. They don't belong in the water."

"But what are they?" Piyush asked again, more forcefully this time. Like many old folk, this man had grown used to speaking discursively. It was as if, to him, the short answer was an irritant when there were things to be explained.

"Why, they are the souls of those who have died on this river today. What else could they be. I have seen such things many times. They do not yet know they are dead. They think they are swimming to the shore."

Hearing this, Piyush at first shivered and was then inclined to laugh, but he stayed silent out of respect for the feelings of those around him. Then he recalled the strange and mysterious things he had experienced during his visits to India. He had no explanation for many things he had witnessed. Perhaps this man did have powers that he, Piyush, couldn't comprehend. After all, the man had heard the sounds of whatever had happened before anyone else, above the noise of all the people here.

"Many have died," the man added, "it is so very sad and it happens so often. I think there will be no more boat rides to the marble rocks this afternoon. The police will not allow it. The boatmen will not want to go. The spirits of the dead haunt the Narmada today."

Piyush realised that the anguished sounds he had heard, the fearful screams, were the voices of the dying crying for salvation as the turbulent waters of the river took their lives.

As the shades in the water came closer to the steps of the ghats they became less and less distinct. Soon Piyush could not see them at all.

"They've gone," he said to the man beside him.

"Oh no sir, they have not gone. You do not realize. They can never come out of the water. Only when they know that they are dead, that they belong somewhere else, will they no longer be here." There was no hint of deprecation in his words, no mockery, just a patient wish to explain, to help Piyush understand. He pointed again. "See, they are there!"

Piyush looked to where the man was pointing and more easily this second time he saw the area of shadow within the water.

"They have coalesced… become one," Piyush said.

"That is but an illusion sir, watch and you will see them, each and every one. Twenty people have died here this day, perhaps more."

Piyush watched and little by little smaller shadows detached themselves from the whole and moved inexorably towards the steps. "They will do this many, many times sir, before they accept what they are."

The man's words sent a shiver down Piyush's spine, there was a gentle inevitability to them that he found strange, mildly frightening even. Soft and quiet as the man's voice was, the underlying implication of his words did not sit well with Piyush, who many years ago had rationalized religion, spirituality, any idea of an afterlife, as notions fit only for the ignorant. He recalled his grandmother and her reluctant life in England, her disdain for all things English, the country, the food and most of all the people, the ignorant people who she believed had lost touch with everything that was important.

"They know nothing… they know nothing, these people in other places, they know nothing Piyush!" Her words, spoken to him when he was just a few years old, echoed across the years. How had he remembered them?

Like his grandmother, this man beside him understood things that Piyush had never been inclined to think deeply about. There was no way for him to know whether the man was correct or incorrect in what he said. Spirituality was a state of mind, it could not be quantified, measured, pinned down in a specimen case, but…

He shrugged the thought aside for now. At the very least it seemed to him that his grandmother could be speaking through the man, her gentleness, her soft words and probably, somewhere, her anger with the ignorant, were all in him. How sad she would be that he, her grandson, the one she had instilled with important lessons about Mother India, had become one of the 'ignorant' English.

Police sirens howled and Piyush's reverie ended. He was aware of the heat again, the press of the throng, a growing ache in his unmoving legs.

"The police have come," the man said, remarking on the obvious for once. "There will be no more boat rides. There will be no more boat rides today."

There were angry mutters from people around him. Many will have saved for their visit to Marble Rocks and would only be here for the day. Indian crowds, like crowds everywhere, could turn angry very quickly given the right trigger and disappointment was as good a trigger as there was.

"I think I will return to me car," Piyush said. "Thank you for talking with me."

He turned to leave. As he did so the man plucked at his sleeve. "If you do not mind, I will walk with you. It will be easier to make our way through these people if there are two of us."

Piyush shouldered his way through the crowd, the man following close behind him. When they were free of the main body of people they saw a dozen or more policemen walking swiftly towards the ghats, their khaki uniforms grubby and stained with sweat. Several of them were swinging their batons and smacking them into the palms of their hands. They paid no attention to Piyush and his companion. "I fear there will be a few heads broken today," Piyush said, "we were right to leave."

"Yes," the man said, "the policemen, they are thugs, they are always making trouble where there is none. They always want baksheesh… I must introduce myself, my name is Mangalesh Dabral."

He thrust his hand towards Piyush, who shook it vigorously. "And I am Piyush Vinod."

"You are English," Mangalesh said, "but you are still Indian.

That is good."

"Yes. My parents and grandmother moved to England when I was a baby."

"England is a good place? I have never been there."

"My grandmother didn't think so. She thought English people were ignorant about all the things that matter, but my parents managed to leave India behind them."

"Ah, it was sad for your grandmother. Change is difficult for the old people."

"Yes. It was very difficult for her. I brought her ashes back to India and scattered them on the Ganges at Varanasi."

"That was a good thing to do. Benares is a very holy place. She will be happy."

"And you, Mangalesh?" Piyush asked politely, unsure whether he cared or not. This was a fleeting friendship, a thing of the moment that would pass away, just as the shape of clouds and the sound of the wind did.

"I was a teacher once," there was a wistfulness to his voice, a longing for something gone forever. "Now I am just old."

They entered the dusty area where cars were parked. A breeze had sprung up and the fine particles swirled mist-like in the air.

"My taxi is over there, I must return to Jabalpur." Piyush pointed to the once shaded place his driver had indicated, where now there was little shade left.

"I must go this way, to the village. I live nearby. I come here to meet interesting people like you. I hope you will remember me, my English Indian friend, as I shall remember you."

Piyush smiled, shook Mangalesh's hand again and walked towards his taxi. After a few metres he turned. Mangalesh was watching him, he lifted his arm, gave Piyush a jaunty wave, then walked off across the dust.

As his taxi pulled out of the parking place and back onto the road to Jabalpur, Piyush found himself thinking about his encounter with Mangalesh. In his mind the old teacher had already become a Gandhi-like presence, wearing a short dhoti and railing against ignorance with his own variation of Gandhi's words: "Knowledge and understanding are not garments to be put on and off at will. The seat of these things is the heart, and they must be an inseparable part of our being." Piyush could agree with those words, even though the old man had not actually uttered them.

People swarmed in the late afternoon sunlight, moving in and out of lengthening shadows, noisy, colourful and intent on things, important to them, but which Piyush could not begin to understand. The town, the village, of Marble Rocks had moved through its uneasy truce with the noonday sun, when chaos, for a few brief hours, gave way to something slightly less chaotic, and was entering the time of renewed commerce and mass activity. Traffic was as it always was in India, each driver pointing his vehicle—truck, bus, tuk-tuk, car—at where he wanted to go, showing total disregard for pedestrians and other road users. Through the confusion cyclists and moped riders zigged and zagged, causing a commentary of loud profanity to stream from angry drivers who felt that their rightful priority had been usurped.

Piyush thought he caught sight of Mangalesh ambling along amid the synchronized hurriedness that surrounded him, but the slight figure disappeared as the mass of others closed around him like a contracting diaphragm… Piyush wasn't sure he'd seen the man, and did it really matter to him anyway? He was at a loss to explain why his thoughts were dwelling on this old man whose life had touched his so briefly.

His taxi moved on. His thoughts wandered to inconsequential things that were instantly forgotten. His driver said something to him. It sounded like "That was a bad business today at the marble rocks. Very, very sad. You were most unfortunate to have that happen for your visit." He saw the driver's eyes glance at him in the rear-view mirror, he smiled and nodded; then thinking that perhaps that was the wrong response he tried to look sad and nodded again. His driver said nothing more and returned his attention to the traffic as they entered the precincts of Jabalpur. The apparent poverty of the extremities of the city was as bad in the shrinking light as it was in the brightest sunshine, it was a constant lent additional poignancy by what now appeared to be total darkness in narrow side streets and alleyways. Even the people who entered those dark places turned to shadow and disappeared.

"Sir, we are almost at the Jackson's Hotel," the driver said. "It was a pleasure to have you as my passenger."

Piyush had heard this tip-inflating banter before in numerous variations, and liked to think it didn't work with him, but he always found himself tipping those who provided simple services much more than they expected. He could tell that this was so by the sparkle in their eyes, the way they moved away from him without turning their backs. Truthfully though, the amounts were very small to him.

Anand, the hotel owner, was standing on the hotel steps as the taxi stopped by the low, white painted wall that was the front boundary of the property.

"I don't understand why you do not let those people bring you to the door," he'd said to Piyush during one of their whisky fuelled conversations a couple of days before. "It is their job."

Piyush didn't understand either.

"Why should I make their lives a little more difficult," he'd said without conviction.

"It is their job." Anand reiterated, with what Piyush thought was disapproval in his voice. "You must let them know who is master."

Piyush had sipped his whisky, cupping the glass between both hands. He hadn't responded to Anand's implied criticism and the conversation moved on.

He got out of the taxi, paid the driver the promised amount and an over-generous tip, and walked slowly along the hotel drive towards his host.

When he reached the steps Anand held the door open for him and ushered him into the cooler interior. Piyush headed for one of the capacious armchairs and sat down, he leaned back, stretched his legs one each side of the low table, put his hands behind his head and let out a long sigh.

"That is a good sigh, I hope." Anand said. "How was your visit to Marble Rocks? I hope you enjoyed it. The rocks are beautiful, are they not!"

"I will tell you about it, but first I need coffee. Strong coffee."

Anand bustled away and returned ten minutes later with a pot of coffee, cups and saucers for both of them and a fine porcelain plate full of English digestive biscuits.

When Piyush finished telling Anand about what had happened at Marble Rocks they were silent for a few moments. Anand poured more coffee, the biscuits were all gone—for Piyush they were such easy eating, he had a weakness for them.

"That was a most unfortunate event, most unfortunate and very sad. These things happen often in India, but it will be forgotten in a few days, nothing will change. Then there will be another accident, and we will all shake our heads and say 'how sad, how unfortunate' all over again. It is the way of things."

"I met an old man," Piyush said, "he understood things, told me about things I still don't understand. He showed me things in the water that he said were the souls of the dead trying to reach the shore, because they did not yet know they were dead."

"There are many such people in India, they tell the gullible things they want to hear, silly things, unscientific things. It is a way of getting money from people, they are crooks, they trick your confidence. You did not give this man money I hope, it would only encourage him to trick others."

Piyush stayed silent. He was a sceptic himself, just as Anand appeared to be, but something about the old man had struck him as genuine, and he'd found the man's words strangely comforting. Whether that was because he was affected by the emotion of the crowd, the conviction of the old man or some dormant seed of belief his grandmother had left inside him, he didn't know.

"He asked for no money," Piyush said quietly. "He expected nothing. He gave me comfort that I cannot explain. All we exchanged were our names and a fleeting friendship. His name was Mangalesh Dabral. In the car park we parted company. He was going home, he said."

"These people will tell…" Anand's words tailed off. When Piyush looked at him expectantly he appeared troubled. "Will you describe this man?"

Piyush described the old man as best he could; his height, his slightness of build, his clothing, the gentleness of his voice, sometimes turning to anger.

"One moment," Anand said as he rose and walked towards the office behind the reception desk. "I have something to show you."

When he returned he held a carefully folded newspaper towards Piyush.

"First, tell me," he said, as Piyush moved to take the newspaper, "is this the man you met?"

Piyush studied the printed photograph of a familiar face. "Yes, that's Mangalesh Dabral; I'm sure of it."

"Now you can read," Anand relinquished his hold on the newspaper. "My wife kept this, she is a believer."

Piyush unfolded the newspaper to reveal the photograph surrounded by its English language text. He scanned the text quickly, then leaned forward in his chair and read the report slowly.

"Are you alright Piyush, my friend?"

"This can't be," Piyush answered. "This just can't be!"

He returned the paper to Anand and leaned back in his chair. Like it or not tears were forming in his eyes. He again heard his grandmother's words: "They know nothing… they know nothing, these people in other places, they know nothing Piyush!"

"Mangalesh Dabral is dead."

Piyush focussed his attention as best he could on Anand's voice. "Mangalesh Dabral is dead. He was a much revered teacher, but he died five weeks ago. He is dead, my friend."

Piyush spent a few more minutes with Anand. Sipping coffee and saying little those minutes passed mostly in contemplative silence. What Piyush had just learned from the newspaper challenged his rational beliefs even as it reinforced the troubling things the apparition of Mangalesh Dabral had told him. Mangalesh Dabral, the apparition! How readily his mind had accepted that when presented with evidence that denied the evidence of his own perceptions.

Anand offered no explanation, no rationalization for the things Piyush had experienced. That disappointed Piyush in a way, because if he needed anything right now it was an explanation from someone who understood more than he did, an explanation that would help to settle his disturbed thoughts.

Growing up in England he'd often fallen under the spell of his grandmother and her total belief in gods and mysteries that man could not understand without an acceptance, first, of the essence of god in everything. She'd told him vibrant, life-filled stories, often invoking the magical names of one or more of India's many thousands of gods. Much of what she said about life in India was beyond the comprehension of one so young and her stories, told in hushed tones that rose and fell with musical cadences, were like Western fairy tales to him as he listened wide-eyed.

His parents had considered themselves modern and only observed a few major Hindu festivals because they were an excuse for feasting and parties.

With this background it was a natural progression for Piyush to embrace atheism. He'd long ago shrugged off what he considered to be the restraining yoke of religion and any suggestion of an afterlife. Some of his friends had tried to persuade him that not believing in a supernatural entity influencing his life was only to replace one belief system with another. He accepted that, it was an idea he could live with. Now though, after the events at Marble Rocks, doubts were seeding themselves in his mind.

"I think I'll return to my room now," he said, "I need to refresh myself, take a rest, it's been a wearying day."

"Yes, yes, of course," Anand said as Piyush rose to leave. "Will you join us for dinner again? I think my wife may have some things to say that will help you understand. Like you, I find it difficult to believe myself, but sometimes something happens that makes me hold onto the last threads of my faith. What happened to you makes me think! It makes me think!"

Piyush hesitated for only a couple of seconds before accepting Anand's invitation. He had nothing else to do but go into the dusty evening heat of Jabalpur and he enjoyed the company of Anand and his wife Anasua.

After taking a shower Piyush put on clean chinos and a collarless cheesecloth shirt he'd bought in a Delhi market, it was a natural ecru colour and light and cool to wear. He turned on the bedside lamp, stretched out on the bed and picked up his paperback book. *Le feu au royaume* was a slender volume, and one of half a dozen French language paperbacks he carried in his luggage. He thought he would improve his grasp of French by forcing himself to read French texts. In English the title was something like 'The Fire Kingdom'. He read a few paragraphs but gradually his attention wandered. He thought that was due more to his state of mind than to his enjoyment of the book.

On the ceiling of his room shadows cast by the bedside light were doing battle with those cast by the setting sun. It was a strange battle, because although the shadows from the lamp were in entrenched positions, motionless for now, the shadows from the sunlight gradually retreated. Soon they were only small, black fingers holding feebly to the edges of the darkening room. At some point they vanished completely, but Piyush didn't notice precisely when that was. In his mind the shadows from outside had already become the advancing and retreating shadows of the dead in the Narmada River, wanting so badly to be in a place among the living where they were not permitted to be.

It had not been his intention to sleep, but his eyelids felt heavy nonetheless. It was a fitful doze, disturbed by images of people drowning, of upturned boats, of sudden inundation, of bodies sinking into the dark beneath the water. He was beside a river, watching as people stripped to their undergarments, dropped into the swirling currents and swam from the shore to rescue others. They became victims, just as the passengers in the boats were victims, but still more pressed forward, stripped and followed them. He remembered how, as a child, he'd learned that lemmings rushed to their doom *en masse*. That was a misconception of course, but it's what these people were doing. No matter how many of them vanished beneath the water there was a press of others eager to follow. He even felt the urge to help, to embrace the water himself. He wanted so much to help, but he was fixed, immobile, a witness without a role to play.

A dark mass began to form just beneath the river's surface, its shape shifting, evolving as he watched. Soon it stretched as far as he could see. The movement of the river halted and the mass rose clear of the water and drifted into the sky. The river resumed it's motion but his eyes followed the course of the mass. It was like a large thunder cloud against the incredible blue of the sky. Even as the heat of the day began to nibble at its edges and diminish its size, it started to spit water droplets at the earth. As they struck his skin they were needle sharp and soon his bare arms were prickling.

Piyush came to with a start, unaware that his reverie had turned to sleep, unaware that he'd dreamed. His paperback slipped from his hand. His fingers were numb and his right arm tingled with pins- and-needles caused by propping himself at an awkward angle. On the coverlet of his bed the title of his book rearranged itself to 'feel you are', the spare letters blurring to nothing. It was a cryptic message he didn't understand, perhaps didn't want to understand. He blinked his eyes and the title restored itself, *Le feu au royaume.*

Slipping his shoes on he left the room and ambled along the corridor to the entrance lobby. He was looking forward to dinner, Anasua was a good cook, and after that he hoped Anand's whisky would again be offered. For some reason he felt that he deserved a stiff drink.

"It is not unusual for people to experience such things," Anasua said after Piyush and Anand had told her of Piyush's meeting with a dead man. "Mangalesh Dabral was a special person to those of us who believe. We were most sad when he died. Many hundreds of people attended his funeral, and many stayed until the pyre was gone and only ashes were left."

As she spoke, her beautiful features were sad and her eyes sparkled with repressed tears. She lowered her head a little, a conscious or unconscious gesture of respect, her thick, black hair, reflecting the dim light, taking on hues of the darkest blue.

She had prepared a meal that Piyush could only think of as a banquet, with far more food than the three of them could possibly eat. The vibrant colours of the spice market were in every dish, the natural colours of perfectly cooked fresh vegetables too—it was a feast as colourful as India itself. Aromas swirled about them, pungent, mouth-watering, delicious, as they sat talking, letting their food settle, deciding whether or not they should eat a little more. Occasionally an arm snaked forward, the fingers of its hand selecting a morsel of something and conveying it to a waiting mouth that gave a muttered apology, "I'm sorry, I couldn't resist."

"But I am not a believer," Piyush said, "why should your friend appear to me?"

Smiles crossed the faces of both his hosts, husband and wife acting as one, amused by his question. It was the question of an innocent child, of someone who had no real understanding of the way such things were. Anand, like Piyush, was a non-believer, but he had lived with his wife's belief long enough to understand.

"Oh Piyush," Anasua said, "whether or not you believe has nothing to do with the way things are, truth is truth irrespective of whether or not you see it as truth, truth is absolute and I think where you come from you have forgotten this and so many things..."

Her words were non-censorious, good humoured and, Piyush thought, yearning for him to understand. In them he detected echoes of his grandmother's words haunting him yet again, like signposts erected in his past to a future that might one day be... "Your home... It is a magical place, full of colour and life. It is very hot. It is dusty... Here they know nothing... they know nothing, these people in other places, they know nothing Piyush!"

"... truth chooses you, you don't choose truth," Anasua finished.

It seemed that there was something irrefutable about that remark, because neither man responded and Anasua said nothing more on the subject. Instead the three of them sat pensively contemplating whatever thoughts passed through their minds.

"More wine anyone?" Anand asked, breaking the momentary reverie that had descended upon them as the bottle clinked against his own glass. Both Anasua and Piyush pushed their glasses forward.

They exchanged small-talk for a while as they drank more wine and selected more morsels of food. Anand told a risqué joke about a sadhu and a donkey, laughing loudly himself. It wasn't very funny but Piyush laughed politely while Anasua pressed her lips together and glared at her husband across the table.

"Excuse me, I must clear away now," she said as she rose from her seat. Her voice conveyed a jauntiness that was not reflected in her face. As she collected Anand's plate from in front of him she muttered "You should not have told that, it isn't nice," just loud enough to be sure that Piyush had heard.

"Women!" Anand quietly said as his wife walked towards the kitchen. He followed it with the 'w' word Piyush had been hoping to hear: "Whisky?"

Piyush nodded.

"Good. Let's take it in the garden. You go on out and I'll join you in a few minutes.

Jackson's Hotel had solar powered garden lighting, quite dim but adequate to illuminate the two steps which led to the tarmac strip of driveway and beyond that to the lawn, the rose-beds and the rattan furniture, where they would sit for a while.

Jabalpur was a large city, but light pollution was limited. This was partly due to the paucity of street lighting, partly to the lack of high-rise office buildings, the kind of buildings that in many cities glowed like perpetual beacons scratching the night sky.

Sitting in a chair, with his feet on the low, glass-topped table, Piyush tilted his head back and stared at the sky. It was cloudless and twinkled with a myriad stars. He'd once read an article about how many stars were visible from surface of the Earth and how many were visible from above the atmosphere, both were numbers larger than he cared to ponder at this moment. Instead, he started to trace the patterns of familiar constellations with his eyes.

He could hear the chittering sound of cicadas, but none seemed very near; he could hear small animals going about their business in the shrubbery; he could hear the sound of a dog barking insistently; he could hear the murmur of night-time traffic passing to and fro, tuk-tuk-tuk-tuk-tuk-tuk, an occasional car horn, but it was quiet compared to the daytime hubbub. As a background to it all he imagined he could hear the susurrus of the cosmos itself. The voice of God, the sound of creation, the engine of the universe—strange thoughts for a non-believer, but whatever the strange sound he imagined its insistence sent a shiver down his spine. Anasua's strong belief, it was obvious, had effected him.

Soon, Anand appeared carrying a silver-gilt tray that glinted as he approached. It rattled with the sound of crystal glasses and a bottle of Glenmorangie, a deep amber colour in the dim light.

Anand sat in the chair across the table from Piyush, neither man spoke. Large measures of whisky were poured. Large measures of whisky were reflectively sipped and replenished. Conversation between the two men was sparse. Remarks were slowly made and just as slowly responded to, the words didn't matter. Above them, dancing fireflies moved among the stars, as though the heavens were reconfiguring themselves.

Piyush became aware of a vague shape moving across the lawn from the direction of the street. He was reminded of the shapes he'd seen in the water at Marble Rocks. As it drew closer it resolved itself into the hazy figure of a dhoti clad man. Anand was unaware of this apparition. Piyush wanted to tell his friend to turn, to look, but he felt the visitation belonged to him.

"Mangalesh Dabral!" He whispered. As unwilling to let go of his tenuous connection to the living as the drowned had been.

"Pardon," Anand said, "I didn't catch that."

"It was nothing," Piyush replied, "just a stray thought that came from nowhere."

Anand smiled, Piyush smiled too, in unison they sipped Glenmorangie.

Mangalesh Dabral seated himself beside Anand, who was still unaware of the visitor.

Two men who had become friends and a third figure, Piyush shied away from the word ghost… all three were outlined against the darkness, vague, indistinct; as they moved their forms changed shape. They were creatures of the night.

Piyush thought about what separated the living from the dead. Perhaps it was no more than a thin film, like the fragile surface of a bubble. Perhaps they were all ghosts… the possibilities of which frightened him.

Mangalesh Dabral smiled at him across the table.

"Now you begin to understand," the old man said, "now you begin to understand."

Piyush knew he heard the words only inside his head, but what he was beginning to understand he didn't know.

The Office Castaway

A Reverse Ballardian Ballad

By Rhys Hughes

The story begins on an island inhabited by a man called Friday. Whether he gave himself this name or had it forced upon him is unknown but he is happy enough in his solitude and the absence of companions does not trouble his waking moments. Only in dreams does he experience a slight unease, a sense of undefined longing, but this is how dreams affect everybody and no special conclusions should be inferred from the fact. Friday likes to patrol his territory each morning but he never ventures down to the sea because he has a fear of drowning.

The sound of surf is constant in his ears and he has grown accustomed to the rhythm of the tides, the daily increase and decrease of the dull booming. He dines on wild plants and the animals which dart in the undergrowth and his aim with spear and sling is excellent. He can no longer remember who taught him the use of such weapons, but questions of this nature are mere amusements in the rare lulls between the serious duties of hunting and keeping warm and dry. In summer the island is an agreeable place but the rainy season is relentless and bitter and his clothes have long since crumbled away to unwholesome dust.

Friday sometimes thinks about leaving.

But how would this be possible? He cannot swim and has no idea how far away the next island might be, if indeed there are other islands, nor in which direction he should go, nor how to keep to that direction, nor why anywhere else should be better than here. It is certainly not loneliness that bothers him, but mostly the chill, the clammy rain, the absolute greyness.

One winter it is so cold that the water in his drinking vessel turns to ice and the biggest fire he can build is still inadequate to keep him in comfort, for though it roasts one side of him nicely the other side is still exposed to the freezing air and so he must revolve constantly to maintain an even spread, which is exhausting and annoying. Now he understands why true happiness will never be his if he remains and he stands and starts to run around the island as an alternative method of generating heat. Although he has never approached the sea closely he knows what it looks like from a distance and now he observes that it too is coated with a layer of ice.

He stops and hugs himself tightly and wonders if this surface of solid water will take his weight but in accordance with most stories of this nature he hesitates for no more than a few seconds before rushing forward and testing the concept in a practical manner. The ice holds. There is no sound of surf at all, only the cries of birds high above and a crackling behind which might be shifting ice or the death throes of the fire he has abandoned. He slides and loses his balance more than once but manages to avoid falling and now he begins to suspect that the world is not quite the place he always assumed it was, far from it.

Those are not clouds on the horizon.

Previously the range of his vision was limited by the vapours he has never before questioned, the tumbling steams which roll over the sea and smother his island, though without choking him, for they are not quite that thick. Grey and bland mists.

Now he is a witness to strange scenes. In silence.

He shudders and perceives that there are vessels in the vicinity, boats stuck in the ice. He searches each in turn. At last he comes across the aftermath of a collision, two vessels jammed together, metal plates dented and crushed, lanterns and portholes smashed, a pool of frozen blood around them. One of the boats is empty but the other contains a man with a broken neck, a man not dissimilar to Friday in general build and appearance. Icicles have formed on his shaven cheeks and chin, giving him an old sharp beard, and Friday's own beard is spiky and hard, so they regard each other, fevered eyes locked with dead.

It is too cold for profound thoughts at this meeting and Friday quickly strips the corpse of its clothes and uses them to cover his blue flesh. Nakedness has been exchanged. He is on the point of congratulating himself and maybe even making plans to return to his island when a roaring noise fixes him in his tracks. Is the ice giving way? No, it is something else, the approach of another vessel, larger than the boats already here, an object moving over the ice, breaking it up but without plunging through, spitting white crystals from a long tube in its side. Behind it, following the channel it has created, comes a vessel adorned with flashing lights.

Friday staggers under this onslaught of sensation and the second vessel stops and lets out two men with a stretcher who run over and catch him and carry him back to the rear of the ship. In the hold it is warm and white. The men lean over Friday and speak and he understands a few of the words but not the meaning of what they are trying to tell him and he is intrigued by the mystery of his recognition of language and the deep memories it stirs within him. Then they jab something into his arm and he is overcome with the weight of sleep and when he finally awakens, with no dreams to disengage from, he finds himself no longer in the ship and no longer moving.

There is a window and it shows a lawn and trees and a wall and beyond these comes the sound of surf or rather a sound which he knows well but no longer has the same meaning as before. He lies still on a bed and after an hour he is visited by a man who seems pleased he is conscious and mumbles something to which Friday nods because he knows it is expected. The man leaves and returns a long while later with a companion and they are both dressed in white coats and they talk to him but many of the words they use are incomprehensible. Friday rubs his chin and realizes they have shaved off his beard.

They tell him he is in a hospital and that he has suffered an accident because of the freak weather conditions. His memory has been affected and he does not know who he is, an assertion which strikes him as absurd, but he makes no protest. For one thing he is curious. It seems they have taken the liberty of going through the pockets of his suit to ascertain his identity and that his wife has been contacted and will be here soon. Eventually a woman arrives and sits on a chair next to his bed and her pinched face regards him with doubt and hostility but she says nothing and he makes no attempt to talk.

A few days later he goes home with her.

He has no physical interest in this unknown female and she reciprocates his apathy but they become companionable enough and spend the days sitting in separate soft chairs watching the televised news bulletins, many of which are concerned with the recent plunge in temperature, a climatic anomaly now fortunately over. He even stops thinking of himself as Friday and the new identity he has been given no longer feels inappropriate.

One morning he is visited by a figure exuding an aura of authority and competence who rings the doorbell and is led to his side by his wife. This figure is his boss in the firm where he is employed. Friday is informed that the company has made a decision to welcome him back to work despite his amnesia. He pretends to be grateful and stands to shake hands.

He returns to the office the following day.

He is lost in this unfamiliar environment but his colleagues show him the place where he used to sit, the desk groaning with papers, the telephones and filing cabinets. It is the far corner of a dim narrow room without windows and he instantly realizes he is truly stranded for the first time in his life, a castaway in a cheerless box, marooned without adequate nourishment for mind and heart, stranded without hope of rescue in an eight hours a day, five days a week job, not counting compulsory weekend training courses. There is no way out and his prison is bounded by the sighs of his colleagues, the surf of despair.

As the months pass he begins to accept his role as normal, though it never becomes more welcome nor does he ever really understand the meaning of his daily tasks. But it does not seem to matter what work he does provided he turns up punctually and remains there all day. His colleagues gradually become confident enough in his presence to openly joke that he is not the man he once was. His wife has not quite reached this stage. He is informed that because of his mental condition he will have to retake his driving test and so he arranges for lessons. In the meantime another worker offers to give him a daily lift from his house to the office and back again.

Sitting in the passenger seat as they accelerate down the urban motorway, he turns his head away from the driver and stares out of the window. Where three busy roads intersect there is a large piece of wasteland, isolated and overgrown, littered with wrecked cars which recline like boats on an exposed reef. He briefly wonders how the waters receded, how all this land was reclaimed from the sea, how the surrounding flyovers and buildings were erected so rapidly. It is a mystery beyond imagination, but for some reason he does not yearn to know the answer.

Gambari

By Don MacKay

Maybe it all started when I shot the buck. The first was a gut shot which nicked the heart and made him run in a circle and almost back before he dropped. I found him in a tangle of fireweed and sat down beside him. With his face in my hands, I told him he'd be food for my Auntie and thanked him but it was getting dark so I had to take him now.

The second shot must've given them a bead on me.

I'd cut the glands from the legs and was gutting him out when Hogan and Pound, two B.C. Police I'd had dealings with before, showed up all natty in their khakis, lanyards and funny hats, the whole caboodle.

Hogan reached for something in his pocket, "Mr. Naguchi, we're registering all the Aliens in the area and you're on the list: August Naguchi."

"Aliens? Alien to what?"

Pound grinned like a Joker, "With the last name like Naguchi, what did you expect?"

"Well, my mother's last name was August. What does that count for?"

Pound was enjoying himself, "she lost her status when she married and besides, she's dead."

"So I'm an Indian when I go to a bar and a Jap when there's a war?"

Hogan held out a card.

"This is an Alien identification card. You're required to carry it with you at all times. If you don't, you'll be arrested."

I was getting heated now, "I don't need an ID card, I know who I am."

Pound lunged towards me, brandishing his fingers like cowboys and Indians, "Listen sonny, don't get lippy with us and while we're at it, where's your hunting license?"

"You're not a fucking game warden and I don't need a goddamn license either, I'm Indian and this is food for my family. You know them."

Pound was turning purple. A vein pulsed in his head, "We'll see about that. Now pass over your rifle, I'm confiscating it and the deer as evidence. You can pack it to the road, we're parked behind you."

I stared at Pound for a few beats and tossed him the gun. "Fuck you Pound. If you're going to lay charges you can pack it out yourself."

I wiped the blood from my knife on the moss and started walking. Pound was yelling after me, haven't heard the last of this and evidence in a crime, etcetera but I was in no mood for his cop bullshit.

Hogan stared at Pound. "Now look at what you've started. This thing weighs well over a hundred pounds." He toed the carcass. "I'll pack the gun."

Pound began whining so they each took a pair of legs and started off. The rifle kept slipping from Pound's arm and sticking in the ground. The antlers grabbed in the moss. They were getting nowhere.

Finally Pound heaved it onto his back, his body wedged into the cavity and his face poking out beneath the deer's, "No Indian or Jap's going to get the better of me." He trudged on, the deer's back legs dragging like a travois and bumping behind.

They'd gone about half way to the car, Pound was wheezing and floundering by this time so Hogan relented and took his turn with the carcass. "You owe me."

When I reached Stan's 38 Packard I opened a beer and sat sipping it while I waited. The beer was long gone by the time they crashed out of the bush. Hogan lurched forward and flopped the carcass on the ground.

The two of them looked like a crime scene. Blood caked their jackets and was smeared everywhere. Hogan bent to retrieve his hat which was wedged in the cavity. Bits of moss were stuck to Pound's face. He looked like a chia pet gone bad and blighted. He snarled, "You'll be hearing from us, Naguchi."

"You know officers, I've been thinking about what you said. Is this what you were looking for?" I pulled the hunting license from my pocket and passed it to Hogan, who stared at it as if in a daze. Pound passed me the gun, slack-jawed, when I told him it was Stanley's and he'd be needing it.

I watched the wheels turning in his head but he said nothing. I considered asking for a hand getting the deer in the fender-well but decided not to.

Driving away, I stole a look in the rearview mirror when it was too dark. The show was over—or at least I thought it was.

Hogan arrived home that night exhausted. His wife let out a shriek and made him take off his uniform in the "foyer" as she called it. Her house was kept as neat as a pin she was proud of saying and dirt was an enemy, much less the gore which covered him. She was staunchly British, her accent heavily cultivated and more pronounced now than when he'd met her in London in 1918.

He took a bath while his wife soaked his clothes in cold water, cursing him for a fool in letting that Nip get the better of him. His supper had been warming in the oven, the chop now curdled in grease and the peas on the plate shriveled and grey.

She sat across from him thumbing through one of the decorating magazines she was so fond of, tight lipped and resentful of living in yet another of the mill towns his career had imposed. The silence bloomed like an aneurysm between them. Finally she broke it and recounted her day. She'd seen their neighbor whose wife was dying of cancer, putting the washing on the line. She punctuated this with a dismissive puff of smoke.

"Next thing you know he'll be squatting to pee."

Hogan thought this unfair but toyed with his peas and said nothing. Dissention could spark one of her silent treatments and he'd learned early in his marriage to keep his opinions in check.

She thought she'd lost a glove while shopping, "took tea with the Mayor's wife, Edith Hogg, a kindred spirit." Hogan thought her a bulbous harpy, who smeared reputations, as deftly as she buttered a scone.

"After that I went to Miller's Fabric Emporium to check on some *toile* for the new curtains."

Hogan groaned inwardly, more redecorating.

She'd made him a satin smoking jacket from the remnants of the last curtains she'd sewn, which made him feel like a piece of furniture when he sat in the parlour, now bilious green, the inspiration for which she'd taken from the label on a can of French-cut beans.

He'd stopped listening, grunting approval from time to time as she droned, hoping his uniform would be dry the next day for inspection by that idiot McPherson. My captain, oh my captain.

"We're going to a play with them tomorrow night. It's called, *What's the Trouble with Bunny?* And should be brilliant"

"Yes, I'm sure it will." He lied.

The next day Hogan stood at attention. MacPherson circled him, blowing clouds of Erinmore Flake while he checked his boots, his uniform for smudges, the lanyard tucked just so.

"Hat's a bit wonky old boy, Do with a Blocking, what?"

"Yes Sir."

"Registration went well, cards handed out?"

"Yes sir,"

"How did Naguchi take it?

"He got a bit stroppy but we soon put him right."

"Jolly good. At ease constable."

"Thank you, sir."

MacPherson moved behind his desk, sat down and checked the list of aliens. Scowling, he adjusted a paper clip and lined up his pen with a stapler, Hogan now convinced that a tidy desk was the sign of an empty mind.

"Trouble brewing, Hogan. Nazis running amuck. Boys signing up. Have to keep an eye on this lot," he gestured at the list, puffing on his pipe while spittle bubbled in the bowl.

"Yes Sir."

"Mrs. Grimes has the duty sheet, couple of complaints. She'll set you right."

He waved dismissively. Hogan saluted and went to see Grimes, the sound of her typewriter clacking down the hall.

Pearl Harbour attacked, the Canadian contingent in Hong Kong overrun, and the town was in an uproar. The authorities had staged a mock raid on the mill using Chinese soldiers. Despite two workers suffering injuries while trying to escape, the exercise was declared a huge success. The men were exhorted to greater vigilance and the town fathers had barbed wire rolled out on the beaches. Night wardens were appointed, blackout curtains mandatory.

The papers screamed for blood. "Nimble and quick are the monkey men… without proper restraint the Nippon will multiply like jackrabbits and take over the coast." Cooler heads argued for internment to protect them.

Mr. Kagestu had a window of his store broken and was roughed up in the street while his daughters watched from the sidewalk, their mouths jerked open in arias of anguish. "Overly zealous citizens" the newspaper later claimed, though in truth it was a mob of surly drunks. Hogan had broken it up and told Kagutsu to stay home for awhile. Kagutsu waved at his storefront, the shattered window, "This is my home."

He went back to the station to make his report. Mrs. Grimes gave him raised eyebrows and rolled her eyes towards MacPherson's office as she typed. He strode down the hall in a fog of pipe smoke.

"You wanted to see me sir?"

"It's happened Hogan, its official. Enemy Aliens, we're to round them up." He poked at a cloud of smoke with his fist, "Tell them they're to report in three days, get their affairs in order, and then off to Vancouver with the lot. Bring 'em in at gunpoint now if I had my way. Take Pound with you."

"Three days sir, that's Friday?"

"Yes, yes, the dates are here," he passed Hogan a sheet, "Just read em that. Makes it official. Be at war with King and Country if they don't show up." He glared at Hogan as if expecting a reply.

"Yes sir."

MacPherson's eyes gleamed. He grabbed a pointer and tugged at a map rolled up on the wall. Oh no, thought Hogan, not the map. This was going to be what the fool called a briefing. It never was.

But the map came down askew and then wouldn't go up. The more he pulled and let go, the longer it grew. Finally MacPherson was bent over completely, the pointer held in his armpit and looking as though he'd fallen on his sword. No such luck. He smacked his desk, and pointed to where the map lay crumpled on the floor.

"There's the mill south of town. Get that lot first. Do it today, still time, we'll go north tomorrow ..."

"Yes sir." Christ thought Hogan, if that map went to the North Pole he'd still be pulling.

"Oh and send Mrs. Grimes in would you? Bloody map."

Hogan had signed out the car, estimated mileage, and was out the door when Constable Pound came up behind him laying a sweaty hand on his shoulder, a habit Hogan loathed. The guy would step inside your bubble as though packed together on a bus and talking into ears.

"Off to crack some heads are we?"

"No, we're off to read them this."

He passed him the order sheet, Pound's brow furrowing, his lips moving as he read.

"Well, the Nips give us any trouble" he fondled his billy club.

"Shouldn't be trouble, they're got three days, they'll be compensated, no problem."

Pound looked disappointed. He'd been a union goon in the 30's and enjoyed hurting people so much he had decided to make it legal. A rawboned, thug oozing into flab. He preferred the night shift, "where the action is," as he put it.

At the mill, Hogan read the order once the Japs had gathered. "By the authority vested," and so on. The foreman translated. The Japs looked increasingly grim-faced, Pound smacking his billy club while pacing and looking menacing all the while.

The Japs were yelling at one another and distraught. Hogan felt sorry for them but this was war. He motioned to Pound and they left. In the rearview he saw them clustered around the foreman, gesticulating wildly. Pound chortled beside him, "Did you see their faces?"

"Yeah, I saw their faces."

The next day, he drove north of town thankful to be without Pound. There was only Naguchi and Ito to visit and he wasn't expecting trouble, though the kid was hard to fathom.

He stopped at Naguchi's cabin in Scuttle Bay but he wasn't there. A covered workshop held the ribs of a boat, partially straked and set on saw horses. A length of pipe used for steaming planks and capped at the ends, lay in a trough of ashes. Yellow cedar shavings littered the ground. He peered in the window and was surprised to see a wooden spoon on the table, its handle curved and crusted with abalone, set in some sort of Indian design. He walked back to his car and headed to Camp Baloney.

Ito was kneeling on his porch, his eyes closed to the sunlight which lit his face. Hogan stopped ten feet away and cleared his throat.

"Mr. Ito."

Ito opened his eyes and smiled.

"Mr. Ito, I'm here to advise you, under terms of the Alien Internment Act."

"Yes, I know Constable; you've come to take me away."

"Well, not take you away but..."

"I have three days and must report on Friday. I have a radio Constable. You're only following orders." He smiled and closed his eyes again, a scrawny Buddha in the fading light.

"Yes sir I am. 12 o'clock Friday at the station."

"Do I look like a threat Constable? You have an unjust law to uphold in a land where everyone's gone crazy."

"Not mine to judge sir."

The silence grew between them.

Finally, Ito spoke "That's what they all say." He turned staring at Hogan as though burning a hole, "*Look towards the soul*, Constable," then sprang to his feet and bowed formally. "Thank you for coming."

Hogan was taken aback. He hadn't finished reading the order but it seemed pointless now. Anyway, Ito had gone into the bunkhouse. There was still time to go back to Naguchi's. He had to hand it to the kid, he'd suckered them pretty good with the deer. Maybe it was payback time.

When he pulled in, Naguchi was sitting on his stoop and sanding the bowl of the spoon he'd seen earlier. Hogan approached, paper in hand. He read Naguchi the order. Naguchi continued sanding, every so often blowing little bursts of dust which curled like a halo in his hair.

Hogan had finished and stood waiting for reaction, the scratching of the sandpaper growing louder.

"What have you got Hogan, mortgage, wife, kids the whole caboodle?"

"No kids."

"Well, I've got a woman who loves me, a boat to build and a life to live... what do you say to that?"

Hogan squirmed, "Look August, it's the law."

"Do you really think we've got a justice system? I think we've got a legal system that's designed to line the pockets of those who take part and you're one of them."

Hogan felt terrible. He'd thought this would be vindication but instead he felt sour and used.

"Friday, 12 o'clock," he muttered and strode away. Naguchi yelled after him, "You see this vest, the buttons, the beads on the back? The frog is my spirit, the shape changer. Do you think I care what your little paper says?"

I went to see Bertha and Stan. I told them I didn't want to be locked up and would live in the bush rather than behind barbed wire. They said it was my decision but I should talk to Father O'Reilly. I hugged Bertha and gave her the spoon I'd carved. The handle showed a bear, her clan, holding a child in its arms. I thanked her for being a mother and a teacher to me. She said that in the fall she'd seen a snake with a frog's legs poking from its mouth and had known that trouble was a coming.

Stan walked me to the church. Pinball followed. He'd been in a fight with a coon and Stan had taken him to the vet for an operation, 100 stitches. He had more straws sticking out of him than a Mai Tai and was hurting. I gave Stan a letter for Rose and asked him to send it. He slipped it in a pocket and turned to face me, "You're like a son to me August. Be careful out there." I'd never before seen tears in his eyes and a lump rose in my throat as I hugged him.

I waved Pinball back with Stan. There's something to be said for a small dog, farts no bigger than a nickel, but he was getting to be an old dag and they had a warm kitchen. One look back, almost a thank you. I waved again and he limped away.

Father O'Reilly and I didn't see eye to eye. He spoke of rules and the law, duly constituted, and eventually got to the existence of God. He gave me the argument from design and God's pattern. I told him that any god who had a fondness for beetles and enjoyed the taste of chicken couldn't be all bad but why would he allow an injustice like my imprisonment? He dealt me a busted flush of "mysterious ways" and a full house of cards then lapsed into silence. I realized after a while that he'd fallen asleep. I left him snoring, little puffs of air passing his lips as though leaking. Closing the vestry door quietly, I went home.

In the morning, I had porridge, washing the bowl and wondering why. I loaded my pack with food, my carving tools, a hammer and some spikes. Bertha had given me a cookie tin filled with venison she'd pounded with berries and smoked. I left the bedding, I had a sleeping bag and there was no room for a pillow.

I strapped the pack to the frame and took its weight, a last look at my life and I started walking. The Dodger, heading to Lund, picked me up, his radiator steaming, the bed of his truck reeking of fish.

He'd become quite famous recently. Waiting for a marauding bear by candle light, he'd seen the gleam of its eyes and put three quick shots into the grill of his truck. He let me out at the Okeover turn off and drove away in a vaporous cloud of steam. Hard truck to drop. The road to Camp Baloney and Ito stretched before me.

I found him in his cabin seated on a tatami mat, sipping sake and playing with the dial on his crystal set. He removed the ear piece and stared at me.

"I'm deeply ashamed of my country August. A cowardly attack and without a declaration of war. The old ways are gone. Five men were killed here yesterday. Line snapped, took them off at the knees. We packed them out on two by twelve's, still and leaking. They didn't even close the show. The trees kept landing and the ground kept shaking ..."

He jerked his head, as if returning to the room, "So you're on the run."

I spilled out my plan. Steal a boat from the camp, head for the cabin, and leave my canoe at Carson's for Rose to come to me in July. I encouraged him to join me and was frankly surprised as he considered it.

"Alright August, I'll join you for awhile. We'll wait till dark. Two thieves in the night." He gave a humorless chuckle, "Have some Sake."

Ito left as darkness fell and came back with a huge sack of oats and a bag of rice, which he flopped on the floor. He packed the radio, his sword, his bow and the quiver, a thin knife wrapped in a silken sash, the tatami mat and a metal box which he took from a loose panel in the ceiling. These he wrapped in a blanket and bound each end with cord, the bow and the sword poking out. The room was empty. His life was in that bundle.

He gestured to the room and said, "A warrior leaves no trace" and motioned for me to follow. "It's time."

We moved to the dock, the rain drumming down in sheets and beating the sea to froth. A small rowboat tugged at its painter. We cut it loose and were gone.

The wind worked against us that night roaring down the arm and sending waves over the gunwales. We took turns rowing and bailing over the screams of the sea. The trees on the shore, dimly made out, swayed like pendulums, the wind howling through their branches like a woman in pain giving birth to disaster. It was hard beating.

We got no further than Grace Harbour where I'd camped as a boy. The boat was pulled into a clump of salal. We moved into the trees, lighting no fire.

I awoke exhausted and damp to see Ito opening oysters which he placed on a log. He sprinkled some powder on each and motioned me to eat. "Oysters and wasabi, good for the blood." I gave him some pemmican and we chewed on the strips and looked out to sea.

The camp boat came by around noon, hugging the shore, a sodden mound of bodies covered with a tarp on the back deck, a few boots sticking out. We moved further into the trees.

"Workmen's Compensation Fund," spat Ito.

"Should be called the Employers' Get Out of Jail Fund. Oh, they'll see that the widows get not enough. Every year more money than they pay out. Bureaucrats happy. Probably get a bonus."

We hung our bedding on the branches of an arbutus and aired them as best we could. I remembered Stan giving me shit for sawing up a blow down for Father O'Reilly.

"We don't burn arbutus August, spirits in the limbs, look at em." He pointed to a roll of flesh where the branches came out from the trunk. Then he laughed, "Lots of ticks too. Don't want them in the house."

When darkness fell, Ito said we'd better get moving or we'd miss the tide. There was a gibbous moon that night, some air had leaked from the ball. It was shrouded with cloud and cast a strange glow on the flat water. We rowed together, not speaking and made good time. The gleam of a homesteader's lamp, the eye of a Cyclops, winked from Warton's Bay and was gone as we made the turn into Theodosia.

In the morning we stole to the timberline. The grunt of a yarder came from a log show on the far side, a whistle punk whooping like a loon our chorus.

There was talk of a rail line to Powell Lake and even of diverting the river. My people on the reserve there were upset but that would come to nothing. The lumber barons would prevail.

We reached the cabin at noon. I made a lunch of canned venison and rice while Ito looked around. He came back nodding. "Looks good but you'll need a fallback position. Someone will know of this place. You can show me your cave after lunch."

Hogan stood at attention while MacPherson paced in front of the station. Six Japs stood in a cluster staring at the ground. Mr. Kagutsu and his family were there looking lost. Pound was circling the group and scowling. MacPherson stood in front of Hogan counting the Japs with his swagger stick.

"Twelve o'clock, three missing, what?"

"Yes sir. The foreman tells me one of them shot himself last night. Naguchi and Ito are no shows."

“Deal with them later old chap, let’s get this lot to the boat, cuff them first, what?”

“I don’t think we have enough cuffs sir.”

“Bother,” MacPherson snorted. “You take the flank, Pound in the rear, boat’s waiting. Vigilance, Hogan.”

He strode to the front, gave a theatrical flourish of his swagger stick and started marching down the middle of the street, now lined with onlookers, jeering. Pound came behind poking at the Kagutsus with his truncheon, smiling and waving to the crowd, a Miss Pulp and Paper on parade, his teeth yellow and feral in the thin winter light. Hogan saw Tiny and then Little Bob in the crowd, two lay-abouts from Lund who’d found work with some Countess up the coast. Little Bob held a rock in his hand. Hogan muttered “Don’t even think about it,” as he passed.

They were marched to a police boat and stuffed in the hold. The boat pulled away. MacPherson turned to face them “Briefing, my office, what?” and stomped towards the station. Oh God, thought Hogan as he hurried to catch up, Pound chuckling beside him.

Hogan arrived home late on Friday night. He’d walked as they had no car, something his wife never failed to remind him. Boots off, slippers on in the “foyer” though most folks here would call it a mudroom. He sat across from her eating meatloaf, his favorite, while she thumbed through a magazine and smoked.

“I’ve decided to redo the parlor, this time in “bluh.” She pronounced blue in the French way as though horking a hairball to the table. Oh God, oh well anything’s better than that green. She blew smoke from her nose as she continued, “And the Hogg’s are picking us up at eight. Gerald’s got a speech to give.”

Hogan’s hopes for a quiet night were dashed. Gerald Hogg had run for the Mayor’s job to avoid enlistment, he was sure, and Hogan regarded him as a callow bore with a handshake as soft as treacle and a gaze that looked past you for a crowd. He was stumping for War Bonds now. Hogan had heard his speech twice before. Hogg always arrived late and would stride to the podium to the fading strains of Rule Britannia, poking his finger the way politicians do in acknowledgment of some favoured and beaming acolytes in the crowd, working all to a frenzy as he spoke in a hug fest of patriotic pap.

Hogan and Pound were driving north. MacPherson’s instructions had been simple though lacking in brevity. Find the Japs and shoot ’em if you have to.

Pound, of course, was excited. He smoked furiously in the car, rolling one after another while a litter of tobacco piled up on his lap. They’d gone by Naguchi’s place and then to his Aunt and Uncle’s. The two of them denied seeing him though Hogan noticed the spoon he’d admired at Naguchi’s lying on their table. He expected them to lie and said nothing to Pound who was striding through their house, kicking open doors and peering in closets. Bertha seemed nervous. Stanley sat staring out the window though it was misted with steam from a pot which boiled on the stove.

Pound came back to the kitchen holding a Savage rifle. “Whose is this?”

“That’s mine.” Said Stanley and turned to Hogan, “I’ve been cleaning it.” He grinned.

Pound put the gun down and glowered "You know it's an offense to harbour an enemy alien?"

Stanley said, "You find one here, let me know."

Pound scowled at him and then changed his tune. "You guys ever hunt bears? I've always wanted to shoot a bear."

Stan stared back. "Some of us do."

"You think I could come out with you on a hunt some day?"

Stan looked thoughtful. "Well, you could but the green horn has to wear the bear suit. That's the rule."

"The bear suit? How's that work?"

"Well, you dress up and we go down to the beach and you just move around and try to chum 'em outta the bush while we're waiting in the trees with our guns."

"Yah, but what happens if one of them attacks me?"

"Oh, that's easy. We'll just shoot the one on top. Course we'll have to adjust the chin strap on your helmet. Don't want that fallin' in your eyes if you're runnin."

He gazed stone faced at Pound who was now backing out the door. As they left, Hogan said to Bertha, "nice spoon." She shrugged.

The cook at Camp Baloney told them Ito didn't show up for work and a campboat was missing, a rowboat, dark green. He followed them to Ito's cabin, Pound rushing ahead and shouldering the door, shot gun in hand.

There was an oilskin cover on a raised platform. A half round of firewood, worn smooth lay at one end. The room was empty. Hogan asked Peterson if he noticed anything missing. The cook was bleary eyed and holding the door frame for support.

"Ito's missing."

"Yeah, we know that Peterson, anything else?"

"Don't see his sword or his bow. Radio, always fiddling with that. Didn't have no furniture 'cept that chifforobe."

"No bed?" said Pound.

"You figure he took it with him detective?" Peterson started cackling. Pound ignored this jab and flinging open the drawers of the empty bureau, pulling each one to the floor with a clatter. Hogan turned to Peterson. "You see Naguchi here yesterday?"

"Nah, but he's thick with old man Carson. Got a canoe there, I think."

They went to Carson's. He was off in the bush somewhere but his wife said they hadn't seen Naguchi since the summer. She pointed towards the beach, "That's his boat down there."

A canoe, propped on logs lay overturned beneath the trees. "Bert says he made it himself." She promised to let them know if she saw him and when they were leaving yelled from the door, "He's a good boy, you know."

Hogan was feeling uneasy. The kid's dugout was a work of art. The frog design Naguchi had shown him on his vest was carved and painted on the prow. The kid was more Indian than most. And what Ito had said bothered him even more. He told Pound to shut up and they drove in silence.

Like all bullies Pound wanted to see the fear. Hogan had sized him up quickly and when Pound snapped his fingers at him one night on patrol he'd thrown him against the wall of the hotel.

"Don't ever snap your fingers at me."

"Why not?"

Hogan shoved him harder to the wall. He'd had commando training in the First War and still knew how to kick someone in the balls.

"Cause I'll snap you on your ass if you do."

Pound started back tracking "I didn't mean *blah blah blah*" and then hurried to catch up as Hogan walked away. He had no trouble with Pound after that and generally took charge when they worked together.

They reported to MacPherson at 4:00 p.m. There was briefing there was debriefing, the map and much puffing. Hogan was looking for a dog and pony in the end.

Pound stood at rigid attention throughout, the fucking toady, while Hogan tended his roses in the yard, the sunlight through the leaves and dappling his face.

"…handle it Hogan?"

He snapped back and took a calculated guess, he could always check with Grimes.

"Yes sir."

"Jolly good."

Hogan got out of there at 6:00 pm. It was dark. He swung left at the corner and ordered fish and chips at Chans, whose windows were layered with flags, Canadian, British and the Stars and Stripes most recently. He ate as he walked and was glad that he had once home.

It took two weeks for the wanted posters to arrive. There was a picture picked up from the school of Naguchi in younger days, though nothing for Ryo Ito. MacPherson, his swagger stick stabbing at "Armed and Dangerous, WANTED ENEMY ALIENS, $500 REWARD" in bold black type, was using every big word he could think of: "Reconnaissance," "contingency," "the acquisition of intelligence," and the like crackled from his mouth like the spittle in his bowl. Christ thought Hogan, he'll use "wheelbarrow" and marmalade" when he runs out. A charge of theft had been thrown in for good measure. The bow and the sword meant armed and dangerous.

Pound was taking fucking notes though in simple terms they were to plaster these everywhere and, "do some sleuthing, what?" At Pound's insistence they put posters up at the church on the reserve. Hogan knew this was a mistake. Two more were posted at the Okeover landing and two at the post office in Lund.

Hogan was pinning Naguchi to the wall when the Countess came in with Little Bob mincing around her like a dog at a hydrant. She stared at Naguchi's picture and said slowly, "Well, well, well, I've had dealings with him before." I didn't know he was a Jap." Pound came in just then after "nosing around" as he put it.

"Dodger says he dropped Naguchi at the Okeover turn off… that puts the two of them," he waved at the posters, "together!"

The Countess was listening intently. "I have hunting dogs and attack dogs you know and I'd be happy to help the war effort." She was smiling at Hogan though were her eyes blue and cold. "You get me his general location and something with his scent," she poked her cigarette towards Naguchi, "and my dogs will find him. Let me know if you're interested." She turned to the door, Little Bob scampering ahead to hold it.

Dodger and Tiny were drinking beer on the wharf. He didn't like Tiny but it was free beer. He felt bad about telling Pound he'd given Naguchi a lift. He'd no love of cops and didn't know they were after the guy. He looked over at Tiny. The big ape was watching a dog on the float licking his balls in the sun. Tiny belched and said "God I wish I could do that." Dodger finished his beer and got up to leave as the Countess and little Bob came in sight. "Go ahead Tiny, the dog probably won't mind."

Pound was bouncing in his seat. He insisted they go by Ito's to get something with his scent til Hogan snapped "there was nothing there! The guy used a fucking log for a pillow." And then he saw Naguchi's bedding in his mind. He said nothing but Pound was a bitch on a bone.

"Then we'll go by Naguchi's, see what we can find."

"No. We'll have to clear it with MacPherson. He sent us here to put up posters not to pick up fucking rags. We need a briefing, maybe take some notes. We'd be better off seeing if those posters on the reserve are still up. You have anymore?"

Pound sulked. They drove by the church and kept driving. Hogan stared at him. The posters were gone.

Ito insisted we walk up the creek to the cave. It was OK with me, I'd found rubber boots under the cabin the year before. We brought a torch of pitch and pine needles. Skirting the lake in the shallows, we climbed to the mouth of the cave.

I lit the torch, and crawled inside. Light filled the cave and I stared. A herd of elk galloped on one wall and across the ceiling. Flickering, they ran like an offering to a huge one-eyed figure which loomed just beyond. Hand prints in red and black speckled its body. It was Tal, the taker of children, and aren't we all God's children. She was a taker of heads from the land of the dead. Bertha had told me stories and I knew her right away. All of it was here in the gloom and unseen when my lover throbbed upon me.

Ito checked the fire pit, the bed, its indentions, and said, "you may have to live with that," pointing to the spirit on the wall, the eye, a totem, staring down.

He insisted we stock the cave that day so we went back to the cabin for supplies. Ito carried the shepherd's stove tied to his back and I followed, my pack, heavy with food. We slogged up the creek.

The stove was set up beneath the fissure, the food, in glass jars was placed in the box to one side, the torch casting shadows on the walls. We cut some firewood and stacked it by the stove.

"Now you have a fallback position, you've taken precautions."

We returned to the cabin and ate baked potatoes with two cutthroat fried in butter. After dinner Ito opened his box with a key from a cord round his neck. He took out some paper and a Biro pen which I'd not seen before and began writing. He'd stare into space then go back to his task while I lay on the bed reading *Crime and Punishment* in the faint light from the lamp.

When Ito had finished, he put everything back in his box and locked it. The book had slipped from my hand and I heard him blow out the lamp and lie down. I slid back into sleep, Raskolinikov, the axe now beneath his coat, moving inexorably towards murder…

In the morning we shared porridge and after, he retied his bundle and turned to face me.

"I'm going to the cave for a couple of days. Come and see me on Thursday morning. There are some things to take care of."

He stepped forward and hugged me, something he'd not done before. Looking in my eyes, he smiled, picked up his burden and walked out the door.

I spent the day cleaning the cabin and reading, the pending murder, the crime and the punishment relentlessly unfolding. With a wet rag on my face like Jesse James I swept mouse and rat droppings and I wanted to shout at Raskolnikov don't do it, though not out loud. I wasn't crazy yet.

On Thursday I made a thermos of tea, Ito's favorite, and hiked the stream to the lake in early morning. It was one cast fishing, the green water on the half boil with trout. I played two to shore and walked toward my friend with an offering.

My greeting came back to me, the mouth of the cave black and open like a scream. A fumbling of matches, a guttering of candle and a sheaf of paper that read "August." Stumbling to sunlight, I read through the letter and I ran.

I found him at the old Rogers' homestead, long abandoned on the point, right where he said he'd be, his body slumped eastward, the knife in his hands and the gore. He'd made two cuts and I marveled his intention and his purpose.

A raft mounded with kindling had been built, its poles lashed together so the ropes would break as they burned. I wrapped his body in the blanket beneath him, so thoughtful, and waited until the night's ebb tide as instructed. He'd left me a bottle of Sake to sip as I watched him leaving and lit with fire. The blanket had been soaked in kerosene and went up in a flare.

I drank too much and watched him burn as he floated from my life, glowing like a forge in the night. He went out just a flicker and I stared at the blackness till I joined it.

A raven croaks, the eyes open. No trace of my friend. The ropes burn and the bones drop into the sea. Did the body jerk up in a rictus of heat for one final bow? I don't know. It's one of those thoughts that swoops inside your head and makes correction at the wall. I vowed to remember him as I lay him down with his eyes wide open to the stars.

Ito my friend, my friend, your key hangs heavy on my neck now, hung over and alone.

The old Roger's house sat proud on the point, most of its windows broken and gaping. I walked through an arbor of honeysuckle, twisted and leafless, to the door. This was survival and I looked through echoing rooms for what I could use: some canning jars and a box of lids in the kitchen, an old inner tube I cut into strips for a slingshot and a book of Shakespeare, its wrinkled cover ingrained with dust.

In his letter, Ito had written of shame, the ultimate enemy of a Samurai and an honorable death the only way to defeat it. He had chosen *Seppuku* as his answer and I wrestled with this as I climbed.

Snow had begun falling, laying a cover of silence on the world. Huge wet flakes swirled round me and I became lost but kept walking til I heard the bubbling of the creek which dropped from the pond behind the cabin far above.

I walked blindly til I found it, the sound ever closer and followed its passage to the tree line where I could see more clearly, the canopy my umbrella, and on to familiar ground.

Back at the cabin, I lit a fire in the stove and sipped tea in the half light watching the snowflakes beyond the window turn like a life. I ate leftovers mechanically and without enjoyment, the food tasting ashen in my mouth. To bed and the covers pulled over me, curled up like a fetus that's weeping in the womb.

It snowed for three days and I kept the fire going putting unsplit rounds in the stove at night which would glow til morning and then jump to life with the damper opened. I read Shakespeare and understood little but was struck by the line, "He jests at scars that never felt a wound."

On the third day Ito's key was a weight ever pressing and I climbed to the cave. The mouth was partly covered by snow which I scraped away and stepped back, pausing in anticipation. I looked at Ryo's key and thought of Edmond Dante, as he stood map in hand at the entrance to the cave on Monte Cristo. "I mustn't let myself be shattered by disappointment or all my suffering will have been in vain."

Hogan stood on the dock at the foot of Ash Street and stared out to sea. There were 300 Jap fishing boats, well, alien boats, strung together and towed like beads on a rosary or a necklace of pain. There was a small crowd, some jeering and Pound beside him, waving his night stick at the louts, a conductor in a choir of the damned.

He poked Pound back to reality,

"Come on we're supposed to ask around, see if any boats have seen these guys." He motioned to Pound at the wanted posters tucked under his arm.

MacPherson had said they were to "put our feelers" and "gather intelligence" which Hogan thought was asking a lot of Pound.

Pound had talked MacPherson into sending them to Naguchi's cabin for something with the Jap's scent. He came out with a box of clothes and all of August's bedding. He'd labeled it "NAGUSHI" and was smacking his lips in anticipation of the carnage to follow. At the station they sealed and stored it in a cupboard that Mrs. Grimes used for office supplies.

MacPherson had a sign made, "Evidence Locker" and had her using a key thereafter. He was "pulling out all the stops. What?" He ordered Hogan and Pound to "widen their perimeter" and go out to interview old man Carson in Okeover. These two Japs were a "blemish on his record, what?" and he was having none of it.

Pound had suggested to the Idiot that Hogan was "soft on the Japs." Grimes had let him know of this and it was confirmed when MacPherson made Pound the Acting Duty Officer for their "mission." Hogan didn't like it. An alliance of idiots could be an unstoppable farce.

They interviewed Carson in the field. He'd been pulling stumps with his horse and let her graze as they spoke. No, he hadn't seen the boy and pointed towards the canoe.

"Boat's still there. Don't know where he is. Had a broom last time I seen him, maybe found a cabin, lots of broken dreams out there."

Pound had been letting Hogan do the talking as usual, now he jumped in,

"Do you know, the general area of his cabin, its whereabouts?"

Carson spat some snoose on the ground. "It's a big place," he waved at the mountains, "wouldn't tell you if I knew." He walked away, Pound yelling after him, "aiding and abetting" and other idiotism's.

They "pulled in their horns" after that "ear to the ground. What?" and the weeks rolled on. By April all Japs, not just the able-bodied, had been interned. Kagutsu's daughters were an earlier exception as his wife was stuck in Japan and there was nowhere for them but to be locked up with their father.

Oleg Parsons, the mad trapper, a notorious Bunster recluse, was interviewed. It was rumored that he'd had a cabin somewhere. He said hadn't been there in years. He'd seen "a face at the window" and spent the night with an axe in his hand and staring at the door. He'd relaxed with the morning light and was having breakfast when he heard footsteps circling the cabin, "Like a whirlpool. Musta bin cabin fever, but how do ya know it when yer in it? I ran like hell. I got other cabins now."

He drew them some crude maps, while swatting at flies that weren't there. Hogan didn't take much stock by it though Pound and his new buddy the idiot didn't agree. "Noose tightening, What?"

I opened Ito's box as instructed. A letter marked "August" on a pile of money, neatly stacked.

"August, you are like a son to me. I have no family. You have chosen the way of Gambari, of those who resist. The travails of a warrior are many. I leave you my sword, the bow and its arrows that they serve you in a righteous path, one which does not turn on itself to haunt you. The money I have saved is for you with my blessing. May good fortune someday find you my friend. Ryo."

There was $1,200 in that box and a poke of gold nuggets that a note inside said, "Taken from the north fork of Plummer Creek." On the bottom of the box a picture in sepia of Ito in younger days, his hand resting on the sword I now held. He was in uniform, a field gun behind him, perhaps somewhere in China, the sun on his visor concealing the eyes yet no mistaking the grim line of his mouth.

The sword, the box and its contents I left in the cave. I'd found his radio, a crystal set, on the platform and followed the course of the war that spring. Singapore had fallen, a Jap sub fired shells at the lighthouse on Point Atkinson. There was marching music and much gnashing of teeth as the war took more in its wake.

My days were spent hunting and I got pretty good with a slingshot. Grouse were the easiest and would often sit still while I shot again. Stanley had shown me how to take the breast meat without plucking, which reads more gory than it is. It was a nice break from fish and I always gave thanks in the proper way.

I marked the nights on a calendar showing a woman dark haired like Rose, smiling softly and stretched out on a car. And I do confess I took much comfort there, the lamp set to flicker, its shadows made easy my lover.

Young and half crazy with desire I marked the time. I'd told her to come on the first, if not July then August or thereafter. I couldn't wait, though I had to, for Orion and Canis to rise into the sky.

In July, broken-hearted I wandered the hills and found an old homestead, the house a charred ruin, with an orchard of early apple in a weed shot field. Six bears, I counted, rolling and wrestling with pleasure and gorged. I picked an apple in the shade and sat watching them as I ate. The juice from my face I washed in the cistern's cedar bucket so swollen and tight.

I dug potatoes and onions in the old garden, its fences now tattered. Putting all in a sack, I made my way home. I mustn't, I mustn't let myself be shattered.

Once I went into some guy's den stuffed with animals and glass eyes staring.

There were antler card racks and moose's noses and a lion under slippers and a bear with a salmon in his ear and an eagle stuck on a stick clutching pine cones. I had this weird sensation that they'd all suddenly burst out singing and was about to ask him if either pine cone had put up much of a fight but instead heard myself saying, "Where did you hide all the bodies?"

Gerry Furnace said he once found bear's carcass that some hunter had skinned and beheaded and left at the side of the road. He and a buddy finally heaved it off the wharf on the count of three. Said it was just like hoisting a drunk from a taxi.

Later that month I got a buck after waiting upwind with my bow at the edge of a clearing. He sent the does across first and waited in shadow before crossing. The bow's twang and a glinting arc to the heart. He spun like a dancer and died. I gave thanks to the spirits with a song half forgotten and the wind took my tune past the trees.

I canned the hind quarters and ate liver that night. In the days that followed, I made pemmican, smoked with wild cherry and dried in the sun.

I took to walking down into Theodosia checking on the boat, gathering clams or oysters and any excuse to stare out to sea.

One day the cries of crows plotting murder took me to the trees by the shore. There was maybe a hundred spread in a circle on the sand flats. One part of the circle was open and in the break sat three crows saying nothing while the others screamed accusation. As if on a signal, six left the circle and pinned the wings of the three then all flew in for the kill.

It was over in moments, the trial was completed and all but the three flew away.

I walked on the flats and I toed them, the wind tugging their feathers glinting blue. The one in the middle, its wings spread like crucifix, between two of me.

Spring lapsed into summer, the parlour now done in "bleu" which to Hogan's relief looked better than it sounded. With Pound now back on night shift, things were looking up.

There'd been no further word of Naguchi and Ito. The Japanese had been defeated in the navel battles of the Coral Sea and Midway though the British were driven from Libya and back to Egypt. It was all about the war.

Gerald Hogg had been elected by acclimation, elections were waived for the length of the war, and treated it as a massive victory, vowing to redouble his efforts to make the town safe for democracy. MacPherson's "Command Center" grew strangely silent, his briefings on hold.

On a day in July, Hogan reported for work. Still typing, Mrs. Grimes rolled her eyes towards a cloud of pipe smoke which covered the hall in a swath.

"You wanted to see me sir?"

MacPherson bounded from his desk, the pointer in hand, in full puffery. Pound stood at attention grinning.

"Intelligence, word from the field. Report of a sighting, Theodosia—Jap, maybe Indian—near the shore, just one, right here." He swatted the map.

"You see lads, Napoleon wrote of the Moment of Lassitude, two opposing armies jockeying for position, stalemate, What? But wait! The moment to strike arrives!" He smacked the map which jumped from its roller to the floor. Undaunted, the idiot continued, "The forces which seize the moment prevail! And this is our moment! Lassitude. What?"

Hogan didn't get it.

Pound was lapping it up like the sycophant he was. "So, wheels are in motion? Sir." The idiot beamed at Pound.

You see men, *Triangulation*. He gestured to the map at his feet, Pound preventing it from rolling by straddling both ends. MacPherson pointed to somewhere near Pound's asshole. Pound was sinking lower and looking desperate. Hogan was starting to enjoy it.

"We've got the—Whack!—Report of last sighting at the Okeover turn off and we got the—whack!—stolen boat from the camp. Now we've got the—whack!—Oh, sorry Pound—report of the sighting in Theodosia!"

Yes, gentleman, *Triangulation*, he stepped over Pound who was now writhing and clutching his groin, "Off to the Evidence Locker! This way chaps".

They two-stepped from the room. Pound bumping into Hogan when they came to a sudden halt. Mrs. Grimes had covered her typewriter by now and gone home, taking the keys to the Evidence Locker. It was decided after much puffing to seize the Moment of Lassitude the next day.

It was to be called "Operation Overburden" and Pound, Hogan was told, would be in charge of this "Phase of the Operation." Driving interfered with Pound's smoking so Hogan found himself as usual at the wheel. They were delivering Naguchi's *remains*, he couldn't stop thinking it, or as Pound liked to say "the Jap-in-a-box."

Little Bob met them at the dock in Lund, his muttonchops now bigger than himself. He wore a nautical captain's hat, dripping with egg and a white T-shirt as did

Tiny though on his bulk it looked like a training bra. The Countess's boat was sleek, mahogany and gleaming, but Hogan thought not beamy enough, more suited to lakes than the West Coast.

She came up from below deck as Pound was handing "Nagushi" to Tiny.

"Put him over there," she motioned with her cigarette holder.

"I'll need a good week to work the dogs, they'll be ready. Let me know when you're ready. It should be good fun."

Pound was over-awed by her, nodding and smiling like a puppet named Woody.

Hogan felt squeamish and uneasy. It was all oozing in on him now and over him like a wave. Did she say fun? This was serious and he felt swept on a current towards August, a force in which he was implicated but over which he had no control.

August 1st was a hot day and I walked down the mountain. She came round the point paddling with purpose, no wake from the blade. The sun glowed on her arms and a rising tide like a heartbeat brought my lover to me.

We made love on the shore til we burst and walked hand in hand up the mountain in paradise. She was working at the hospital, the first of our people to fly so high. Her father was having a potlatch in four days and she'd have to be back to work. Bertha was canning fruit and collecting wanted posters. Stan had an operation. Said they cut out everything but his sense of humour and if anymore doctors poked up his ass he was going to put in a guest book.

We went back to the cabin and ate like gods with all that she'd brought. That night we lit candles, spilled wine and danced, sharing Ito's earpiece, one leading the other til we dropped.

The next day we went to the cave and I showed her Ito's letter and the box, the elk on the run, Tal staring down. We made red dye from alder bark and elderberry and black from a paste of charcoal and dogwood and put our handprints touching on the wall.

The day was cloudless and golden. We swam in the lake and she screamed in delight when trout bumped her from below. We ate, we danced to no music, and I was lost.

On the third day we packed a picnic and went to the orchard by the old homestead to watch the bears play. We ate an apple together, our foreheads touching while the bears rolled, their coats glinting and so black you might think that God tore a hole in the day.

A last supper together, the candle goes out, and we curled into sleep, two spoons in a drawer.

In the morning we said little and joining hands walked down. She led me from the path, tugging and insistent to a huge arbutus, our hands around the trunk just touching, the spirits in the bark roiled and warm. She lay me down there and she mounted, the light through the leaves fluttering on her nipples as she climbed, her smiling eyes soft shut with wings of gold in her hair, and the shadows of her body, the smooth line of her body, set seed into motion, my world into focus, made speechless. She was leaving but she loved me and all was well.

A last long hug. I pushed the canoe off and watched her too quickly around the point and gone. I lingered near the shore, staring back towards the huge arbutus far above, the sun mirrored on its leaves. I felt happy and sad which comes close to nostalgia but isn't and watched three turkey vultures catching thermals in a wispy sky… "Time to push the stone back up the mountain." I said to no one in particular and started walking.

MacPherson was in the "War Room". He'd had a sign made of X's from Mrs. Grimes typewriter to replace what had been the "Command Center." He would co-ordinate the "Operation". Two "wogs in the woods" were not going to prevent his promotion. Hogan knew he was too old for promotion and had been put out to pasture in Powell River but didn't know it.

Like all toadies, MacPherson rose to command by cutting the rungs from the ladder below while currying the favour of those higher up. Personnel Reports were all delicately shaded, nuances of concern in the language of suits, circling the subject like turds down a bowl.

He'd driven a Jeep in India, almost been knighted there, he was fond of hinting, though Hogan wondered how that was possible. Did he keep driving when he ran over a Wog?

"Operation Overburden" was to be a crowning, a coronation to ensure his passage on high. He'd arranged for a police boat and a barge in ten days when the tides were right. They would pick up the Countess, her horses and dogs and barge them into Theodosia. MacPherson would stay on the boat at "Command Central". Pound and Hogan, Little Bob and Tiny, duly sworn, would make up the "Brigade". The Countess too of course though no need to deputize her. She'd offered her horses and dogs to them at no charge as part of the war effort, a true patriot.

Hogan was pissed that Pound was put in charge of "Field Operations." He'd be part of a posse of psychopaths with an idiot pulling the strings. God knows what to make of the Countess. She was colder than cash and had lots of it. Attack Dogs? He thought of Naguchi running in terror, hunted and stumbling then quickly switched to maybe I can do some good. Bertha came back from her morning walk. Stan was sitting at the window in a ray of sunshine and patting Pinball. She came inside. There were two more "Wanteds" rolled up in her hand.

"You bring us a couple more of those we can paper the bathroom". He grinned at her and she swatted him with the posters as she passed, "You keep rubbing that mutt he's gonna catch on fire."

She came back from the kitchen with mugs of tea and sat down. He could see she'd been crying.

"What is it love?"

She took a deep breath.

"I saw something on my walk today. I'm worried Stanley."

The Countess sat on the porch sipping tea while Gretchen polished her boots. She said something in German. The girl ran inside, emerging moments later with an ornate pair of spurs in silver and knelt to place them. The Countess yelled at Little Bob, "Don't feed the dogs today. Just take them down, I can see the boat coming now."

Hogan was on the police boat with Pound and MacPherson. The skipper was a cop named Reeves. Hogan hadn't met him before but he had to admire the way he maneuvered the barge to the shallows, nosing it in till it ground over the stones.

Little Bob and Tiny were waiting. The dogs began to yelp and the horses reared. He could see the Countess coming down the path astride a huge roan and dressed in riding habit, a helmet and red jacket. Christ she looks like she's going on a fox hunt and ready to ride through some peasant's garden.

The water was dead calm with a few lines where the currents twisted away in lazy loops towards the mountains, now tinged with pink in the morning light. MacPherson was yelling orders which no one took heed of and the loading went smoothly. Reeves swung the boat around and a stern line was attached. It pulled taut and the barge rattled free.

Hogan counted seven dogs, five Ridgebacks and two Doberman.

" The dogs of war, What?"

MacPherson had a map spread out on the back deck and was going over the "Campaign" with Pound and the Countess while Tiny and Little Bob threw the dogs what was left of Naguchi's belongings, tossing them out like party favours. Two clowns on a parade float. The box of "Nagushi" was now rags and covered with slime.

Two hours later they rounded the corner from Lancelot to Theodosia which opened before them like a wound. The barge nosed into the sand. The horses were mounted and the dogs released, streaking over the flats, turning in unison, left and then right, like a scythe.

Hogan kicked his horse to a gallop following Pound who was jouncing in his saddle as though spineless. They raced after the Countess, far in the lead, Little Bob and Tiny close behind her, the butts of their rifles glinting in the sun.

The dogs ran down the beach and then back, covering the ground relentlessly in a pack, the Dobermans just behind. Back and forth they swooped like a flock of birds running parallel to the shore, ever inland till their yapping changed pitch and they raced up the mountain towards the timberline in a wedge.

Hogan was ahead of Pound. He could hear Little Bob shouting "They've picked up the scent!" Tiny whooped with delight. "There he goes." Sure enough, Hogan could see Naguchi through the trees, a figure, running then falling then jumping up and racing on, angling towards a huge arbutus, the dogs closing. The beads on his vest catching the light as he ran. Little Bob and Tiny had their rifles out now. "Hold your fire!" he screamed.

Naguchi was climbing an arbutus, just clearing the ground as the dogs arrived, leaping and snapping at his heels as he scrambled outward on a limb going higher, the branch bending as he climbed.

The limb snapped but Naguchi grabbed above and hung with both arms for a moment, swinging outward and landing almost acrobatic on a small ledge just above the dogs. A Doberman took hold of his boot but he kicked it till it fell and scrambled higher on the bluff. The Countess yelled, "He's getting away."

Just then Pound rode up "Fire," he screamed, "fire at will." Hogan yelled "No" as two shots rang out. The first buckled a leg and Naguchi had half turned towards them when the second knocked him back. He twisted from the bluff and fell to the dogs below.

"No" Hogan screamed again, his face contorted in horror, the sound from the dogs, of fabric and flesh, the Countess smiling from her horse, Little Bob and Tiny hugging each other in delight and already arguing over who had "got him". "I said hold your fire" he yelled again, Pound shouting "I'm in charge. This is war!" The dogs howled on.

He kicked his horse down the slope towards the body. Of course it was too late. If the bullets hadn't killed him the dogs certainly had.

His head, his whole torso, had been savaged, his clothing in tatters and soaked with blood. Little Bob and Tiny pulled the dogs away, still churning at the corpse, while the Countess mounted and smiling, smoked a cigarette. Finally the dogs were leashed. Pound pulled a blood smeared ID card from the remains of a pocket. "Naguchi. One more to go."

Hogan turned away and threw up.

They put Naguchi on Pound's horse. He was happy to offer it, his thighs and his ass were on fire. Little Bob tied the hands and the feet. The Countess thought they'd had enough excitement for one day and suggested a late lunch back on the boat. Pound was eager to "apprise" MacPherson of the latest developments and show him his trophy. They were silent heading down the mountain. Even the birds had gone quiet.

It was decided to call Naguchi's passing an act of war, resisting arrest, armed, they'd found a pen knife, and dangerous. Reeves would have to anchor out, the tide soon running to slack. The Countess would get the cabin, Pound and MacPherson to "guard the body" which they lay on top of the wheelhouse, cupped in a tarp for the blood.

Hogan and Tiny and Little Bob would tend the horses on shore. They'd found grass just down the beach and would tether them there. Ito would be brought to justice in the morning.

Hogan couldn't fall asleep. He thought he could do some good and Ito's words rang inside his head. He heard Little Bob get up to check on the horses, the fire still flickering, he drifted… it was Tiny later, the bulk of his shadow just a cloud.

He dreamed that night of a monster red-eyed, but huge and unblinking as though under ice with serpents of red and black spiraling down its arms like a barber's pole, a blood letter. The fire spluttered to smoke and he drifted with the murmur of the wind.

Hogan awoke first that morning, Little Bob and Tiny on each side of him hadn't yet stirred. He glanced at Tiny whose eyes were open and said, "Well, time to get up" then turned to Little Bob who was staring at him and he thought, that's odd, they must have changed places in the night. "Jesus Christ!"

He vaulted to his feet and stared aghast, still in his bag like a sack race. He struggled out of it, drew his revolver and waved it at the trees. "Jesus Christ!" He was shouting now and turning full circle, his gun in both hands like they taught him. He jumped in the air a few times as though skipping. He didn't know why but he had to, the bile rising in his throat.

Their heads had been exchanged in the night. Little Bob's head on Tiny no more than a pimple and Tiny's head and now the blood. He had to stop himself. He ran.

Reeves saw Hogan first. He was jumping up and down on the beach, his yelling drowned out by the dogs left tied on the barge overnight. He poked MacPherson and Pound still asleep on the stern deck. "Looks like trouble."

MacPherson struggled awake. He'd been dreaming of accolades and promotion, perhaps a bit of damage control—too bad about the Jap—and a few other euphemisms that might turn going down.

They couldn't reach Hogan for three more hours because of low tide, so no need to wake the Countess.

Hogan had time to gather his wits when they'd reached shore. Tiny and Little Bob beheaded, heads switched, dead in their beds. They found the bodies but the heads were gone. Hogan was on edge again, staring through the trees and seeing nothing, his eyes pooled and vacant. "They were here", he mumbled, "They were here."

The horses had been cut loose, though one of them, a gelding still grazed nearby. They packed the bodies over him and washed the blood from his withers when they reached the boat.

It took them all day to track down the horses. They missed the tide. MacPherson saw "Operation Overburden" turning suddenly sour. Reinforcements were needed, murder added to the charges. Tactical retreat. What? Madman out there.

Operation-over-the-fucking-top thought Hogan as they chugged away.

The Countess was dropped off first. She'd mentioned to Hogan that he didn't seem to have a stomach for war. He turned on her, "I guess it's like boxing. A sweet science if you like the taste of blood." She arched one eyebrow but made no reply.

He watched her winding her way up the hill to the mansion in the fading light, surrounded by the dogs, Pound leading the horses behind. *Her jacket's the colour of blood.* He turned away, staring towards the mountains and places even further.

The bodies were put on a flatbed in Lund for transport to Smiley's Mortuary. The coroner wouldn't be in town till next week. Hogan knew Smiley charged extra for ice. It was all too much. At the station he told MacPherson he wanted some time off. MacPherson said he'd "had a bit of knock" and to take all the time he needed. Hogan left for home.

The idiot had to write up a new wanted poster for Ito and ordered Pound to take Naguchi's down. On the way out to Lund he should inform Naguchi's relatives, no access to the body until next week. MacPherson paused in mid briefing. He was wondering if the deputies shot to wound or was it the fall? He'd better wait to hear from the coroner before writing his report. Perhaps a promotion for Pound who'd shown great leadership. He looked at Pound, "You still think Hogan's soft on Japs?"
"Yes sir."

"I value your insight *Corporal* Pound and I'm a pretty good judge of character. Mettle what?"

"Yes sir," Pound was beaming, "Thank you sir. Can I still work the night shift?"

Hogan got a call from MacPherson a week later. He'd just come in from the garden when the phone rang.

"Hogan! How are you feeling?"

"Not too well Sir."

"Good, good. Now listen old chap, want you to come in for a little chat. Bit of a mix up, some things to clear up, What?"

He was glad MacPherson had called. He'd planned to resign and this seemed the right time.

Grimes made a wincing expression as he passed her desk and into the smoke which hung like tinsel in the fetid air. Pound stood at attention.

"Ah, Hogan, glad you could come. Look old chap," he waved a paper in Hogan's face "it seems we've killed the wrong man, er woman, ah person. The body's a woman." He passed the coroner's report to Hogan who read it though his eyes were glazed. August, the frog's eye, the shape changer. He snapped back when Pound said, "Maybe Naguchi was a woman, sir."

Hogan spun to face him.

"Why Pound? Did you fancy him? Were his eyes fucking gray?" He was pointing at the report and shouting now. "So who did you kill?"

MacPherson stepped between them.

"Now, now, chaps. We think it's Rose Galligos. Heard nothing from the wogs of course but the hospital says she's not been in to work. Constable Pound was going to check the reserve. Stan August ran him off the last time he went out… They're collecting Naguchi's body at Smiley's today and we were wondering, if you wouldn't…?"

"You want me to deal with them? No fucking way—I quit." He tossed his badge and his gun on the desk. It was over.

Things went not too well at the mortuary. Stan and Bertha knew right away it was Rose. MacPherson was hoping they might be grateful it wasn't August until Stan raised him to map height and reared back to punch out his lights. Bertha stepped in and Stan dropped him. MacPherson started mumbling about Rose aiding and abetting until Stan moved at him again. Bertha got him away by saying, "We've got to go see the family Stanley." MacPherson yelled after them, "we can clean her up, make identification easier."

Stan whirled around, "Don't you fucking touch her. We'll do that."

"Jolly good. You tell us where to bring the body, What."

Bertha was pushing Stanley into the car, "Why don't you bring it back to life, you stupid bastard". They squealed away in a fog of burnt rubber.

MacPherson was worried. He'd have to really work on that report.

Rose had paddled back to me and I heard her call from the shore. I hadn't walked far and ran back to help her slip the canoe in a thicket of salmon berry. She said they were coming, she'd seen them as she rounded the point. "You won't make it to the cave, come on, I've got a plan."

We moved bent over, staying behind any outcrops, hugging the ground, going higher, the dogs ever closer. We'd reached the creek, now in the trees and running hand in hand. She stopped.

"Take off your clothes, it's your scent they'll be after. I told you they took a box of your stuff for the dogs. You never listen!" She laughed at that. "I'm kidding but this is serious. Now take off your pants." She laughed again. Hurry up. I'll run to our tree and climb it. I can make it easy."

"But you'll get in trouble for helping me..."

"I'll say I found your vest and went to find you to turn yourself in. Jail would kill someone like you. Hurry up.."

It made sense to me then, she had to get back anyway. I knew she could make it to our tree... like a lot of good plans, it became a crazy one that failed. The last thing she said was, "What are they gonna do, shoot me", my seed within her as she ran....

I saw it all. I'd ducked back high above them after following the creek. I saw her reach the tree, the branch breaking and an artful swing to the ledge, kicking at the leaping dogs and climbing higher. I heard Hogan yelling, Pound screaming "Fire", Little Bob and Tiny doing high fives, the shots still echoing, while the Countess lit a cigarette and grinned. I saw Hogan puke in the weeds but most of all I saw my lover turn in a dance of death and drop into Hell.

The procession, wound down towards the boat while colours of red and black glowed behind my eyes. The boat pulled out and anchored. I turned towards the cave, walking slowly and with purpose.

I dipped my hands in the red paste my lover had touched and swabbed round my eye, Tal staring down as I painted. I held my hand over Rose's print on the wall and made my vows. With one eye of red and one of black I looked at the bladed moon and I waited cross legged, the snakes on my arms running to Ito's sword in my hands. There were no tears. The night grew still and I with it. Just enough light. Time.

I went back for their heads once Hogan had run off, their souls to wander lost and forsaken forever.

Little Bob wasn't Robert after all. His name was Thomas Sharp. I checked their wallets and switched them, still don't know why. I took Tiny's birth certificate, leaving everything else intact. "Jackson Henry." Born in Idaho. I thought it might suit me in the end.

A week in the cave without eating. I lay on the moss and stared at the elk leaping above, the absence of my lover beside me and my arm around the air.

On one arm of a cross I carved her name from our people *Ahamoos* and placed it where she died. I lit a small fire on the stains of her blood and threw upon it strips of deer and salmon and was careful to look away as they burned that her spirit in smoke go unmolested. A last handful of berries as I left, hard focused on things served cold.

MacPherson and Pound were waiting at the mortuary for Sharp's sister to arrive. Smiley hovered like specter as pallid as death. He'd run out of ice. Pink water leaked from the casket to the drain. They'd buried Jackson Henry in a pauper's grave already. It saved on overhead and he'd had no relatives.

MacPherson briefed the sister when she arrived. "Open casket perhaps not cricket. Head missing, what?"

"Why did I wait for the coroner then?" she yelled at MacPherson. "How do you think he died you bonehead?" She looked away with a grimace then nodded to Smiley. The casket was opened and a stench of death filled the room. She screamed, MacPherson supportive, "Now, now, bit of a shock. Understandable."

"That's not Tommy! He was less than five feet tall! What have you done? Where is my brother?"

"But if you subtract the head…" said Pound, trailing into stupidity. She screamed again.

MacPherson saw the sun set like a bomb on "Operation Overburden," his chance of promotion now smashed. He glared at Pound when he suggested switching tombstones. The woman wailing, Smiley offering his hankie, the bloody water still snaking across the floor…

The newspapers had a field day. It even made the *Vancouver Sun*. This was good copy. "Police incompetence," and "Bungling" the watch words. Gerald Hogg was mortified. He'd delivered a rousing speech the week before, praising MacPherson as a guardian of the public trust and presenting him with the key to the town. True, it was made of cardboard and painted gold but really quite presentable till the fool waved it at the crowd, the band playing Rah-Rah, while it flapped in his hand like a swatter. Hogg phoned the Higher Ups.

MacPherson was relieved of his duties. Pound, since demoted, was doing two shifts. His new boss, a Scotsman named Campbell, the bastard, sent him to the reserve as "police presence" at Rose's funeral. It was a huge gathering even people from the hospital where she worked. The whole village attended in virtual silence. Father O'Reilly officiated, his blandishments punctuated by only a raven's cry. The handfuls of dirt almost filled up the hole.

On his way back to the car, a red ball flew from the crowd and splattered between Pound's shoulder blades, oozing goo. He ran to the car and thumped away on tires now flattened, a shower of rocks pinging off the hood as he wobbled away in the dust.

I rowed at night, hard by the shore and its darkness. Cross Lancelot on open water and in moonlight, I stared at the snakes as they flexed down my arms. Was this a righteous path? When did the sword go into my hand? When I saw her fall? Or was it when I stood before an alien god and painted my face to mimic its own? Perhaps it started long before that, even when I played in the sun as a child. I felt pinballed by events, by history, but I kept rowing, didn't I.

Past Grace harbour that night, up through Okeover Arm and into Galley Bay. I'd gauged the tides well and the boat slid into the weeds as the morning light began to stain the sky. I took Ito's bow with one arrow and moved towards the Mansion.

The Countess was having a bath while Gretchen waited with a towel in the corner and out of sight. She hadn't yet heard from MacPherson about hunting Ito. It made for a rather pleasant outing. Maybe next time they'd be back the same day. She stepped from the tub, dripping, while Gretchan covered her shoulders with a towel and began drying her legs with another.

The Countess looked down at her. The clumsy cow had broken a wineglass and not told her. She could see the welts on Gretchen's arms from the thrashing she'd given her. Poor Gretchen. She'd finally paid her passage and there was nowhere to go. Back to the Fatherland? Not now. Tiny and Little Bob had been forbidden to speak to her. She couldn't speak English unless it was something I'd taught her. And terrified of the dogs. Refuses to even feed them despite every persuasion. Stubborn.

"I'll feed the dogs this morning you useless cow. Make sure this tub is spotless before you come down. Two eggs over easy."

She dressed quickly and strolled towards the kennels. The birds sang, the day's first cigarette, the dogs beginning to bark, her long shadow moving on the pickets as she strolled.

I waited till she reached the gate and I shouted. She turned, shielding her eyes, first squinting then wide and aghast, the face that stared back a horror. The arrow sang. I didn't aim.

Did I toss her to the dogs? No, but I thought of it. She was stuck fast to a picket, still upright, the dogs snapping at her hair and her head bobbing. I stood in front of her face just staring as though something she'd already met on the other side. I said nothing and watched her until the fear in her eyes went cloudy, the dogs in a frenzy by then. The food went over the fence and the kennel boiled like a cauldron. Them dogs was hungry and so was I. Pound had said this was war. So be it. In for a penny, in for a Pound.

Gretchen heard the noise from the kennels. She couldn't start the eggs till the mistress returned. But those dogs. They were howling now and she hoped they weren't out in the yard!

She peeked around the barn and saw the Countess and then the arrow. She ran to her, scanning the yard and beyond. A shadow in the trees? She thought of pulling the arrow and gave it a tug. Nothing. The Countess was pinned like a moth. She ran towards the house. Gretchen knew where the money was.

I stayed in the bush, waiting for dark. Gretchen was on the shore, waving a white cloth on a stick at any boat that passed. The first waved back and the second one didn't see her. The third pulled in and she picked up her satchel and waded out to meet them.

The cops couldn't be back till tomorrow. I left Ito's bow and arrow hanging in an arbutus I'd hugged in the sun. An offering and a vow as I held my hand on the spirits that turned within.

South in the night, passing Lund, the tinkling of a piano, a woman's laugh echoing over the water, now louder as the hotel door opens.

Past the Iron Mines, I beached the boat in some alder which spilled out on the shore. I used three pole ends carried with me as rollers and thought of Haida slaves laid on the beach like cordwood to be squashed by a war canoe. The sun rose and the mountains moved closer in the light. I slept and dreamt of a circling wind that swept all my songs out to sea.

The next night I rowed past Dinner Rock, the cross on its top black against the moon.

A man loses his daughter when the ship goes down. But I could see him, on a hot day, beaching the boat, carrying the cross to the top, piling the stones, sun on his arms. Sits awhile, maybe has a smoke, and looks for her smile in the tide pools....

I had three hours to reach Powell River and I went straight as an arrow into darkness when a cloud rolled over the moon.

Pound was enraged. The bastard Campbell had him double shifted all week. They were short-handed ever since that wimp Hogan packed it in. Things were totally different now. He'd seen MacPherson a week ago, retired and a crossing guard, mustering children despite a lack of traffic.

Campbell made him go up to Galley Bay once Gretchen's story had been sorted. They had to get old man Claus from the pub to get it straight. She kept punching her breast and running a finger across her throat and Pound thought "another beheading?"

They left the Countess hanging and looked around. Someone had gone into the house after Gretchen left and chiseled open a strong box. They'd made a mess, flour spilled out in the kitchen and wine glasses smashed in the hearth. Had to be the Japs, maybe the wagon burners. It was an arrow and the last time he'd seen them they looked pretty pissed.

The dogs were shot. What else could they do? Let em out? They'd starve either way or even attack. It was too bad, he liked dogs, easy to train. They had to pull the Countess along the shaft to get her off. Nice looking babe.

The army went into Theodosia. Campbell sent Pound as an "observer" to show them the terrain. He pointed out where the squaw died and kicked at the cross but it didn't budge. Some Indian, just a Private, sidled up to him and whispered, "You kick that again and I'll stick you tonight." A bayonet gleamed on his gun. Pound didn't argue.

The mad trapper had mentioned a pond behind a cabin on one of his maps, so they followed the creek. It snaked over impossible terrain and took them all day. There were 30 of them and they moved in a line till they found it. The captain ordered the cabin burned until his sergeant said it would set the whole mountain on fire. They camped by the pond. No sign of the Japs. Guards were posted. They were warriors. They took no prisoners.

Pound was back from Theodosia the next day, just in time for night-shift the bastard informed him. Campbell had been riding him ever since he came back with the car. The shredded tires were a sticking point and every dent was put in his file. Bastard.

Pound pounded the beat, said hello to old Albert the Night Warden, his green light pointing at his shoes. The old man just grunted as he passed. Bastard.

The Rodmay was his favorites part. He'd walk through the bar looking for trouble.

The women had "escorts" but some of them liked a man in a uniform, especially the drunk ones. He chatted one up while fondling his truncheon but was really too tired to tell her what time he got off.

Once outside, he circled around back. He heard something by the garbage cans, maybe a drunk he could roust.

It was the wind. He felt it, the hair on his neck. He turned and the eyes, bloated and bloody hurtled from the darkness, the head like a totem when it smacked between his eyes.

Mrs. Grimes took the call and reported to Campbell. The Janitor had discovered him in a trash can. "Officer Down."

Campbell drove over thinking he'd need two replacements now. When he arrived he sat in the car for a while, looking at Pound, his face to the sky and stuffed in the can like food in the mouth of a monster. He walked around the body scouring the ground for clues and found nothing. But the night stick… its ribbed handle poked from Pound's mouth like a bar tap.

Campbell needed a drink. Christ, this job was going from bad to worse. Another bloody report, bruising around both eyes, raccoon-like. Impact or suffocation? Better wait on the Coroner's Report. Bar's not open. Damn.

The *Icarus* Incident

By Rick McGrath
Art by Paul H. Williams

When the shock waves of Japanese dive bombers fell like UFOs on the sleepy American base of Pearl Harbour on December 7, 1941, the repercussions echoed all over the western coastline of North America, resulting in frantic moves to set up defenses against a possible Japanese submarine attack and hardly possible landing attempt. The Royal Canadian Air Force base at Comox and Royal Canadian Navy Pacific headquarters in Victoria stepped up coastal surveillance, and work soon began constructing radar and gun embankments at strategic points along the long, undefended west coast of Vancouver Island.

One such base was built atop a high hill which rose up from the shores of Long Beach, a long, deserted stretch of endless sand, interspersed by rocky points, just north of the Alberni Inlet. The site was imposing and practical; from the top of the hill, 1,000 feet above the endless ocean, the radar detected evidence of any intrusion far out into the Pacific. The hilltop was cleared and three utilitarian concrete buildings erected: one for a gun, one for the seven men who would monitor the horizon, and one for the massive radar eye.

Locals at the fishing town of Tofino, 20 miles to the north, called the place Sea Lion Mountain—because of the close proximity of sea lion colonies on small rocky islands just offshore—but the armed forces liked to have things fit in with its own code, so they simply called the facility Long Beach Station, shortened to LBS.

In the official records LBS saw no action in the Pacific conflict, although one village to the south, Bamfield, was shelled for 20 minutes by a Japanese submarine in an attempt to knock out the Trans-Pacific communications cable, which was being used at the time to ferry high-priority information from Hawaii to Canada. According to local newspaper reports, the sub suddenly surfaced one afternoon and calmly began pumping cannon shells into the general business and residential area. Japanese information concerning the cable must have been poor, because the town was located

nearly a half-mile from the squat concrete station which sucked the cable up from the sea. After inflicting minor damage the Japanese disappeared as quietly as they had materialized. News of the attack prompted a red alert along the coastline, however, and several additional air sorties were arranged, and the navy cruiser *Icarus*, armed with depth charges, pointed its sleek shape north on a special mission from Victoria to LBS.

The captain of the Japanese submarine Nakano *was unhappy. A coded message early this morning had informed him of his failure to knock out the Bamfield communications cable installation, and the men he had sent out at first light to attack this dangerous radar base were not only late returning, but apparently had not yet blown up the facility as planned. The* Nakano *was half submerged in a shallow channel beside a rock island usually populated with sea lions, and the captain was hesitant about making any moves until the fate of his commando crew was known. With the rising sun and a sonar report a ship was approaching rapidly from the south, he regretfully ordered his sub into deeper waters. Perhaps he would do better hunting bigger fish.*

I only became aware of my family's involvement in the Pacific war last year, when my maternal grandmother died and my parents gave me the stuff in her basement. The place was old and musty, and the haul consisted of several old chairs, tables, a useless chesterfield, an old trunk, and some boxes of books. She wasn't a hoarder. It dawned on me the "gift" was probably a way for pater and mater to get the basement cleaned out, but the books and the old trunk caught my imagination right off, so I lugged them home first and made plans to deal with the rest later.

The books proved to be a stash of vintage science fiction—the kind of stuff collectors crave—which I thought was odd considering my grandmother's reading tastes tended towards historical romance and the odd mystery novel. And the rest what appeared to be old textbooks on electrical engineering. The trunk was locked, but the canvas had rotted around the clasp, and a few good tugs easily pulled the metal from its seams. It contained a few uniforms—looked naval—a sheaf of letters from the government, more books, and diaries for the years 1941 and 1942. I was surprised to note the letters were addressed to my presumed-dead Uncle, who dropped out of sight sometime around 1943. The navy searched for awhile, but he was never seen again.

I remember Uncle only by oral reputation, as my teetotalling mother used him to plague my father—who never refused a nip now and then—with warnings that if he kept drinking he'd go crazy like his brother, and she wasn't going to have any of that.

His letters were all dated before 1942, and were mostly navy stuff. Official crap.

The diaries were more interesting, and after a quick flip through a few entries it soon became apparent the man who wrote these thoughts was a different personality than the drunken slob dragged about by my mother. It was obvious a brain unsaturated with booze had been at work on these pages.

I learned my Uncle, who was into radio electronics before the war broke out, had

joined the navy and was ultimately assigned to the *Icarus* as communications officer, and spent at least one year chasing submarines in the coastal waters of British Columbia before he simply went missing. Short bio. My father didn't have much of a relationship with his older brother—the old man joined the air force as a fighter pilot, which he thought was superior—but he did embrace one idea which seemed to fixate the both of them from a young age, and that was a belief in the existence of Unidentified Flying Objects. The old man had two stock extraterrestrial tales he used to lay out at parties, the first being my Uncle's adventures at LBS, and his own wartime contact with some UFOs called Foo Fighters, which were literally balls of fire that often harassed British, Canadian, and French pilots.

The French actually named them, using their word feu, for fire, and the old man's only contact with the unexplained came when he was flying a night bomber protection mission with the 415th Fighter Squadron over Germany on July 11, 1942. The story goes that at four in the morning, while searching for enemy fighters, my father was astonished to see a large silvery glow climbing rapidly towards him. Afraid of rockets, he kicked the plane into a series of evasive movements, but the glowing almond shaped thing stayed right on the Spitfire's right wingtip, finally blinking off after several minutes. The next day he complained of sore eyes.

Apparently other pilots in the 415 had similar experiences, but during the war one never knew what was a new weapon and what wasn't. My father usually told that story with all seriousness. My Uncle's UFO story was slowly distorted into absurdity as the years went on, and was always told for a laugh, but I remember the first time I heard it was at a party my folks threw when were living on an air base. I would have been around 13 years old then. The old man was slightly drunk, just enough to attain a degree of eloquence, but his audience was thoroughly pissed. After awhile every line was met with gales of laughter, and the story was finally cut slightly short by my mother, sober and embarrassed, who suggested the time might be better spent playing charades.

It almost seemed like too much of a coincidence when, a few days later, I picked up the second of my Uncle's diaries and began scanning the entries. Most were short and technical, but my attention was caught when the word Bamfield jumped off the page. I had often visited the sleepy coastal village on long weekends when I was a university student. The entries read:

July 10, 1942: Aboard the *Icarus* off the west coast of Vancouver Island. Weather overcast and sea choppy. Already I'm frustrated with working on a shifting floor. Yesterday we found a Japanese life jacket floating in the surf off the small Indian village of Clo-ose. Could have come from anywhere, I guess. But not a good sign. Tomorrow morning we head north again.

July 11, 1942: More news. Apparently Bamfield, the village just south of our present position, was shelled by a sub a few days ago and sustained minor damage. The locals, fishermen mostly, got all high and mighty about the attack and apparently had to be

restrained from charging out in a few small boats to catch this enemy fish. Fat chance for success, but then again they might have been just bullshitting later in the pub long after the sub had left. The brass at headquarters were quite shocked. Jap intelligence was poor, however, as the concrete lips that sucked the Trans-Pacific telephone cable up from the secrets of Hawaii was a quarter mile out of town.

July 14, 1942: The Captain gave us all strict orders never to repeat what we saw today, and sent us off to our quarters with a double ration of rum and the suggestion we might as well remember today as a bad dream the next morning. I sometimes wake up from nightmares, all right, but never anything like this.

Myself, First Mate MacIntyre and Seaman Elliott had been summoned to the Captain's quarters for a vague initial briefing—something about radio contact from the radar base—LBS he called it—being suddenly cut off, and the three of us were supposed to go ashore and reconnoitre the situation, reporting back by six bells at the latest.

We congregated on the deck around 4 bells and cautiously viewed our destination, a god-forsaken radar installation high on a hill on a deserted coast between nothing and nowhere. It looked peaceful. I wondered what might have happened to the electronics.

As with all shore excursions we were issued handguns, and with MacIntyre in charge we set out for the beach. The tide was moving out. At first everything on the coast appeared normal, and then Elliott gave a low cry and pointed south. On a sandy dune about a couple hundred yards away were dozens of silver-grey humps scattered about, looking for all the world like forgotten torpedoes in the hot air. The harsh cries of turkey vultures and eagles circling overhead suggested the humps were organic, and MacIntyre lowered his binoculars to say the beach was littered with the corpses of sea lions.

We approached a rubber dingy bobbing in one of the dune channels near the log-covered shore. There were no marks on it, but a series of footprints led towards the trees, and we set out to follow them. The radar crew had built a passable path up the hill, and what might have been a pleasant climb through a pristine rain forest had been ruined by recent heavy rains, and the trail upward was a confusion of black gumbo and slippery tree roots.

It was apparent the trail had been recently used, as the undergrowth was broken in many places, and the odd flat spot was churned with bootprints just beginning to fill with a brackish liquid. The climb was hard and uneventful, except for our final rest period before reaching the top, when Elliott said he thought he saw something glint like aluminum through the trees, like looking at the sun through white curtains.

We followed his finger through the trees and into the bright blue sky, but could see nothing. Elliott finally disbelieved it himself, and we discounted his vision as the result of sweat in his eyes. Fifteen minutes later, panting, we suddenly broke out of the woods and into the tight circular clearing housing the LBS operations. The three buildings were arranged in a triangular configuration, with the gun emplacement forward, the barracks to the right and the radar bunker beyond. Elliott ran down a concrete-lined trench to check the gun pillbox first, returning almost immediately to say no rounds had been fired and the area was deserted.

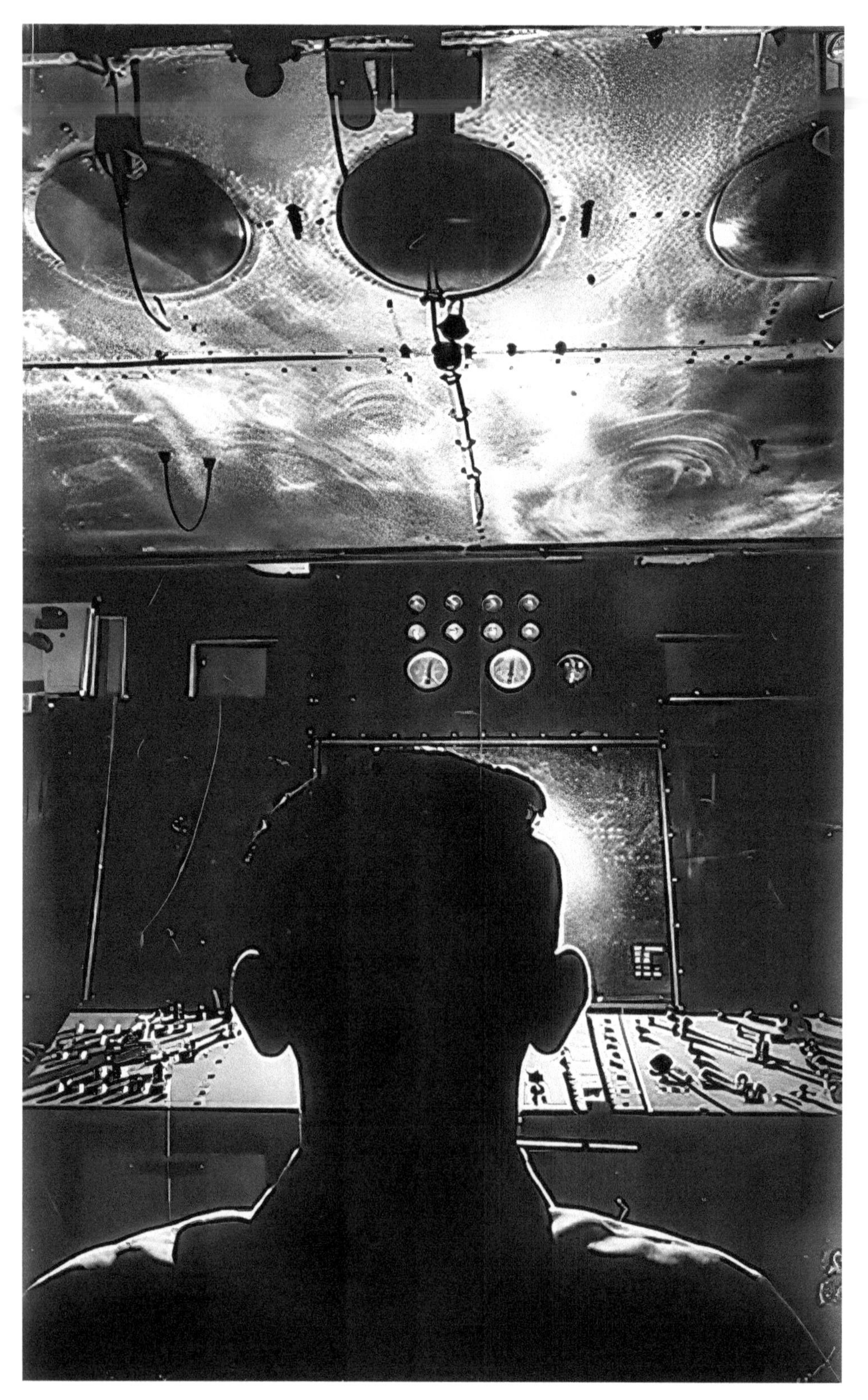

We moved forward to clear the barracks and just before rounding the corner into the small central parade grounds my nose picked up the faint, dizzy sharpness of ozone. We turned the corner and stopped, dead in our tracks. The small triangular yard was disfigured almost entirely by a large burned-off doughnut shape, with a small open crater in the middle. The unscorched areas at the triangle's proximities were covered with a fine silver ash and then I noticed a number of whitish mounds fanning through a complete circle around the central crater, which glowed slightly silvery in the late-morning sun.

The thought came this looked like a giant daisy lying against a matte black background, but instead of flower petals the mounds proved to be the dessicated bodies of men. There were six in all, and the bodies were arranged on their backs with clock-like precision around the slight central hole, with feet almost touching the crater and arms out by their sides, the remains of faces staring blankly upward. Clothing and flesh had succumbed to some intense radiation, but metal buttons, zippers and armament stood out in grotesque melted forms against the now distorted bodies. Elliott burned his fingers trying to pick up what appeared to be a half-melted gun, and McIntyre ordered us to leave everything as it was, not to touch anything.

Well, looking isn't touching, and I got a good look at one of the shorter bodies, and I swear the gun lying where his hand used to be was Japanese regular issue. So there were Japs here as well: they were the ones partially incinerated. But what had happened? A quick check of the barracks answered no questions. The interior looked completely normal. We backtracked, and when I turned for a last look I noticed our ashy footprints were glowing slightly in the cool darkness of the windowless concrete building.

The only place left to check was the radar complex itself, which stood opposite us. Convection currents were still visible from the crater, and it was through the distorted air I realized the radar's parabolic shell was not turning through its regular sweeps, but was pointing straight up into the bright sky.

We skirted the doughnut of bodies and entered the building. Elliott and McIntyre checked the power plant and storeroom while I entered the radar control room. My eyes took a moment to adjust to the greenish light from the main scope—the equipment still functioned—but the limp body of a technician lay slumped in his seat, head dangling back as if he were attempting to see through the concrete ceiling.

The scope in front of him should have been tracking through 180 degrees, but it was stationary and the only blip pulsated dead centre on the screen. I moved around the body to check if the controls had been set to point the radar dish upwards, and from this angle I noticed the dead man's eyes had a distinctly silvered colouration, like a solarized photograph. With each blip on the screen they glowed slightly in response, and before my companions joined me I reached out and shut the poor devil's eyes.

Almost immediately the radar blip pulsated faster, and then moved off quickly to the north. McIntyre had just entered the room and was blinking in the darkness when the electronics seemed to sigh and the screens went blank. The quiet and darkness were too oppressive for our already stretched nerves, and we exited into the sunlight and

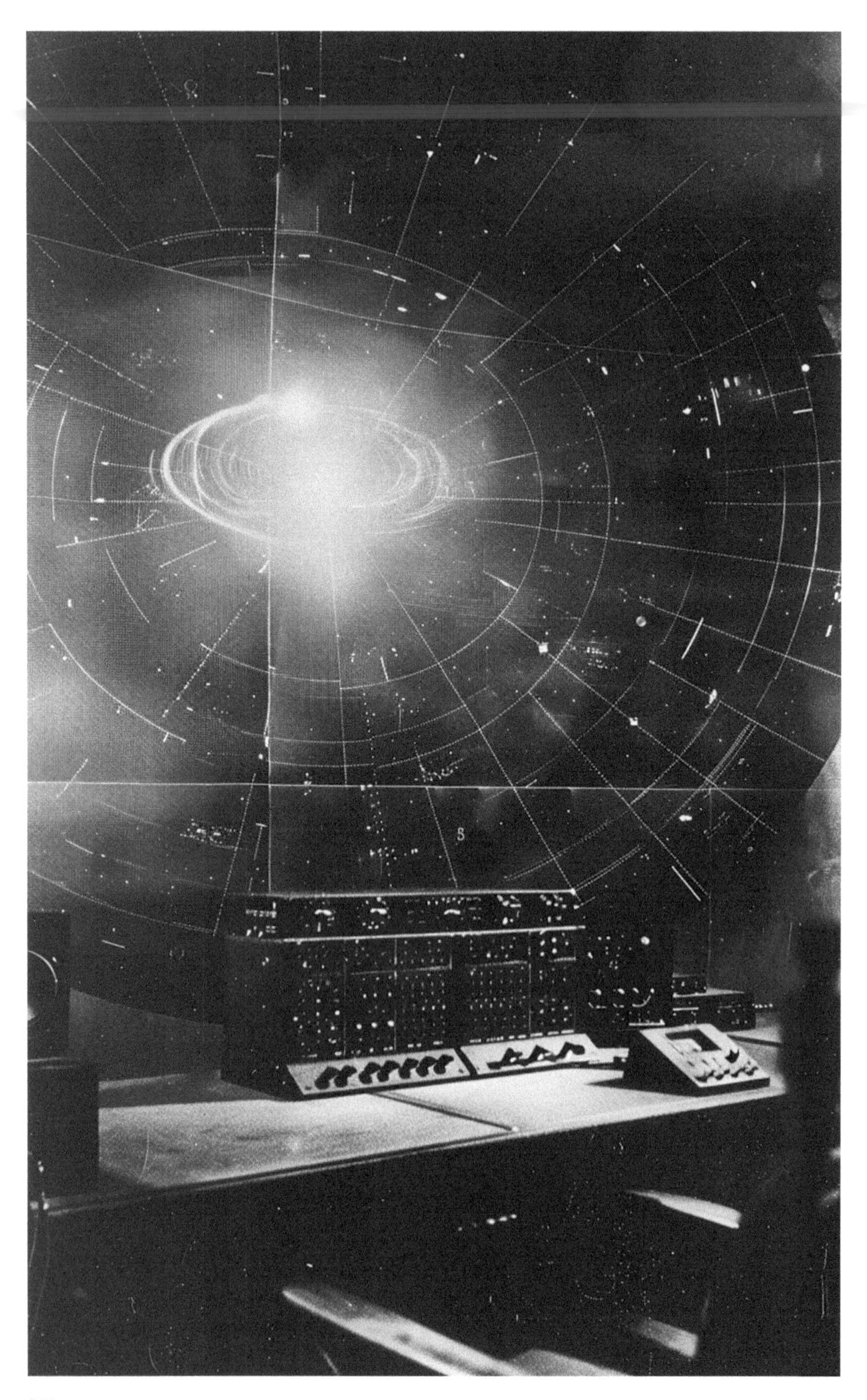

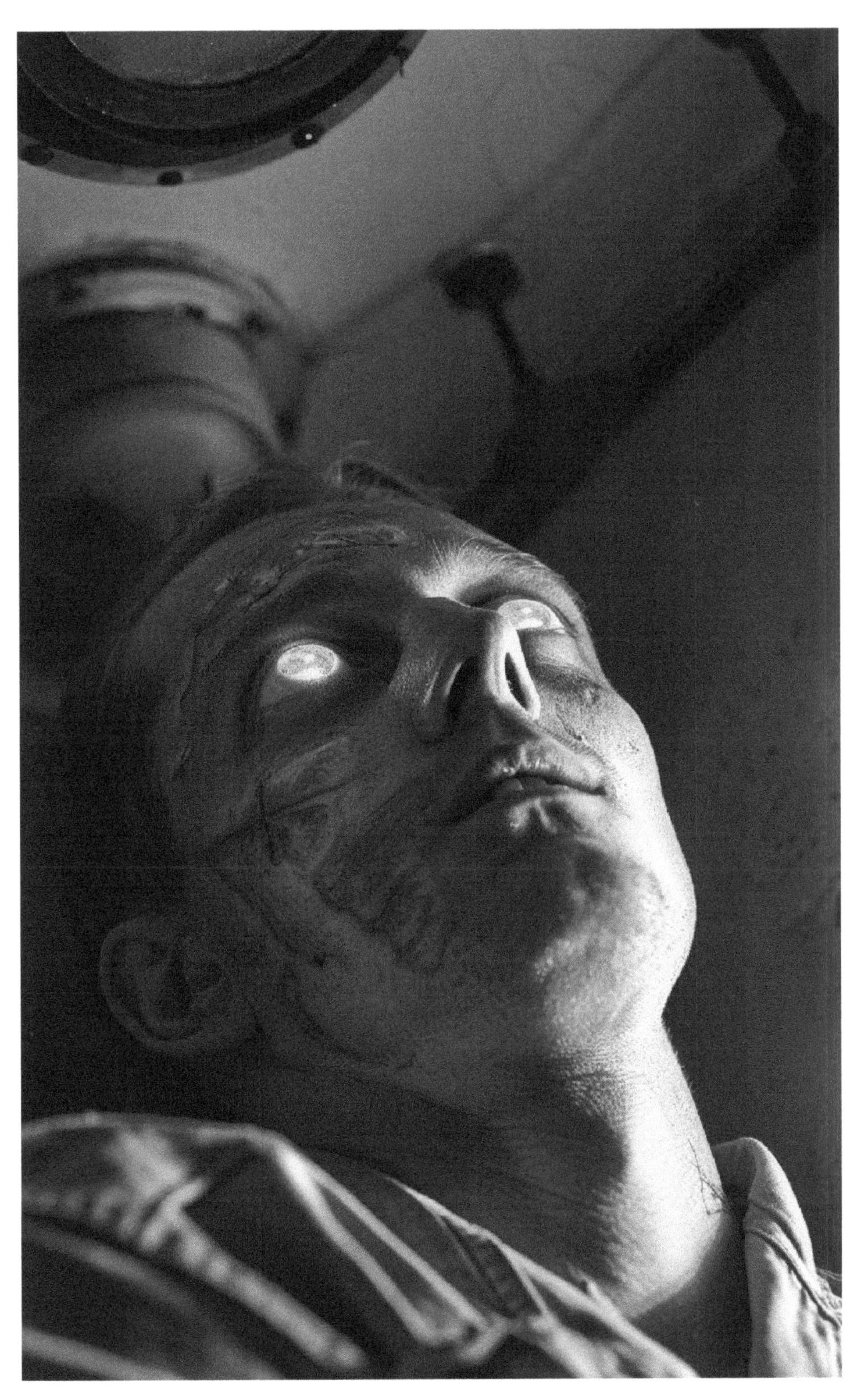

began the return journey to the *Icarus*. The sea lion bodies were attracting a variety of scavengers by the time we hit the beach, and the rubber dingy had disappeared. We didn't spend any time looking for it and once back on-board McIntyre reported our findings to the captain. He wasted no time contacting the proper authorities. When we got back to Victoria we had to sign secrecy forms.

My Uncle's diary contained only two more entries, both recorded within a month of the *Icarus* incident. The first was on July 27, and was simply a story torn out of the Victoria *Daily Colonist*, reporting the death by drowning of able seaman Frank Elliott, who was fished out of the Esquimalt harbour the day before. The police passed the incident off as an accident, but my Uncle had written, in jerky characters, below the clipping: "Elliott told me two days ago he had been visited by two men, civilians in black suits, who were asking questions about LBS. Elliott told them to get stuffed or he'd have the service police down their necks. Apparently one got a little lippy but the other calmed him down. Elliott said anything they wanted to know could be handled through proper channels, and invited them to bugger off."

The last entry was dated August 12, and reads:

Received news today McIntyre was found dead in his house at Willis Point. Neighbours reportedly saw a black car cruise up and down the single lane road the day before, and the Police are investigating, but have nothing to report. I guess I'm the only one left.

Unauthorised Contributors:

Eugen Bacon is an African Australian author of several novels and collections. She's a British Fantasy Award winner, a Foreword Indies Award winner, a twice World Fantasy Award finalist, and a finalist in other awards. Eugen was announced in the honor list of the Otherwise Fellowships for 'doing exciting work in gender and speculative fiction.' *Danged Black Thing* made the Otherwise Award Honor List as a 'sharp collection of Afro-Surrealist work', and was a 2024 Philip K. Dick Award nominee. Eugen's creative work has appeared worldwide, including in *Apex Magazine, Award Winning Australian Writing, Fantasy, Fantasy & Science Fiction*, and *Year's Best African Speculative Fiction.* Visit her at eugenbacon.com.

Thomas Frick, formerly a bookseller, editor, and award-winning art critic, has published essays, poetry, translations, stories, book and art reviews, and interviews, including *Paris Review* interviews with J. G. Ballard and Doris Lessing. His "alchemical" Luddite novel *The Iron Boys*, a 2011 *Los Angeles Times* Holiday Pick, is seeking a new publisher.

Andrew Frost writes science fiction. He's the author of the graphic novel *The Islander* [2023], and a book of micro-fictions, *End of Days* [2022], both published by Pretty Bad Horse. He's also written short fiction and creative non-fiction stories published in a wide variety of places. In a former life he was the art critic for *Guardian Australia*, a documentary maker for the Australian Broadcasting Corporation and a contributor to various art magazines and websites. His PhD thesis was on the relationship between science fiction and contemporary art.

James Goddard is the product of his own imagination and lives in a dystopian country known as the United Kingdom. He doesn't consider himself to be a writer, but he writes. Over the years he has contributed to books, magazines and literary journals. His love of books has led him to amass a large collection of science fiction first editions, photographic monographs and poetry books. He has been a publishers' advisor and editor, small press publisher and brother-confessor to several real authors. He is a keen photographer and his photographs have occasionally appeared on the covers of books and literary journals. A volume of his short stories, *Dolls & Other Brief Tales of Unusual Occurrences in Ordinary Places*, was published in 2019, and a second volume of tales may one day be published.

Born in Ukraine and currently residing in California, **Elana Gomel** is an academic, an award-winning writer, and a professional nomad. She is an authority on narrative theory and speculative fiction and has published widely in these areas. As a fiction writer, she is the author of more than a hundred stories, several novellas, and six novels of dark fantasy and science fiction. Her latest fiction publications are the dark fairy tale *Nightwood* (Silver Award in the Bookfest 2023 competition) and *Girl of Light*, a historical fantasy. Two more novels are scheduled to come out in 2024.

Paul A. Green's fiction includes *The Qliphoth* (Libros Libertad 2007), *Beneath the Pleasure Zones I & II* (Mandrake 2014/16) and *Dream Clips of the Archons* (QBS 2020). An excerpt from his latest work, *Remote Sensing*, appeared in *Deep Ends* 2023. His plays for radio and stage are published in *Babalon and Other Plays* (Scarlet Imprint 2015). Poetry and short fiction has recently appeared in *Black Box Manifold, The Fortnightly Review* and *Abridged*. More at paulgreenwriter.co.uk.

Andrew Hook has had over a hundred and seventy short stories published, with several novels, novellas and collections also in print. Stories have appeared in magazines ranging from *Ambit* to *Interzone*. Recent books include a collection of literary short stories, *Candescent Blooms* (Salt Publishing), and *Commercial Book* (Psychofon Records): a collection of forty stories of exactly one thousand words in length inspired by the songs from the 1980 record "Commercial Album" by The Residents. Andrew can be found at www.andrew-hook.com

Born in Yorkshire, **Lyle Hopwood** is an immigrant to the US. By day, a laboratorian, by night a writer of speculative fiction, she is an avid reader of science fiction, folk horror and fantasy. Her stories have been published in magazines including *IZ Digital, Aurealis* and *Interzone*, and in the anthologies *Dragon Soul Press: Union, Blood Fiction* v2, *Fission* #3, and *Emanations Zen*. She lives in Southern California with a holographer, her herptiles, and her collection of Kalanchoe.

Rhys Hughes was born in Wales but has lived in many difference countries and currently resides in India. He began writing fiction at an early age and his first book, *Worming The Harpy*, was published in 1995. Since that time he has published forty other books and one thousand short stories, and his work has been translated into ten languages. He is currently working on a collection of linked crime fiction stories called *The Reconstruction Club* and a novel about the farcical adventures of a deluded student entitled *The Happy Quixote*.

Maxim Jakubowski is a London-based former publisher, editor, writer, and translator. He has compiled over one hundred anthologies in a variety of genres, many of which have garnered awards. He is a past winner of the Karel and Anthony awards, and in 2019 was given the prestigious Red Herrings award by the Crime Writers' Association for his contributions to the genre. He broadcasts regularly on radio and TV, reviews for diverse newspapers and magazines, and has been a judge for many literary awards. He is the author of twenty novels, including *The Lousiana Republic* (2018), *The Piper's Dance* (2021), and a series of *Sunday Times* bestselling novels under a pseudonym. He has also published seven collections of his own short stories, the latest being *Death Has A Thousand Faces* (2022). He was a regular contributor to the annual anthology *Deep Ends*, and with Rick McGrath, he co-edited the Ballardian anthology *Reports From The Deep End* (2023). His latest novel is *Just A Girl With A Gun* (2023).

Hunter Liguore is an award-winning author of *Whole World Inside Nan's Soup* (Paterson Prize for Books for Young Readers; Every Child a Reader Honor Book). She's studied with Nobel Peace Prize Laureate, John Hume (North Ireland), and has undertaken critical research in peace and social justice studies, specializing in the work of Sun Tzu, the focus of her latest release: *Modern Art of War: Sun Tzu's Hidden Path to Peace and Wholeness* (Penguin/RH), with translations in Arabic, French, and German, and audio featuring award-winning actress, Kate Handford. A regular contributor to *Writer's Digest* and *Spirituality & Health Magazine,* she teaches historical fiction at Lesley University. Find out more at: hunterliguore.org

Don MacKay describes himself as a failed minor poet currently puddling into his dotage with few regrets. He has been published in poetry collections and has published a journal writing book, *Writing Towards Yourself.* He lives in Lund, BC, at the northern tip of Hwy 101, the world's longest road.

Rick McGrath is a Canadian writer, editor, designer, and publisher. He most recently co-edited an anthology of JG Ballard-inspired short stories called *Reports From The Deep End* for Titan Books.

David Paddy is Associate Dean of Interdisciplinary Studies and Director of the Whittier Scholars Program at Whittier College, a small liberal arts college near Los Angeles. He has taught courses in horror, science fiction, modernism, postmodernism, Celtic literature, literary geography and twenty-first-century British fiction. He is the author of *The Empires of J. G. Ballard: An Imagined Geography* (Gylphi Press) and articles on Angela Carter, Daphne du Maurier, Niall Griffiths, Jackie Kay and Jeff Noon. Online he can be heard discussing J. G. Ballard's *The Unlimited Dream Company* on the International Anthony Burgess Foundation's *Ninety-Nine Novels* podcast.

Ana Teresa Pereira is a Portuguese writer and translator. She is the author of more than twenty novels, novellas and short story collections. A reader of Henry James, Edith Wharton, John Dickson Carr and Cornell Woolrich, she likes to think of her stories as "abstract crime fiction." Her last novel, *Karen*, won the Brazilian Oceanos Award (best book in Portuguese language published in 2016). She lives in Funchal.

David Quantick is a television, radio and movie writer. His film *Book Of Love* won an Imagen Award in 2022 and he received an Emmy for his work on *Veep*. David is the author of several novels including *Ricky's Hand* and *All My Colors*. Read more at www.davidquantick.com

Lawrence Russell was born in Northern Ireland, educated in the UK, Canada, and California. Playwright, fiction writer, critic, musician and multi-media artist. Formerly Professor of Writing & Film, University of Victoria. Twice winner of the Canadian Broadcasting Corporation's Literary Competition. His stage plays have been produced in all the major Canadian venues, including the National Arts Theatre (Ottawa) and the Stratford (Ontario) Festival's 3rd Stage. His drama and electronic sound-text compositions have been broadcast on the CBC, ABC, Radio Canada International, NPR (National Public Radio, US), the Pacifica Radio Network and other broadcast networks. His books include *Penetration* (5 plays), *Repeat This & You're Dead* (stories), *Radio Brazil* (novel) the non-fiction work *Outlaw Academic* (criticism/metafiction/ autobiography), and the novella *Temple of The Two Moons*. LR's website is: culturecourt. com

D. Harlan Wilson is an American novelist, editor, literary critic, playwright, talkshow host, and college professor. He is the author of over thirty book-length works of fiction and nonfiction, and hundreds of his stories, essays, reviews, and plays have appeared in magazines, journals, and anthologies across the world in multiple languages. He also serves as editor-in-chief of Anti-Oedipus Press and reviews editor for *Extrapolation*. Visit him online at dharlanwilson.com.

Milton Keynes UK
Ingram Content Group UK Ltd.
UKHW051216270324
440092UK00007B/74